# The
# Midwife
## Of
# Berlin

BOOKS BY ANNA STUART

*WOMEN OF WAR*
*The Midwife of Auschwitz*

*THE BLETCHLEY PARK GIRLS*
*The Bletchley Girls*
*Code Name Elodie*

*The Berlin Zookeeper*
*The Secret Diary*
*A Letter from Pearl Harbor*

# The
# Midwife
## Of
# Berlin

ANNA STUART

*bookouture*

Published by Bookouture in 2023

An imprint of Storyfire Ltd.
Carmelite House
50 Victoria Embankment
London EC4Y 0DZ

www.bookouture.com

ISBN: 978-1-83790-742-7
eBook ISBN: 978-1-83790-741-0

*For Kate, my wonderful agent,*
*without whose wisdom, persistence, understanding and support I*
*would be nowhere.*
*With thanks and love from one strong woman to another!*

# PROLOGUE

## AUSCHWITZ-BIRKENAU | DECEMBER 1943

*ESTER*

It's a miracle. Every time she's assisted at a birthing, it has seemed magical, but it is only with her own baby that she understands it is a miracle. How can she have made this perfect miniature person? How has she brought forth this tiny human from her emaciated body? How has she produced the milk that is sustaining her daughter? And how on earth, here in hell, can she keep doing so?

No baby belongs in Auschwitz-Birkenau; but no baby should be taken away.

'I must hide her,' she says, time and again, but there is nowhere to hide amongst the stark wooden bunks.

There are no rugs in Auschwitz-Birkenau, no cushions, no chairs. No woman has more than the striped suit on her back, no mattress has more than a handful of straw, no blanket is thick enough to cover even a frozen limb. Ester has only kept her baby alive for these two precious days through the kindness of others sparing her rations they can ill afford to do without. Even if she hid her baby in the deepest recesses of the barracks, it would only be to die.

She strokes sleeping Pippa's downy hair. It is blonde. That, too, is a miracle. They like blonde babies, the Nazis. She knows they will take her child and they will give her to a 'wholesome German woman' and that will keep Pippa alive. That will keep her safe.

But it will not keep her with Ester.

Is it better, in the end, for your child to die with you, or live without you?

These are the sorts of impossible questions that the camps demand of you. Ester has seen the agony of it so many times in other women but now it twists its evil way into her own still-pulsing womb like a dagger. Pippa may no longer be inside her, but the essence of her daughter is in every cell, and when they take her away, it will rip them all open.

And they *will* take her away. Ester cannot hide Pippa from the all-knowing, all-hating eye of National Socialism, but there is one thing she can do.

'I must mark her.'

She reaches for the tattooing needle. It is not permitted to ink a number onto the arms of Jewish babies but Ester can tattoo her own number into Pippa's armpit, hiding it in the creases of the infant's skin. One day, when this dark madness is over, she might find her again. It's a grim hope, but that hope might stop enough of her cells from bursting open to keep her alive through the terrible moment when they steal her precious newborn.

She lifts the needle, makes the marks. The baby's eyes fly open in shock and she lets out a bleat of a wail but does not protest further. Perhaps she is too weak or, perhaps, somehow, she understands.

'There, there,' Ester soothes. 'It won't last long. It will be worth it. It will make you truly mine.'

But will it? For two more days she keeps Pippa in her arms. 'I love you,' she tells her over and over. 'I love you now and I will love you forever and I will never stop looking for you.'

Pippa blinks her blue eyes up at her.

But on the fourth day a call comes from the barrack doorway. 'A car! There's a car.'

They are here then. They have come. The pain of the impending loss spikes through Ester and she holds her baby close, kissing her blue eyes shut so that she will not see her mother hand her over to the ravening clutches of the enemy.

'I'm sorry, Pippa,' she weeps. 'I'm so, so sorry.'

The doorway fills with the snaking darkness of the SS. Manicured hands reach out of a tailored coat and claw at her baby like a raptor at its prey.

'Don't hurt her,' she begs.

'Why would I hurt her?' the man sneers. 'She's a good daughter of the Reich.'

A cackle of cruel laughter, the rap of a warm boot, and they are gone. Ester falls to the floor and waits. The pain is intense but her cells do not, after all, burst open. Nothing so kind. Instead, they knot into hard, angry tangles of bitter determination. She will not let them get away with this; she will not let them win.

It *is* better, in the end, for your child to live. Hope is the greatest pain but also the greatest strength. Finding her little girl is now Ester's goal, her challenge, her driving purpose. Finding her baby again is now Ester's reason, amidst the dirt and cold and fear of Auschwitz, to stay alive.

PART ONE

# ONE

*OLIVIA*

It wasn't the thud on the door that woke Olivia, it wasn't even the man's voice, measured but taut with the expectation of obedience, or her mother's steady reply. It was her father's concern that snuck into her sleep and pulled her out of bed. Her father was a gentle, peaceful man, but tonight he sounded angry.

'I go with her, or she doesn't go at all.'

'No men allowed,' came the curt reply.

Heart racing, Olivia reached for her dressing gown, then changed her mind; you didn't face the Stasi in your nightwear. Instead, she grabbed yesterday's clothes that had been flung hastily onto the chair. Her mother would have been cross if she'd seen – she was a stickler for tidiness – but Olivia had been too tired to fold them into the drawers. Glad now, she tugged on the blue blouse and black skirt of the Freie Deutsche Jugend – the Free German youth – not bothering with the woollen tights or the blue and white neckerchief.

The conversation was still going on downstairs but the

man's patience was clearly wearing thin and she hastily opened her door. Her parents were standing shoulder to shoulder in the hallway before a thickset man in a heavy overcoat, straddling their doorstep as if he owned it.

'The Stasi are the shield and sword of the party,' Olivia muttered to herself. It was what they'd been taught at school. 'There is nothing to fear from the Ministry for State Security if you are a good socialist.' Up until now Olivia had believed this, but with the officer standing in her hallway in the darkest part of the night, she couldn't stop fear creeping, unbidden, through her veins.

'Your wife will be quite safe, sir,' the officer said, the sir an afterthought and the guarantee little more.

Olivia's mother, Ester, looked up at her husband, her crisp midwife's uniform so glaringly white in the moonlight slanting through the hall window that she seemed almost ghostly.

'It's only a birthing, Filip. It's only a mother.'

'It's a prisoner, meine liebling,' he replied. 'She could be dangerous.'

'Which is why she is under full guard,' the Stasi officer snapped.

He was getting angry and *that*, Olivia knew, was dangerous.

'I'll go.' They all looked round and, feeling exposed, she wished she'd taken the extra moments to pull on her tights. She hurried forward, glancing to her younger brothers' door to be sure she hadn't woken them. 'I'll go with Mutti.'

'You don't have to do that, kindchen,' Ester said.

'I don't have to, but I will. I want to.'

'Good,' the Stasi officer said. 'Come then. There's no time to lose. She was screaming the place down when I left.'

Ester allowed herself a small smile. 'They do that.'

The fear was still twisting in Olivia's gut but her mother's calm stilled it and she slipped her bare feet into her school shoes. The man glanced at her FDJ shirt and, with a curt nod of approval, took the coat Filip was holding out and helped her into it.

'Thank you.'

'Take care,' Filip said, giving them both a kiss.

He still looked uneasy but Olivia felt more confident now. They were not in trouble but helping the state, as they should do, and the fear was beaten down by a rising excitement. She'd assisted her mother at birthings before, even done a couple in the night, but never with such drama. Wait until she told everyone in school tomorrow!

The moon was high in the sky above Stalinstadt, casting a silvery hue over the new, perfect socialist town. The symmetrical rows of accommodation blocks stood out as solid shapes, and the smoke of the iron foundry it was built to serve danced upwards as if pulled towards the glow. Car headlights picked out two yellow spots on the great obelisk to German–Soviet friendship opposite their block, and Olivia saluted it automatically, but then saw the vehicle before them and her heart quailed again.

'In, please.'

The officer opened the door of the stark, grey van but Olivia shrank back. Everyone knew these vans and no one wanted to see the inside.

'I don't...'

'In!' He all but pushed them into the tiny space.

'Are we...?' Olivia stuttered, but her words were cut off by the slam of the door and they were shut inside.

'We're not in trouble, Liv,' her mother said softly. 'Sit down and try not to worry.'

The van was divided into five miniature cells, each with a stark, hard bench and a hook for handcuffs. The cell doors, at least, were not locked, so she could see her mother sitting herself neatly in one, back straight, feet together, medical bag held tightly in her lap. Heart pounding, Olivia tried to fit into the next one but, standing almost a head taller than her mother, she barely fitted. She was 'big-boned' – a hulk of a cuckoo in a nest of slight, slim sparrows – but at least it meant she could use her long legs to keep the door open and her mother in sight.

'Where are we going?' she asked.

'We'll find out soon enough, my sweet.'

Olivia nodded reluctantly. No one in East Germany knew more than they needed to. It was for the best. The state had it all under control and the job of the individual was to fulfil their part as directed. *We are all*, Olivia reminded herself, *just pieces in the great jigsaw of communal life. If we slot into our allotted place then the picture will work.* Even so, it would be nice to know if she would be in this terrifying van for minutes or hours or—

'Oh!'

The gasp jerked out of her as the van lurched to a stop. They heard a rattle of garage doors opening, then the van juddered forward, and then they heard the garage close again.

Ester reached out and took Olivia's hand. 'We're not in trouble,' she repeated.

But Olivia had to fight to believe her as the door opened and they were nudged out into a blank white garage and up two steps into the thin, starkly lit corridor of a Stasi prison. Running down both sides were heavy metal doors with huge locks and thick grilles over tiny windows.

'Don't look,' Ester whispered.

But it was impossible to resist and Olivia caught glimpses of men and women, most curled, foetus-like, upon thin, hard beds without even the comfort of a blanket. The officer was hurrying them along, deeper and deeper into the fearsome building, and it took every ounce of Olivia's trust in her mother to keep following her into hell.

'There!' The officer put up a hand as a thin wail leached into the corridor. 'Listen to her. Is there any need for such fuss?'

'That's what we will find out,' Ester said. 'There may be complications.'

The officer shuddered. Stopping before one of the iron doors, he rapped on it three times and it was opened by a woman wearing the grey-green uniform of the Volkspolizei and a pained expression.

'Midwife,' the Stasi officer said and gave Ester a small push inside.

'At last!' The vopo – everyone's nickname for the Volkpolizei – took Ester's arm. 'Something's wrong with her, it has to be.'

Olivia followed Ester into the small room and gasped at the sight before her. The prisoner was a thin scrap of a woman, surely not much older than Olivia's seventeen years, with a huge belly and short, startlingly green hair. She was writhing in agony, straining against the handcuffs that held her to a pipe as if trying to climb the stark wall.

'Something is very wrong,' Ester agreed, striding forward. 'The poor woman needs to move about.'

'Not possible,' the vopo said. 'She must stay secured. She could be a threat.'

'Does she look threatening?'

'Well, no...' She looked to the door but the Stasi officer had gone and, as the prisoner reached the end of a contraction and slumped against the wall, they heard the tap, tap, tap of his smart shoes echoing away down the corridor.

'You look a capable woman,' Ester said crisply to the vopo, 'and my daughter is very strong. We'll be fine.'

The vopo looked from Olivia to the prisoner.

'Very well, but it's on your head if this goes wrong.'

'Of course.'

The vopo unlocked the cuffs and the young woman fell to the floor. Ester stepped to her side, nodding at Olivia to help guide her onto the rough bed.

Her eyes opened and she looked up, confused.

'Have I died?'

Ester smiled at her. 'Quite the reverse, my dear, you are about to give birth. What's your name?'

'Claudia.'

'Well, Claudia, let's get a rest and then... Oh, looks like we're off again.' Claudia writhed but Ester held her firmly and looked deep into her scared eyes. 'Breathe, Claudia, like this – in through the nose, out through the mouth. Good. Work with the pain, my dear. This is simply your body opening up to let Baby out. Breathe, that's it, that's wonderful.'

Olivia stood back, blinking away stupid tears as she watched her mother working magic with Claudia who, contraction ended, relaxed on the bed.

'Lovely,' Ester said easily. 'Let's have a look and see where we're at, shall we? Ooh, excellent, you're very close, Claudia. That's why it hurts so much – Baby is getting ready to come out. If you listen to me, it'll be over very soon and Baby will be in your arms.'

Claudia gave a weak smile. 'I wish Frank was here.'

'Is that your husband?'

She nodded. 'He wanted to be with me. I know it's not conventional, but he wanted it, said it was only right that he should support, support...' Her sentence ran out on a sob and then a new contraction wracked her thin body and she could only concentrate on her breathing.

Olivia glanced to the vopo, who'd retreated to the doorway, then back to Claudia.

'Why are you in here?' she whispered.

Claudia pointed weakly to her hair, tugging on the green tips.

'I'm a subversive.'

Olivia gaped. They were warned constantly of the evils of

rebelling against the all-caring state, but she'd never met anyone who'd actually done it.

'You are?'

The girl shrugged.

'Apparently. I only dyed it for fun. My clothes were like sacks so I thought...'

Olivia frowned.

'But you must have done something too. You must have...'

'Olivia!' Ester's voice was sharp. 'Now is hardly the time for political discussion.'

Olivia jumped.

'No, Mother. Sorry, Mother.' She leaned in. 'But it's awful in here, so—'

'This isn't awful.'

There was a tight steel in Ester's voice that pulled Olivia up short. He mother was so calm, capable and loving that she forgot, sometimes, what she'd been through.

'I'm sorry,' she said again.

Ester gave a tiny shake as if casting off the past, and smiled at her. 'There's nothing to be sorry for, my sweet. Now, fetch water, please. And that towel. It looks like Baby is crowning!'

Glad to escape, Olivia grabbed what her mother needed then stood back, careful to stay by Claudia's head. Babies were a wonderful gift, she knew that. It was every woman's duty to have as many as she could to replace the poor men lost to enemy guns in the war and, when the time came, she would do her duty. She just wasn't sure she wanted to know quite so much about it beforehand.

Claudia was clawing at her green hair, shrieking as if she were being torn apart, and Ester was calmly stroking her back and telling her how well she was doing.

'It's coming! Baby's coming, Claudia. One more push.'

And then, suddenly, with a roar from Claudia, there was a new life in the room.

'It's a boy,' Ester said as he broke into a lusty wail. 'You have a boy, Claudia, a son.'

Ester cradled the baby in her steady hands and Olivia crept forward to look. He was so big. How on earth had Claudia managed that? Ester held him out to Olivia.

'Me?' She glanced to the vopo, but she was staying near the door, talking through the grille.

'Please,' Ester urged. 'I have to cut the cord.'

Olivia held out her hands and her mother passed the baby into them. He was a bit gunky but his skin was so soft and, as he kicked out his little legs, she was flooded with awe.

'He's beautiful.'

'Isn't he just?' Ester snipped the pulsing cord and nodded. 'You can hand him to Mutti now.'

Already Claudia was sitting up, her agonies dropping visibly away as she reached for her child and covered him in kisses.

'My boy. Oh, my süße boy.'

His lips puckered and when she opened her top, he latched eagerly onto the breast. Claudia winced but then shifted and settled, her fingers caressing the downy hair on his head as he suckled. The baby gave a mew of contentment and his hand came up to his mother's, his tiny fingers closing reflexively around one of hers.

Olivia stepped back as far as she could in the cramped cell to give Claudia a little privacy but she couldn't take her eyes off the new mother and child.

'Is that how it was for you?' she whispered to Ester, who was busy checking the placenta. Ester jumped and Olivia looked at her in surprise. 'With the boys, I mean, with Mordy and Ben.'

'Oh. I see. Yes. Of course. The first moments with a new baby are very precious.'

She seemed flustered and Olivia looked at her curiously but Ester ducked her gaze and stepped back up to the bed.

'Well done, Claudia.'

Claudia tore her eyes from her child.

'Thank you. Thank you so much. I couldn't have done it without you.'

'There now, of course you could. Baby knew what to do, didn't he?'

She nodded, smiled.

'I shall call him—'

But her words were cut off by the door slamming open. They all looked up as the Stasi officer strode back in and stared at the baby.

'A boy,' he said. 'Good.' He reached out and snatched him from Claudia's arms, so swift and sure that she had no time to react. 'I'll see him well homed.'

'What?' Claudia gasped. He was already turning to the door and she leaped out of bed, blood running down her thin legs, and scrabbled at his arm. 'What do you mean? What are you doing? He's my baby!'

'Not any more,' was the cold reply. Olivia stared in horror at the officer, the baby a squirming pink bundle against the black of his overcoat. 'You are a subversive, a danger to the state,' he continued. 'We cannot trust you to bring up a baby. He will go to a good home, a socialist home.'

'I'm not a subversive. I promise you I'm not.' Claudia was on her knees now, sobbing. 'I only dyed my hair for fun. It doesn't mean anything. I'm in the FDJ, I've taken the oath, I'll raise him well, I swear it.'

'We can't trust you, I'm afraid.' The officer gave a shrug, as if he was taking away a chocolate bar, not the life she had battled to bring into the world.

'Please,' Claudia cried.

But he turned for the door, oblivious to her pain.

And that's when Ester stepped in front of him.

'No,' she said. Everyone in the room froze. Ester was small but her voice filled the space. 'You cannot do that, sir. You cannot take this baby from its mother.'

'Cannot?' His eyes narrowed.

'It is cruelty, repression – everything, surely, that we fought against?'

'How dare you?' he snarled.

But Ester was oblivious to the threat, her whole body quivering with emotion.

'I've seen this before. I've seen babies ripped from their mother's arms. I've seen the harm it does, the distress it causes. Nazis take babies from their mothers. I thought we were better than that? I thought socialism was about building a future together. I thought it was about family and community and shared values.'

'It is, and this woman, this subversive, does not share ours.'

'She's still his mother. He came from her body.'

'Which is an instrument of the state. We are not going to be cruel to the child. He will be safe and well cared for.'

'But not by her.'

'Because she is not worthy.'

'But—'

'Midwife! You have done your job, now let me do mine. If this woman proves herself loyal, she can have another child.'

'It's not the same!' The words seemed to rip out of Ester, raw with pain.

The officer recoiled. 'Maybe, Midwife Pasternak, you are a subversive too?'

'No!' This time it was Olivia's turn to speak out. 'My mother is loyal and good and honest.'

'Then make sure she stays that way or you will see the inside of this building again.'

And, with that, the man was gone, the unnamed baby with

him. Ester collapsed on the floor with Claudia and they wept together.

The van dumped them back on Alte Ladenstraβe as the first threads of light cut across Stalinstadt. Olivia scrambled out, never more relieved to see her home, as the officer gave them a curt 'thank you' and shot away.

'I'm sorry you had to see that, Liv,' Ester said. 'But I'm very grateful for your help.'

'I'm glad you didn't have to go in there on your own, Mutti.'

Ester gave a small, dark laugh. 'I've known worse, my sweet, much, much worse.'

This was always what it came down to with her mother. Olivia knew why; she knew that when she was the age Olivia was now, Ester had been sent to *that place*. She knew her time there sat at the base of all her mother was, but tonight had been something new, some well of pain that went even deeper than Olivia had previously understood.

Ester looked at her and gave her a sad smile. 'It looks like it's time.'

Olivia's heart jolted.

'Time for what, Mutti?'

'Time for the truth – the full truth.' She took Olivia's hand, drawing them onto a bench in front of the obelisk. 'I was going to save this for your eighteenth birthday, kindchen, but it seems God has other plans.' She drew in a deep breath and gave Olivia a sad smile. 'You know that you were born in *that place*? You know your mother died and you were taken away and that we found you in an orphanage and brought you home?'

Olivia nodded. There had been no secrets about her adoption and she wanted to say how grateful she was, how happy she'd been as part of Ester's family, but the words stuck in her throat because, for the first time, she saw it was not the extent of the story.

Ester swallowed.

'There was another baby, taken as you were, but her mother wasn't dead. Her mother was... Her mother was me.'

Olivia felt Ester's fingers tighten around hers, just as that poor little boy had held onto Claudia for the brief moments they'd been allowed together.

'You have a sister, Olivia,' her mother went on, her voice cracking. 'We never managed to find her but, pray to God, somewhere out there you have a sister.'

Olivia stared at her, Ester's unusual distress becoming as clear as the icy morning air.

'You have a daughter?'

'*Another* daughter,' Ester corrected gently. 'And, yes, she was taken from me in Auschwitz-Birkenau when she was just a few days old.'

'You've never found her?'

'Never.'

Ester looked down, plucking nervously at an imaginary loose thread on her immaculate uniform.

'You're still looking?'

For a long time Ester stared at her hands, then she suddenly looked up and straight at Olivia. 'We stopped.'

'You stopped looking for your daughter?' Grief flared in Ester's eyes and Olivia hated it. 'I mean, I'm sure you had your reasons. I'm sure—'

'We stopped,' Ester said. 'There were reasons. Well, one main reason. Were we right? I don't know. It was the hardest decision of my life and every day – every single day – I question it. But, yes, we stopped.'

Olivia opened her mouth to ask why but something in Ester's pain-filled eyes stopped her.

'Tomorrow,' Ester promised. 'I will tell you more tomorrow. For now, let us snatch what sleep we can.'

Olivia nodded and let herself be led into their apartment but somehow the pretty rooms seemed a little less cosy than before, her bed less safe, and she lay staring at the sun coming up on a world that apparently, somewhere, held a girl who was more her dear parents' daughter than she was.

# TWO

*KIRSTEN*

'Can I suggest a doughnut with that, sir? We have the finest in Berlin.' Kirsten flashed the young man her prettiest smile and he looked to the confectionary display, clearly tempted by the pair of doughnuts left on the stand. 'I can let you have the second at half price if you buy them both.'

'But then I'd have to eat two,' he said, one eyebrow raised.

He was cute. Not, perhaps, Kirsten's usual type – leaner and more serious-looking – but definitely cute.

'Do you have no one you could treat?' she asked, looking up at him from beneath the flop of her fringe and hoping the curls she'd spent ages twisting into her blonde locks this morning were still in place.

'No one special enough for the finest doughnuts in Berlin.'

Kirsten giggled. 'Then I guess you *will* have to eat them both yourself.'

'Or I could give one to you.'

Her heart skipped a beat. He had to be in his twenties and was with the cool crowd from the technical university.

'I'm not allowed to eat on duty,' she said, allowing herself a little pout.

'I could save it until you're done.'

'Well, I—'

'Move over, Kirsty,' her co-worker Sasha said cheerily, squeezing past, 'some of us have work to do.' And with that, she reached out and scooped up the two doughnuts.

Kirsten could only stare, open-mouthed, as Sasha served them to a large older lady with two mewling kids tugging at her skirts.

The cute boy gave an exaggerated sigh. 'Guess that's both of us saved from temptation,' he said.

'I'm not so sure about that,' Kirsten replied, without thinking.

He laughed and she felt herself flush furiously. What an idiot! The boy, however, leaned in and said, 'You might be right about that. I'm Dieter, Dieter Wohlfahrt.'

'Kirsten,' she stuttered.

'I know.'

'You do?'

He pointed to her name badge and she flushed deeper. He'd think she was a naive little schoolgirl – and he'd be right.

'Kirsten Meyer,' she elaborated hastily. 'That'll be one mark, please.'

'Thank you. Maybe we can do doughnuts next time.' Placing a mark on the counter, he picked up his coffee and turned to join his friends, but then looked back and added, 'I like your dress by the way. Very... different.'

He was gone, joining the raucous crowd in the window seat, before she could find a response. One girl pointedly made room on the bench and Kirsten watched Dieter squeeze in next to her and tutted at herself. Why would handsome, smart student Dieter have any time for a seventeen-year-old waitress who made her own dresses? He'd just been being polite.

Forcing her best smile, she turned to the next customer, trying not to sneak too many looks to the window table but it was hard. The girl sitting next to Dieter was very pretty, with glossy chestnut hair and fashionable clothes. Kirsten watched her enviously, admiring the Levi denims that fitted her shapely form perfectly. How she'd love a pair of those but there was no way she'd be able to afford them.

*He liked your dress*, she reminded herself, glancing down at the red gingham A-line frock that she'd spent hours making, copying it from pictures in *Twen* magazine. She was pleased with the final product but she knew it didn't have the gloss of a shop-bought piece or the cachet of a brand like Levi.

It was rubbish being poor, she thought crossly, and then told herself off. Her mother worked hard to keep her and her brother happy and it was mean of her to want more. It was just that she knew they'd once been rich, and life would be much easier if they still were. There was a photo of herself as a baby with her parents on the doorstep of an enormous house in Charlottenburg, but that had been during the war. After it, her father had disappeared, and the house with him.

So many kids at school had lost their fathers in the war that Kirsten had never felt the lack of hers, but she did feel cheated of the house. They'd inherited her grandparents' cosy apartment on Bernauerstraße, across the road from her widowed Tante Gretchen, and she knew she should be grateful, but it was hard not to wonder how Gretchen had kept her apartment, which was far bigger and fancier than theirs. Both sisters' husbands had fought for Germany but one, it seemed, with honour and the other...

If Kirsten ever dared to ask her mother what had happened to her father, Lotti blew up angrily, saying Jan was 'dead to her', and refused to speak about him. She'd never stated he was actually dead but Kirsten supposed it amounted to the same thing. Her brother, Uli, said he must have been a Nazi and had lost all his property for 'having hateful ideologies', which sort of made sense but wasn't something Kirsten wanted to think about too hard.

'Move it, Kirsten, there's customers waiting!'

Kirsten jumped. 'Sorry, Frau Munster.'

Her boss was a nice lady, but stern, and it wouldn't do to cross her. She had to focus.

For the rest of her shift, Kirsten made coffee, handed out cakes and cleared up dishes with the beaming smile expected of her. As the evening unfolded, the university crowd moved on to schnapps and became louder and louder. Kirsten could swear that Dieter kept looking over at her and, when she had to go and collect a round of glasses, he leapt up to help.

'You should join us for the next round,' he suggested.

But she'd never be so bold and, besides, Marlene Dietrich came on the jukebox and the glossy-haired girl got up to sing, so Kirsten beat a hasty retreat.

The girl's voice was mellow and husky and, when she was done, everyone in the café clapped and the students shouted 'bravo, Astrid'. Sasha rolled her eyes and said, 'of course the damned girl can sing as well,' which made Kirsten feel a little better, but she was glad when the clock ticked towards closing time and she could start wiping down tables. She was edging towards Dieter and his gang when her younger brother Uli walked in and, with excruciating timing, tripped over his gangly fifteen-year-old legs right in front of them all.

They laughed uproariously as Uli scrambled to his feet, scarlet in the face.

'Hey, Kirsten,' he said, far too loudly, 'Mutti sent me to fetch you home.'

Kirsten could have died. She felt the scar in her armpit itch and resisted the urge to touch it. She'd got it in an accident with a hot pan when she was a toddler and it always seemed to flare up when she got too warm, but the last thing she needed right now was to scratch at it like a monkey.

'Careful, Kirsten,' Astrid called, 'or you'll be flat on your face too.'

'She'd be better flat on her back,' one of the other boys said.

'Jensen, hush!' Dieter snapped at him, for which Kirsten supposed she ought to be grateful, but she was too mortified to care. Why couldn't they go?

She was very relieved when Frau Munster came out, arms crossed, and told them sternly that she was closing up. They flocked out, laughing and discussing what dance hall they should go on to, and Kirsten tried, again, not to feel resentful as she reached for her only dancing partner of the evening – the smelly old mop.

'Sorry for embarrassing you,' Uli said as they let themselves out a little later and made for the U-Bahn.

'It's fine,' Kirsten said. 'They were just stupid students.'

Uli offered his arm like a grown man and, after only a moment's hesitation, Kirsten took it. It was Friday evening and the centre of Berlin was alive with people, out for dinner or the cinema or, like Astrid and Dieter, heading to one of the many dance halls that had proliferated in a city battling to recover from its woes in the war. There were still holes all over the place where bombs had taken out many homes, and the rest were marked with bullet holes, but new buildings were going up all the time and, with the economy booming, Berlin was determined to enjoy the good times.

Kirsten looked around, enjoying the sights of her home city at play. Berlin was a place of contradictions, split in two politically but still operating as a whole. When Germany had been divided after the war beneath the command of the victors, the Russians had taken the eastern half of the country and the British, Americans and French the western half. As the Russians had slowly and insidiously taken control of every government in the Eastern bloc, including the Deutsche Demokratische Republik, the Iron Curtain had fallen across Europe – a line of barbed fences, patrolled by sentries that stopped the people behind it from leaving.

The only exception was this wonderful city of Berlin. As Hitler's capital, it had been deemed a special case and, despite being deep into Eastern Germany, was also divided in half. West Berlin was connected to Western Europe by designated road and rail links, and East Berlin was divided from West Berlin by nothing more than a nominal line running along ancient district divisions. Kirsten's own Bernauerstraβe, for example, was a district border. The people on her side were in the Allied zone and the people on the other – including her Tante Gretchen – in the Soviet one, but no one paid it any attention.

As a result, those who didn't like life in the East could travel to Berlin, walk freely across the city and catch a train to freedom. The authorities were trying to clamp down, stopping anyone with suspicious amounts of luggage and sending them back, but there was little more they could do without a solid border and no one, surely, would be mad enough to build such a thing across a city? So, the Berliners got on with life, travelling between the zones and choosing the bright rock'n'roll bars of the West, or the smoky, edgier ones in the East as it took their fancy. And on this warm May night everyone seemed to be out.

'Shall we go for a Coca-Cola somewhere, Uli?' Kirsten suggested on impulse.

He looked startled.

'Wouldn't that worry Mutti?'

Kirsten sighed.

'I suppose so. Come on then, home it is.'

She turned down the steps into the U-Bahn and instantly the music and chatter of the street was muted.

'But we could,' Uli said, 'if you wanted to. I mean, I don't mind. I—'

'It's fine, Uli. I'm worn out anyway.'

He looked anxiously at her and Kirsten gave his arm a fond squeeze. He was a worrier, her brother, the opposite to her in so many ways. Where she was conventionally blonde and blue-eyed, his hair was darkest brown and his eyes the colour of oak bark. He was slimmer than her too, especially since he'd had a growth spurt, and, although she supposed he might be good-looking in a year or two, for now he was lanky and awkward. Sweet though.

'Come on,' she said as the train pulled in, 'what animal would you like to be tonight?'

He grinned gratefully at her. This had been their game when they were small and their mother, Lotti, had taken them regularly to Berlin Zoo. It had been their favourite place in the whole city and they'd happily spent hours chasing up and down outside the monkey cages or pressing their faces to the glass of the beautiful hippo house. Inspired, they'd invented 'what animal would you like to be', opting for a giraffe if they were stuck in a crowd, a hippo if they had a day out at one of Berlin's many lakeside beaches, or a monkey in the playground. Uli had once, at Sunday dinner, picked up the last of the chicken carcass and said he'd like to be a vulture, but Lotti had snatched it off him and said there were 'enough vultures in Germany, thank you very much,' so he'd never said that again.

'I'd be a manakin,' he offered now.

'The bird? Why?'

'Cos they're great dancers, so I could take you out tonight.'

She laughed.

'We can dance at home.'

'Yeah!' Uli brightened. 'Maybe Mutti will get the gramophone out and put on some of Grandpa's old swing records.'

'Sounds wonderful.'

Kirsten smiled at him again and tried not to picture Dieter and Astrid and their cool friends dancing to all the latest tunes in the Wanne or the Eden Saloon.

'What would you be?' Uli asked.

'Sorry?'

'Animal, stupid – what animal would you be?'

'Oh, right. Erm, a sea lion, because then I could charge people to come and watch me do tricks.'

Uli squinted at her. 'Why would you want to do that?'

She shrugged. 'Money, I guess. Wouldn't you like to be rich, Uli?'

'I suppose so.'

'We were once, you know, in the war.'

'Well, yeah, but that was Nazi wealth, gained from the suffering of others.'

'Sssh!' Kirsten put a hand over his mouth, mortified.

'It doesn't mean we're the same,' he mumbled against her fingers.

'I know that! Even so... it's not something you want to broadcast, is it? If it's true.'

'Course it's true,' he hissed. 'You've seen the uniform Vati's wearing in that photo.'

'Yeah, but everyone wore a uniform. It was wartime.'

'Not everyone wore the death's head.'

'The what?'

'Look at his cap when we get home – it has the skull and crossbones on it. That was the SS symbol.'

'Was it?'

'Don't you know anything?'

She wrinkled her nose. 'I don't want to know that stuff. It's in the past and we should forget about it. Germany is about industry now, and sport and, and...'

'Zoos?' he offered.

He was trying to make her feel better, she knew, but he was

the one who'd brought up the damned SS. Kirsten didn't know much about them – they weren't exactly taught it at school – but she was pretty sure they'd been Hitler's elite, the ones who'd run the ghettos and the concentration camps. She didn't want to dance now. She didn't even want to drink the cocoa she knew Lotti would have ready for her, or talk about her day; she just wanted to go to bed and sleep.

'It's our stop, Kirsty. Nearly home.'

Her brother was still darting her anxious looks and she fought to stay patient with him in the short walk up Bernauer-straβe to No 106. Desperate to hide in her bedroom and dream of Dieter asking her to dance, she ran up to their first-floor apartment, stepping inside with a relief that swiftly dispelled at the sound of voices.

'Has Mutti got someone here?' she asked Uli.

'Not that I know of. Maybe it's Tante Gretchen?'

They paused, listening, then looked at each other in concern – the voice was deep and hoarse and unmistakably male.

'Mutti?' Kirsten called out, putting an uncertain hand to the living-room door.

'Kirsten? Is that Kirsten?' The door swung open to reveal a large, blond man in a rough shirt, too small for his muscular arms. 'Well,' he said, spreading them wide. 'Guess what – your father's home!'

# THREE

*OLIVIA*

Olivia turned her key in the lock and slipped gratefully into the apartment. Inside she could smell freshly baked Sabbat bread and chicken soup and hear the soft hum of her parents cooking together in the kitchen. Her friends were always amazed that her father cooked. Some had even been disparaging about it until it had come up in class and he'd been hailed as a socialist hero.

'In the Deutsche Demokratische Republik,' the teacher had said, 'all comrades are equal. Gender roles are a Western oppression, stopping half of the workforce from contributing to the national good.'

That had shut everyone up, but at home the truth was gentler. Filip said he'd learned early in their marriage, when he had not been allowed, as a Jew, to work under the Nazi occupation, and that he enjoyed it. He sometimes joked that he was better at it than Ester, who always countered that he was welcome to do it all. Olivia enjoyed meals from them both but liked it best when they did it together and paused in the hall-way, drinking in the comfort of home.

It had been a strange day at school. She had been tired out from being up half the night and even more so from her moth-er's revelation. She had not, in the end, told her friends anything about the van, or the prison, or the green-haired mother deprived of her child, and had only wanted to get home to learn more about that other baby, born into the same hell as herself.

Olivia had always known she'd been born in Auschwitz and always known she was adopted. Ester and Filip had made no secret of it, telling her of her birth father, shot by the Nazis, her birth mother, Zofia, who had died of grief when Olivia had been taken from her at just two days old, and an aunt who'd gone to the gas on arrival in *that place* and after whom Olivia had been named. They'd told her of the miracle of finding her in an orphanage and knowing it was her from the number – 58031 – that Ester had carved into her armpit and that was still there today.

They'd told her time and again of their pleasure in making her a part of their family, and she had no reason to doubt it. Even when Mordecai and then Ben had been born to them – proper, biological sons – she'd felt secure in their love and, perhaps, in her status as the only daughter. But all along there had been this other girl. All along they must have been searching. Of course they must have; it was the only rational thing to do. Olivia under-stood it totally and was not foolish enough to think it meant they loved her any less. But it was still a shock to find that she wasn't quite enough. That she wasn't their only daughter after all.

'Olivia? Is that you?' Ester came out of the kitchen, a pinny over her uniform and a smear of flour on her flushed cheek. She rushed forward and took Olivia's hands. 'I'm so glad you're back. That makes all the family in for Sabbat.'

The word 'all' was pointed, as if her mother had seen into her thoughts and wanted to reassure her, and Olivia smiled gratefully.

'The boys are here?'

Ester gestured into the living room where Mordecai and Ben were sitting on the floor with a Meccano set. Olivia had passed a gang of lads playing tag in the open area before the obelisk on her way into the apartment and knew her brothers, at ten and twelve, would like to be out there, but Friday evenings were sacred in the Pasternak household and the boys waved happily at her.

That the family were Jewish was not a secret, but neither did they wear their faith out in public. That wasn't unusual in the DDR. The Christians also kept their heads down in a country in which religion was considered an unnecessary distraction from the all-consuming life of the state. That was fine by Olivia. She liked their religion as a private act, shared by the five of them. She liked how on a Friday her father and brothers would put their kippahs on their heads, finely embroidered by Filip. She liked the way that she and her mother would light the Sabbat candles and pour the kiddush wine and they would all sit down and break bread together.

'Why don't we have a synagogue?' Ben had asked recently when Filip had been reading the scripture to them.

'We do,' Ester had told him. 'It's here, in our home, and in our hearts.'

He'd nodded solemnly. 'You built it there in *that place.*'

'I did, Ben. I built it in my heart where only God could see it and it stands there still – in my heart, and in all our hearts.'

It was a lovely sentiment and one Olivia held dear but, like everything else, it seemed it wasn't the whole story. If they hadn't been Jewish, her parents would probably still be living in Łódź, where they'd grown up. Her mother would not have had to endure Auschwitz, or her father the killing fields of

Chelmno. They would still be speaking their native Polish and still going to a real, bricks-and-mortar synagogue with others. But the Poles had not been keen on having their few surviving Jews back after the war. There had been intimidation and persecution and when, in the summer of 1946, forty innocent Jews had been killed in a violent pogrom in Kielce, just two hours south of Łódź, Ester and Filip had decided to leave their homeland.

They'd talked to Olivia about the painful irony that they'd ended up in Germany, but once Ester had completed her midwife training in Berlin, they'd moved to Stalinstadt, just outside the capital. It was a brand-new town with brand-new ideas and, with three young children to care for, they'd taken the chance to start again, even changing their daughter's name from the Polish, Oliwia, to the German, Olivia. Ester had become a valued midwife and Filip ran the womenswear department of the state textiles store, using his skills with a sewing machine to do 'alterations' that improved both the fit and style of the standard Konsum garments for the lucky ladies of Stalinstadt. Life here, they always insisted, was good.

'Do you want to change before dinner?' Ester asked now.

'Do *you*?' Olivia laughed, pointing at her mother's uniform.

Ester looked down at it and shook her head.

'I totally forgot. Come on, let's get spruced up together.'

It didn't take long to get into their best frocks and join the menfolk at the table. They all stood, heads bowed, as Filip recited the kiddush, then the food was served and the chatter began. Mordecai had been selected for the chess team and Ben had won a prize for science. Filip had received a whole chicken from a grateful customer, delighted at the embroidered trim on her standard-issue housedress, and the soup was rich and delicious.

Olivia shared that she'd been asked to captain the tennis team in a youth competition next week and her family, although

largely baffled by her interest in sport, toasted her enthusiasti-
cally. She thanked them and swallowed down her unease at this
clear sign of how different she was. What, she couldn't help
thinking, was their real daughter good at? Was she as fine-boned
as her parents and their birth-boys? Did she want to be a
midwife like Ester? Might...?

She stopped herself. This was silly. She was very lucky to
have such a wonderful family and if the number hidden in her
armpit didn't match the one on her mother's arm, so what?
They had chosen her and they loved her and that was a great
blessing.

Even so, she longed to know more.

After their plates were scraped clean and cleared away,
Filip produced a precious bar of chocolate and they sat down in
the last rays of sun slanting through the window, savouring the
rare treat.

'Tell us a story, Mutti,' Ben said, squirming between his
parents on the couch.

'Oh yes! Tell us a story.'

Mordecai was up immediately, sitting eagerly at Ester's feet,
but Olivia shifted uncomfortably. She was never sure why her
brothers were so keen for Ester's stories. They were not the
usual type of bedtime tale; there were no fairies, or witches, or
dragons in her accounts. Or perhaps there were – just very real
ones.

'Why do you do it?' she'd asked her mother one day. 'Why
do you keep telling us about *that place*? Would it not be better
to forget it?'

'It *would* be better,' Ester had agreed, 'but it's impossible.
This way, I can parcel it up into almost-bearable snippets, and
open them one at a time. If I tried to push it away, all the memories would rise up and swamp me. This is the only way to
control them. Plus, of course, you need to know – you all need

to know what mankind is capable of. You must be on your guard, always.'

Olivia wasn't sure that the boys took the stories as a warning, more as juicy horror – every bit as remote as witches and dragons – save when they looked into their mother's eyes and saw the pain. That, none of them ever took lightly.

'Tell us the one about the Christmas tree,' Mordecai asked now.

Ester drew in a shaky breath and smiled at him. 'You know how to pick them, Mordy.' She looked at Olivia over his head, her eyes swimming with meaning, and Olivia felt her Sabbat dinner churn in her stomach and snatched up a cushion, cuddling it to herself for protection from what might come. 'If you're sure?'

'We're sure.'

Ben slid down next to his brother and they sat cross-legged before Ester like students before a rabbi.

'Very well. It was Christmas 1943, deep into the middle of the war, and I had been in *that place* for eight months. Olivia had been born three months before and had gone to, well, to wherever she went before some kind soul took her into the orphanage where, with God's blessing, we found her.'

The boys shifted in surprise. This was a new detail in the story, one Olivia was sure her mother had added to prepare her for the revelation to come. They looked curiously to their adopted sister but she wasn't what really interested them.

'Tell us about the tree,' Ben urged.

Ester smiled at Olivia and turned back to the eager faces at her feet.

'We were forced out into the snow, in darkness, by Irma Grese.'

'The guard with the whip?'

'They all had whips, Ben, but the one keenest to use it, yes. She said the authorities had a treat for us and, sure enough, when we got out into the bitter cold, there was a giant fir tree in the middle of the camp and guards were lighting candles clipped onto the branches, as if this were the middle of any cosy German town. For a moment we thought they did actually have hearts somewhere under their SS uniforms, but we couldn't have been more wrong.

'The next thing we know, they were whipping sheets away and underneath the tree, piled gruesomely high, were dead bodies, naked and with red ribbons trimming the top ones. I still think, sometimes, about the people who cut that ribbon and tied it round dead limbs, taking time to be sure the bow was perfect, just to make us even more miserable than we already were.' She coughed and spoke again, more a growl than speech. 'I say people, but they weren't people – they were monsters.'

Filip put an arm around her and even Ben and Mordecai sat silently, remembering that this story wasn't invented, but truth – their mother's truth. Ester coughed again and lifted her head high.

'But then Ana – your Grandma Ana – began to sing.' Olivia closed her eyes and tried to picture the kind older lady who had been her mother's greatest friend in Auschwitz and had stood as their surrogate grandmother ever since. 'She sang "Silent Night",' Ester went on. 'And one by one we joined in, all of us, even the Jews. We didn't know the words but it didn't matter because the tune was beautiful and while we sang, however briefly, we were human again – not animals scrabbling in the dirt and ice for scraps of bread, but humans who could feel and care and love. They didn't rob us of that, however hard they tried and, in the end, love won.'

Filip held her tight and Olivia saw her mother wipe away a tear and was scared all over again. Ester rarely cried, not even over her stories. She told them with tight control and always with the same ending – love won. But it seemed now that love had also lost and she watched Ester's fingers fold and refold her dress as Filip rose to usher the boys to bed.

'Oh Vati, do we have to?'

'You do. We're going fishing tomorrow, remember?'

'Yeah!' Ben leapt up. 'I'm going to catch a fish, Mutti, and bring it home for you.'

'I'm going to catch a bigger one,' Mordecai said, throwing his hands wide to indicate the size of the fish he was almost certainly not going to land.

'And we will share them both,' Filip said firmly. 'Now come on, bed.'

They clattered noisily through to the boys' bedroom, chattering about rods and nets, and suddenly it was just Olivia and her mother.

'Come and sit here, kindchen.' Ester patted the sofa and Olivia moved next to her. 'Mordy picked a hell of a story for tonight. Almost as if he knew.'

'Knew what?' Olivia's voice came out stupidly husky but Ester didn't seem to notice.

'That Christmas Eve was the day I went into labour.'

'With... with my sister?'

'With Pippa, yes.'

Pippa. Olivia tested the name on an in-breath and felt it seep into her. Pippa. Filipa. It made sense – her mother's labour and her father's name.

'Tell me,' she whispered.

Ester clutched at her hand.

'My waters broke right there, in the snow. They rose up in a cloud of steam and it was only thanks to the wine the guards had drunk and their smug pride in their sick "gift" that they didn't notice. Ana and Naomi – my Greek friend – got me into the barracks and I laboured through the night. I missed roll-call the next morning. That would usually have been instant death, but Pippa had chosen to come on the right day and the pigs were too busy gorging themselves on their Christmas feast to care.

'She was born a few hours later and, for a while, for the first time in *that place*, I was happy. Actually happy. Other women were very kind. They brought me their bread and margarine and beet – though Lord knows they didn't have enough to keep themselves alive, let alone a baby – and my milk came in and for four whole days I had her to cherish. It was magical. And then they came.'

'Who came?' Olivia asked.

'The SS officers, the same ones who took you. They were something high up in the organisation of *that place* and they rode in, in a fancy car, and took babies. Snatched them, like the Stasi officer last night snatched Claudia's. That's not right, is it, Olivia? That's not fair. You cannot take a woman's baby from her.'

'Of course not,' Olivia agreed, picturing poor Claudia on her knees, weeping and pleading as if the man had pulled away a part of her very soul. 'What were they called?'

'Meyer,' Ester said, 'and Wolf. Wolf was a woman. Imagine that! She was a woman and still she took our babies. I sometimes wonder if she ever had children of her own and if, when she did, she thought of what she did to us.'

'Surely she went to prison?'

'Maybe, maybe not. You'd be surprised how few of them did. Some ran away, got new identities, fled the country. Even those who *were* caught didn't do so badly. Apart from the top lot, they got a year or two in prison and were out again, romping around Germany as if nothing had happened. I'm only glad we're in the East as no fascist would dream of living beneath the communist yoke. They're happy as fat capitalists while millions of people fight to pick up the pieces of their ruined lives.'

'And one of those pieces, for you, is Pippa?'

Filip slid back into the room and placed a hand on Olivia's

shoulder. 'You know we love you as our own, dear daughter, Liv?'

Ester looked up and horror flashed over her face.

'We do,' she agreed. 'We absolutely do. Finding you was a miracle and Pippa is nothing to do with that. Please don't think—'

Olivia squeezed her hand.

'I don't. I love you both and I've been so lucky to be a part of this family.'

'Not as lucky as we've been to have you. It just...'

Ester ran out of words and Filip finished for her.

'It just would have been nice to have you both.'

'You tried to find her?'

'Of course,' he agreed, coming to sit on her other side. It was a bit squashed but Olivia welcomed the press of their love. 'We tried every avenue we could, for years – the synagogues and orphanages all over Poland and Germany, the Jewish Relief committee and various national bodies. The Red Cross did a lot in the early years, and the United Nations had a relief and rehabilitation unit with a child search team. That's how we found you, Liv. The tattoos Mutti had put into the babies' armpits helped and a few turned up but...'

'But none of them were Pippa,' Ester said. 'Then we thought we'd found her. We thought...'

'There was a report of a baby,' Filip filled in, holding his wife's hand tight. 'Well, a child by then. It was 1950.'

'Five years after the war?'

'Yes. And seven after you were born. And... and Pippa was. We'd all but given up hope.'

'And then?'

'It doesn't matter.' Ester's voice was tight and hard, brooking no opposition. 'It doesn't matter, Olivia. Filip and I found each other, against all the odds, and we found you, and then we had

Mordy and Ben. We had many, many blessings, especially compared to most people we knew... before. It was enough.'

Her voice told Olivia that the subject was closed, but the tears behind it spoke another story. They were a happy family, Olivia knew that, but it was *not* enough, that much was clear, and God help her, she longed to know more about the missing daughter.

# FOUR

## EAST BERLIN | JUNE 1950

*ESTER*

'There's someone asking for you, Midwife Pasternak.'

Ester looks up. She's washing the blood of a new birthing from her hands and is dog-tired. It was a breech labour and needed all her new skills, but both baby and Mutti are doing well and Ester is looking forward to her bed.

'I'm not the only midwife in Berlin.'

'But you're the best.'

Ester smiles gratefully at the woman, a glowing new oma. Her partiality is understandable after the night they've just had, but Ester is no use as a midwife right now.

'Anyway,' the oma says. 'I'm not sure this one is here about a birthing.'

Something spikes in Ester's heart. The only messages she receives that are not about babies due to be born, are about babies recently found, but surely this cannot be about Pippa. Not now. No tattooed children have been found for over a year.

At first, when she and Filip moved into the chaos of post-war Berlin, babies were regularly found with numbers in their armpits. Every time, the news filled Ester up with glorious, painful hope and every time it was cut out by the wrong digits. As the years unrolled, infants, then toddlers, then lively pre-schoolers were found and reunited with the surviving fragments of their families, but Baby 41400 was never located.

'It's a woman,' the oma says, but that's nothing unusual.

Even now, in 1950, there are four women to every man in Berlin. Enough males have limped home from war, recovered from injuries, or grown from boyhood to provide babies, but the women still look after each other. And Ester looks after the women.

It was Ana's idea for Ester and Filip to come to Berlin. Ester protested bitterly but Hitler's capital had become an occupied city, run by the Allies and, in a deep irony, one of the safest places for the people he tried so hard to eliminate.

'I have a friend in a hospital in the Soviet zone,' Ana told her. 'She will train you. She will look after you.'

'Not as well as you've done.'

'And not with as much delight in having you either. I so wanted you to train with me, Ester, but God moves in mysterious ways.'

'Perhaps because Łódź already has a talented midwife?'

'Perhaps because Berlin needs one. I hear there are many swollen bellies there.'

Which was true. There was a rush to produce children – bright, beautiful babies, innocent of the scars of war and the tangled taint of Nazism, and Ester was instantly busy. But more enticing than the work were the records and the reports available in the capital of the ex-Reich, the agencies and the charities searching for the lost.

Every few weeks, at first, reports came in of possible Pippas that lifted Ester and Filip – then dropped them every time. Ester is dog-tired of that too. Recently Filip has been muttering about leaving the capital. He has brought home a leaflet about a new town they are building outside the city: Stalinstadt – a bright, clean place where families can live a good, socialist life. It is tempting, but Ester has always felt that if she is to find Pippa it will be here, in Berlin. Hope never dies.

She dries her hands carefully. 'What sort of woman?'

'A smart one, in a suit. Fancy shoes. American accent.'

Ester's heart pounds. It was often Americans immediately after the war – well-meaning matrons, arriving in Europe to 'do their bit' and homing straight in on the myriad lost children teeming around in Germany's broken capital. They saw it as a treasure hunt and Ester supposes it was – *is* – but the treasure for her, and other mothers like her, is beyond any price these bumbling women can imagine.

They've mainly gone now, back across the Atlantic to their bring-and-buy sales, cookie bakes and charitable balls. The orphans are largely gone too – returned to found families or adopted by new ones, off to England and Israel and the USA. They are making lives and that is wonderful, but it leaves Ester with part of hers still missing.

'She's waiting outside.'

Ester nods her thanks, not trusting herself to speak. She bundles her bloody apron into her bag with shaking hands and tidies her hair. Stupid really – what does hair matter if Pippa is found?

Suddenly desperate, she darts out of the bathroom and down the short hall to the apartment door. Outside, in the hall-way, stands a perfectly coiffed woman, her manicured hands holding a slim folder.

Ester's heart throws itself against her ribs. She has seen these folders many times before – scrappy details of a whole life parcelled up in beige cardboard.

'Frau Pasternak?'

Ester nods, her eyes fixed on the folder.

'We've had a report of a child. A girl around seven.'

That would be right. Olivia is seven. Their adopted daughter is, as well as her glorious, happy, loving self, an unknowing barometer of her parents' shadow-child.

'Where?' Ester chokes out.

'In a private home.'

That makes sense. Ester has known for some time that if her baby is still alive, she must be hidden within the treacherous family that stole her.

'She's in Berlin. Someone reported her – saw her playing on monkey bars and spotted the number in her armpit.' Ester staggers and the woman darts forward and holds her up with surprising strength. 'We're sending someone to investigate. We'll have more information soon but, well, we thought you'd like to know.'

'I would,' Ester gasps. 'I mean, I do. I do want to know.'

Pippa, her Pippa, might be right here in Berlin with the woman who stole her, and Ester might be able to take her back at last. It is almost too wonderful to bear.

# FIVE

*KIRSTEN*

Kirsten stared at the man framed in the living room doorway.
Was this really her father? She'd always assumed that, if she
saw him, she'd feel the pull of their biological tie, but this man
was a total stranger and his bulk loomed over her home in a
most unsettling way.

'Hello,' she stuttered, looking to her mother for assistance,
but Lotti was hovering helplessly in his shadow, her face
blotched and her eyes cast down. Her mother was an attractive
woman, with an enviably voluptuous figure, but tonight she
looked shrunken and afraid.

'Pleased to see your old man, hey?' he demanded. 'Back
from the dead like a miracle.'

He cast a mean glance at Lotti and her head shot up.

'I never said you were dead, Jan.'

'You never said I was alive. Come on, Kirsten, where's my
hug?'

He threw his arms wide and Kirsten felt sucked forward

into his embrace. His body was rock hard and quivered with raw strength, and she was glad when he released her.

'You're a pretty thing, I must say.' He nodded approvingly. 'So grown up though. Makes me realise how long I've been away. How old are you?'

'Seventeen, sir, er, Father.'

'Seventeen! Last time I saw you, you were barely weeks from your mother's womb.'

'Jan,' Lotti said, with strange urgency.

Jan threw his wife another mean look, then strode over suddenly and kissed her, hard, on her mouth.

'But, then, your mother is very pretty too. Always was. Pick of the bunch, my Lotti. Sagged now, of course, but still lovely.'

He kissed her again and Kirsten saw her mother's body tense and fought for a way to distract his attention.

'Have you travelled far, Father?'

He swung round.

'Travelled far! I like that. Very good. Yes, little Kirsten, I've travelled all the way to hell and back. But I'm here now, so time for some fun at last. I bet you know how to party, don't you, girl? And who's this? Boyfriend, is it?'

He gestured to Uli, cowering behind Kirsten, and she squinted at him.

'No, Father, of course not. This is Uli.'

'Uli?' He shook his head. 'Never heard of him.'

Kirsten looked to Lotti, who was wringing her hands. Her brain whirred. Uli had been born in February 1946, nine months after the end of the war. Had Jan been gone by then, off to wherever they'd taken him?

'He's my brother, Father,' she managed. 'He's your son.'

'My...?' Jan went a curious shade of purple and a vein pulsed in his temple. 'No. No, he can't be.'

Kirsten heard Uli whimper and reached back her hand for him to clasp.

'Mutti?' he whispered.

Lotti's face was still blotched and her eyes red around the edges, but they found Uli with bright certainty.

'You're my son, liebling,' she said. 'My much-loved son.' She smiled at him but the word 'my' sat between them, pointed and prickly.

Then Jan sprang. He grabbed Lotti, flinging her against the wall and pressing his face into hers.

'What have you been up to, you whore?'

'Don't!' Kirsten cried. 'Leave her alone.'

'Or what?' he growled.

'Or I'll call the police.'

'Good. I need to report adultery anyway.' He turned back to Lotti, spittle flying from his lips. 'Who've you been fliking while I've been shut away, wife? God, the lad must be, what, fifteen? You didn't hang around, did you? You tart, you—'

'Get off me.' Lotti's voice rang with fury. 'I "fliked" no one, Jan, but plenty fliked me. While you were off fighting for the dying Reich, I was left in Berlin with the Russians marauding around the city taking everything – and everyone – they wanted.'

They all stared at Lotti, who pushed her chin up defiantly.

'"Komm, Frau," that's all the German they knew. They'd walk into a room, or a cellar, or a broken-down church where we were desperately trying to hide and they'd cast their eye around and then: "Komm, Frau." There was nothing you could do – nothing. They were so strong and there were so many of them and they had guns. They'd grab you, breathing like rabid dogs, and they'd bend you over the nearest pile of rubble and hold you down while they, they...'

Tears sprang to Lotti's eyes and Kirsten tried to go to her, but she put up a hand to ward her off and even Jan retreated in the face of her taut rage.

'Days it went on. Or, rather, nights. They slept in the light but as soon as dusk fell, they were at the vodka and not much later they were hunting us down again. There was nowhere to hide. It was like they could smell you out. And they were insatiable.'

'Bastards,' Kirsten said.

'Bastards,' she agreed, 'but, then, they were on a revenge mission, weren't they?'

'Revenge?' Kirsten asked.

Lotti's eyes went to Jan.

'Oh yes, revenge, because when our brave, noble German soldiers were invading Russia, they did exactly the same. They took every mother and sister and daughter they could find on their rampaging way to Stalingrad, so...' She spread her hands wide. 'Once they'd fallen back and left their own womenfolk exposed, we were payback.'

The fury was draining from her and she crumpled against the wall.

'How many had you?' Jan stuttered.

'Too many to count. I was well-fed, you see, kept nicely by my high-ranking husband, and they loved a bit of flesh on a woman. I was first every time. The only blessing was that it stopped them taking poor young virgins. We got them the best hiding places because, well...'

She grabbed at Kirsten's spare hand and Kirsten held it tight, aware of Uli's sweaty grip on her other one.

'So, I'm...' Uli stuttered, 'I'm Russian?'

'Half Russian,' Lotti said hoarsely, 'but *all* mine.' She let go of Kirsten and hugged Uli. 'It doesn't matter, Uli.'

'Of course it does. You were raped, Mutti.'

He tried to pull away but she held him with surprising strength.

'It was a dark, dark time. There was little water, little food, little comfort. The women of Berlin were alone and vulnerable and the enemy attacked us with all they had. It was war, Uli, and it was awful. But one good thing came out of the horror, one bit of light in the darkness, and that was you.'

'You were happy to bear him?' Jan stuttered, leaning heavily against the nearest wall.

'Not at first,' Lotti said. 'I was devastated, but I was far from alone. A lot of women had abortions but, well, I had Kirsten to care for and, anyway, a life is a life, right? It was hardly Uli's fault and I couldn't bring myself to get rid of him. He was like a little miracle.'

'Hardly a miracle,' Uli said miserably. 'It would have been more of a miracle if you hadn't got pregnant.'

'Not true,' Lotti said, but she looked at Jan and Kirsten saw something strange pass between them – a quiver of a time when they had been together and, she assumed, happy. It lasted only a second, though, before Jan hit out at the wall and they all jumped and huddled together.

'Wunderbar!' he said. 'Welcome home, Jan. Good to have you, Jan. Here's a commie cuckoo in your nest, Jan.'

'It's not Mutti's fault,' Kirsten protested.

Her head was spinning, but on this she was clear. Jan's eyes, however, narrowed dangerously.

'You think? I'm not so sure. Tell me, Lotti, how come you could never—'

'Jan!'

He shut up, curiously submissive before her, then wheeled away.

'I can see I'm not welcome here. Years I've waited to come home to you, Lotti. Long, hard years dreaming of home and now here you are, with your own apartment and your own verdammte kids and no use for me at all. Well, fine, I'm going.'

'Where?' Lotti asked.

'Do you care?'

She hesitated a moment too long and, with a roar of fury loud enough to shake the whole block, Jan was gone. They ran to the window to see him storm off down Bernauerstraβe, his big form casting bristling shadows under every street lamp until he reached a bar and marched inside.

Lotti collapsed into an armchair and Kirsten and Uli sank at her feet.

'Is that man really our father?' Kirsten asked.

'He's not mine,' Uli said.

'Lucky you,' Kirsten told him.

'Because mine's a rapist Russian?'

Kirsten grimaced.

'Sorry, Uli. But, look, it's not what matters is it? Fathers are more than simply seed. Fathers are people who care for you and keep you safe and bring you up. Neither of ours have done that, but Mutti has. Mutti is who joins us, who holds us together, aren't you, Mutti?'

'I am,' Lotti agreed, but her voice quivered and, with this fierce father tearing up their happy home, Kirsten had no idea how long any of them would be able to hold anything together.

# SIX

*OLIVIA*

'Olivia! Olivia Pasternak, are you paying attention?'

Olivia blinked at her teacher. The honest answer was that she'd been so busy thinking about her mother's stolen baby that she hadn't heard a word of the lesson, but an honest answer would definitely not be best.

'Of course, Frau Werner. It's very interesting.'

'I'm glad to hear it and perhaps, therefore, you will oblige us with a concise summary of the benefits of collective farming?'

Olivia pushed herself slowly to her feet, forcing her brain to work.

'The process of collectivisation involves co-opting small and inefficient private holdings into a far larger one that can be farmed as a collective, or soviet,' she said. 'Working together, the group can create a fair and efficient system that ensures all work equally for equal gain.'

'Very good,' Frau Werner agreed grudgingly. 'And how can the same socialist principles be applied in an urban setting?'

Olivia bit back a groan, but this was a favourite topic here in

Stalinstadt, the ultimate socialist town, and she knew the answer backwards.

'The identical principle of pooling individual skills for the common good can be applied. The doctors provide medical skill, the iron workers technical skill, the kindergarten teachers caring skill. All contribute equally to the communal good, so all are paid on a work quota established by the state. No one is unjustly rewarded on a spurious value-system that rates some skills higher than others, and all goods needed to sustain life are available at a set price so that no false external worth is placed on unnecessary symbols of shallow wealth. That way we can create a truly equal society, free of the trammels of capitalist inequity.'

'Right. Yes. Well done, Olivia.'

Frau Werner actually smiled at her and Olivia smiled back. It wasn't hard. They'd had this explained to them endlessly at school and by the FDJ. Besides, it made total sense. In the West, people climbed to great wealth simply because they could work dark magic with money, using it to make *more* money that they could spend on ridiculously overpriced clothes and houses while others, whose skills were, say, working a machine or tending the sick, could barely scrape by. It was all wrong and Olivia was glad to be in the East, where they were working to a fairer society. Even so, the thought of poor Claudia having her baby taken away just for dyeing her hair a non-state-approved colour niggled at her.

'Nazis took babies from their mothers,' Ester had raged at the Stasi officer and the ugly word – 'Nazi' – still rang in Olivia's ears. She'd always believed communists were the antithesis of Nazis but the events in that sordid basement last night had shaken the solidity of her convictions and it was almost a relief to speak some of the core socialist values out loud. They were working to a better way of living, but it was hard. Humans were an essentially selfish species and they all had to learn how to put communal good above private gain.

Her thoughts crept again to her parents' missing baby – the girl who should have been in her place. What would have happened to her if they had found their Pippa first? They'd spent her life assuring her of their love and she wasn't foolish enough to doubt it, but she'd never before realised there might be a comparison out there. Was Pippa prettier? Smaller? Neater? More like Ester and Filip? And why had they stopped looking? Olivia had a horrible feeling it had been to spare her, to stop her feeling the clawing doubts she was feeling now. But the awareness that her parents might have given up their real daughter for her clumsy, awkward self only made things worse.

She was relieved when the bell rang into her tortured thoughts and everyone leaped to their feet. The next lesson was physical education and Olivia headed for the smart sports hall with the rest, keen to lose herself in the rigours of tennis practice before the match tomorrow. She was cross, therefore, when they were stopped at the entrance.

'OK, team!' Herr Neumann, the head coach, boomed. 'We have a treat today – a top East German sports champion is joining us, Herr Erich Ahrendt.'

'Erich who?' someone asked.

'Erich Ahrendt, the great javelin thrower.'

Everyone around Olivia looked as blank as she felt.

'He threw for the DDR at the Rome Olympics last year.'

'Did he win?'

'He threw a very long way. Over 70 metres. Can any of you throw over 70 metres?'

Herr Neumann's eyes raked the crowd and they all cast their eyes down. Olivia tried to picture how far 70 metres was – about the length of three tennis courts, end to end. That *was* a long way.

'Well, you'll get a chance to find out,' Herr Neumann went

on. 'We're having a special session – a talk from Erich and the opportunity to throw a javelin yourselves.'

The students offered a dutiful if thin cheer.

'Does this mean no football?' a lad in front of Olivia asked his mate and it seemed, as they were ushered towards the bleachers along one side of the sports field, that it did indeed mean no football. And no tennis either.

'He'd better be good,' someone said in her ear and Olivia turned to see one of her fellow tennis players looking crossly at the man standing on the grass before them.

He was very tall with an impressively triangular physique and was holding a long, silver-tipped javelin striped with the red, black and gold of the DDR. Olivia looked at it with interest.

'It's a cool implement.'

'You like the look of his spear?' her friend giggled, and Olivia nudged at her.

'Shut up, idiot. I don't need to be dragged out again this morning.'

It seemed, however, that the fates were not with her. Erich talked surprisingly eloquently about life as a professional athlete and the excitement of going to the Olympics, and Olivia found herself so caught up in it that when they asked who would like to try the javelin, she shot her hand up without thinking.

'You! Olivia Pasternak. Come on down.' Herr Neumann turned to Erich and said, loudly enough for everyone to hear, 'She's a good choice. A top tennis player and a big girl, as you can see.'

Olivia could have died. He meant it as a compliment but she could already hear the boys jeering and was sure that 'big girl' was all she'd get for weeks to come. Her thoughts flew to her family, all so much slighter than her, and then on – relentlessly – to the real daughter who might be somewhere out there, no doubt petite and sweet and a natural carer like Ester. Her guts curled and she glanced to the exit, desperate to pick up her feet and run away, but that would only make things worse.

'I think you mean strong, sir,' Erich Ahrendt said, smiling at her. 'And perhaps we should have a few more volunteers, so she's not stuck out here on her own?'

Olivia smiled gratefully at him and he grinned back as Herr Neumann went along the bleachers selecting more boys and girls to join her while Erich explained the basic principles of throwing the javelin.

'The key,' he said, 'is not so much to throw it hard, but to generate speed in your run-up and convert that into motion through the javelin. It's about being smooth and straight. You have to throw the javelin through its own point.'

Olivia and her fellow guinea pigs squinted at him and he laughed.

'It means simply that the body of the javelin should follow the same trajectory as the tip, rather than wobbling all over the place. Here, I'll show you.' He lifted the javelin, whipping it expertly up above his right shoulder. 'I'll only do a short run-up, so don't expect it to go too far.'

He ran five quick steps, turning sideways and crossing his feet over as lightly as a ballet dancer as he increased his speed before releasing the javelin into the air. It flew up into the blue sky, arced gracefully above their heads and came down, the red, black and gold stripes spinning mesmerisingly, before landing almost at the perimeter of the field. Everyone broke into spontaneous applause. Olivia watched the javelin quiver in the grass, and felt pure awe ripple through her.

'That was amazing,' she gasped.

Erich grinned again.

'Your go then.'

Olivia stepped forward, self-conscious in front of the whole class but desperate to try this magical implement. She listened carefully as Erich showed her how to do a three-step run-up and how to hold and release it.

'It's a bit like a tennis serve,' she commented.

'Very like,' he agreed, 'only aim up not down.'

Olivia laughed.

'Whatever you say.'

It was now or never. Gripping the javelin as he'd showed her, she blocked out her fellow students, blocked out all the thoughts that had been troubling her over the last few days, and focused on his instructions. The javelin felt powerful in her hand and, closing her eyes, she lifted it high, took the steps and released it with all she had. She heard a small whoosh and, daring to open her eyes, saw it fly. Not as far as Erich's, of course, not even a third as far, but a satisfying distance all the same. It landed, point sticking into the ground and she looked to Erich.

He was gaping at her.

'Did I do it wrong?' she asked nervously.

'No. God, no. You did it exactly right. Have you done this before?' She shook her head. 'Right, well, you really should think about doing it again. Let's measure it.' He grabbed a long tape and sent Herr Neumann trotting out towards the javelin with one end while he read the other. 'Thirty-one metres! Are you sure this is your first go?'

'Beginner's luck?'

'Maybe,' he agreed. 'We'll see. Next.'

Olivia stood back as a tall boy came swaggering forward and took the javelin.

'Watch this,' he instructed his fellow students, but as he ran forward he lost his footing and the javelin wobbled through the air and landed barely 10 metres in front of them. The students roared with laughter. 'I tripped,' he said crossly. 'Let me try again.'

'Of course,' Erich agreed, retrieving the javelin but,

although the boy managed a smoother run-up, he didn't send it much further.

'It doesn't go straight,' he moaned loudly.

'It did for Olivia,' was all Erich said. 'Next.'

One by one the others took their turn, with varying degrees of success, but not one of them got it past 20 metres. Olivia stood awkwardly as they looked at her with a mixture of respect and fury.

'Yours must have been a fluke,' the last one said as his javelin turned tail over tip and bounced awkwardly across the grass.

'Would you like another go, Olivia?' Erich asked. She shook her head, embarrassed. 'I think you should but, perhaps, without the crowd?'

He looked to Herr Neumann, who nodded.

'Agreed. Off you go, the rest of you. Lunchtime!'

It was a magic word and everyone scrambled away, leaving Olivia standing awkwardly next to the Olympian.

'Now,' Erich said, 'let's see what you can do with a little more coaching.'

She took a deep breath and paid attention. It was easier without an audience and, oh, she did love the feel of the beautiful implement in her hand. Her stomach grumbled but this was far better than any grey school dinner and she focused hard as Erich showed her how to do the crossed-feet thing and encouraged her to get up some speed. The javelin flew from her hand and into the air, several metres past her first mark. Erich looked at her.

'You're good, Olivia. Tall and strong and with an excellent command of your body.' Olivia blushed and looked down, but Erich took hold of her chin, lifting it up again. 'It's a good thing, girl. You have a gift. I'm out in schools looking for individuals with potential and you, Olivia, have bags of it. You like sport?'

'Oh yes,' she agreed.

'Olivia is our best tennis player,' Herr Neumann said. He'd come swiftly back from kicking the others out of the hall and was fawning around. 'We've done all we can to encourage her.'

'You like tennis, Olivia?'

'I do,' she agreed, 'but not as much as I like this.'

She indicated the javelin, already keen to throw it again, but what Erich said next caught her up short.

'Good. I'd like to put you forward to attend one of the DDR's sports schools.'

'What?'

'Olivia!' Herr Neuman snapped. 'Manners.'

'Sorry. I'm very sorry, sir, but, what did you say?'

Erich smiled easily. 'We have special schools where talented sportspeople can study and train all on one site. To date it's been mainly football, but we're widening our scope and I've been tasked with identifying raw athletic talent to be brought in for specialist coaching.'

'I see,' Olivia said, though in truth her tired mind was reeling. This, on top of the news of her mother's lost baby, was an awful lot to take in. 'Is there one near here then?'

Erich shook his head. 'Not near enough. You would have to board, Olivia.'

'Board? You mean, leave home?' Her head spun. She thought of her mother and father and their cosy home. She thought of her brothers, of the games they played and the fun they had. She thought of Sabbat meals and trips out at weekends. How could she leave all that? Especially after what Ester had just told her. The javelin felt hot in her hand and she set it down awkwardly. 'I'm not sure.'

Erich smiled kindly.

'Don't worry, you can talk to your family. But let me say now that the place I'd be recommending is the best in the country. It's looking for athletes to become the Olympians of the future and that could be you, Olivia. Are you interested?'

Olivia looked at the javelin sparkling in the May sunshine, bright with possibility, and then up to the blue heavens above. She had to admit that home didn't feel quite as home-like since the revelations of the Stasi prison. She was newly aware that there should have been someone else in her family – someone as small, neat and quietly clever as the rest of them. Perhaps this man's strange proposal was a God-sent opportunity to make the parents who'd taken her into their nest proud, to prove to them that their big-boned cuckoo had been worth choosing.

'I'm interested,' she agreed. 'I'm definitely interested.'

# SEVEN

## FRIDAY, 26 MAY

*KIRSTEN*

Kirsten paused while collecting a jumble of cups and plates and looked out of Café Adler's long windows onto Friedrichstraβe. Usually, she loved the buzz of central Berlin, but these last few days she'd been finding the crowds daunting and had had to keep a tight grip on herself to stay smiley for the customers. At least at work, like at school, she was spared the arguments and tears that had characterised her home life this week, and there was no way she wanted to lose her job.

Jan had, unfortunately, returned to the apartment that first evening, hammering on the door in the early hours and staggering into the living room to pass out on the couch. Lotti, ill-equipped to deny her legal husband a place in her home, had got Tante Gretchen over first thing the next day to help her face him. Her younger sister was a richer, more glamorous and more confident version of Lotti, and had told Jan in no uncertain terms that if he was to live on Bernauerstraβe, he had to get some decent clothes and a proper job. He had not taken kindly to that but had, at least, disappeared into the city, nominally to take Gretchen's advice, but in reality, judging by the smell of him on his eventual return, to tour Berlin's many bars.

'Don't give him a key,' Gretchen had instructed them all. 'He can stay here if that's what you want, Lotti, but this is our apartment, inherited from Mutti and Vati, and he has no rights over it. He lost those when he went to prison for killing Jews.'

Lotti had gasped as Kirsten and Uli had looked at each other, astonished. 'Gretchen!'

'Well, I'm sorry, but they need to know. I'm afraid, kids, that your father was part of the team who ran the Auschwitz KZ.'

'Ka-Zet?' Kirsten stuttered. It was the German shortening for konzentrationslager – concentration camp – and was a dark, ugly word, never spoken lightly.

'I'm afraid so, I'm sorry. He was one of the sick bastards who thought that the most humane way to deal with the so-called "Jewish problem" was to build great big gas chambers to exterminate a whole nation who, let's face it, had never done anything to deserve such hatred.'

'Gretchen!' Lotti had cried again. 'Have a care. They're young.'

'Kirsten will turn eighteen next year and it's hardly the worst news Uli has had all week, is it, schnuki?' She'd put a fond arm around him and he'd squirmed, but not pulled away, from her easy comfort. 'People in this country – many people – did terrible things and we have to face them to be sure we don't do it again.'

'*We* didn't,' Lotti had protested.

'Really?' Gretchen had raised a finely plucked eyebrow. 'Did you ask where Jan worked? Did you query how he'd got all those fine stripes on his uniform? Or why you had such a beautiful big house? Or where...?' She'd cut herself off. 'I'm not criticising, Lot. We all did it. We let the men fight the war and got on with thinking we were better than the rest of the world when, all along, it turned out we were worse.'

It had been a most depressing conversation and Kirsten had gone to school with a heavy heart. She'd heard of Auschwitz, of course, as she'd heard of Buchenwald and Dachau and the terrible conditions that had been unearthed in those hellholes at the end of the war, but no one really talked about them. They were nightmare places, far away in Poland, and had not felt like part of her life – not until Jan had brought them lurching into it. Lotti had assured her that he'd once been a loving husband, but it was impossible to see how that better man could ever be excavated from the prison-hardened ex-Nazi who staggered onto their sofa every night.

Shaking off thoughts of her father, Kirsten balanced her tray on her arm and wiped the table just in time for a group of girls to grab it. They were laden with shopping bags and Kirsten peered enviously into the nearest one, catching sight of a pair of bright red mules. They'd look amazing with her gingham dress, she thought, and bent down to try to see the price tag.

'Everything all right there?' one of them asked, pulling the bag close.

Kirsten bit her lip.

'Yes. Sorry. I just... I love those shoes.'

The girl simpered.

'Gorgeous, aren't they?! I got them in the sale – only fifteen marks.'

'What a bargain!'

Kirsten backed hastily away. Fifteen marks was almost two weeks' wages; she'd never be able to afford that. She stomped back to the kitchen, battling not to feel resentful. It had annoyed her before that her family were struggling with money, but since Jan had come home, she'd found out that even the money they'd once had, had been tainted.

'You're going to have to make sure you earn a decent living, Kirsten,' she told herself sternly. But how would she do that? She was decidedly average at school and could barely concentrate long enough to keep down a simple job as a waitress – who would give her proper employment?

Grumpily, she forced herself back out to the counter and was working so hard that she didn't realise Dieter was next in the queue until a soft voice asked, 'Any doughnuts for a hungry young man?'

'Dieter!'

He smiled.

'You all right there, Kirsten? You looked miles away.'

'Bad day, sorry. Let me see if...'

She moved towards the confectionary display but he reached out for her wrist, stopping her.

'Forget the doughnut. How would you like to get a proper bite?'

Her heart thudded.

'A proper bite? With you?'

'Maybe a dance too, if you fancy it?'

'I'd love it.'

'Good. When does your shift end?'

'You mean tonight?'

His smile broadened.

'If you're not busy?'

'No! I mean, no, I'm not. That sounds fun.' She glanced at the clock. 'I finish in half an hour actually, so...'

'So, I'll wait here. One coffee please.'

'Coming right up.'

She made the coffee with shaking hands. A bite to eat, with Dieter! And dancing! That was a date, wasn't it? An actual, proper date. She'd have to let her mum know, but she could call Gretchen's telephone from the pay booth at the back of the café. It would cost her but, oh, it would be worth it. Forget the red mules; she could dance in her old pumps any day if she was holding Dieter Wohlfahrt's hand.

'Have you been to the Wanne?' he asked.

She shook her head.

'But I'd love to, Dieter. I hear it's really cool.'

He smiled.

'I don't know about that, but it's a fun place and the music is great if you like jazz. Do you like jazz, Kirsten?'

Kirsten had no idea.

'Love it!'

'Perfect. We can get a currywurst on the way. Unless you'd rather sit down to eat?' He hit his head with the flat of his hand. 'What am I doing offering you street food on our first date?'

'It's fine. Perfect. Really.'

Almost as perfect as the fact that he'd said 'date'. *First* date.


'What are you studying?' she asked Dieter as they ordered from a stand on Zimmerstraße.

'Chemistry,' he said.

'You must be very clever.'

'I don't know about that.' He gave her a shy smile. 'Chemistry's just about how things are put together. It's the physics lot like Astrid that are the clever ones. I never have a clue what she's on about.'

Typical! Astrid already had the glossiest hair, best clothes and finest voice; now it seemed she had brains too. Still, Dieter was here with *her*, which was what counted.

'Did you grow up in Berlin?'

'I did. My dad was Austrian but he came here after the Anschluss and met my mum. He teaches at the Humboldt university, so we lived in East Berlin after the war.'

'Was it all right?'

He shrugged.

'I never knew the difference, but my parents aren't keen on the Russians and they didn't let me join any of the communist youth groups. You know, the young pioneers and the Freie Deutsche Jugend and all that.'

Kirsten wasn't sure she did know, but didn't want to say, so gave a nod and bit into her wurst.

'Well, if you don't join them, the state doesn't like it. Makes life very hard for you. I wasn't allowed to do sixth form.'

Kirsten nearly spat curry sauce across Dieter's smart shirt. 'Why?!'

'Only those in the Party are allowed the "privilege of further education". I'd have been shipped off to a collective farm or factory and I didn't want that, so I moved in with my aunt over here in West Berlin. There was a school offering "east classes" for kids like me who'd moved over, and it was an eye-opener, I can tell you. I learned so much about the world, about different cultures and attitudes and political systems. In the DDR there's only one way to do things – *their* way – and you're not even allowed to know the alternatives.'

'Isn't that a bit paranoid?' Kirsten asked.

Dieter roared with laughter.

'It is, Kirsten. It absolutely is. But that's them all over. I mean, what sort of country has to put barbed wire around its borders to stop their people getting out! And it's not working, not here in Berlin at least. I volunteer at the refugee centre in Marienfelde and they're getting around a thousand people a day coming out of the Soviet Zone. A thousand! Most of them come to Berlin from elsewhere in the DDR because the border is open here, and they're all young – people in their twenties like us who can see the fatal flaws in their nasty brand of socialism.

'East Germany is leaking workers out of Berlin left, right and centre, Kirsten, and the only way the Ossis know to stop it is with laws and guns and nasty, sneaky spies. It's sick and I'm very glad, these days, to count myself a Wessi instead.'

'Me too,' Kirsten mumbled, though she'd been distracted by

him saying 'people in their twenties like us'. How old did he think she was? And should she enlighten him? She thought not, especially as they were now arriving at Wanne – the Bathtub – and she'd been dying to go here for ages.

She followed Dieter inside, drinking in the smoky atmosphere and the buzz of chatter. A band was playing something very lively on a piano, clarinet and saxophone and she felt the lilt of it pull at her feet.

'Dance?' Dieter asked.

'Yes please!'

She was shockingly inexpert but he guided her around the other couples with a firm hand, so that she quickly got the hang of it. The evening flashed past and it was only when a nearby girl exclaimed she'd missed her curfew, that Kirsten realised it was almost eleven. Her mother would have a fit! Reluctantly, she tugged at Dieter's arm.

'I think I'd better get back, Dieter. Mutti might worry.'

'You live at home?'

'Er, yeah. It's, you know, cheaper.'

'Sure. What are you doing? With your life I mean. You don't work in Café Adler full-time, do you?'

'Just while I, you know, sort out what I want as a career.'

'Right. I thought with all your cool clothes that you might be at design college.'

'You did? I mean, that would be good, but not yet. I'm, er needed at home for, you know...' She waved an airy hand, trying to imply important, grown-up things rather than the prosaic fact that she was still at school. 'It's very dull.'

'Right. Come on then, I'll walk you home.'

'I'm right out on Bernauerstraβe.'

'Then we'll take the tram. I have to see you safe; it's late.'

Kirsten flushed, delighted, and even more so when he took her hand as they left the club, lacing his fingers naturally into hers. Was he going to kiss her? she wondered. Anticipation raced around her blood as if she were still jazz-dancing so that it was hard to make coherent conversation.

'This is me,' she said when they reached the start of her block. 'It's not posh or anything.'

'It looks lovely.' He paused, tugging on her hand so that she was pulled to a stop. She looked up at him. 'You're lovely, Kirsten.'

'I am?'

'Very. May I kiss you?'

Oh goodness! She nodded, tipping her head back, and then his lips were on hers and he was pressing her against the wall and, oh my, if the anticipation of his kiss had been jazz-dancing then the reality was a Parisian can-can. She threaded her hands around his neck and he gave a small groan and slid his tongue into her mouth. Not just kissing, but French kissing and, wow, it was good!

'So lovely,' he moaned against her lips.

His hand moved down her back, cupping her buttock and she gasped. She hadn't been expecting that and now his other hand was tugging at her blouse and his fingers were creeping upwards across her skin and it felt good, but wrong too. The scar in her armpit prickled as his breathing grew ragged. She thought of her mother talking about rabid-dog Russians and, frightened, pushed him away. He stumbled, falling awkwardly sideways, and a man passing on a bike rang an angry warning on his bell.

'What did you do that for?' Dieter demanded angrily.

'I'm sorry. It was... too much. Too fast.'

He stared at her, his eyes dark, but then he crumpled.

'God, I'm sorry. I got carried away. You're so lovely, Kirsten and I... I'm so sorry. I didn't think, I...'

'It's fine.' Kirsten wasn't scared now, just embarrassed. She must seem so naive. 'I'd better go in.'

He caught at her arm.

'A little longer, please. I really am sorry. I wouldn't have hurt you, I promise, or made you do anything you didn't want to.'

'Of course not. I didn't think you would. You're no Russian.'

'What?' He stepped back, puzzled. 'What do you mean by that?'

'Nothing, sorry.'

He was the one looking offended now and her gorgeous night was getting tangled into a stupid, sticky mess.

'Why would I be a Russian, Kirsten?'

Oh God! All the information she'd found out recently seemed to sit permanently at the top of her mind but it wasn't meant to come blurting out like this! Now she was going to have to explain, which was mortifying.

'It was a stupid thing to say. I just... I found out the other day that Russians, you know, forced themselves on my mother after the war.'

'No?! Oh, Kirsten, how awful.'

'It was a long time ago, in the battle of Berlin. They were angry, she said, out for revenge.'

'That's no excuse. The poor woman.'

'Yeah. Days it went on and she got pregnant, too, with my brother.'

'The lad in the café the other day?'

'That's him. That is... You won't tell anyone, will you? I mean, I know it wasn't her fault, and it certainly wasn't his, but they'd be mortified. I shouldn't have—'

He leaned in and quieted her with a kiss, light and soft and so tender that Kirsten melted.

'Of course I won't, Kirsten. That's terrible. No wonder you're... wary.'

'I'm sorry. It's not you.'

'Just one more thing to blame the Soviets for, hey?'

She nodded and wished he'd kiss her again and forget about

it all, but he was looking at his watch and asking which was her door and her date, it seemed, was at an end.

'Thank you,' she said. 'I've had a great time.'

'Me too. Goodnight, Kirsten.'

'Goodnight.'

She leaned hopefully forward but he was already turning away, so she let herself unhappily into her apartment block. Had she blown it? It was hardly the romantic ending to the evening that it should have been and she feared that her first date with Dieter Wohlfahrt might also be her last. What had possessed her to say anything about the damned Russians? She'd just had such a nice night and Dieter had seemed so genuinely interested in her that her stupid tongue had been unable to resist the urge to confide her recent troubles. What a mistake! She trudged up the stairs, cursing herself, but as she slotted her key into the lock, the door flew open and there was Lotti.

'Kirsten! Oh, thank God. I was worried sick.'

'I'm sorry, Mutti. I was dancing. I lost track of the time.'

Her mother grabbed her shoulders, looking closely at her.

'Dancing? You've been on a date, schnuki?'

'Sort of.'

'With a boy?! I hope he treated you right. I hope he—'

'He was lovely. Really.'

'Lieber Gott! My Kirsty courting. Did you hear that, Gretchen? Kirsty is courting.'

'I'm not. It was just a date. What are you doing here, Tante?'

'Waiting for you.'

Kirsten grimaced.

'I'm sorry.'

'And keeping an eye on *him*.'

Gretchen gestured to the sofa where Kirsten's father was lolling, his eyes half closed and a cigarette burning down to his thick fingertips. As if sensing their eyes on him, he started awake and sucked automatically on the fag. Kirsten shuddered in distaste.

'Do we have to let him in?' she asked.

'Unless your mother does the sensible thing and divorces him, yes,' Gretchen told her.

Jan pushed himself up, fury burning in his red-rimmed eyes.

'Divorce me? That's rich, that is. Fifteen years away from my dear wife and when I find my way back, she wants to divorce me.'

Gretchen put her hands on her hips.

'You weren't "away", you were jailed for crimes against humanity.'

'A made-up charge. Didn't exist before 1945.'

'Because it didn't need to. Did you, or did you not, run a death camp, Jan?'

'I did not.'

'You're denying it was a death camp?'

'I'm denying I ran it. I was one of the management team. My job was the smooth processing of the... the goods.'

'The people? The Jews?'

'They weren't all Jews.'

'Oh, sorry, you happily gassed other people too.'

Jan pointed a meaty finger at Gretchen.

'I didn't see you or any of your pious ilk asking us to stop, did I? Christ, I didn't see you speaking out against the yellow stars, or the ghettos, or the trains full of people heading east. Out of sight, out of mind! At least some of us were prepared to stand up and make sure it happened as humanely as possible.'

'Fair point,' Gretchen said weakly. 'Not the humane bit, that's scheiβe, but the out of sight stuff.'

'And it wasn't only killing, actually. I saved lives.'

Gretchen rolled her eyes but Kirsten stepped forward, intrigued.

'How?'

'I got people out. Little people. Babies.'

'Jan...' Lotti said, and Kirsten caught the same warning in her voice that she'd heard on his first night in the apartment. She looked to her mother, who twirled her finger at the side of her head. 'He's lost it, Kirsten. Not surprising, really, after fifteen years inside, but sad all the same.'

Jan gave a low growl.

'I have not lost it, woman. I saved babies. I took them out of that place and got them to good homes, safe homes – as well you know.'

'Jan,' Lotti said again, pleading now.

He gave a sly smile but Kirsten wasn't buying it.

'I don't believe you,' she told him. 'How could there be babies in a KZ?'

Jan turned her way and she looked into his pupils, black pinpricks in his stained eyeballs.

'Oh Kirsten, little Kirsten, you have no idea, do you? You're as stupid as your mother. And, it seems, every bit as much of a tart.'

'I've been dancing.'

'That what they're calling it now, is it? Learned from the best, you have – from pious Karlotta and her Russian brat. Divorce me, Lotti. Suits me. It seems you're keener on nurturing Jews and commies than good German babies, anyway.'

'Jan!'

'Oh, shut up! I'm fed up with the lot of you, whining all the time, I'm going to sleep.'

And with that, he flung himself back on the couch, curled his big arms around his prison-hard body, and said no more. Kirsten looked from him to her mother, whimpering in Tante Gretchen's arms. Above them the clock struck midnight and Kirsten felt like the worst Cinderella ever. Just an hour ago she'd been happily dancing in the Wanne; how had the evening gone so badly downhill?

'What did he mean, Mutti, about you only nurturing Jews and commies? Am I not his child either?'

The question quivered in the air between them, but then Lotti broke free from Gretchen and ran to her.

'Of course you are, schnuki. You're every bit as much his as you are mine, though I, at least, treasure you. Now come on, bed. It'll all look better in the morning.'

Kirsten let herself be led away but, glancing back at the man snoring on the couch, she very much doubted it would look better in the morning, or any time soon.

# EIGHT

*OLIVIA*

'If you could slip your clothes off, my dear.'

The nurse said it kindly but that didn't make it any less strange.

'My clothes?'

'So we can make sure everything's working properly. Your body is in the service of the state now, you know, so we have to look after it.'

'Right.'

Slowly Olivia began undressing, wondering what on earth she'd got herself into. It had all happened so fast. She hadn't really believed Erich Ahrendt about the sports school so it had been a shock when she'd been summoned to the principal's office a few days later to find a fidgeting Herr Neumann and both her parents. Ester and Filip had looked small and bewildered, but had offered Olivia wide smiles and pulled her into a seat between them as the principal had explained that she'd been identified as an 'asset to the state' and they wanted to move her schooling to Dynamo Berlin.

'Berlin?' Olivia had gasped. She had vague memories from being there as a little girl when Ester had been training as a midwife, but she hadn't been back since.

'That's almost an hour in on the train,' Ester had protested. 'She'll be exhausted.'

'You don't understand, Frau Pasternak, she'll be boarding.'

'She'll... she'll leave home?'

'To become an elite athlete, Frau Pasternak, and represent the DDR on the international stage.'

'But... but who'll make sure she eats properly?'

He'd smiled condescendingly.

'She will eat better than any of us, I assure you. It is in the state's interests to ensure it.'

And that had been that.

'Are you sure?' Ester had asked Olivia, again and again as they'd rushed around packing. 'Are you sure you want to go? Are you sure you want to leave us?'

'Sure,' Olivia had said, afraid that if she thought about it too deeply, she'd clutch at her mother and beg to stay there where she was safe, where she was loved, where she was still a child. But she'd grown up fast in the last week and now God had sent her an opportunity to grow and she'd had to take it.

Closing her eyes against the nurse's probing examination, Olivia thought unhappily back to the farewell dinner Ester and Filip had organised at the Aktivist, Stalinstadt's premium restaurant. She, Mordy and Ben had often peered through the tall, stained-glass windows of the restaurant, dreaming of eating there, but it was usually full of Soviet officers, and as both Ester and Filip tended to flinch near uniforms they'd never been. For Olivia's last night in Stalinstadt, however, they'd made an exception.

It had been a disaster from the moment they'd stepped inside. They'd sat there, stiff and uneasy in the high-backed red chairs, as the soldiers at the next table had drunk vodka after vodka, their riotous bonhomie only good to cover the family's awkwardness.

'Why does Olivia have to go?' Ben had asked Filip.

'I'm right here,' Olivia had said.

He'd turned fiery eyes on her.

'Very well then – why do you have to go? Don't you like us any more?'

'Of course I do, Bennie. It's not that. This is a chance to further my education.'

'Throwing a spear isn't education,' Mordecai had shot at her. 'It's what cavemen did.'

'Boys!' Filip had admonished, shocked. 'Olivia has been chosen to train for her country. It's an honour.'

They'd looked at each other sulkily.

'Why can't we all go to Berlin, then?' Ben had demanded.

'Berlin is not nice,' Ester had told them in her tightest, sternest voice.

'So why is Olivia going? Does she not want to be a part of this family any more?' Mordecai had whined.

The waitress had arrived then, with greasy-looking bowls of dumplings, and they had all sat there miserably with the accusation floating between them.

'Of course I do,' Olivia had wanted to scream, but the fact that it was even a choice had dug into her skin and she'd been almost glad when one of the soldiers had thrown up centimetres from Mordy's shoes and attention had been diverted.

Even back in their apartment, just the five of them, it had been heartbreakingly stiff and she'd been half-relieved to leave for the train early the next morning. They'd be just the four of them now. Perhaps they'd be happier like that.

Olivia shook the thought away as the nurse, thankfully, finished the examination and produced a mound of clothing – two full tracksuits in the red and gold of Club Dynamo, five polo shirts, two pairs of shorts and a competition kit.

'Is that all for me?'

'It is.'

'How much will it cost?'

'It's all provided, dear. Remember, you're an—'

'Instrument of the state,' Olivia completed.

Her astonishing situation was truly starting to sink in and it was with mounting excitement that she pulled on her new uniform and looked in the mirror. There, before her, was a whole new self. In this outfit her height and strength looked purposeful and imposing rather than awkward. She had been right to leave, right to come to Berlin. This cuckoo had found her nest and she set her shoulders back and gave herself a tiny nod.

'That's it, girl,' the nurse said. 'You're elite now – enjoy it. Here.' She handed her a jar of small, blue pills. 'Vitamins, newly developed by our clever scientists in Leipzig to help you train more effectively. We introduced them last month and are seeing excellent results, so take one a day please, when you first wake up. And one of these too.'

She added a foil pack of tiny, white pills.

'What are they?'

'Contraception.'

'Why? I'm not, you know...'

'Having sex? Oh, you should do. It's marvellous fun and very good for the circulation. We encourage all our athletes to explore the potential of their bodies in every way, but we don't want you getting pregnant, do we? Hence...' She nodded to the packet. 'One every morning, dear, and you'll be quite safe. It regulates your cycle too so that we can be sure you're in peak condition, though you may find your periods stop anyway.'

Olivia looked at her, surprised.

'Why?'

'Oh, all the training – the weights and that – have an effect, that's all. Still, something you can do without, yes?'

'I suppose so,' she agreed, because who wanted periods if they didn't have to have them? As for the sex thing... The state encouraged intimacy within a secure relationship, but her parents were keener on marriage first. Bless them, though, they were old-fashioned and, besides, they'd been lucky enough to fall in love the moment they'd met each other. Sometimes Olivia watched the shining bond between them and wondered how she would ever come close to that herself, so she had no qualms about trying out a few people first. The only problem was that she'd not met anyone worth doing it with.

With her spare clothes and her tiny pills in a smart Dynamo kit bag, Olivia was ushered out of the medical room to go meet the school principal. She was glad of her new outfit to make her feel more a part of this astonishing place, but it was still impossible to hide her awe at the facilities. The main building was new-built, in the Stalinesque style familiar from home – big, chunky blocks in austere grey with grand neo-classical columns at the imposing entrance – and round the back were sports fields, training halls and swimming pools like none she'd ever seen. At the far side of the complex, a round stadium proclaimed itself the home of Dynamo FC.

'The football club is Erich Mielke's pet,' the nurse told her, 'but it's high time we expanded. First we had swimmers, then gymnasts and now you athletes. It's good to have women here.'

'Erich Mielke?' Olivia asked, swallowing at the mention of the head of the Ministry for State Security.

'Yes. The Stasi headquarters are somewhere nearby – no one knows where, of course – and he often drops in.'

'Sounds scary.'

'Maybe at first, but you'll soon get used to being watched.'

'By the Stasi?'

'By everyone! The price of fame, my dear.'

Fame! This was ridiculous. Olivia felt horribly like an impostor and could only pray she lived up to Dynamo's expectations or she'd be on the train back to Stalinstadt within weeks. *And safely with my family*, she reminded herself and felt better. They'd always be there for her, so she just had to do her best.

'In here, please.'

The nurse paused at a dark door and rapped confidently on it. A brass plaque bore the words, *Herr Braun, Schulleiter*, and Olivia sidled inside feeling nervous all over again.

'Olivia, welcome!' Herr Braun, a trim man with a neat moustache and a big smile, came towards her, hand outstretched. 'You must be feeling a little overwhelmed.'

'It's all happened rather fast,' she admitted.

'Sorry about that. Dynamo have been given an urgent remit to recruit talented track and field athletes before the Olympic cycle hits, so it's all go. You see there.' He took her to a big window, pointing past a run of football pitches to where diggers and men were busy in an open patch of land. 'That will be our brand-new, rubber and asphalt track. Once completed – hopefully before Christmas – it will be the best facility in the country. Exciting, isn't it?'

'It is,' Olivia agreed, enjoying his enthusiasm. 'But at the moment?'

'Straight to the point, Olivia, I like that. At the moment, the athletes are training on the city track about four kilometres further into Berlin and are housed in a hostel right near the track. I'll take you there now if you're ready?'

Olivia nodded dumbly and followed him to a smart Trabant, peering out the window as he drove her out of the quiet suburb of Hohenschönhausen and into the busier streets of inner Berlin. She had vague memories of the capital from her pre-school years but had not been old enough to notice much beyond the nursery school and apartment and now she stared in surprise at the higgledy-piggledy streets of the city. Many of Berlin's buildings were new, but they were squeezed into bomb-holes between old ones and built in a variety of designs so that the effect was curiously crowded and mismatched.

'Wait until you see the Brandenburg Gate,' Herr Braun told her, as if reading her thoughts. 'It's very grand and so is Stalinallee – a most impressive new monument to the power of the DDR. The Western side of the city think they're so smart with their shiny shops and marketing boards but we're the ones creating monuments for the future.'

'The Western side?' Olivia asked nervously.

'That's right. It's only a couple of streets away.'

'And I can just walk across?'

'You can if you wish to, but I wouldn't recommend it; there's nothing there but empty promises. Now, here we are at your hostel, let's get you inside.'

Following him into a shabby building, Olivia found herself in a brightly painted lobby. It had white walls, dotted with swirls of red, black and gold, with three words scrolled in bold letters on the back wall: *Citius, Altius, Fortius.*

'Do you know what that is?' Herr Braun asked. She shook her head. 'The Olympic motto: Faster, Higher, Stronger. It's what we're all about here and in Tokyo '64 we're going to prove it to the world. You, Olivia, can be a part of that. Is it not wonderful?'

'Wonderful,' she agreed, looking around her and blessing Erich Ahrendt for this astonishing chance.

'Good. Excellent! And now, here are Herr and Frau Scholz, your hausmeisters, to show you around.'

A thin-faced couple approached, both in stern, dark suits, with not the hint of a smile between them.

'Olivia Pasternak?' Frau Scholz asked in a gravelly voice.

'Yes,' she squeaked.

'Welcome. You will be in the girls' dorm under my charge. I expect absolute tidiness in your cubicle and absolute discipline in your behaviour. Breakfast is at 6 a.m., lunch at midday, and supper at 7 p.m. If you're late, you miss it. Your coach, Trainer Lang, will provide your training schedule and, if you have time, you are permitted into the city for two hours a day. No alcohol or drugs under any circumstances, and curfew is 10 p.m. – all girls in bed and all boys out of the dorm by that time. Do you understand?'

Olivia glanced to Herr Braun, her enthusiasm faltering, but he gave her a blithe smile and said, 'The rules are strict but fair. Herr and Frau Scholz are in loco parentis here and will see you safe and well.'

Olivia looked again at the forbidding pair and could imagine no one less like her mild-mannered, soft-hearted parents but she supposed that if you were in charge of a large group of youngsters you had to be stern and she certainly didn't want to get on the wrong side of them.

'I quite understand, Frau Scholz, thank you.'

'Good. Now, we're far too busy to show you around, I'm afraid, but I've recruited one of our second-year students. Hans?'

She gestured to one side and a young man jogged in. He was wearing the same red tracksuit as Olivia but open at the front to reveal an exceptionally toned chest beneath a tight-fitting polo shirt. He had dark hair, cut short at the sides but with bouncy curls on top, and his eyes were the colour of Western chocolate – and just as tempting. Best of all, he was smiling fit to burst.

'Olivia, right? Our new javelin thrower. I'm Hans Keller – discus. Welcome to the throws team, the best one in the whole verdammte place.'

'Language, Hans,' Frau Scholz said, but with a glimmer of a smile for the lively athlete.

'Sorry, Ma. Big training session. I'm a bit pumped.'

'As you should be, Hans, as you should be.'

She shot him an indulgent look and waved him towards Olivia with clear reluctance.

'This your luggage?' Hans asked, swinging her heavy suitcase up as if it were a bag of feathers. 'Excellent. Let's get you settled in. This way.'

He led her out of the big hall and, as they headed up some stairs away from Herr Braun and the intimidating Scholzes, Olivia breathed more easily. Through the landing window, she glimpsed the athletics track and, beyond it, the roofs of central Berlin.

'Not a bad view,' Hans said. 'You've got lucky here, Olivia – us athletes may not have the shiny facilities of Dynamo proper, but we have a lot more freedom.'

'We can go into the city, right?'

'Right. The schedule's pretty hectic so we never get long, but it's possible. What are you after? Shops? Bars? The West?'

She recoiled.

'Not the West!'

Hans laughed.

'I felt like that when I first got here – I'm from Leipzig – but West Berlin's not the weird place they tell you about, honestly. Wessis are just like us, really, but with a bit more gloss.' Olivia frowned uncertainly and Hans squeezed her arm. A thrill shot across her skin and when she dared to look up, his lovely chocolatey eyes met hers with genuine interest. 'It's a funny place, Berlin, but cool when you get used to it. I'll happily take you into the city if you want.'

'Thank you.' He was still holding her arm and it felt delicious. 'As long as we meet Frau Scholz's curfew?'

Hans laughed.

'Don't worry about Ma Scholz. She thinks she's in control, but she doesn't know the half of it.' He winked and opened a door and Olivia found herself in a common room packed with youngsters. They were chatting in a small kitchen area, lounging on beanbags, and gathering around a ping-pong table at the far end. 'Welcome to Dynamo AC, Olivia. We're here to train as hard as we can, but we're here to have fun too. Life's for living, right?'

'Right!' Olivia agreed happily.

'And what our parents don't know won't hurt them!'

It was a throw-away comment, designed to make her feel at ease, but it had the opposite effect. Instantly, all Olivia could see was Ester's tortured face when she'd told her about their missing daughter. They didn't know where Pippa was and now she'd left them too. For all the right reasons, perhaps, but for the first time it occurred to her that Ester and Filip might think she was running away from the secret they'd finally shared.

*Well, they ran away from it too*, she thought bullishly, but it didn't help much. Thoughts of that painful last meal spiked through her. 'Does she not want to be a part of this family any more?' Mordecai had asked, but he couldn't be further from the truth. She just couldn't help feeling, now, that she had to justify her place within it. She shuddered. *Faster, Higher, Stronger* was a good motto, but her strength came from her family and she just prayed that coming to Berlin had not eroded that forever.

# NINE

## WEDNESDAY, 31 MAY

*KIRSTEN*

'You made these yourself? Is that not very difficult?'

Kirsten looked down at the three-quarter length trousers she'd laboured over for hours, and back to Dieter.

'Not really. It's only a bit of sewing.'

Dieter shook his head.

'There's no "only" about it, Kirsten. My mother once made me try to sew a button back onto a shirt after I'd torn it climbing trees and I couldn't even thread the needle. I think you're very talented.'

She flushed, delighted. She'd been so sure that Dieter wouldn't want to have anything to do with her after the embarrassing end to their date, but he'd come straight over to order for his crowd when they'd arrived in Café Adler. Astrid kept throwing her dirty looks and now she sauntered across to join Dieter with a false smile for Kirsten.

'Hey, it's my favourite waitress. Nice slacks.'

She looked pointedly from Kirsten's home-sewn trousers to her own denims, but her dart missed its mark.

'Aren't they great?' Dieter enthused. 'She sewed them herself.'

'You don't say!' Astrid's eyes narrowed. 'I don't know how you find the time with your job and, of course, school.'

'School?' Dieter looked to Astrid and then back to Kirsten. 'You're still at school?'

Kirsten wondered how easy it might be to poison Astrid's doughnut but then remembered that the svelte student never ate confectionary.

'One year to go,' she admitted.

'Right. You, er, you didn't say.'

'No.'

'Why not?'

There was nothing for it but the truth.

'I was embarrassed.'

Astrid gave a nasty laugh, but Dieter looked sideways at her and said, 'You shouldn't be embarrassed. I'm even more impressed by your sewing now.' Astrid snorted and, snatching two coffees from the counter, stalked back to the others. Dieter leaned in. 'And even more ashamed of my, er, behaviour the other night.'

'Please don't be. I should have said.'

'Perhaps you'll give me the chance to make it up to you another evening?'

'Really?! I mean, yes. Please. I'd like that.'

He grinned.

'It's a date.'

Kirsten smiled at him, astonished, and it was only Sasha nudging at her to serve the next customer that brought her to her senses.

'He's cute, Kirsty, but you need this job, right?'

'Right,' Kirsten agreed. Lotti couldn't afford to give her any pocket money and there were so many nice things to buy, so she applied herself to her work.

It was busy and time shot past with only the chance to look for Dieter, oh, about every minute. At least Astrid was deep in conversation with another boy – something very earnest-looking, no doubt about planets or forces or whatever physicists were into – and she could enjoy watching Dieter as he joked with his friends. It must be so cool to go to university, to study something that interested you and hang out with so many people your own age. Perhaps she should apply. Hadn't Dieter said he'd thought she was a design student? So why not?

She shook away the foolish thought. She wasn't clever enough for university and the best people on the design courses probably ran up simple trousers in an hour or two instead of swearing the apartment down evening after evening.

Not that she was the one doing the swearing there now. Every evening, by around ten o'clock, she, Uli and Lotti would tense up, expecting Jan to bang through the door. The world – the free, peaceful world – seemed to be enraging him more with every day and he would take out his anger on anything that fell into his sights – Lotti's pretty pastel chairs; their basic wireless set; the coffee table he disparaged as 'stupid American nonsense' but always put his big feet on.

Lotti tiptoed around him offering food, as if sausage or potato salad might appease his rage, and poor Uli hid in his room. Kirsten hated Jan for making her brother feel so worthless and stood up to him when she dared, but he was big and strong and she'd taken a few bruises for her troubles. So had her mother. Lotti should throw him out but he was so intimidating that none of them – not even feisty Gretchen – could work out how.

Kirsten sighed and glanced to the clock. Nearly her shift's end. Uli would be coming to collect her – Lotti insisted on it when she was on lates – and she prayed he'd wait outside. But no, here he was, sidling in as if looking for a gap in reality to absorb him. Kirsten tried to wave him behind the counter but he hovered dead centre and Sasha bumped into him in a clatter of cups.

'Watch out, kid,' she said, unfazed, but the noise had attracted the attention of Dieter's group.

'Well look who it is,' Astrid purred.

'Astrid,' Dieter warned, but there was a glint in her eye as she rose and patted Uli on the head.

'Come to pick your sister up, have you? How gallant.' Uli looked up at her, dazed, and she beamed down at him and added, 'Especially for a bastard.'

The people nearby gasped. Confusion swam in Uli's eyes and leaked out as a tear. He turned and ran straight back out again and, mortified, Kirsten ducked into the kitchen. She stood there, digging her fingernails into the wood of the chopping board, hating herself for her cowardice. She could hear Sasha shepherding people out and wondered where poor Uli had gone. He felt hated at home and now he must feel hated here too. It wasn't fair.

Setting her shoulders, she went back out to see Dieter hovering unhappily at the counter as his friends gathered up their bags.

'You told her,' she accused him.

'I didn't. I promise.'

'Then how does she know?'

'I've no idea, really. I promised I'd keep it secret, didn't I?'

'You did but it seems you couldn't resist filling your friends in on your juicy bit of rape gossip.' Dieter looked shocked. 'Oh, I'm sorry, am I not allowed to say "rape"? Is it so shameful that we can't speak about it, despite it not being my mother's fault or that of any of the hundreds of other German women who were so hatefully abused?'

'Of course not. It was you who wanted to keep it quiet.'

That was true. Kirsten felt as confused as poor Uli had looked, but she knew one thing – Dieter might be cute and clever and a great dancer, not to mention a very fine kisser, but if she couldn't trust him, he wasn't worth dating.

'I think it's best if we don't see each other again.'

He looked pleasingly distraught.

'I honestly didn't tell her. Astrid! Astrid, come over here!' Kirsten's stomach lurched. She just wanted to get away and find Uli, but Dieter was grabbing Astrid's slim arm and pulling her across. 'You didn't hear about Kirsten's brother from me, right?'

Astrid flicked her glossy hair.

'I can't remember.'

'Well try.'

The force of his voice clearly surprised her and she flinched.

'I heard it from my brother,' she admitted petulantly. 'And he heard it the same way as the rest of Berlin – some bloke called Jan getting drunk in the Eden Saloon and spitting bile to anyone who'll listen. My brother said he was raving on about how his damned son is a Ruskie bastard and his damned daughter a stupid waitress at the Adler, so I figured he must be your father, Kirsten. That boy's as dark as any Slav.'

'Astrid!'

She shrugged Dieter off.

'Well, he is. Poor thing,' she added in a half-hearted attempt at sympathy. 'Anyway, must get going, essay to write.'

And with that, she flounced off, the rest of her group in obedient tow. Dieter hesitated.

'You see, it honestly wasn't me, Kirsty.' She sized him up, wanting to believe it, and he gave her a little nudge. 'Why don't you go down the Eden now and see for yourself?'

'No, thank you.' She turned to the nearest table, reaching for the dirty cups. 'I'm not going to grace him with the attention.' Already, though, her mind was racing and once Dieter was gone, she found Sasha. 'Where's the Eden Saloon again?'

Sasha looked at her in concern.

'Are you sure, süße? I mean—'
'Where is it?'
She sighed.
'Damaschke Straße.'


The Eden Saloon was buzzing. As Kirsten approached, she could see myriad dancing shadows behind the fogged-up windows and feel the bass of the music shaking the pavement. Someone had propped open the doors and a square of multi-coloured light fell onto the dusky road as laughter and chatter spilled out like froth on the top of a stein. Kirsten bit her lip and looked nervously to Uli. She'd found him cowering behind the bins around the back of Café Adler and apologised for not standing up for him.

'No matter,' he'd said. 'I wouldn't stand up for me either.'

She'd hugged him close.

'I should always stand up for you, Uli – you're my brother.'

They'd headed for home, arm in arm, but, with Dieter's words niggling at her she'd insisted on this detour. Now she wasn't so sure.

'He's probably not in there,' she said. Uli nodded in dumb agreement. 'It sounds a bit young for him, don't you think? Perhaps we should go home?'

Another nod, more enthusiastic, but then Kirsten heard a familiar voice over the happy hubbub: 'The world's gone to sheiße, that's the problem. There's no discipline any more, no order!'

She glanced at Uli, who grabbed her arm, finding his voice. 'Let's go home, Kirsty. He sounds really drunk, so what's the point in going in?'

Kirsten considered.

'The point, Uli, is that he's badmouthing us to half of Berlin.'

'He's badmouthing everyone by the sounds of it. What good will it do?'

Kirsten wasn't sure but Jan was off again.

'It's these Slavs hanging around, acting like they own the place. This isn't their country and I can't believe everyone is letting them act as if it is. I'd shoot 'em all. Even that snotty little mouse in my own damned home.'

Uli shrank back, but that was it for Kirsten.

'You stay here,' she told him and, blood boiling, she marched inside.

The Eden Saloon was rammed, though most of the people were too busy dancing to pay attention to the ageing, blurry-eyed bloke holding forth to a raggle-taggle group near the door. Kirsten marched up to him.

'Hello, Father.'

He squinted at her.

'Kirsten? What are you doing here?'

'Listening to you spouting off like a Nazi,' she shot back.

The other men gasped and even the band seemed to stop, but it was simply a beat in their bouncy tune and no one looked round.

'We were all Nazis,' Jan drawled. 'It used to be a good thing and just because someone else decided it isn't any more, we have to pretend that we've changed.'

'I wasn't a Nazi,' one of the group said hastily. 'Were you, Heinz?'

Heinz threw up his hands.

'No way.'

Jan rolled his eyes.

'Very good, boys. Play the game like the cowards you are.'

Heinz leaped to his feet.

'Who are you calling a coward? I fought in Stalingrad, I did.'

'And now you lick the Ruskies' boots.'

Jan was up too, flexing his muscles, and Kirsten started to doubt the wisdom of this visit. She glanced to the door and saw Uli creeping in nervously.

'I think,' she said, 'that we can all be a bit more tolerant nowadays. Why does it matter where you were born?'

Jan's eyes narrowed and he turned away from Heinz and advanced on her.

'Why?! You see, this is what's going wrong. But then, what can I expect from you, stupid girl. You're no more German than your bastard brother.'

Kirsten felt the pub throb around her.

'What do you mean?' she stammered. 'I'm your daughter, I—'

He cut her off with a nasty laugh.

'You're not my daughter, Kirsten. Christ, that's not even your name. I found you, girl. I gave you to your mother as a present because her goddamned womb was too sour to give us a baby of our own and look where that got me!'

Kirsten's head spun.

'Found me? Found me where?'

'In a hovel, in a ditch, in hell itself. Does it matter? You're as much of a bastard as he is!'

He pointed to Uli. Kirsten grabbed at him and he put an arm around her waist and stood at her side.

'I'm glad you're not my father,' Uli said, loud and clear. 'And I'm glad you're not Kirsten's either. In fact, it's the best news I've heard in weeks.'

Kirsten gaped at him but as a stunned Jan lifted his fist, Uli turned and ran and she ran with him. They fled the Eden Saloon, shooting past the happy light of the windows into the welcome shadows beyond.

'Let's go home, Kirsty,' Uli was babbling, over and over. 'Let's get you home. Let's get you safe.'

But they both knew that home was no longer safe, because it

was also home to the man who was not, if he was to be believed, father to either of them. Uli was taking comfort in that solidarity but Kirsten felt as if her world – maybe even her very self – was imploding.

*That's not even your name,* Jan had said and what was she without her name? Empty, confused and afraid, she clung to Uli's arm and hastened through streets that now felt full of shapeless shadows waiting to engulf her, and home to an apartment full of secrets.

# TEN

*OLIVIA*

Olivia stared out the window, trying to ignore the angry babble
of voices at the front of the bus. This was the furthest she'd ever
been from home and the first time she'd been into the Federal
Republic of Germany. The Dynamo bus had been ushered
through the Inner German Border at the checkpoint and she'd
pressed her nose to the window, eager to see the vulgar West,
but it had looked remarkably like the East.

Most of the three-hour trip to Wolfsburg had been through
fields and woodlands without the brash lights and branding of
rampant capitalism that she'd been expecting. Even Wolfsburg
itself, built to house the workers at the Volkswagen factory, had
been quite like Stalinstadt in its order and calm, and Olivia had
stared at it in confusion and been very glad to get into the
athletics stadium for the competition.

Now, with dusk casting a pastel pink across the open countryside, they were heading back to school. The competition had
gone well. Dynamo's fledgling team had stamped their mark on

German youth athletics and the coaches had been triumphant as red tracksuits had flooded the podiums. They were not so happy now.

Olivia touched her fingers to the medal around her neck. She still couldn't believe that she'd won the silver and couldn't wait to tell her family. This would surely show the boys why she'd left? This would surely make Ester and Filip proud of her, their cuckoo daughter?

Olivia pictured her home, with them all cosy within it, and felt the now-familiar ache. She'd written to them several times, and they'd replied with messages of love. The boys had even sent pictures of her throwing her javelin, their anger at her departure apparently forgotten, but every day without them made her doubt her decision to leave and this, at least, was something to hold onto.

She'd been battling for weeks to learn the many complex elements that went into a good javelin throw, always afraid she'd be unveiled as an impostor at Dynamo, so when her third throw had flown sweetly out of her hand and travelled close to the 40 metres line, she'd been unable to believe it. It had only been Hans going mad on the sidelines that had assured her the mark on the board was truly hers. Stepping onto the podium and hearing her name over the loudspeaker had filled her with joy and she'd been so proud to take her place in the sea of red tracksuits for a happy team photo.

It hadn't been happy for long, for that photo had been short of two athletes and the arguments had begun moments later.

'Anyone sitting here?'

Olivia looked up to see Hans and gladly snatched her bag off the seat.

'No. Please.'

She waved him in and felt a tingle of warmth flood across her skin as his thigh touched hers in the tight space of the double seat. She'd met so many nice people in school. None, however, as nice as Hans.

'You did so well today,' she said, nodding to the golden medal around his neck.

'As did you. Silver in your first ever comp.'

She laughed.

'I think it was a fluke.'

'I think it was brilliant. You've got so much talent, Liv. Sorry, can I call you Liv?'

She nodded.

'My parents call me Liv.'

The thought of them made her heart ache. If only they could have been here today. They'd have been leaping up and down, confused but clapping fit to burst, just like they'd always done at her tennis matches.

'You miss them?' Hans said.

'I do. I'm really happy to be here but I do miss them.'

'Me too. My mum and dad used to come to all my comps, so it's weird when they're not there. Today I looked round several times expecting to see them, my mum shouting that I was doing brilliantly, and my dad offering me useless tips like "throw it further, lad".'

He smiled fondly and Olivia instinctively reached out to pat his leg, then felt very self-conscious. Hans, however, placed his hand over hers and they sat there, quiet suddenly, and absorbed the closeness.

Suddenly, 'I'm not the verdammte sprints coach, am I?' came shrieking down from the front.

'But you *are* the head coach. This is on you as much as it's on me.'

The two men were squaring up to each other, Trainer Lang trying to separate them.

'Not here,' he said urgently, nodding to all the athletes

watching curiously. 'We can sort this out when we get back to Dynamo.'

'*We'll* be sorted out when we get back to Dynamo,' the head coach growled. 'We'll have Mielke himself on our backs and all because two of this joker's dummköpfe sprinters jumped ship while he was chatting up Western high jumpers.'

Olivia grimaced at Hans as the men were, thankfully, pulled into separate seats and the argument simmered to low growls. Two of the school's best sprinters had gone missing at the end of the competition – disappeared into the orderly streets of Wolfsburg or, more likely, spirited away on another club's bus – and there would be hell to pay back at Dynamo. Republikflucht – fleeing the republic – was a crime punishable by up to three years in prison and losing young Eastern talent to the ravenous West was a grave sin in the eyes of the state. No wonder the coaches were on edge.

'Why would they go?' Olivia asked Hans.

'Freedom?'

'To do what? Dynamo has the best training facilities in Germany.'

'True, but things are quite controlled in the DDR, aren't they?'

'So that everyone gets fair pay for a fair day's work and there are no gross inequalities in living standards based on spurious value-judgements about worth.'

'Yes.' He smiled. 'You're right. It's a much more decent way to live.'

'And will pay dividends soon. We'll be stronger, healthier and better off than the decadent West, as long as people give themselves to community living and don't go chasing personal glory.'

Hans leaned over and took her medal in his long fingers.

'Is this not personal glory?'

Olivia shifted uncomfortably.

'A bit, I suppose, but we compete for Dynamo and for the DDR. We're—'

'Instruments of the state, you're right. And you, Olivia Pasternak, are a very pretty instrument.'

Olivia blinked, uncertain she'd heard right.

'Pretty?'

'Very.'

She laughed.

'Quatsch, Hans. I'm big and tall and, and...'

'Magnificent,' he filled in. 'Not to mention kind and good and funny.'

Olivia flushed and looked around. They were alone near the back of the bus and Hans was deliciously close.

'You're only saying that because I'm dangerous with a spear,' she dared to tease.

'There is that,' he agreed. 'It's a risk, but I like risks. And I like you.'

He let go of her medal to bring his fingers to her face, softly tracing the line of her jaw before brushing along her lips. Olivia leaned into his touch and then his lips were on hers and his kiss rippled across her every fibre. Winning silver today had felt good, but not half as good as kissing Hans, and she shifted sideways to let his arms go around her, giving in to the delicious feel of his body against hers as the arguments of the coaches faded into glorious nothingness.

It did not seem to take very long at all to get back to Berlin; not nearly long enough for Olivia. The few kisses she'd had at FDJ dances had been nothing like this. She liked everything about Hans – his easy-going nature, his sense of humour, his commitment to his sport and, yes, his handsome face and very well-honed body. She could have stayed locked into his embrace all the way across Europe and was glad when she heard the head coach telling the driver to take the ring road around the city.

'But, sir, it's further and it's late and...'

'And you'll do as you're told. We're not going through West Berlin.'

'It's not like the kids can jump off,' the driver pushed. 'Besides, they can walk into West Berlin any day of the week if they want to.'

'Not any more,' the coach snarled.

Olivia looked to Hans, who groaned.

'There goes our freedom, Liv. We'll have the Scholzes watching us like we're kindergarten kiddies from now on.'

'So we'll be stuck in our dorms?' she said, looking up at him. 'What *will* we do with ourselves?'

He grinned.

'Olivia Pasternak, you are a wicked girl.'

Then he was kissing her again and the Berlin ring road flashed past as fast as the rest of the trip until they drew close to the hostel and the head coach got up to address them.

'Well done, all of you,' he said, calming himself with visible effort. 'It's not your fault that your fool compatriots have seen fit to flee into the West and I hope that you will train extra hard to beat them into oblivion next time you meet them. Dynamo is the future of sport, as they will see when they come weeping over the line behind you, weak on decadent living and ill-discipline while you grow strong and fast. Freedom is an illusion; success is real. Your families will be proud of you and we will be writing to each and every one of them about your triumph today. Congratulations.'

Olivia felt a squirm of pride in her stomach, imagining her parents' faces when that letter arrived. It would be even better than coming from her.

'Your folks are in Stalinstadt, aren't they?' Hans asked as people began to shift around collecting bags.

'Yes, my mum, dad and my two little brothers. Have you got siblings?'

'A sister. Older. We argue all the time when I'm at home, but I miss her.'

Olivia smiled.

'My brothers are both several years younger than me so it's not quite the same.'

'No sister then?'

Olivia shook her head and then caught herself. She looked at Hans.

'I didn't think so – until recently.'

'What?' He stared at her. 'What do you mean? How can you not know you have a sister?'

Olivia bit her lip.

'I'm...' She cut herself off, not ready yet to admit she was adopted. 'I found out a few weeks before I came here that my mother had a baby during the war, a little girl. She was taken from her and they never found her again.'

Hans stared.

'That's so sad. How come?'

Olivia winced.

'She was in Auschwitz.'

He gasped.

'Your mother was? And she survived?'

'Somehow. She was a nurse, working with an amazing midwife there – my grandma Ana.'

'Your grandma was in there too?'

'Not my real grandma. She sort of adopted my mother because her mum died in the train on the way there.'

'God, Liv, how awful.'

His blue eyes were swimming with horrified sympathy and Olivia wished she hadn't started on this. She was weary and wanted to get into her bed and turn over the events of her day, but Hans looked so sad on her behalf that she couldn't just walk away.

'It was terrible for them both, but they had each other and they had the maternity ward. They brought nearly three thousand babies into *that place.*'

Hans looked as if his handsome head might explode.

'I can't begin to imagine it.'

'It's best not to. Mutti tells us "stories" of it sometimes – snippets, she calls them – but they're enough to make me weep with the horror of it, so trying to imagine all of those put together day after day is impossible. She's very calm, my mother, very controlled. She keeps so much inside because that's the way she learned to survive, but she's warm too and very loving. When I found out that she lost a daughter – that she's *still* lost a daughter – it broke my heart.'

'I bet.' Hans gripped at her hand. 'I'm so sorry, Liv.'

'Don't be. What's past is past, as Mutti always says, but I can't help thinking about this baby. They tried so hard to find her after the war but she'd vanished and then, for some reason, they stopped looking. They said it was because of having me and my brothers, but there was more to it, I'm sure there was. Mutti had that Auschwitz-look on her face when she told me.'

'Auschwitz-look?'

'The one that says I'll never understand. And when it comes to the camps, I won't, but this feels different. I worry, Hans, that she gave up Pippa for me and I... I'm not sure I was worth it.'

Hans stroked her back.

'Oh Liv, don't be silly. Of course you were worth it.' She touched her fingers to her medal but he pushed them gently away. 'Not because of this – because you're you. Lovely, kind, caring you.'

Olivia gave him a grateful kiss.

'I'm being self-indulgent, I know. I just wish I could do something to help.'

'You do?'

Hans was looking at her sideways and she frowned at him.

'Of course I do. Why would I not?'

'It's not that. It's just... You know that all the records are kept in Berlin?'

She stared at him.

'What are you saying?'

'Nothing really.' He ran a hand through his hair. 'I mean, it's not my place to say anything, but if I was looking for a missing person, this is where I'd start.'

'You mean *I* could look for Pippa? Where?'

'The Rathaus, I suppose. But, Olivia, don't listen to me. There might be a good reason your mother stopped looking. Nothing to do with your worth as a daughter, there just might be things they don't want you to know.'

Olivia sighed.

'Maybe, Hans, but they were going to tell me at eighteen anyway, so I'm only a few months early.' Olivia felt excitement begin to bubble within her. Why had she not thought of this before? She grabbed Hans' arm. 'Mutti has spent her whole life trying to protect us all from hurt but all along she's been nursing her own, terrible pain. Imagine if I could help lift that!'

Already, she could picture Ester's face when she told her she'd found Pippa. She'd light up and all that hurt, all the darkness forced into her by *that place*, would be pushed out of her with the joy of a new future.

'The Rathaus,' she said determinedly. 'I'll go tomorrow.'

'Tomorrow, Liv? Steady on. The Scholzes will be on high alert when this all gets out.'

'So? It's not a crime to ask after your lost sister.'

'Of course not. But they may not see it that way, especially after today.'

Hans nodded to the coaches, bickering again as they pulled into the Dynamo car park. Olivia felt sorry for them, but this was important. Her parents had gone hunting for a missing daughter and found her instead. In the end, it seemed, they had given Pippa up for Olivia, and she could think of no better way to repay that precious debt than by bringing Pippa back – whatever it cost her.

# ELEVEN

## EAST BERLIN | JUNE 1950

*ESTER*

Filip is excited.

'It's a sign,' he says when Ester tells him about the American woman with the beige folder and the little girl on the monkey bars, joyously exposing her KZ number to the curious woman below.

'Our patience is being rewarded,' he tells her later, in the dark of their bedroom, with Olivia sleeping in her tiny room next door and Mordecai settled in the crib at the foot of their bed.

His hand creeps round her waist, pulling her close and stroking her stomach. It is flat yet, except to the two of them who know there is a new life growing within.

'Three is a good number,' he had said when they'd been sure she was pregnant again, and it's true, but they both know that four would be a better one. Maybe now...

'You were right about us staying in Berlin,' he says, kissing her neck.

'Not necessarily, Filip.' She's nervous of this precarious optimism. 'Stalinstadt looks good.'

'It does,' he admits. 'They're opening a big Konsum store there and my manager says he'll recommend me to run the womenswear department.'

'Run it? As manager?'

He nods, buries his face in her neck in a way that tells her he is blushing. She twists in his arms to face him and takes his face in her hands.

'Then we should go, Filip.'

'Not now!'

Mordecai shifts at the bottom of the bed and they both freeze.

'We'll go when we've got Pippa,' Filip whispers when their son settles again.

'We don't know it's her yet,' Ester protests. 'I tattooed at least a hundred babies in *that place* and, to our knowledge, only thirty-two have been found. That's at least sixty-eight still out there. The odds aren't good.'

'I have faith.'

Ester's heart aches for him. He has never met Pippa, never looked into her blue eyes or stroked her hopeful blonde hair.

'I have faith too,' she tells him. 'I have faith in God and faith in us and faith in our lovely children. I have less faith in a stray report from a well-meaning American.'

'We'll see,' Filip says and that much, at least, is true.


'I've been to visit the child,' the American, Mrs Jefferson, tells them two days later. 'She is healthy and well cared for.'

Ester frowns. She's delighted that the child is well, but well cared for, that's harder. Her guts churn with anger at the thief-mother blithely raising this child as her own. If it is Pippa, *she* wants to care for her. *She* wants to love her, not in the shadows of her heart but in her arms.

'She has a number?' she asks.

'She does. It's a little indistinct. They stretch, you see, as the child grows.'

Ester nods sharply; the number is not the only thing that has stretched over the years. Her patience is dangerously thin. So, it seems, is Filip's.

'What is it?' he demands. 'What does it say?'

Mrs Jefferson opens the file.

'We believe it might be 41400.'

Ester's knees give way. The weight of all that hope, all that possible joy, is too much for them. Filip clutches her tight, propping her up so close against him that she can feel his heart thudding against hers.

Mrs Jefferson puts up a hand.

'Or it might be 41406. It's hard to tell.'

'I'll be able to tell,' Ester says keenly. 'I put the numbers there.'

Mrs Jefferson closes the file.

'Good. Does tomorrow suit? Four p.m.?'

It does not suit at all. Filip will be at work in his dress factory and Ester will be doing her rounds, Olivia and Mordecai safely in the state nursery. But that matters little.

'We'll be there.'

'Good,' Mrs Jefferson says again. She offers them a smile, but it's a nervous one. 'Just so you know, there will be another mother there too.'

Ester feels her whole self contract.

'Number 41406?'

'Exactly.'

Ester looks to Filip and his fingers entwine in hers. Someone, it seems, will find their child tomorrow. The odds are improved to 2:1 but it still feels like a long shot for a mother with a hole in her heart.

'We'll be there,' Ester says again.

Is it wrong, to pray for your own good fortune if it must come at the expense of someone else's? Probably, but that night Ester and Filip pray harder than ever in their lives before that this child, right here in Berlin, is their own dear, stolen daughter.

# TWELVE

## WEDNESDAY, 7 JUNE

*KIRSTEN*

Kirsten lay on her bed, staring at the last of the sunlight casting unbearably pretty colours across the ceiling as she struggled to make sense of what Jan had thrown at her last week.

'You're not my daughter, Kirsten,' he'd said. 'I found you, girl. I gave you to your mother as a present because her goddamned womb was too sour to give us a baby of our own.'

It made a certain sick sense. She thought back to how tense Lotti had been that night Jan had found out about Uli. She'd repeatedly tried to warn him not to talk about something – had it been that Kirsten wasn't his child either? Indeed, if Jan was right, she wasn't even her mother's child. That made her less a part of this family than Uli, who at least had Lotti's blood in his veins.

Kirsten's hand fumbled for the book she'd snuck from the living room, hoping it might have some answers. She should talk to her mother, she knew, but it was hard to find a way to start. Lotti had been snoozing on the couch when she and Uli had got in on the night of Jan's revelation, and Kirsten had asked Uli not to say anything. She'd wanted time to absorb the news before she had a conversation with her mother... *adoptive* mother.

Time, however, wasn't helping much and Kirsten sat up and opened the book. The family photo album was sparse as only Gretchen had a camera. Kirsten flicked past early snaps of her parents as a happy young couple, standing on a lakeside beach, at a party, on their wedding day. She paused at that one, looking at Jan in his uniform and noting the SS death's head on the cap held proudly under his arm. Lotti was pretty in pure white with flowers threaded through her blonde curls and was looking up adoringly at her smart husband. Was it true what Jan had said earlier – had everyone been a Nazi? The way the older genera-tion told it now, Hitler had coerced or tricked every last one of them into supporting him, but that couldn't be true, could it?

Kirsten faced the wearying realisation that the world was a complicated place and turned the page. There she was – baby Kirsten, dressed in a lacy christening gown with her beaming mother holding her and her father standing at her side. It was a photo she'd seen many times – there was a framed copy on the side in the living room – but she'd never before noticed how Jan stood slightly apart, or how he held his shoulders as rigid as steel. Shivering, she moved on. Here was Lotti pushing her in a perambulator, Lotti laughing as she fed her, Lotti holding her hands as she took her first steps. No more Jan. It had been the war, of course, so not really the time for cute family pictures, but there was one of Gretchen and her husband, Mark, before he'd been killed under Rommel in Africa, and another of the four adults out at dinner – just none of Jan anywhere near Kirsten. Why had she never noticed that before?

Slowly, Kirsten turned the page and there she found a blank. Four stick-on corner pieces suggested a photo had been displayed at some point but it was missing now and by the next page she was a plump toddler with cute blonde bunches. Then there was a two-year gap until she appeared again, clutching a dark-haired baby and beaming proudly for the camera as if she had borne him herself.

'Uli,' she murmured softly.

She'd felt so bad for him when he'd found out about his anonymous Russian father and now she was in a similar position. Or worse. She had no idea how or where she'd been born, or to whom. Flicking back to the missing photo, she stared at the faded square as if it might hold the answers but, in the end, she'd only find them out one way.

'Mutti,' she called, feeling the raw irony of the word even as it fell easily from her lips. 'I need to talk to you.'

Lotti looked up as Kirsten marched into the living room.

'What's wrong?' Lotti asked.

Kirsten held up the album. She heard Uli's door open and felt him slide into the room behind her.

'Why is this photo missing?'

Lotti flushed.

'Goodness, what are you doing with that old thing? I don't know, schnuki. It must have fallen out.'

Kirsten dropped the album onto the table next to Lotti's cup of tea.

'I saw Vati last week in the Eden Saloon. He told me something.'

Panic flashed across Lotti's pretty blue eyes.

'He'd have been drunk.'

'He was, yes, but lucid all the same.' Lotti cowered and it was all Kirsten needed. 'It's true then? You didn't give birth to me? You're not my mother?'

'No! That is, it's true that I didn't give birth to you, but I *am* your mother. I've brought you up, Kirsty, done everything I possibly can for you, cared for you all your life.'

'Not quite *all* of it,' Kirsten shot back.

Her head was spinning and her mouth dry. She'd half

hoped Jan had been lying to wound her, but now Lotti was confirming his story.

'Almost,' Lotti said desperately. 'You were less than a week old when you were brought to me.'

'By whom?'

Lotti waved an airy hand.

'Men. Your father's men. You were a gift, Kirsty, a wonderful, treasured gift. Haven't I looked after you? Haven't I loved you like my own?'

'*Like* your own, maybe, but not *as* your own. Why didn't you tell me, Mutti?'

Lotti wrung her hands.

'I was going to, many times, but what good would it have done? You're mine, Kirsten, in every way that matters.'

'Bar one.' Kirsten picked up Lotti's cup and drank the dregs of her mint tea. It was cold and thin but it eased her dry throat and gave her time to think. 'Who gave birth to me?'

'I don't know, truly I don't. She died, the mother. The father too. You were a helpless orphan. If I hadn't taken you, Lord knows what would have happened to you.'

Kirsten took a step forward.

'How do you know I was an orphan?'

'I, I... The men who brought you told me your parents were dead. Why would they lie?' It was a fair point, but this was the SS they were talking about. They'd lied to a whole nation, so what difference would one little baby make? 'Truly, Kirsten.' Lotti reached for her hands. 'You were destitute, alone. You didn't even have a name.'

Now it was Kirsten's turn to flinch. She pulled away from the woman she'd known as her mother all her life.

'How do you know, Mutt— Lotti? How do you know I didn't have a name?'

Lotti began to cry.

'I don't, I suppose. I don't know anything. I'm just a foolish, naive housewife who took the baby I'd wanted more than anything in the world and brought her up. I didn't ask questions, nobody did. I simply took my gift and loved her. I love her still. Have I not brought you up well, Kirsty? Have I not done my best for you?' Her voice rose, sharp and hysterical, and she dropped to her knees, clutching Kirsten around her legs. 'Do you not love me?'

Kirsten felt tears rise and fought back the urge to fling Lotti away. She *had* brought her up, despite all the hardships, to feel cared for and safe – until he'd come back, spitting poison.

Spitting truth.

Kirsten placed a hand on her mother's head.

'I do love you, Mutti, of course I do, but I want answers. I want to know about my real parents. Is that so bad?'

Lotti's eyes narrowed.

'If your "real" parents are alive, why have they not looked for you?'

Kirsten's skin prickled.

'Maybe they have. How would they find me with a new home and a new name and a new mutti?' Lotti sucked in a hurt breath and Kirsten felt bad but this was too big to brush under the rug.

'What was in the missing photo?' she pressed. Lotti began weeping hysterically, but Kirsten stamped her foot. 'Is it too much to ask?'

Uli rushed forward, putting his arms around Lotti.

'It seems to be too much right now, Kirsty. Perhaps you could try Tante Gretchen?'

Kirsten stared at him.

'Excellent idea, Uli.' She dropped a kiss on his dark head. 'See you soon.'

Uli looked startled.

'You're going over there now?'

'Why not?'

'It's late.'

'Yes,' she agreed. 'Seventeen years late and I'm not hanging around any longer. Don't wait up.'

With a wave at Uli and a despairing look at Lotti, she let herself out of the apartment. Outside, night had fallen, but Gretchen kept late hours and Kirsten could see her lights burning. She lived almost exactly opposite them, but in a far grander, two-storey apartment with four bedrooms and an enormous sitting room, furnished in grand style. She and Mark had bought it when they'd married and, as Mark had died with his reputation untainted by the state, she'd been allowed to keep it after the war. If only Jan had done the same, Kirsten thought bitterly, but then reminded herself that if he had, she might never have known about her true birth.

Perhaps that would have been better.

Gritting her teeth, she rang the doorbell and stood back to wave up at Gretchen when she inevitably looked out the window to see who was visiting at this late hour. Her lipsticked mouth formed an O at the sight of her niece, then she disappeared and footsteps sounded down the stairs before the door opened.

'Kirsten, what's wrong? Is someone ill?'

Kirsten shook her head.

'Not ill, Tante, but not exactly well either. My supposed father has been telling me a few things.'

Gretchen winced.

'I wondered when this might happen. Come in, schnuki, come in. Let's get a brandy, hey, for the shock?' She ushered Kirsten onto her squishy sofa and produced a fancy bottle from a fold-down cocktail cabinet. Pouring generous measures into two crystal glasses, she joined Kirsten. 'Drink a little. It will help.'

Kirsten took a cautious sip, thinking guiltily of Uli, left to handle Lotti while she fled to the calm of their aunt's apartment. The brandy burned her throat but sent warming tendrils around her blood – until she remembered why she was here.

'You knew then?' she said.

Gretchen sighed.

'Even I wouldn't have missed my own sister being pregnant.'

Kirsten rolled her eyes.

'You didn't think *I* deserved to know?'

Gretchen considered.

'The reverse – I felt that you deserved to be protected from that knowledge. Do you feel better for it?'

'No!'

'There you go then. You have to understand, Kirsty, it was chaos after the war, especially in Berlin. Half of Europe ended the war in the wrong place and they all seemed to come through here to get home. Everyone had lost people, and the kiddies were the worst of it. There were so many orphans needing a home that your case didn't seem very special. I'm sorry if that sounds harsh, but it's just how it was. You had a home, and loving parents – well, a loving mother – and that was more than most, so I considered you were lucky and let Lotti get on with it.'

Kirsten took another sip of her drink. What Gretchen was saying made sense, but that didn't make it any easier to take.

'Where did I come from, Tante?'

'Must you call me "Tante"? It sounds so old.'

'Sorry, *Gretchen*, but don't dodge the question.'

'I wasn't!' Gretchen protested robustly but she took a large glug of her brandy and looked around her elegant room as if she might find a handy answer waiting.

'So...?' Kirsten prompted.

'So, your father sent you, we assumed, from the front.'

'Because he was fighting there?'

'So we assumed.'

'And now?'

Gretchen fidgeted with the golden bracelet around her slim wrist.

'Shouldn't you be asking your mother this?'

Kirsten groaned.

'She got hysterical. I left her with Uli.'

Gretchen stood up.

'Is she unwell? Should we check on her?'

'No,' Kirsten said, 'she's not unwell and Uli will fetch us if he's worried.' She reached out and grabbed at her aunt's hand. 'Please, Gretchen. I just want to know. Wouldn't you?'

Gretchen sighed.

'Probably. Whether it would be wise or not is another matter.'

Kirsten drank more brandy; it was definitely helping.

'Is it anything to do with the missing photo in our family album?' Gretchen jumped and two spots of colour appeared high on her cheekbones, more precise than any blusher. 'It is! Tell me, please.'

Gretchen sighed again.

'Better than that, I can show you.'

'You have the photo?'

Kirsten leaned eagerly forward as Gretchen moved to her mahogany bookcase. Carefully, she extracted a slim, leather volume and opened it up.

'Are you sure, Kirsty?' she asked.

'Is it so horrible?'

'No! Just... a bit odd. We took the photo when you were very young and then, after the war, Lotti thought it best if we had it removed.'

Kirsten fought to understand.

'Had what removed?' she asked.

'This.'

Gretchen held out the photo and Kirsten peered at what

seemed to be a soft fold of skin marked with a rough, black number.

'41400,' she read slowly. 'What is that? What does it mean? And what's it on?'

'It's an armpit,' Gretchen said. 'In fact, it's *your* armpit, Kirsten.'

Kirsten's hand went to the scar nestling beneath her arm. She felt the raised line of it and stared again at the number on the photo.

'The pan injury?'

Gretchen shrugged.

'We had to tell you something. The surgeon was the best Mark's money could get, and he did a good job, but he said it was bound to scar. Still, we figured a white lie was better than... than that.'

She jabbed a finger at the ugly number.

Kirsten fought to understand. She'd only seen numbers like that on arms – arms of KZ survivors. She looked back at her aunt, who sank slowly next to her and took her hand, moving it gently away from the scar.

'We think it was tattooed onto you at birth, Kirsty. We think it was your mother's number.'

'I was born in a konzentrationslager?' The information felt as if it was coming at Kirsten like a hailstorm and she stared again at the photo. 41400. This was a thread to the woman who'd brought her into the world. 'She could still be alive,' she burst out.

'Don't get your hopes up, schnuki. Very few people made it out of those places. You were born at Christmas 1943, a full year before the Russians made it into the first camps.'

Kirsten shrank back at the mention of the Russians. While some of them had been raping her poor, adoptive mother, others could have been liberating her real one. Yet more tangles.

'But it's possible,' she insisted. 'People did survive.'

'A handful perhaps but—'

'Which one?' she demanded. 'Which KZ?'

'We don't know,' Gretchen said. 'But it seems only one KZ tattooed its inmates and given where it emerged that your father worked...'

'Auschwitz,' Kirsten breathed. 'I was born in Auschwitz?'

The word fell like poisonous gas into the scented air of her aunt's apartment and Kirsten battled not to breathe it in. A month ago, the worst she'd had to worry about was not being able to afford a pair of Levi's; now, she didn't even know who she was.

'If your "real" parents were still here,' Lotti had shot at her, 'why have they not looked for you?' But how could they when she had cut their only clue away? Gretchen was right – she really hadn't wanted to know, but she did and, now she'd got this much, she had to know more. Much more. She had to trace her mother; she had to know if she was still alive.

# THIRTEEN

*OLIVIA*

Olivia stared up at the Rotes Rathaus and tried to muster the courage to go in. With everyone at school in a fluster over the lost athletes it had been easy to take the tram a few short stops to the central administrative building of the DDR government but now she was here, she was scared.

'Let me come with you,' Hans had begged when she'd told him her plan, but she'd refused.

'No point two of us getting into trouble. I've left a note for Frau Scholz telling her I've gone to check some family records so no one thinks I've fled, but you can confirm that if they ask.'

'Don't be long.'

'I won't, I promise. If it drags on, I'll leave. I'll definitely be back for afternoon lessons.'

She'd kissed him, loving how easy it felt to do so, and headed off into the sunshine before she could do anything silly like change her mind, but now she was here, the building looked so big and imposing and official.

'There might be a good reason your mother stopped looking,' Hans had said. 'There just might be things they don't want you to know.'

She shook her head. She was an adult now – or almost. At her age, Mutti and Vati had been shoved into a ghetto and then out to concentration camps, so why were they trying to shield her from a few inconvenient facts? She could do this – for them. She could find the daughter they'd lost to prove she was the one worth choosing.

Setting her chin high, she headed up the steps and into the vast atrium, trying not to be intimidated by the sound of her footsteps echoing across the marble floor.

'Can I help you?'

The groomed young woman at the reception desk looked at Olivia's tracksuit in disdain and then clocked the Dynamo insignia and straightened.

'I'm looking for records of my sister,' Olivia said. 'She was taken from my mother's arms in Auschwitz, and I'm hoping there might be some way of tracing her.'

'Auschwitz?' The receptionist gawped at her.

'That's right.'

'A baby in Auschwitz?'

Olivia couldn't stop herself tutting.

'There were many born there. A few were shipped out and given to Nazi-friendly families.'

'And you're looking for records of that?'

'I am. She had a tattoo in her armpit. It would match my mother's number.'

The receptionist looked even more incredulous.

'How do you know?'

Olivia drew herself up tall.

'Because my mother told me so. And because I have one myself.'

Now the receptionist was gawping at her like some sort of curiosity in the zoo.

'*You* were in Auschwitz?'

Olivia hadn't ever thought of it as baldly as that.

'For two days,' she admitted. 'I was born there. But this isn't about me. I'm looking for my sister, Pippa Pasternak. Number 41400.'

'There were that many babies in Auschwitz?'

Olivia resisted the urge to scream at this vacuous woman.

'No! But there *were* that many women in there and every one of them deserves our compassion.'

'Yes, of course, I know that. I just...'

'Look,' Olivia said, 'I don't have much time. Can you help me?'

'To find a baby, a Jewish baby?'

'Does that make a difference?'

'No. Not at all. I'm simply looking for clarity.'

'As am I. Do you have konzentrationslager records here?'

'Erm, maybe. I don't know.' The woman was panicking now. 'Come through and take a seat and I'll fetch an adviser.'

'Thank you.' Olivia let herself be ushered into a small room. 'But, please, if you could be quick – I'm due back at school very soon.'

'Of course, fräulein. It won't be long, fräulein.'

Olivia sat, resting her hands in her lap and trying to stay calm, though the conversation had shaken her. She had pictures in her head of *that place*, gleaned from her mother's mini-stories, but she'd never before placed herself in there. She knew about the big wooden barracks with the tight rows of bare, triple-storeyed bunks into which at least ten women would be crammed with little more than a blanket between them. She knew about the concrete pipe-casing down the middle on which the poor labouring mothers would give birth, and about the dirt on the floors, and the enormous rats who would nibble on the sick long before they had succumbed to death.

She knew about the long roll-calls standing in the cold in ill-fitting striped outfits, and the inhuman disinfections in which prisoners were submerged in near-neat bleach to kill the fleas that bit typhus into their ailing bodies. She knew about the sudden 'selections', where anyone sick or weak or just unlucky enough to attract the wrath of the guards could be yanked out and marched to the looming gas chambers at the rear of the camp to be crushed into a cruel suffocation of a death, clawing their desperation into the concrete walls with their nails. She knew about all of that, but had never pictured her own, pink, innocent little body amongst the terrible carnage.

She turned her face into the private synagogue Ester had taught her to build in her heart and thanked God for bringing her out of there and, somehow, to her wonderful adoptive parents. Her heart twisted at the thought of them. They'd been through so much in the war, Ester making it to liberation more than half starved, and Filip escaping the guards at Chelmno and joining the resistance for the final fight into Berlin. They'd fought to find each other and they'd fought to find her; the least they deserved, now she was all but an adult herself, was for her to find Pippa.

But, still, no one came.

Eventually she stood up. She had twenty minutes to get back for class and it wouldn't do to be late, today of all days. As she was stepping into the atrium, however, a man came striding towards her.

'Fräulein Pasternak? So sorry to have kept you. Busy, busy, busy!' He gave her a broad smile that went no deeper than his ice-grey eyes and ushered her back inside.

'I'm afraid I don't have time now. My school...'

'Will be informed you are with me. Take a seat.'

Again the smile, like a fox assessing its prey. Olivia glanced around, but the receptionist studiously avoided her eye and reluctantly she sat back down.

'May I ask who you are?'

'Of course. I'm Klaus and I'm with the Ministry for State Security.'

Olivia's gut clenched and for a moment she was back in a grey van, being driven deep into the pain-filled corridors of a Stasi prison, but she shook the stupid thought away.

*You're doing nothing wrong*, she reminded herself and tried to stay calm.

'I'm sorry to trouble you, sir. I think the receptionist may have called the wrong person. I was looking for a record of my, er, my sister.'

'So I gather. You are an Auschwitz survivor, Olivia?'

'Sort of.'

'That has made you strong.'

'I don't think so, sir. I think it was my parents' genes that made me so.'

'Perhaps, though they were Polish Jews, were they not, from Rejowiec?'

'I believe so,' Olivia said. She should not be surprised that he knew; the Stasi knew everything, including, perhaps, where Pippa was.

Klaus smiled his thin smile again.

'And now you are a fine athlete. You won a medal yesterday, I gather.'

This was more frightening. It had been less than twenty-four hours since the precious silver had been hung around her neck but, then, Dynamo was run by the Stasi so she supposed it should be no surprise either.

'I was proud to win it for my club, sir. I am very happy there.'

'I'm glad to hear it, Olivia. You are a fine citizen of the DDR. You have commendations from your FDJ unit back in Stalinstadt and good reports from school.'

'I do?'

'Of course. You are the sort of excellent young person upon whom the future of the DDR rests and we are here to help you.'

'Find my sister?'

'If possible, yes. The fascists perpetuated awful crimes on good people all over the world and we wish to see those repaired wherever we can. If that brings you personal satisfaction, so much the better.'

'Thank you, sir.'

'Klaus, please. I hope we can be friends.'

'Friends?'

'Of course. You can, I think, help me too. Would you do that, Olivia? Would you help me?'

Olivia swallowed.

'I'm not sure what I can do, sir.'

'Klaus. And there is much you can do. As you know, Olivia, two fine young people did not return to Dynamo last night. They were seduced into the West by corrupt and evil forces.'

'I know,' Olivia agreed. 'They were very stupid.'

Klaus' smile this time was almost genuine.

'Indeed they were, Olivia, but sadly not all young people are as clear-sighted as you and there are wolves out there – wolves who would rather prey on our carefully nurtured Ossi talent than grow their own from amongst their weak ranks. Do you want that, Olivia?'

'Of course not.'

'Neither do we. And that is why it will be so useful to us if you can keep an ear out around school. Nothing more. We are not asking you to spy or to report on anyone or betray any friends, Olivia. We are simply asking you to listen out for anything that sounds like some of your weaker fellow athletes might be open to corruption so that we can help them to resist.'

Olivia looked at him uncertainly; it sounded like spying to her.

'A team is built on trust, sir – Klaus. I cannot betray that.'

'Of course not, Olivia, of course not. We're not looking to hurt or punish anyone, simply to keep them safe. What makes a good socialist state work, Olivia?'

'Community,' she said promptly. 'Working together for the common good instead of pursuing individual desires.'

'Exactly! Your good reports were understated. But individual desire is so much more insistent, at least for some people. The perfect society is coming, but it takes time and it takes sacrifice. Just as an athlete trains to be at their peak for a competition, so we must train ourselves to work as a nation in order to fulfil our potential. It is exciting, is it not?'

'It is.'

'And we must throw all our efforts into it, including helping those weaker than ourselves, for is that not an underpinning principle of socialism?'

'It is,' Olivia agreed again.

Klaus beamed.

'Good. So, we are agreed. I will personally look for records of your lost sister. It may take time – the KZ records are tangled and incomplete – but I will do my very best for you and your dear family. In return, you will keep an ear to the ground on the training field and in the common room, yes?'

Olivia thought about it. She was under no illusion that she had any choice, but what Klaus said made sense. Those sprinters were idiots and whoever had poisoned their minds against Dynamo and the DDR were criminals. If she could help others resist being seduced in the same way, then everyone won.

'Yes,' she said. 'I agree.'

There was a squirm of unease in her stomach as Klaus showed her out, but she pushed it down. The Stasi did not arrest you if you had done nothing wrong and if this man could find Pippa for her long-suffering parents, that was, surely, worth a little of herself.

# FOURTEEN

## FRIDAY, 9 JUNE

*KIRSTEN*

'Kirsten?' Kirsten turned round from the coffee machine, her most hospitable smile at the ready. 'Kirsten Meyer?'

Her smile faltered.

'How do you know my full name?'

'It's my job. Do you have a minute?'

She shook her head.

'No. Sorry. I'm very busy.' The man looked pointedly around the café. It was 2 p.m. – after the lunch rush and before kaffee und kuchen – and the place was almost empty. 'I'm not meant to leave the counter unattended,' she said uncomfortably.

'No problem. I'm happy here.' He slid himself onto one of the bar stools. 'Mint tea, please, and one of those delicious strawberry tarts.'

There was little Kirsten could do. He was a paying customer, sitting on a free seat, but that didn't mean she wanted to talk to him. His eyes were too dark for her liking, his hair too slicked back, and his confidence too, well, confident. Reluctantly she made his tea and fetched his tart.

'Cream?' she asked.

'Why not? Might as well make the most of a little luxury while I'm over here.'

Kirsten frowned.

'Over from where?'

'The East of course, the DDR. A fine place, far more decent than this side, but I have to admit the cakes aren't anywhere near as good.'

He bit into his treat with relish and Kirsten watched, unsure what to make of him. Three older ladies arrived and she gladly moved to serve them, but he was still there when they'd finished dithering over the cakes and waved her imperiously back to him.

'So, Kirsten, you like nice clothes?'

'Who doesn't?'

'Indeed. Expensive though, aren't they? Especially over here. All those fancy brands.'

'I make my own clothes, thanks.'

'And very well too. Not the same though, is it? Not as... cool.'

'It's not—'

'As it happens,' he pushed on, reaching into a bag at his side, 'I picked these up today.'

He laid a pair of brand-new Levi 501s on the counter and Kirsten had to dig her hands into her skirt to stop herself reaching out. 'They're your size,' the man said.

'How do you know?'

'I told you, Kirsten, it's my job.'

'Your job is to know my measurements?'

'My job is to know everything about you. About everyone, actually.'

He said it matter-of-factly and Kirsten's stomach turned over. Was this one of those Stasi officers she'd heard people whispering about? What had Dieter said? Something about

East Germany leaking workers and 'the only way the Ossis know to stop it is with laws and guns and nasty, sneaky spies'. She looked to the door, hoping desperately for more customers or, even better, for Frau Munster to return from buying supplies, but it stayed resolutely closed.

'What do you want?' she demanded.

'A little information, nothing more. This café is right on the border, as I'm sure you're aware, and it's a hive of activity – not all of it innocent.'

Kirsten stared at him. Café Adler stood on the corner of Friedrichstraße and Zimmerstraße. Zimmerstraße was the border between the districts of Mitte and Kreuzberg and, therefore, between the American and Soviet zones, but no one paid that much attention. People passed up and down all the time. Ossis came to work in the West, or to visit the many cinemas nearby, and Wessis headed East for the cheap services and cool bars.

'I don't think we should worry about borders,' she said. 'Berlin is Berlin and everyone should live together.'

He raised an eyebrow.

'Sweet. You're right, of course, but not everyone is as generous-spirited as you. We've had word that there are subversives meeting here and we'd like to know more about them.'

'And you think I'd do that? Listen in to people and report to you? That would be wrong.'

'Not if what they're saying is bad.'

'Bad for who? No, thank you.'

'Shame.'

He slid the jeans back into his bag.

She laughed.

'Were those a bribe?'

'I'd prefer to use the word "reward".'

'Of course you would, but no thanks to that too. They're not worth it.'

'I see.' The man nodded thoughtfully. 'Very commendable. Brands are the work of the devil anyway, but I have other things to offer.' She moved pointedly away, but he spoke again. 'You're looking for your mother, Kirsten.'

Kirsten froze.

'How do you know that?'

'I told you—'

'It's your job,' she finished warily. 'It's also a secret.'

'No such thing. I know about her, *all* about her.'

Kirsten felt herself pulled towards him like a nail to a magnet.

'You know who she is?'

'I might do.'

'That's not good enough.'

'OK, I *do*. I know she had a number. I know she was in a KZ. I know she was Jewish.'

'She was?'

Kirsten's voice came out harsh and hoarse. It had always been likely, of course, if she'd been in Auschwitz, but it was still a shock to have it confirmed. 'How do you know?'

He put up a thin finger.

'Come now, Kirsten, you're a good little capitalist, you know how it works – everything has its price.'

'And to find out about my mother, I have to spy on my customers?'

'Exactly!'

Oh, it was tempting. It was so very tempting, but the price was too high for some name on a gas-chamber record.

'No, thank you. I'm no spy.'

She turned away, busying herself with polishing glasses, but then he spoke again.

'She's alive, Kirsten.' The words jolted through her like an electric shock and she stared at him. 'I have her name, her address. Don't you want to meet her?' Kirsten did, of course she did. 'I'm not asking you to spy on people,' he wheedled, 'just to—'

The bell above the door rang out and Kirsten looked over with relief.

'Dieter!'

He came bounding in, waving something glossy.

'I brought you this, Kirsty. It's a brochure, for the university. They do a course in design that looks perfect for you so I thought...' He dried up and looked from Kirsten to the customer. 'Is this man bothering you?'

She swallowed.

'He is a little.'

Dieter squared up to him. He was slight but tall and his arms, as he crossed them over his chest, rippled with quiet muscle.

'I think you should go, sir.'

'And you are...?'

'The assistant manager,' he lied easily. 'What's your name, please?'

The man got down from his stool.

'That doesn't matter. I'm going. It's a terrible café, anyway. That was the worst strawberry tart I've had in ages.'

And on that petty note, he snatched up his bag and stalked out. Kirsten reached over the counter, pulled Dieter to her, and kissed him long and hard.

'Whoa!' he said, when she let him surface. 'What was that for?'

'Turning up at the right time. That man was trying to bribe me to spy on customers in the café.'

'Bastard! What did he offer you?'

'Levi's. They were very nice ones, very tempting, but not as tempting as his other offer – information about my mother.'

'Oh, Kirsty.' Dieter slid under the counter and took her in

his arms. She'd told him about her father's revelations and he'd been very supportive.

'He says she's alive, Dieter.'

'He would do. It's more tempting that way.'

'*So* much more tempting. I so wanted to know more.'

'I don't blame you, but don't worry, this is the West – you can just go and ask. I hear the landesarchiv has all sorts of records these days. You might get lucky.'

'Really?'

'Really. And without stupid Ossi spies making unfair demands on you. Now, take a look at this brochure – I swear, it's perfect for you.'

Kirsten tried. It was kind of him to bring it and the description of the course did sound amazing, but she'd never make the grades and, besides, how was she meant to concentrate on sewing when her mother might be out there? She had to get to the landesarchiv as soon as she had time and, until then, stay clear of sweet-toothed Ossi foxes.

# FIFTEEN

## THURSDAY, 15 JUNE

*OLIVIA*

'Silence for the great Soviet leader!' Herr Braun called but it was half-hearted at best.

Nikita Khrushchev had been ranting on for some time now and even the teachers were losing focus. The school was under orders to tune into this state broadcast of the Russian leader talking about German reunification but he'd been at it for over an hour and spirits were flagging in the sports hall.

'Shall I bring out some snacks?' Olivia heard Frau Scholz suggest to the principal and was very grateful when he agreed.

'I wish I understood what he was saying,' Olivia said to Hans, who sat next to her, his hand entwined in hers.

A translator was doing her best to turn Khrushchev's words into German but the man spoke fast and the cameras had clearly been instructed not to waver from the great leader, so it was hard to hear her.

'In essence,' Herr Scholz said at her shoulder, making her jump, 'Khrushchev is furious at the Western powers who have signed peace treaties with all the other states who fought with

Herr Hitler, including Italy and Japan, but still arrogantly refuse to sign one with us. This, despite clear indications that Germany – especially East Germany – is the very antithesis of fascist.'

'That doesn't seem fair,' Olivia said.

'It is not fair, Olivia. It is mean-spirited and backward, designed to punish us and hold us back.'

Olivia frowned.

'Why won't they sign it? There are still bullet holes riddling Berlin, so why would we fight again?'

'Precisely!' Herr Scholz said, favouring her with a smile that reminded her chillingly of Klaus, the Stasi agent. 'Yet the city is filled with occupation forces as if she were still at war. I tell you, Olivia, they do not want us to heal. They are angry that we are recovering our prosperity and want to ram their nasty Western boots on the back of our necks to keep us in the mud.'

'But we're not in the mud!'

He grinned.

'That is our victory. But they must acknowledge it. They must let us sign a peace treaty and they must take their damned troops out of Berlin and either give her to the East – as is only right and fair – or, if they persist in treating her differently, make her a free, self-governing city. That, my dear, is what Herr Khrushchev is saying.'

'Thank you.'

Herr Scholz favoured her with another smile and went off to help his wife hand out dumplings to a suddenly animated crowd of students. Olivia turned to Hans.

'It sounds reasonable,' she said.

He nodded.

'It does.'

'So what's stopping them?'

'Fear, I suppose.'

'That Germany might grow too strong again?'

'Maybe, but more, I think...' he glanced around and lowered his voice, 'fear of the Russians. Khrushchev is proposing that the West sign a peace treaty separately with East and West Germany, then leave us to negotiate reunification ourselves. The West would rather we reunify first, then sign a joint peace treaty.'

Olivia considered this.

'Why should we not sort out our own country ourselves?'

'I think the West feel that if we are left to do that, it will, in the end, be the Soviets who sort it out. We all know that Walter Ulbricht does whatever Khrushchev tells him. Our precious president hid in Moscow for the entire war and was flown back into the DDR as soon as it ended. He owes everything to Khrushchev, so he's his puppet.'

Olivia stared at Hans.

'Should you be saying that?'

He coloured.

'Not really, but it's true. And it could be a good thing. The Russians have been doing socialism a lot longer than us, after all. Now, shall we grab a dumpling before this greedy lot eat them all?'

He dropped her hand to head across and catch Frau Scholz's rapidly emptying tray and Olivia followed as Khrushchev finally wound up his speech. For the last week, since her visit to the Rotes Rathaus, her head had been filled with thoughts of her missing sister and, God forgive her for a terrible socialist, but at the moment, finding Pippa felt far more vital than all these tangled politics.

'Will he get the treaty, do you think?' she heard Julia, a tall high jumper, asking the group.

'The West have to give in at some point,' Franz, a fellow javelin thrower, said. 'They can't keep troops in our country forever; we're not at war any longer.'

'We *are*,' one of the gymnasts pointed out. 'It's just a cold war.'

'But it could get hot quickly if either the Russians or the Americans decide to press the nuclear button,' another said.

'Which is why the dummkopf Americans have to agree to negotiate before Khrushchev loses his patience.'

This last comment was from one of the many footballers. Olivia's neck began to ache from looking from one speaker to another.

'But then what will happen to Berlin?' Julia asked.

'They're talking about a free city.'

'Meaning?'

'Dunno. That it's sort of independent, rules itself.'

'That'd be hard though, right,' said Julia, 'with it being in the middle of the DDR?'

'Yep,' one of the swimmers agreed. 'It's stupid the West having a hold on it. They've got Bonn as their capital, so why can't we have Berlin? Greedy bastards need to just let it become part of the East.'

'I don't think Kennedy will let that happen, though,' Hans said. 'It's America's foothold behind the Iron Curtain.'

'Which is unfair,' Lisel, a talented sprinter, objected. 'We don't have a "foothold" in their half, so why should they have one in ours?'

Olivia's head was starting to spin. Out in Stalinstadt she'd never really thought about all this. They'd been taught about socialist principles, of course, but in a very applied way – labour quotas and social care, rather than politics. At home, Ester and Filip had always been glad to close the doors on the outside world and just be their family – a loving unit working for each other's good. That, to Olivia, was socialism, and she found all these threads very hard to understand, though she knew she had to try. This was exactly the sort of thing Klaus would want to hear; the sort of thing that might get her the information about Pippa that she needed.

'You all right, Liv?' Hans asked. 'You've gone a bit pale.'

'Just tired. It was a heavy weights session today and I'm ready for my bed.'

He kissed her and she leaned gratefully against him, but now the television was switching from Russia to their own DDR, where President Ulbricht was stepping up to a podium.

'Let's see what Spitzbart's got to say then,' Franz called.

Spitzbart – goatee – was the nickname of the neatly bearded president of the DDR and everyone laughed, but settled down to listen all the same. Ulbricht was standing before a sea of journalists and, bristling with an even greater air of importance than usual, he began droning on about the peace treaty again. He said Khrushchev would be meeting Kennedy in Vienna later this month and the West had to 'come to the table with an open spirit.'

'What about Berlin?' a journalist asked him.

'That's what I said,' Julia cried, delighted.

The students laughed but quieted again as another reporter stood up, cutting through Spitzbart's bluster about a free city. She was a short, plump woman with a smiling face, but her eyes were sharp as she fired off her question to the president: 'Does the creation of a free city, as you term it, mean that the state boundaries of the DDR will be erected at Brandenburg Gate?'

A hush fell over the sports hall and the students leaned forward. Spitzbart cleared his throat and stroked his beard. He looked nervous.

'As I understand it, Frau Doherr, you are asking me if we intend to build a wall across the city?' The reporter nodded and the students, along with the rest of Berlin – indeed the rest of the world – held their breath. Ulbricht hesitated a second longer, then waved a dismissive hand. 'I am aware of no such intention. There will be no wall in Berlin.'

The crowd of journalists went mad, leaping up and shouting out questions, but Ulbricht refused to re-address the subject and steered the conference into far duller economic waters.

'A wall?' Julia said, shaking her head. 'Surely they can't build a wall?'

Herr Braun stood up.

'As you'd have heard if you were listening properly, Julia, Herr Ulbricht said specifically that there was *no* intention of building a wall.'

'At the moment,' one of the footballers sneered from the back.

Herr Braun's eyes raked the room.

'Our leaders will decide what is best, as we elected them to do.'

'As the only choice on the ballot,' someone else muttered.

Olivia spun round trying to see who, but the room was packed and the lights low, so it was impossible. Klaus was right, there was clearly subversion – or at least objection – all over the place and that was very worrying. Herr Braun waved for the screen to be turned off and the lights brought up.

'This is not your concern,' he told them.

'Why make us watch it then?' another voice called.

Herr Braun rapped loudly on the podium.

'Because,' he said icily, 'I thought you were mature enough to be able to engage with the wider politics of the DDR, the country we are all working to be able to represent. Obviously, I was wrong.'

The room collectively hung its head.

'This is not your concern,' he repeated. 'Your concern is to work hard, train hard and apply yourselves to being the best you can possibly be. Your job is to make the very most of the opportunity that the DDR is offering – and paying for. If you don't like it, hand in your tracksuit, give up your training, and walk over the verdammte border.'

The silence was heavy. The composed headmaster rarely shouted and the athletes hardly dared look at him, or at each other. Herr Braun let it draw out a little longer and then smiled.

'You are good people,' he told them, 'and great sportsmen and women.' Heads lifted. 'Wherever our borders lie, we will wear our flag with pride and see it run up every flagpole, in every sporting stadium across Europe. Across the world!' Someone cheered and Herr Braun smiled more widely. 'With the perfect socialist combination of technology and hard work, we will show the world that East Germany does not need to fight to win. Sport, my dear students, is the new battleground and we – *you* – will be victorious upon it.'

A swimmer stood up and shouted: 'Long live Dynamo, long live the DDR!' and suddenly everyone was on their feet, echoing his cry, and the hall rang with enthusiasm. Olivia shouted with the rest, feeling relief course around her veins.

'We're so lucky to be part of this,' she said to Hans.

He said something in reply, but it was far too loud to hear him and she lifted her hand into the air and gave in to the release of the communal spirit with relief. Dispute was troubling; solidarity uplifting. It was far easier to forget her petty personal concerns in this rush of noise and she gladly joined the cheers, which went on and on until Herr Braun called time and ushered them out of the hall.

The swimmers, gymnasts and footballers peeled off to their on-site hostels, leaving the athletes to gather at the tram stop for the trip home under the watchful eye of the Scholzes. It was good to get into the fresh air after the humidity of the hall but unusually noisy on the street. The air felt charged with more than simply summer giddiness and Olivia caught the word 'Spitzbart' frequently and 'mauer' – wall – even more often.

The tram, when it came, was packed, and Olivia was forced into a group of men smelling of beer and tobacco.

'They can't build a wall,' one of them said behind her.

'Of course they can't. You don't just split a city in two. It's all bluster, pressure on the Allies to sod off and leave Berlin to us.'

'Will it work?'

'I damn well hope so. My wife loves a uniform, so the sooner they're out of here the better!'

The group laughed uproariously and one burped in Olivia's ear. She counted the stops until the hostel, but in central Berlin the streets were even busier. She'd got used to the refugees milling around, easily identifiable by their hefty packs and bewildered looks, but tonight there seemed to be more of them than ever. Climbing down, she accidentally bumped into a woman dressed in layers of clothing far too warm for the summer night, dragging a heavily laden pram with two toddlers trailing behind.

'I'm so sorry,' she said, trying to sidestep her, but the woman reached out and grabbed her arm.

'Get out, girl,' she hissed. 'Get out while you still can.'

Olivia wrenched away.

'Don't be stupid,' she snapped. 'I've been to the West and it's not as glittering as people make out. The DDR is the future.'

'The DDR is a trap,' the woman hissed. 'Leave now, if you value your freedom.'

She shook her head at Olivia as if she, with all her advantages, was the one to be pitied, and it stung.

'Freedom is an illusion,' Olivia told her robustly.

'Not if the people you love are on the other side of a wall,' the woman shot back, then she was gone, off into the West with the remnants of her life in tow.

Olivia watched her walk away, her head spinning. What if Pippa was in Berlin but the government, somehow, kept them apart? Was that possible? She shook her head, furious with herself. Spitzbart had said there would be no wall, so she had to believe him. This was all just hysteria. People were being seduced by the West, as Klaus had said, and they would find themselves sorely disappointed.

Reaching for Hans' hand, she made for the safety of the stadium at speed. *What if your sister is out there?* a voice whispered insistently in her head, but she pushed it away. Pippa was a family matter and finding her was nothing to do with politics. Nothing at all.

# SIXTEEN

*KIRSTEN*

Kirsten watched, fascinated, as a group in scarlet tracksuits flowed off the tram and across the marketplace towards the athletics stadium. They were chattering together, their big, lithe bodies alive with purpose and strength as they bounded inside, and they made a stark contrast to the straggles of lost humanity drifting down the streets around them. She sighed and sank onto a bench. She'd come out for some fresh air, fed up of the sound of Jan's strident complaining, and found half of Berlin out too – and half of East Germany besides.

She wasn't sure how long she'd been sitting here, watching the stream of poor people heading wearily down Bernauer-straβe. Berlin was full of refugees these days. With the university term over, Dieter had started working full-time at the Marienfelde refugee centre – the first port of call for any East-erners moving across Berlin into the West. The border was still officially open but republikflucht was a serious crime now and there were more and more guards trying to stop anyone attempting it. The poor refugees often had to come with little more than jewellery sewn into the linings of their coats with which to buy themselves a new life, and the workers at the centre were kept endlessly busy trying to process them.

Watching one woman juggling a pram and two crying toddlers, Kirsten wondered what might make someone leave their home, their friends and their whole community, but couldn't imagine it. This wasn't war; was it?

Wearily, she stood up to return to the apartment. At least she had warm rooms, a comfy bed and a mother and brother who loved her. And by now, she hoped, Jan would have gone out to drown his Nazi self-pity in beer. Letting herself in, she made for the kitchen to grab a cocoa and head for the blissful comfort of her bed, but as she opened the door, she saw Uli and Lotti sitting at the table with the ominous shape of Jan on the far side. She froze, but too late.

'Aah, Kirsten, come on in and join our happy family supper.'

Kirsten looked to Uli, who was sitting, shoulders rigid, and cutlery clasped like weapons in his hands. Lotti's head was down but Kirsten could see her red eyes and knew she'd been crying. This was all she needed.

'Thank you, but I'm very tired. I think I'll just—'

'Sit down, Kirsten!'

His voice was sharp and it dug at her already sensitive skin.

'No.'

'What?'

'I said no. You're not my father, as you delighted in telling me, so I don't have to do what you say.' Jan looked stunned and she took a step forward. 'I found something else out today, actually. I found out my mother was Jewish. How does it make you feel, Hauptsturmführer Meyer, that your wife has been bringing up a Jew all these years?'

Jan leapt to his feet and Lotti shrieked.

'Kirsten, don't!'

'Why not, Mutti? Why are you letting this man trample all over you? He's a Nazi, a criminal, and a piece of sheiβe.'

'Kirsten!'

'Well, he is. He's spent fifteen years in prison not repenting the horrific things he oversaw, not learning or changing but simply festering, and now he's out and seeing how the world is prospering without Nazis like him and he has nothing left to do but hate.'

Uli edged to the side of the room, away from Jan, but Kirsten had had enough.

'Jewish, Jan,' she said, stabbing a finger in his direction. 'You have a Jewess here, in your home. How does that make you feel?'

For ages the question hovered in the air unanswered, then Jan stepped up.

'You want to know how it makes me feel, Kirsten? You really want to know? It makes me feel sick to my very stomach. The Jews are the scum of the earth, dirty, rattish people who—'

'Enough!' Kirsten snapped, cutting him off. 'We don't need your outdated bigotry. We're a more tolerant society now and it's a far, far nicer way to live. No race has the right to exterminate any other, surely you can see that?'

'No!' Jan shouted. 'No, I cannot see that; it's not what I was taught. The only thing I know is that I have to be ashamed of everything I am. I have to spend my life grovelling because I used to obey orders, orders issued for the good of the German people, though they're too weak to realise that any more. I'm sick of it.'

He sank against the table and Kirsten looked at him curiously.

'Can you really not see how a world in which everyone has an equal right to be here is a better one?'

He gave a funny snort, then he was up again, grabbing her and pushing her against the wall.

'Stop!' Lotti cried. 'Stop, Jan, don't hurt her.'

But Jan was caught in a fury of his own.

'You see that,' he said, forcing Kirsten's face against the wall. 'What colour is it, Kirsten? What colour is the paint?'

'It's white,' she gasped.

'Is it though? What if it's black?'

'It isn't black.'

'How do you know?'

'How?' Kirsten struggled to think. Her cheek ached against the wall and she could feel the pressure of Jan's considerable strength as his hands crept closer to her neck. 'How?!' he roared.

'I don't know. I learned it when I was little, I suppose.'

'Exactly! That's what it's like for me. I learned the colours of the world from the Hitler youth. I learned that Aryan was the only decent race. I learned that Jews and Gypsies were dirty. I learned that cripples and loonies were a drain on society. I learned that we had to get rid of them all to make space – space for the good, strong, bold people to thrive. That was my black, Kirsten, and now you're telling me it's white. You're all telling me it's white but it doesn't feel it. It still feels black. Everything feels black...'

He let her go and she collapsed against the wall, gasping for breath.

'I'm sorry if that's the way it feels,' she said. 'But you simply have to relearn. Nazi ideals were evil. You – if you persist in them – are evil.'

'Enough, Kirsty,' Uli pleaded. 'Stop now, please stop.'

Lotti had crept up to Uli and they were huddled together. It made Kirsten mad that they were forced to feel so cowed.

'No,' she insisted. 'We're not the ones in the wrong. We're not the ones who should be keeping quiet. We're not evil.'

'Neither am I.' Jan drew himself up, his eyes glinting with a pale light. 'The Nazis had a solid, well-thought-out plan and I can't shake it off. I don't even see why I should. You lot, you're pathetic. Look at you – a KZ Jew, a bastard commie and a shrivelled husk of a wife. If this is the new world, I don't want any part of it. It disgusts me.'

He reached into his pocket and, to Kirsten's horror, drew out a gun. It was some sort of service pistol, old but cleaned with care, and he wielded it with studied expertise.

'Where did you get that?' she demanded.

He gave a wolfish grin.

'Not everyone is as goody-goody as you lot. There are other "evil" bastards out there, other people hiding in the shadows waiting for everyone to come to their senses.'

'That won't happen,' Kirsten said, as calmly as she could. 'We've already come to our senses. We've acknowledged our mistakes and we're moving on.'

He nodded slowly.

'I see that. I see good German people pandering to the glitter of the greedy, look-at-me Americans. I see them yielding to Coca-Cola and rock 'n' roll. I see them going meekly to work for Jews and Slavs and kowtowing to cocky occupation soldiers. "We were wrong, world. We're sorry, world. Please don't hate us, world." Well, I will not do that. I've always been a man of action and fifteen years in prison hasn't changed me.'

He pointed the gun at Kirsten and she crushed up against Uli. Lotti put an arm around them both, pushing them behind her curvy frame as she took a step towards her husband.

'Don't do this, Jan. It's not our fault.'

'Did I say it was? You're weak, that's all. Hitler had his flaws, for sure, but at least he wasn't weak. And at least, when he was in power, Germany wasn't weak either. It's not your fault, but you have to take the consequences all the same. The earth needs ridding of scum, is that not right? Before, that scum was the Jews, now it seems it's the National Socialists and everyone is just as happy to hunt us down.'

'It's not the same,' Kirsten protested desperately. 'The Jews were innocent.'

'Lucky them,' Jan snarled. 'But enough. You're making my head hurt. Everything makes my head hurt. The earth needs ridding of scum,' he repeated, and flicked off the safety catch.

Kirsten clutched her mother and brother and closed her eyes. Uli was quivering violently and she hated herself for provoking this.

'I'm sorry,' she said. 'I'm so sorry. I didn't know he had a gun.'

'Hush, liebling,' Lotti said, her voice calm now, her body steady against them. 'I love you. I love you both, I—'

The bang, when it came, was loud enough to shake the abandoned crockery on the table. Uli cried out and Kirsten's eyes flew open.

'Uli. Uli, are you hurt? Are you...?'

She dried up as Uli lifted a hand to his head and then, with a shake, pointed across the kitchen. Turning, she saw Jan sinking slowly to the floor, the gun falling from his hand and blood spreading out from a perfect hole in the side of his temple. She felt bile rise in her throat and clutched at the side-board to stay upright as Lotti let go of them both and leaped forward, falling to her knees beside the limp man.

'Jan? Jan, are you there? Are you...'

Her words trickled out as she took him in his arms and he flopped uselessly across her knees.

'He's dead,' Uli said.

'He's dead,' Lotti confirmed. 'Oh God, he's dead.' She leaned over, stroking his blond hair away from the blood-laced hole in his temple. 'He's dead. He's at peace.'

'At peace?' Kirsten asked and Lotti looked up at her, tears swimming in her eyes.

'You heard him. This wasn't his world any more and it tormented him. He wasn't always like this, I promise you. The man I married was bright and lively and full of optimism about the future. He wanted to make Germany great and that didn't seem such a bad idea back then, when we were all crippled by the Great War. But somewhere along the line the Nazi plans got dirtier and dirtier. They sucked him in and this, I suppose, was his only way out.'

She bent and dropped a kiss on the unsullied side of his head and Kirsten ran to her.

'I'm so sorry, Mutti.'

'Don't be. He'd clearly planned this and it's for the best.' She started weeping. 'It's just all so... so sad, such a waste. He was a good man once.' She rocked Jan against her, then looked up at Kirsten again. 'He brought you to me, Kirsty. I know that's hard for you. I know it's been a shock and I know it looks evil but, for me, you were a gift – a wonderful gift. I blessed him for it then and I bless him for it still, whatever else has happened.'

Kirsten reached for her across Jan's dead body.

'You've been a wonderful mother. You *are* a wonderful mother.'

'But you want to know if your real one is still out there?'

'Is that so strange?'

Lotti shook her head.

'No stranger than anything else right now. You have my blessing, Kirsten. Find out who she was, find out who *you* were but, please, don't leave me.'

Kirsten shook her head, her own tears falling now. She reached for Uli and pulled him down at her side.

'I won't leave you,' she promised. 'We're a family. A funny-shaped one, perhaps, but a family all the same.'

They clung together, three beating hearts over the stilled one of the man who had crashed into their lives a month ago and had now crashed back out again in the darkest way possible. And they wept together for all they had lost, and all they still had.

# SEVENTEEN

## SATURDAY, 15 JULY

*OLIVIA*

Olivia stretched out on the grass at the edge of the athletics track, feeling the luscious warmth of the sun across her skin. It had been a hard training session and her body was aching, but it wasn't an unpleasant feeling and she pushed her arms out, arching her back to ease it.

'God, Olivia, you are one gorgeous woman.'

Hans dropped down beside her and ran a hand over her stomach. She had tucked her training vest into her bra in the heat and it was bare, brown and pleasingly toned. Six bumps of muscle were starting to show, taut against her skin, and she had to admit that she loved it. The amazing training programme, the good food and the special vitamins seemed to be working magic and her javelin was flying further and further. Trainer Lang was delighted and, with the sun high in the sky every day, life felt good. She reached up for Hans, pulling him down to kiss her.

'You're pretty gorgeous yourself. Good session?'

'The best,' he agreed. 'I've finally nailed my hip drive and it feels so much better. The discus was flying today.'

'And now we're all done and there's ages until dinner. What on earth will we do with ourselves?'

Hans let his hand creep upwards, threading under her tucked-in top to tease at her breast.

'I have an idea.'

'Do you indeed?'

She grinned up at him and he glanced around, but they were alone and he leaned over to kiss her again, deeper this time. Intimacy was encouraged at Dynamo so there was no fear of reprimands, but it was still unusual for him to be this demonstrative.

'I was wondering, Olivia...' he said, colouring.

'Yes,' she encouraged.

'Well, I was wondering if you, er, if you'd like to have sex with me?'

She thought about it. Hans was very handsome and he sent delicious sensations across her body when he kissed her, so why not see what more was on offer? What was it the nurse had said to her on her very first day here: 'It's marvellous fun and very good for the circulation.'

'Olivia? Have I offended you?'

She laughed.

'Goodness no. I was just thinking. I haven't done it before.'

'Me either. I know it's allowed and everything, but I haven't really met someone who seemed, you know, worth it. You though...' He let out a low moan. 'You I simply cannot get enough of, Olivia Pasternak.'

She giggled.

'Thank you.'

'So – have you thought about it?'

'I have.'

'And?'

'And it sounds lovely.'

'Really? Excellent.' He kissed her. 'I think it does too. Shall we...? I mean, when would you...?'

She sat up and took his hand.

'How about now?'

'Now? Now sounds wonderful! Come on.'

He leaped up, yanking her after him and making for the hostel. They bounded up the stairs and into his dorm, falling into his private cubicle where he kissed her once more, long and searching.

'I can't believe I get to see you naked,' he said.

She giggled.

'More than just see me, I hope.'

'Much more,' he confirmed. 'Oh, and I have, you know, protection. They gave it to us when we arrived.'

'Us too. I'm taking a pill so you don't need to worry. The nurse told me sex was, er...'

'Good for the circulation?'

'Yes!' She laughed. 'Do you think that's true?'

'If it is, our blood is in for a treat.' He kissed her again, then took hold of her vest. 'May I?'

'Of course.'

He lifted it over her head and then reached around to unclasp her bra.

'Oh my! Oh, Olivia, you really are so gorgeous.'

He trailed his lips down her collarbone and over the curve of her right breast, exploring every centimetre and sending glorious sensations across her skin. She yanked off his shirt and reached for his shorts.

'May I?'

'Yes! Yes, please.'

What she saw wasn't a surprise. They'd seen pictures in school, had lessons, but the way people fitted together had seemed merely curious back then. Now it made total, blood-rushing sense and Olivia reached down to touch, loving the gasps she could draw from him with the slightest stroke.

'Oh God, Olivia, I think we might need to get on with this or I'm going to burst.'

Olivia scrambled out of her shorts and drew him to the bed. There were a lot of limbs to fit together and a shot of pain, but only like the ping in your muscles when you pushed them hard. Then he was inside her and moving slowly and it felt amazing. He looked into her eyes and she drew him down and kissed him, losing herself in the combined power of their bodies and thinking that her circulation was going to get a lot of activity if sex was this good, before the sensations built and she thought about very little at all.

Afterwards, they lay cuddled together, getting their breath back and sharing kisses.

'I can't quite believe we've done it,' Hans said, stroking his hand down her side.

'We should probably do it again, to be sure,' Olivia suggested.

He laughed.

'We probably should – but after a little rest, hey?'

'A rest! Aren't you taking your vitamins, Herr Keller?'

Hans tensed slightly.

'Do you think they're all right, Liv?'

'The vitamins? Why wouldn't they be? I feel brilliant. Don't you like them?'

'I do. I mean, I'm training really well and all that, but sometimes I wonder if they make me a bit, well, angry.'

'Angry?'

He shook himself.

'That's not the right word. Not angry, but quicker to get riled. With myself, that is, not with anyone else, not with *you*.'

She stroked her hand across his chest.

'Is that not just competitiveness? Wanting to do well?'

'Maybe, but it seems worse since they introduced the blue pills.'

'That might be because the pressure is higher with the season progressing?'

He nodded.

'That's probably it. There's some big comps coming up, right, so I'm bound to be nervy?'

'Exactly. And you'll be great. You're throwing really well.'

'Yes. Absolutely. It's just... Some of the others were talking the other day and they feel the same, especially the girls. Lisel, the sprinter, says she gets mad at the slightest thing now. And...' he coloured, 'she says she wants sex all the time.'

'That I can understand,' Olivia laughed. 'I've already got a taste for it, so you better brace yourself.'

Hans laughed but it was thin and he still looked worried.

'All I'm saying, Liv, is keep an eye on yourself. On how you, you know, feel. Not everyone is happy with the regime.'

Olivia sat up.

'The regime? Who said that? What did they mean?'

Hans looked up at her, alarmed.

'Nothing. It's nothing. Just the vitamins that's all.'

'But who?'

'Sorry, this is so unromantic. Forget it. Lie down again, please.'

He tugged her down and she let herself be pulled into his arms, loving the feel of his body against hers.

'Are you rested yet?' she teased.

'Not quite.' His laugh was more genuine this time. 'Perhaps we could just chat for a bit? Hey, did you get anywhere with looking for your sister?'

It was Olivia's turn to tense.

'Are you trying to distract me, Hans?'

'No! Just asking.'

'As it happens, someone from the Rotes Rathaus has been in touch to say they're looking into it for me.'

'Right. Good. Is that good?'

Was it? Olivia thought of the man, Klaus. He'd turned up at school a few days ago, ostensibly to tell her he had leads on Pippa, though he'd been far keener to talk about the students' reaction to Ulbricht's press conference.

'People were worried about Berlin,' she'd told him, 'about a wall.'

'There will be no wall. Honestly!' Klaus had leaped to his feet, striding up and down the small backroom he'd summoned her to. 'Ulbricht said clearly that there would be no wall, so why does everyone think there will be?'

'I suppose,' Olivia had dared to say, 'that it's put the idea in their heads.'

Klaus had stopped his striding and nodded.

'I suppose so.' He'd leaned on the table, looming over Olivia. 'You're a clever girl, Olivia. Very clever, very observant. That's good. Did anyone, anyone at all, suggest leaving the East?'

'Not in my hearing, no. Everyone was cheering Dynamo and the DDR. People know what a great place it is, Klaus, they're not going to throw that away.'

He'd patted her on the head.

'Don't be so sure. The madness is catching and we must make sure it doesn't get in here, agreed?'

'Definitely.'

'Good. Keep listening, Olivia. I need to know, even if it's little things that don't seem important at the time. It all builds up, especially in young heads not as steady as your own. We must be alert.'

'Yes, Klaus.'

He'd pressed his face closer to hers.

'I heard this morning that the Ministry has a lead on your sister – a strong lead. We may be able to find the KZ records that could take us to her. They're classified of course, but...' he'd given a thin laugh, 'we're the Ministry for State Security. You came to the right people, Olivia, and I hope to bring you some news very soon.'

'Thank you,' she'd exclaimed. 'Oh Klaus, thank you so much.'

'My pleasure. And, Olivia, when I do, make sure you have news for me too, yes?'

The words, laced with the threat of grey vans and dark prisons, had chilled her at the time and, remembering them now, she curled in closer against Hans.

'It's a bit strange, maybe, but I'd love to know more, and Mutti...' Her breath caught in her throat. 'She was so anguished, Hans, when she saw the baby being taken from the poor woman prisoner. She's usually a very calm person, very controlled, but she lost it. It must have been so painful, mustn't it, to have your baby taken from you?'

'Awful. And that on top of all the other horrors in the KZs. It's amazing she survived.'

'And my father too, in Chelmno. Only about five of them made it out of there and one was him. He always says God kept them safe for each other, but they didn't find Pippa. Mutti had her for four days and Vati never saw her at all, never even knew she existed until after the war.'

Hans shivered.

'They must be very strong people. And here am I worrying about a few pills. I feel stupid, Liv. I'm sorry.'

'Don't be. My Tante Leah, my mother's sister, was smuggled out of the Łódź ghetto and lived the war in the hills. She married a farmer up there and for her the war was largely a happy time. She knows Mutti suffered and hates it, but she doesn't get it, and Mutti says that's fine. She says that the fewer people who carry that hell, the better. She says it makes her happy to see others' innocence.'

'Even so... It would be amazing if you could find her baby for her. She deserves that.'

'She does. I'm praying every day they'll find something for me.'

He ran a finger down her cheek.

'They haven't asked you for anything, you know, in return?'

Olivia shifted as a grey van drove across her mind.

'Of course not.'

'Are you sure, Liv?'

'Like what?'

'I don't know. You just have to be careful around here.'

'Not if you're not doing anything wrong.'

'No.' He sighed. 'Everything seems so tense in Berlin at the moment. There are so many refugees now, and they're not only poor folk. I see all these young, well-dressed people flowing past the Brandenburg Gate.'

'Idiots. Don't they know that socialism is the only fair way to live?'

Hans sighed.

'I'm not so sure humans are capable of being fair.'

'Hans!' Olivia leapt up, straddling him. 'Don't say that.'

'Sorry.' He put his hands on her waist and gave her a lopsided smile. 'One of the lads in the dorm has a radio and the other night he was listening to some American news programme. The presenter was interviewing a US senator and he said: "I don't understand why the East Germans don't close their border."'

'He did?'

'Just like that. And more. He said, "I think they have a right to close it." The presenter was all over it and we thought this bloke would get into real trouble with the president, but

Kennedy hasn't said a word and you've got to wonder – if the Americans are saying that, what's Spitzbart thinking?'

Olivia shifted and he looked up at her with a moan of appreciation, but now he'd got her worrying too.

'You think there'll be a wall?' she asked.

'Something like that. Maybe. I don't know. Everyone is on the campaign trail for the elections in September so it should be fine for now, but come the autumn, we could be cut off, Liv.'

She thought about it.

'Wouldn't it be West Berlin that was cut off?'

'Well, yes, from the rest of the DDR, but not from the rest of the world.'

She shrugged.

'The DDR is better. Maybe if we had a proper border, we could get on with socialism without all the capitalists stopping it working properly.' Hans thought about that, chewing on his lip in a most distracting way, and suddenly Olivia had had enough of politics, enough of the worries of who should do what, or think what. 'Is there anything we can do about it?' she asked, moving again and feeling him twitch against her.

He let out a hoarse laugh.

'I don't think so. I don't know. How am I meant to know anything with you on top of me looking so utterly stunning?'

'You don't even know what we might do with the rest of the time until dinner...?' He ran his hands up her back, pulling her closer and flicking his tongue across her nipple. 'Forget politics,' she murmured. 'There's nothing we can do about it, even if they do build a wall.'

'True,' he agreed, moving to her other breast. 'And we have all we want right here, don't we?'

'We do. Dynamo, our families, each other...'

He kissed her and she kissed him back but that word – family – dug into her heart.

'I hope to bring you some news very soon,' Klaus had

assured her, which was amazing, but somehow all she could hear was: 'And Olivia, when I do, make sure you have news for me too, yes?'

She kissed Hans again, determinedly banishing the Stasi from her mind. If their attentions were the price she had to pay to find Pippa, then pay it she would, for it seemed that, in the DDR, there was no such thing as free information.

# EIGHTEEN

*KIRSTEN*

Kirsten stared up at the imposing facade of the landesarchiv, a vast building in the top quarter of West Berlin, and told herself this was easy. All she wanted was a little information and, frankly, after spending the last week talking to officials about arranging Jan's burial, that was a doddle. They'd had to call the police of course, after the shooting, but it had all been clear-cut and, given Jan's record, no one had cared anyway.

'Good riddance,' Kirsten had heard one of the officers mutter and, although she'd agreed with him, it had hurt all the same.

The only positive was that Lotti had given her blessing on seeking out her biological parents and so here she was at the landesarchiv. They would be dead, of course, she understood that. The Stasi man had just been trying to hook her in and she wasn't going to fall for it. She'd found a few articles on the KZs in the library and, of the millions of people who'd been shipped into them in cattle carts, barely a few thousand had survived. The odds of either her mother or father being one of those few were tiny, but at least if she had a name, it would fill in the new gaping hole in her personal history.

'I know about your mother,' the man in the café had said. That, surely, meant there was something to know, though, of course, he could have been lying. There was no telling with snakes like him.

'Come on then, Kirsty,' she told herself.

The clock on the vast building said it was approaching eleven o'clock already and she had to be on shift at midday. Uli had offered to come with her, and she wished now she'd taken him up on it, but it was the last day of the school term, so not one for him to miss. Besides, she'd thought this was something she ought to do alone so, gripping her handbag tight across her chest to protect the precious photo of her mother's camp number, she marched up the steps. Inside, there were several desks, but the nearest one was marked 'information', which seemed encouraging, so she headed that way.

'Can I help you?'

'I hope so. That is, I'm looking for a record of my mother. My biological mother.'

'I see.' The woman was middle-aged with greying hair and kind eyes. 'What information do you have about her?'

Kirsten swallowed.

'She was in a KZ, that is, a konzentrationslager.'

'She was? I'm so sorry. Which one?'

The woman was very matter-of-fact and it made Kirsten feel slightly better. She could hardly be alone in this sort of request. Millions of people had disappeared into those places.

'Auschwitz.'

'I see. Well, the good news is that quite a few records have been recovered from Auschwitz in the last few years. Do you have anything to go on? A name perhaps?'

'I don't have a name,' Kirsten admitted, 'but I do have a number.'

'A number? A tattooed number?' She nodded and fumbled the photo out of her bag. The woman stared at it for some time, but if she saw anything odd in it being an armpit not an arm, she kept it politely to herself. 'This should be a big help, dear. The original documents are kept on site at Auschwitz. It's a museum now, you know, run by a former inmate.'

'It is?'

Kirsten could hardly believe it. A museum? Who would want to do that?

The woman read her mind. 'It is a little hard to grasp. Many wanted to raze it to the ground to wipe away the evil, but the inmates believe it's better preserved as a memorial and a caution.'

Kirsten nodded.

'I can see that. And you say the records are there? Where is it?'

'It's in the middle of Poland, a long way away.' Kirsten's heart sank. 'But don't worry – we have copies.'

'Copies? Of the records? Here?'

'That's right.'

'That's amazing!' Kirsten couldn't believe it. Thank God she hadn't let that snake of a Stasi bribe her. 'Can I see them?'

'We can check them for you, yes, if you come this way. The Nazis kept full lists of names against numbers, but I have to warn you, we don't have them all. Certain sequences are missing, so please don't get your hopes too high.'

'Of course not,' Kirsten agreed, but her hopes were already battering against the celling of the huge building and it was impossible to keep still as she waited in the side room for a 'special adviser'.

It didn't take long before another woman walked in, younger than the first, with darker hair but similarly kind eyes. In her arm she held a set of ring-bound files and Kirsten's breath caught.

'Are those the KZ records?'

'What we have of them, yes. I must warn you, they're not complete.'

'Your colleague said that.'

'So we might not have the number you seek.'

'I understand. But you might?'

She smiled.

'We might. Could I see the photo?' Kirsten placed it on the table and the woman pulled it towards herself with immaculately clean fingertips, then produced a magnifying glass and scrutinised it closely.'

'This isn't an arm.'

'No,' Kirsten agreed. 'It's an armpit – my armpit. Well, mine from when I was a baby.'

The woman looked at her with something alarmingly like admiration.

'You're an Auschwitz baby?'

'Erm, yes, it seems so.'

'You didn't know?'

'Not until recently.'

'I'm so sorry. I must seem very insensitive. We've heard of babies being taken out and even a few stories of them being found again, but I've never met one myself.'

'Well, here I am.'

Kirsten spread her hands wide and smiled awkwardly. The woman stared at her a second longer and then shook herself.

'Sorry. You're not here to satisfy my curiosity, but to know something vital about yourself. This, I believe, says 41400. Do you agree?' Kirsten nodded. She'd read it over and over and doodled it a thousand times on a pad of paper. 'Then let's have a look, shall we?'

She opened the third of her many files and began assiduously turning pages. Kirsten's eyes followed every movement, desperately trying to scan the numbers, but there were so many of them. So many individuals corralled with such administrative precision into this roll of death. Had Jan overseen these? Had he stood in an office on the outskirts of that hellhole and calmly scrutinised the lines of inmates, turning people with lives and cares and loved ones into blank, featureless numbers, easy to consign to the gas? She feared he had.

And, yet, he had also rescued her and 'gifted' her to Lotti. That scrap of humanity inside him had brought her a loving mother and happy childhood.

You owe him nothing, she told herself crossly. Without him and his ilk she would have been born to her natural mother, brought up in peace and love, and had to face none of the confusion and trauma of the last two months.

But she wouldn't have had Lotti. And she wouldn't have had Uli.

Oh, it was all so confusing.

'Ah, yes.'

Kirsten's heart almost stopped and she stared at the woman as her finger came to rest on a single number, halfway down a page.

'Have you found her?'

'41400,' she read out. 'I believe I have. Would you like to see?' Kirsten hesitated. Was it really this easy? She'd thought she was at the start of her search, not the end, and she felt jittery with nerves. The woman cleared her throat. 'How about I read it out to you?'

'Please,' she whispered, clasping her hands together and wishing, again, that she'd agreed to let Uli come. But she was here now and so, it seemed, was her mother – or at least her mother's name.

'Prisoner number 41400,' the woman read in a warm, steady voice. 'Name – Ester Pasternak. Place of origin – Łódź, Poland.' She stopped, looked at Kirsten. 'Are you all right, dear?'

'I think so.'

'It's a lot to take in. Shall I write it down for you?'

'Yes, please.'

Kirsten sat, stunned, and watched her write the words in a careful hand.

'This whole sequence is from Łódź. There's a woman ahead of her called Rebekah and one after called Ana Kaminski. Curious – that's usually not a Jewish name, though the rest around here are. I believe they were clearing the Łódź ghetto around this time.'

'When?'

'Spring 1943.'

Kirsten felt misery creep up inside her. 1943! Auschwitz hadn't been liberated until January 1945. There was surely no way her mother, or any of her friends, could have survived that long?

'Are there any records of... of deaths?'

'There are, but they're kept separately and we don't have nearly as many. Needless to say, the Nazis were keener on recording labour in than out, but I can check what we have. Are you all right to wait?'

Kirsten nodded. She'd be late to the café, but even stern Frau Munster would surely understand when she explained. She sat staring at the name on the paper: Ester Pasternak. Łódź. Poland. She was Polish! She'd never even been to Poland. Well, obviously she had, but only in the first few days of her life.

She tried to picture Auschwitz, but had only hazy pictures of barracks, fences and emaciated workers to call on, nothing that fitted with a baby. Yet she had been carried out of those dark gates and driven across Poland to Berlin where she'd been neatly slotted into the life that she had, until Jan had slammed into the apartment, believed to be her own. Since then, its foundations had been excavated from under her, but filling them back in was proving almost as tricky.

She nearly jumped out of her skin when the woman returned.

'I'm sorry. Did I scare you?'

Kirsten almost laughed out loud – everything was scaring her about this – but she shook her head politely. 'Did you find anything more?'

'Nothing in the death records, but I took the liberty of checking our more up-to-date registers.'

'Sorry?'

'Today's names and addresses.'

Kirsten gasped.

'Today's...? And?'

'And I have an Ester Pasternak listed as a midwife in Stalin-stadt, that's a town about an hour east from here.'

'She's alive?'

The woman put up a warning hand.

'I have *an* Ester Pasternak. It's not an uncommon Jewish name, though it does list her birthplace as Łódź, so maybe... It's certainly worth checking.' She held out another piece of paper. 'She lives with a husband, Filip, a daughter, Olivia, and two sons, Mordecai and Benjamin. I've written it all down here, with their address.'

'Address?' Kirsten took the paper, unable to take in the names upon it. That fox in the café had been right! 'Is it really this easy?' she blurted out.

'Sometimes,' the lady said. 'If you get lucky.'

Kirsten wasn't sure she felt lucky, but this was certainly more than she could possibly have hoped for when she'd taken the steps into the landesarchiv. This fragile record could be her family; her natural, birth family. Somewhere out there could be the people who shared her blood, who, without her ever knowing it, had created her history. All she had to do now, was find them.

# NINETEEN

## WEDNESDAY, 26 JULY

*OLIVIA*

'Chop, chop, girls,' Frau Scholz snapped, striding into the changing room. 'We're due in front of Herr Braun and he won't be happy if we're late.'

'He's not happy full stop,' Julia muttered as they all obediently trooped out of the showers to dress. 'Verdammte Lisel.'

Olivia shivered. Lisel, their top sprinter, had disappeared from Dynamo last night. Alarms had sounded when she'd failed to turn up for training, but an extensive search had found no sign of her. She'd gone, taking her medals with her, and no one was stupid enough to think she'd be anywhere in the DDR. The mood had been dark ever since and Olivia had spent the morning looking out for Klaus, certain he would be onto her immediately. So far he hadn't appeared, but it was only a matter of time.

She rubbed herself dry hastily, but then paused and stared down at her chest, unable to believe what she was seeing.

'Is that a... a hair?'

Julia looked over curiously.

'Goodness, I think it is.' She reached out and tweaked the thin, dark hair between Olivia's breasts. 'That's weird.'

Olivia flinched, but Magda, a shot-putter, laughed.

'Not so weird, I get them all the time. Here.'

She brandished a pair of tweezers. Olivia took them uncertainly, but had the hair out in a second and searched herself for more. There were plenty in her armpit, hiding her tattoo, but that was nothing new. Her upper lip though, was definitely a shade darker than before and she rubbed at it in concern.

'You can get cream for that,' Magda told her. 'Ask the nurse. It's perfectly normal with all the weight-training we're doing.'

'Not for blondes,' Julia said, stroking Olivia's golden hair and then preening at her own straw-coloured locks.

Magda scoffed. 'You beanpole high jumpers barely touch a dumb-bell.'

'Because big fat muscles would break up our graceful flight through the air,' Julia retorted merrily and tripped away to dress.

Olivia sat down next to Magda.

'Do you think we're training too much, Mags?'

'Too much?! Is that possible?'

Olivia chuckled but then leaned closer to her friend.

'It's not just the hair. I think my periods have stopped.'

Magda gave an easy shrug.

'Mine too. Didn't the nurse warn you about it?'

Olivia thought back to her first medical and smiled in remembrance.

'She did actually,' she agreed, relieved. It had been worrying her but if it was a normal part of the process, then who was she to question it?

'Great, isn't it?!' Magda went on and Olivia laughed.

'I guess so, for now at least, but what if we want to have babies?'

'Then we stop training, silly, and the periods come back.

But who wants that right now? I'm so much stronger than I was when I first came here and I'm putting metres on my throws. Coach says if I carry on like this, I might make DDR selection next summer.'

'That's fantastic.'

'Isn't it? And I bet you will too, Liv. Your throw at the weekend was brilliant – a DDR U20 record is amazing.'

Liv gave her a grateful smile and handed Magda back her tweezers. She'd been stunned when she'd pulled out the winning distance at the Youth Games on her sixth and final throw last weekend. A journalist had taken loads of photos of her and then, spotting her giving Hans a congratulatory kiss for his win, had insisted on snapping the 'golden couple'. The whole school had teased them about that when *Neues Deutschland* had come out the next day, but Olivia hadn't cared. Magda was right – success like that was worth a few small changes. Wasn't it?

'Something wrong, girls?'

She and Magda jumped as their hausmeisterin loomed over them.

'No, Frau Scholz, nothing at all.'

'Excellent. Then – get a move on!'

'Yes, Frau Scholz, of course, Frau Scholz.'

Pulling on their tracksuits, they headed out into a miserably drizzly day to catch the tram to the Dynamo main building.

'That Lisel's an idiot,' Magda said as they found seats. 'She's thrown away the best club in Germany for what – Coca-Cola and Levi's jeans? We'll not see her at the Olympics now!'

'Does anyone know why she went?' Olivia asked casually.

'Weren't you mates with her, Julia?' someone said.

'Oh no,' Julia said hastily. 'She mainly hung out with the sprinters. Frieda?'

'She never said anything to me,' Frieda, a young 400-metre

runner, said with a nervous glance to Frau Scholz. 'I thought she was happy. God knows who got to her.'

'You think someone talked her into it?' Olivia asked.

'I reckon. One of the boys probably. She was always hanging around them.'

'Looking for sex!' Magda said, and they all laughed.

'Who was she sleeping with?' Olivia pushed, looking out the tram window to hide the colour flooding her face at her questions. Surely she was being far too obvious? But no one else seemed to notice.

'Who *wasn't* she sleeping with?' Julia chuckled, adding hastily, 'Not your Hans of course, Liv, but anyone else who'd oblige. I heard she even did it with Herr Manzer in the—'

'Julia!' Frau Scholz snapped. 'Enough. Come on, all of you – we're here.'

Julia rolled her eyes but everyone obediently trooped out of the tram and Olivia looked around at her fellow athletes, thankful no one had said anything 'subversive'. Klaus, she was ominously certain, would be turning up very soon and she could honestly tell him that she had nothing to report.

Sure enough, as they crossed the car park she saw the Stasi officer striding towards her and was forced to stop and wait as the other girls hurried out of the rain into Dynamo. She looked to the sodden skies, fighting tears and a sharp longing to see her parents. If only she could go home for a few hours and cuddle them all, with no one watching her, or asking questions, or expecting anything.

She'd hoped they'd come to watch her throw at the Youth Games, but Ester had been on call and Ben had been running a fever and it hadn't been possible. She'd sent them a copy of *Neues Deutschland* with her photos inside and could picture their pride when they'd opened it, but it wasn't the same as being able to reach out and hug them. She hadn't seen them for over two months and the only thing keeping her going until the season ended in two weeks' time, was the thought that she might be able to bring them some news about Pippa.

On that thought, she pushed herself upright to face the Stasi officer.

'Klaus.'

'Olivia. Glad to see you're still here.'

'Of course I am. I like it here.'

'And you're doing very well. Quite the poster girl.'

'I wouldn't say that, Klaus, I'm only—'

He put up a hand.

'People are leaving Dynamo, Olivia.'

'I know,' she agreed. 'Lisel—'

'Was one of our most promising talents. She came to the club with glowing reviews from her school and her FDJ – as you did – and now she's gone. That doesn't happen without someone getting to her, so who can it be?'

'I don't know, Klaus.'

'You don't know?' His eyes narrowed and he stepped closer. 'I asked you to keep an ear out, Olivia. Can you not do that? Can you not *even* do that?'

Olivia tried to step back but the railing was in her way.

'The other girls think it was a boy,' she offered.

'What?' Klaus' stare sharpened. 'What boy?'

'I don't know. Apparently she's, er, been with a few.'

'Has she indeed. Names?'

'I don't know!'

He jabbed a finger into her face.

'Then find out. It's vital, Olivia. Whoever this is could be working on any number of athletes. They could be working on you.'

'No!'

'Prove it.' He grabbed her wrist, his thin fingers digging into her flesh. 'Get me names. Soon.'

'Klaus, please, you're hurting me.'

He loosened his grip.

'I'm sorry, Olivia. I don't want to hurt you. I'm just passionate about keeping those Western bastards from poaching our talent. It's all lies, what they tell them, all mean, calculated lies.'

'I know that.'

'Of course you do, of course.' He gave her an unconvincing smile. 'Ooh look, your meeting is about to start, you better run along.' She turned with relief, but then his fingers closed around her wrist once more. 'Oh and Olivia, I got more news of your sister today. That's why I came. Silly me, I got so caught up in all this terrible republikflucht that I forgot.'

'My sister?'

Her heart leaped. Perhaps she'd misjudged Klaus.

'It's good news. I'm told that the girl you know as Pippa lives in Berlin.'

'She does? Amazing! What name does she go by now?'

Klaus smiled.

'That, Olivia, I will be delighted to tell you.' She looked at him keenly but he laughed. 'A name for a name, my dear. You bring me the boy who sowed subversion into Lisel's ear, and I'll bring you your sister. That's only fair, yes?'

'I...'

'Yes,' he repeated.

Then he let go of her wrist and tapped away, leaving Olivia alone with her world spinning in grey vans around her.

'Olivia! Why are you lingering out here? We're starting.' Frau Scholz waved urgently from the foyer.

'Sorry,' she said, biting back tears. 'Coming.'

The hausmeisterin looked curiously at her. Something almost like sympathy crossed her dark eyes, but then it was gone.

'Hurry up then,' she snapped and hustled Olivia into the hall.

The doors closed and Olivia drew in a shaky breath as she was absorbed into the communal safety of Dynamo – at least for now. She thought of Ester and tears threatened again so, yanking her hair loose of its ponytail, she dipped her head and let them fall. She was desperate to find Pippa for her dear mother, but the cost of that prize seemed to be rising all the time and she was starting to wonder how on earth she was going to meet it.

# TWENTY

*KIRSTEN*

Kirsten looked around the schick Eden Saloon, trying desperately to enjoy herself, but the ghost of her last visit was threading its bitter presence through the happy lunchtime crowd. She could almost see Jan lolling near the door, spitting general poison before delivering his final dart – that she wasn't his daughter. That had been less than two months ago and now the name of her actual father was burning a hole in the pocket of her gingham dress. She turned back to the stage, trying to forget it all for an hour or two.

'OK?' Dieter shouted over the music.

'Fine.'

He was deep in the band – an East German group called Renft who were playing versions of Chuck Berry and Bill Haley to a rapt crowd – so thankfully didn't probe further. In truth, he'd been distant all week, wrapped up in helping the refugees out at Marienfelde, and she hadn't yet told him about finding her parents' names.

'They just keep coming, Kirsten,' Dieter had told her

earlier. 'We had almost two thousand Ossis yesterday and there's no sign of it letting up. Everyone is worried that after the September elections there'll be a clamp-down on the border and they're getting out while they can.'

'Isn't it a bit of an over-reaction?' Kirsten had said.

'Maybe. Maybe not. My parents have been agonising over it, but at least with Austrian passports we should have some freedom. For everyone else, the thought of the Iron Curtain finally closing is hard.'

She'd been glad when he'd suggested coming to see Renft, hoping he could relax, and he certainly looked happy as he ducked a sputnik – the groovig metal canisters on overhead wires that delivered beer to the tables – and grabbed her to dance to 'Rock Around the Clock'. Kirsten gave in to the beat, kicking Jan's ghost away with her heels.

The reality of her real father, however, was harder to escape. She'd plucked up the courage to tell Lotti and Uli about discovering the names of her birth family and he'd been pleasingly happy for her.

'That's great, Kirsten. Well done.'

'Do you think?'

'Of course. There was something you didn't know and now you do.'

He'd made it sound so simple, but this wasn't like learning the capitals of Europe or how to do algebra. This was discovering the identity of the woman who gave birth to you.

'You're lucky, Kirsty,' he'd said. 'I have no chance of finding my father.'

'Do you want to?'

He'd thought about it, but only for a second.

'No. He was a sheiße.'

Uli rarely swore so it had surprised her. It was a fair point, though, and, of course, *her* father could turn out to be a sheiße too. Knowledge was a dangerous thing. And impossible, once you had it, to escape.

'You sure you're OK, Kirsten?' Dieter asked and, to her embarrassment, she realised she'd stopped dancing and was standing stock-still in the middle of the leaping crowd. 'Come on, let's get a drink.'

He steered her towards the bar and she leaned heavily on it as he waved for attention. Newspapers littered the surface and she pushed a tattered copy of *Neues Deutschland* to one side and gratefully accepted a beer. Up on stage, Renft announced they were taking a break and Kirsten and Dieter could hear themselves speak again. No excuses now.

'Is it your father?' Dieter asked.

Now there was a question!

'Not really.'

'Have they buried him?'

'They buried Jan, yes. It was only us there and it was very quick. Mutti cried, but not for long. It's not him.'

'Then...?'

He looked around and with a sinking heart Kirsten saw Astrid and a couple of the other students coming through the door. They were all volunteering at the centre and full of it; she would lose his attention any minute.

'I got the name of my parents – my real parents.'

His eyes swung instantly back to her.

'No way?!'

'Yep. They're Polish.'

'Polish?'

'And, and Jewish.'

'You're a Polish Jew?' It sounded so stark like that, so utterly different from everything she'd thought herself to be. 'That's cool.' Kirsten looked sideways at him. 'Sorry. Stupid thing to say. How do you know?'

'I got my mother's name from the tattoo number and they

found her on a register. She lives in Stalinstadt with a husband and three children.'

'Stalinstadt? That's less than an hour out of the city.'

'An hour east.'

'So what? There's no wall, Kirsten – not yet.'

'Don't!'

'So we can go and look for them.'

'We?'

'Why not? Astrid has a car.' Of course she did! 'I bet she'd drive us out there.'

Kirsten shook her head.

'Thank you, but no. I have to do this on my own.'

'You don't want me there?'

'I don't want Astrid there.'

'Someone calling my name in vain?'

Astrid bounced up, all glossy hair and smiles.

'Don't say anything,' Kirsten hissed at Dieter.

He looked surprised, hurt even, but this was her business and if he couldn't see that, then he wasn't worth being around. She turned away as he asked his friends about the refugee centre and they fell into earnest discussion. Taking a sip of her beer, she pulled *Neues Deutschland* back towards her, as if she was the sort of girl that regularly stood at bars reading the news. It wasn't even today's, she noticed, and idly flicked through a couple of pages, then stopped.

There, in the middle of a spread of photos entitled 'Dynamo: the Future of DDR Sport', was a picture of a girl throwing a javelin. It was an arresting shot, caught as she was releasing the implement into a clear sky, but that wasn't what caught Kirsten's attention. What grabbed her, what reached into her guts and seemed to pull them right up her throat, was the caption beneath: *Gold medal winner, Olivia Pasternak*.

Could it be?

She grabbed the tatty newssheet and carried it to the window for better light but the name was still the same.

*Pasternak is not an uncommon Jewish name*, she reminded herself, but combined with Olivia – one of the names listed in Ester's household – it was striking. Was this glorious-looking athlete, then, her sister? The paper shook in her hands. This girl could have been one of the red-tracksuited athletes she'd seen the night of Jan's death – the ones who had looked so strong and purposeful. If Ester and Filip Pasternak had this amazing daughter, why would they want little waitress Kirsten?

She let the paper drop to her side, but quickly snatched it up again. That wasn't the point. If this Olivia was her sister, she had to find her. The article said that the Dynamo sports club was right here, in Berlin, and the track and field athletes were training at the city track. That was just up Bernauerstraβe, above the marketplace. Kirsten had been there last week, picking up vegetables for Lotti, and all along her sister could have been training on the other side of the fence.

She darted back to Dieter, deep in conversation with Astrid. 'I have to go, Dieter.'

He looked round, confused, but she didn't have time to explain and, besides, he'd be quite happy in his cool bar, with his cool friends, listening to his cool band. With a hasty wave, she made for the door, the newspaper still clutched in her hand.

The tram ride back to Bernauerstraβe felt like forever. She got off as if heading home, but marched straight past her front door and on to the athletics stadium. It was starting to rain but the air was hot and the droplets steamed off the pavement as she all but ran onto the marketplace. Kirsten felt the newspaper crumple in her hand and saw the print smudging her skin, as if imprinting the picture of her sister right onto it. Or perhaps that was just being over-dramatic.

'Over-dramatic!' she snorted. She could be about to meet a

sister she'd only recently discovered existed. Was it possible to be over-dramatic?

Climbing up the grassy slope to the stadium, she looked down into the track through gaps in the fence. There were lots of people training, all in matching scarlet kit and all looking strong and purposeful. There didn't seem to be any javelins so she had no way of picking out Olivia or, indeed, knowing if she was there, but at least the club wasn't away at a competition. Her heart beat ridiculously hard in her skinny chest and she paused outside the rough entrance to catch her breath. Now, though, the waiting felt like agony and, before she could lose her nerve, she pushed open the door and marched through.

It was cool and dark inside and Kirsten was grateful for the murky air as she suddenly felt very conspicuous. There was no reception desk, but a thin-faced woman was sitting at a table overlooking the track, going through some sort of ledgers and tutting to herself. Kirsten screwed up her courage and approached.

'Hello. I wonder if you could help me?'

'I doubt it.'

Not an encouraging start. The woman was looking at her as if she were some sort of bug dragged in on the bottom of a trainer, but Kirsten wasn't going to let that bother her, not now. She could see the athletes more clearly from here and the thought that one of them might be her sister spurred her on.

'I'm looking for an athlete – Olivia Pasternak.'

'Why?'

'I think she might, er, know my family.'

'I see. Well, I can't give out the names of athletes. Confidentiality, you know. If you'd care to put something in writing, I could check.'

Kirsten looked down at her. This was ridiculous.

'I know she's here because it's all over the newspaper.' She thrust the article at the woman, who looked down with disdain at the crumpled mess in her hand. Even so, the picture of Olivia was clear to see, propelling her javelin into the sky between them. 'It can hardly be confidential if it's been reported to the whole of Germany.'

The woman pursed her lips.

'Even so, I cannot summon athletes to meet strangers. There's no telling who you might be.'

'I'm her sister.' It burst from Kirsten on a sort of yelp and the woman blinked.

'Then you will surely, young lady, have your own way of contacting her?'

Kirsten stamped her foot in frustration.

'I don't, because she doesn't know it yet.'

'Doesn't know she has a sister?'

'No!'

Kirsten sized up the woman, wondering if she could push past and run down to the track, but then a voice behind them said, 'I think you'll find she does.'

'Hans!' The woman leaped to her feet. 'What are you doing here?'

'Filling up my water bottle,' the young man told her, waving it, although his eyes were on Kirsten. He was tall, handsome and intimidatingly broad. 'Are you Pippa?'

Kirsten put a hand to her chest.

'Pippa? No. I mean, maybe. I don't know. I'm Kirsten, Kirsten Meyer, but I think Olivia might be my sister. That is, I think her mother, Ester Pasternak, might be my mother too.'

Hans smiled.

'I think you might be right.'

Kirsten felt her knees give way and it was only Hans darting forward to clasp her arm that kept her upright.

'How... how do you know?'

'Because Olivia has been looking for you too. Come on, I'll take you to her.'

'You will?'

This was all happening rather fast. Not that she didn't want it to. She did want it to, but even so...

'Hans,' the thin-faced woman said desperately, 'strangers aren't allowed on site. It's in the rules.'

Hans turned a bright smile on her.

'Didn't you hear, Ma? She's no stranger, she's Olivia's sister. She's Olivia's long-lost sister and the sooner we get them together, the better, don't you think?'

It was clear the woman did not think that but she was help-less before broad Hans, who still had a hold of Kirsten's arm and was steering her past the table, between the rows of shabby bleachers, and down to the track. It was raining harder now, the water pinging off the cinders of the old surface, but no one seemed to care. Hans led Kirsten past a group of runners doing sprint starts, two hurdlers curving their way over the barriers with astonishing grace, and a boy scissoring his long legs over a bar higher than Kirsten's head.

'She's over here on the weights,' Hans said, indicating a group in one corner and there, in the middle, was the girl from the paper, squatting in front of a vast dumb-bell.

As Kirsten drew close, she suddenly threw her legs apart and jerked the bar clean up into the air above her head as if it weighed no more than a tray of empty coffee cups.

'Wow,' Kirsten whispered.

'Amazing, isn't she?' Hans agreed with a very fond smile. 'We'd better wait until she puts that down before I introduce you, or who knows what might happen!'

He laughed easily but it warped in Kirsten's ears as if she were underwater. In what seemed to be slow motion, she saw Olivia put down the bar, smile as another student clapped her on the back, and then turn to Hans. She felt him lift her arm, heard him say the word 'sister', and saw Olivia's mouth gape open, her hands fly to her face, tears fill her eyes. Then she was running, running up to Kirsten and taking her hands and saying, 'Is it you? Is it really you?'

And it seemed that it really was.

They sat in the corner of the common room, people buzzing all around them, but with ears only for each other.

'I only found out about you a few months ago,' Olivia told Kirsten, 'when my mother – *our* mother – admitted that she'd had a baby taken off her in Auschwitz. It was quite a shock.'

'Tell me about it... I found out when my father came home, after years away, and told me I wasn't actually his.'

Olivia's blue eyes softened.

'I'm sorry. That must have been awful. I'm adopted too.'

'What?' Kirsten was truly confused now. 'You said, "our mother".'

'Our parents found me in an orphanage after the war and took me in. Mutti was the one who tattooed babies' mother's numbers into their armpits so that they might find each other again if they ever got out. My tattoo was the first one she did, which is why they found me, or that's how they always told it. It turns out, they were looking for you. They were always looking for you.'

'I'd say they did pretty well with the baby they got.'

Olivia smiled at her.

'Thank you. That's very kind. They've been wonderful parents, *are* wonderful parents.'

'Tell me about them.'

'Of course. Mutti is a midwife. She was a nurse before the war, but in Auschwitz she helped Grandma Ana with all the babies and she loved it, so she retrained here in Berlin once she got out.'

'Grandma Ana?'

'Ana Kaminski – a midwife from Łódź, where Mutti and

Vati came from originally. She's still there now, still bringing babies into the world, although I think she's about sixty-five, and we visit her when we can. She's not really my grandma – she sort of adopted Mutti after her real mother died on the train to Auschwitz – but Mutti says you don't need blood to form bonds of love.'

Kirsten thought of her own upside-down family and felt comforted.

'I think she's right, though there seem to be an awful lot of adoptions in this story.'

'That's war for you. We all had to find care where we could. Did you? Find care, I mean?'

'Oh yes. My mutti, Lotti, she's been a wonderful mother and I have a brother, Uli. We're very close, though it turns out he's not actually my father's child either.'

'How come?'

'It's complicated.'

Olivia laughed.

'You can say that again, Pippa. Sorry, Kirsten.'

'Pippa?' Kirsten turned it over on her tongue. 'It's a nice name.'

'It's for our father, Filip. You were Filipa in full, but Mutti called you Pippa.'

'My father.' There it was, the man who could step into Jan's dirty shoes. 'What's he like?'

'Vati? Oh, he's lovely. Kind and gentle and patient. He's a tailor.'

'No!' Kirsten looked down at her handmade dress. 'I like to sew too.'

'There you go then, it's in your blood.'

The words thrilled through Kirsten. There were so many names to grasp, so many connections to make, so many people to find out about. It was exhausting, but exciting too.

'Are you all right?' Olivia asked.

'Yes, I think so. Are you?'

'I think so.' She reached out and took Kirsten's hand. 'I always wanted a sister.'

Kirsten clasped it. Olivia's hand was big and strong and marked with callouses, but felt infinitely soft around hers.

'Are you my *big* sister?'

'I think so, yes, though not by much. I was born in September 1943 and you the following Christmas Day.'

'Christmas Day?! Mutti always told me it was December twenty-seventh.'

Olivia shook her head.

'Christmas Day. A Christmas miracle! Though we're Jewish, of course.'

'Of course. I mean, are you? Jewish? Still?'

Olivia laughed.

'We're Jewish still. It doesn't go away.'

'No, of course not. Silly thing to say, sorry. It's only that, for me, it's kind of just come.'

'I suppose so.'

They sat there silently while Kirsten fought to process all she'd heard and all she was still to hear.

'Christmas Day,' she muttered, 'what on earth does that look like in a KZ?'

'Not pretty,' Olivia said grimly. 'Mutti will tell you the story when you meet her.'

'When I...?'

'You *will* meet her?'

And there it was – the next step. Kirsten's heart faltered again but she'd come this far and there was nothing to do but push on.

'I will meet her, I'll meet all of them. I'd... I'd love to.'

Her voice caught and Olivia's hand tightened around hers.

'Scary, right?'

'Scary,' Kirsten confirmed, 'but at least, now, we can do it together.' She shook her head at this amazing new sort-of-sister. 'Can you believe we were born in Auschwitz?'

'And both made it out alive. We must be so lucky.'

'Sounds like it was all down to, to...'

Kirsten couldn't bring herself to say *Mutti* yet. Mutti was Lotti, always had been, but she had to find a slot for this new woman now, this brave survivor who'd carved numbers into her baby's armpit in the desperate hope of one day finding her again. It had not, it seemed, been such a desperate hope after all and in just a few days Kirsten could step back into her arms. All it would take was a little organisation – and a lot of courage.

# TWENTY-ONE

*OLIVIA*

Olivia sat on her bed, cradling a picture of her family in her hands and thinking of the girl who should be in it with them, should, in truth, be in it instead of her. Pippa – Kirsten – had left hours ago, but Olivia was still in a daze and had shut herself in her room to take it all in. It was amazing, of course, marvellous, wonderful, all that. And yet... Fantastic as it was to have found Ester's stolen baby, and lovely as Kirsten seemed, Olivia couldn't help a sneaking wish that she'd never existed at all. Sitting opposite her had been like looking at a younger version of her mother – neat, petite and fine-boned – and it made Olivia painfully aware of how different she was.

'That's just selfish, Olivia Pasternak,' she told herself sternly.

At least Kirsten's appearance confirmed that she'd found the right baby and wouldn't offer her parents more heartbreak, but there was another thing niggling at her. Ester had said they'd chosen to stop looking for Pippa. What if her news wasn't welcome?

Hans had been up several times, asking if she was all right, and she'd assured him she was but needed time alone. She couldn't believe Kirsten had found her from that article in *Neues Deutschland*, and found her before she had to say anything to Klaus that she would regret. Not that she should regret helping to prevent people from stupidly leaving the DDR, but it still felt uncomfortable.

She looked at the picture again and shook all the complications out of her head. What was going on in Berlin was not important right now. She had found her parents' lost baby. She had found Pippa. Or, rather, Pippa had found her. A miracle had occurred – the miracle Ester had been praying for since she'd carved her inky number into her tiny baby's armpit – so surely she would want to know? Leaping up, she ran to find Hans.

'Liv! Are you all right?'

He gathered her into his arms, concern in his handsome face, and she smiled up at him.

'It's been a bit weird,' she admitted.

'Did I do the right thing bringing her to you? I know it was a shock, but Frau Scholz was going to send her away and I didn't think you'd want that and—'

'Hush, Hans.' She kissed him quiet. 'Of course you did the right thing. It was amazing to meet her.'

'But weird?'

She shrugged.

'She's my mother's real baby, Hans, her real daughter.'

'And you're the one she chose. That's every bit as real.'

'You're right.' She kissed him again. 'Thank you.'

He held her tight.

'I love you, Olivia.'

She froze against his chest, then dared to sneak a glance up at him.

'You do?'

'I do. I love you and I want you to be happy. Always.'

She smiled.

'I'm not sure that *always* is realistic – what about if I only get a silver?'

He gave a soft chuckle.

'Not then, obviously, but in life.'

She threaded her hands around his neck.

'I love you too.'

She felt shy saying it out loud but it was true, had been true for weeks, and it felt good to speak the words and to see the flush of pleasure across his face.

'This is a bit weird too,' he said and she giggled, but then he sobered. 'I also want you safe, Olivia.'

'Safe? Why would I not be safe?'

'I'm not sure, but I worry. The Stasi are sniffing around with all these defections and Kirsten seemed very, you know, Wessi.'

'You think that will be a problem?'

'I think we'll find out.'

'Klaus.' His name dropped from Olivia's lips before she could stop it and Hans pounced.

'Who?'

She sighed.

'That's the name of the man who was looking for my sister.'

Even as she said it, she wondered if he'd ever looked at all. Kirsten had told her she'd walked into the archives in the West and been given all their names almost immediately. If it was that easy, the Stasi must have known the same details from the minute Olivia met Klaus in the Rotes Rathaus.

'He's Stasi?' Hans asked, his voice tight.

She nodded.

'There was nothing I could do, Hans.'

'That's the problem with them – there's never anything you can do. You need to talk to your parents, Liv. You need to tell them that you've found her before...'

'Before what?' She looked up at him, panicked. 'Before what, Hans?'

'I don't know.'

'You're scaring me.'

'I'm sorry. I don't want to. It might be nothing. I mean, what's wrong with finding a sister? A victim of Nazi oppression?'

'Exactly.'

'Even so, you should talk to your parents.'

'Before the Stasi find out?'

He gave a dark laugh.

'Oh, they'll know already. You didn't see Frau Scholz's face when I brought Kirsten to find you.'

'You think she'd talk to the Stasi?'

Hans gave a weary sigh.

'Of course she would. It's what she's here for.'

'It is?'

He reached down and tipped her face up to his, kissing her tenderly.

'Life must be very innocent in Stalinstadt.'

Olivia bit her lip. She supposed perhaps it had been. Suddenly, she was desperate to get back there, away from the refugee-filled capital, away from the pressure of school, away from Klaus. If only term were over. But, then, if it had been, Pippa – Kirsten – would never have found her.

'Your mother is ill,' Hans said.

'What?' She looked at him, horrified. 'How do you know?'

'No, silly, that's what you need to say. Go to Herr Braun, now. Tell him your mother is ill and he will give you a pass to go home. There's no comp for a whole week so he'll allow it if you're convincing enough.'

'Can't I just tell him the truth? He'd understand, wouldn't he?'

'I don't know,' Hans said, shaking his head. 'And I'm not sure it's worth the risk.'

An hour later, Olivia sat shakily on the train as it pulled out of Friedrichstraße station. Her fear had, at least, helped her in front of Herr Braun who, seeing how upset she was, hadn't quibbled about a 48-hour pass to go home. She would have been excited to be taking the short trip to Stalinstadt if it hadn't been for the lie burning her up inside – though of course, if her mother had truly chosen to stop looking, perhaps this news *would* make her ill.

All too soon, it seemed, they arrived and Olivia stepped onto the small platform and out into her hometown. It was so quiet, so neat, so small. Hefting her Dynamo kit bag onto her back, she traced her way through the familiar rigid grids of the purpose-built apartment blocks towards her family's. Ducking through the final archway, she came out onto Alte Ladenstraße and saw the stark obelisk of German–Soviet friendship piercing the darkening sky ahead.

A handful of kids were playing tag in the open square and her heart leapt as she spotted Ben and Mordy. She went to call out, then stopped herself. She wasn't sure what her parents' reaction would be, so it might be better if the boys weren't around when she first imparted her news. Forcing her lips shut, she edged around the group and made for Block 4 and up the achingly familiar steps to Apartment G. There it was – her front door, lovingly painted in a pretty blue. She pressed her ear to the wood and could hear the murmur of voices, the clang of spoon on pan. Her heart lifted. They were here! Hesitating no longer, she rapped on the door and heard footsteps coming towards her.

'Have you forgotten your key again, Mordy?' her father's voice said, trying to be stern, then the door swung open and he gasped, his lovely face comic in its shock. 'Olivia! Oh, Olivia!' He pulled her into his arms, then almost immediately pulled back again. 'Are you ill? You don't look ill. You look amazing. Has something happened? Is something wrong?'

'Nothing is wrong, Vati,' she said, smiling at him, 'but, yes, I suppose you could say something has happened. Is Mutti here too?'

But already Ester was coming down the corridor, pulling her inside and hugging her tight enough to squeeze all the breath out of her.

'What is it my sweet?' she said. 'Why are you here?'

Olivia swallowed.

'I have some news.'

'News? What's happened? Is it a good thing?'

Olivia took her hands.

'I hope so. Oh God, Mutti, I hope you think so. I've found her, Mutti, I've found Pippa.'

For a heartbeat, Ester just stood there, staring at her, then she fell to her knees, her slender body shaking all over as she buried her face in her hands. Olivia looked down at her in horror as Filip crouched too, his arms around his wife.

'Truly?' he asked Olivia. 'You've found her? Alive?'

'She's alive, yes, and she found me.' She looked down at Ester. 'Mutti? Did I do the right thing?'

Ester said something but it was unintelligible through her tears and Olivia's heart quailed.

'Where is she?' Filip asked.

'She's in Berlin, Vati. She's called Kirsten Meyer, and she lives in West Berlin with her mother – well, her adopted mother – and a brother called Uli.'

'I knew it!' Ester suddenly looked up, her eyes wild. 'I knew it, Filip, didn't I? I said she'd be with a German woman.'

'You did,' Filip agreed uneasily but now Ester was turning to Olivia, clutching at her legs.

'How do you know it's her, Liv? How can you be sure?'

'Because I've met her, Mutti, and, truly, she's a mirror-image of you. It turns out she was searching for me too. She had a photo of her tattoo and someone in West Berlin gave her our names, then she saw me in the paper and she came to the club and, and... there we are.' There we are. Three such simple, inadequate words to conclude nearly eighteen years of hurt. She dropped down next to Ester. 'Mutti? Did I do right, Mutti?'

Ester looked at her, tears shining in her eyes, then threw her arms around her.

'Did you do right? Oh, Olivia, my angel, how could you ever doubt it?'

'Because you chose to stop looking, Mutti. You told me that. You said you had to stop and I thought, maybe it was because of something bad.'

Ester gave a sad smile.

'Not bad as such, more a different way of seeing things.'

'Was it me? Did you do it because of me?'

'No! Oh no, my sweet girl. You made it more bearable, but it wasn't because of you.' She shook her head. 'Look at us, sat on the floor like dummköpfe! Come through, Liv, come through and sit down and let me tell you a story.'

'Of Auschwitz?'

'Of after Auschwitz. Of Pippa. Of mothers and daughters and why life is never as simple as it should be.'

And pulling Olivia onto the sofa at her side, she drew in a deep breath and began.

# TWENTY-TWO

## EAST BERLIN | JUNE 1950

*ESTER*

The street is smart. A little bomb-damaged, but what street in Berlin isn't? They stop outside No 25 and peer at the window behind which Pippa might be playing.

'It will be a shock for her,' Filip says.

Ester looks at him, surprised, but he is right. The child behind that bright red door will not carry any memory of her four days with her mother. She will not have been looking. She will not even have been wondering. The witch who stole her has most likely told her nothing of her origins, has most likely claimed the girl as her own – just another Nazi stealing lives that don't belong to them. She grinds her teeth.

'Steady, liebling,' Filip says.

She looks up at him, astonished. How can she be steady when her whole world is shaking?

'Where's Mrs Jefferson?' she frets. 'What if we're too late? What if the thief has run away?'

'Why would she? They told her it was just a routine check, remember?'

Ester remembers but still eyes the red door warily; she cannot have Pippa slip through her hands again. Footsteps on the pavement make them both spin round, but it is not Mrs Jefferson. It is a frail-looking woman, not much older than Ester and with the same desperate hope in ice-bright swirls across her eyes.

Prisoner 41406.

Ester recognises her. She was, after all, only six steps behind her in the arrival line at Auschwitz or, rather, six steps behind in the workers' line. At least twenty others were probably weeded out between them and sent to the gas, but it is best not to think of that now.

'Adela?' she asks, the name coming to her in a haze of rats and flies and guards with guns.

The woman nods.

'Ester?'

'Yes.'

They hug, but it is stiff, awkward. They are displaced, dislocated, with no way of linking up in this pretty Berlin back street – no way but one. Ester can remember Adela giving birth amidst the grime of Auschwitz and Adela, no doubt, can remember her own Christmas Day labour. Now here, behind a door whose bullet holes have been painted over in bold scarlet, is a child. A child that belongs to one of them. They shuffle apart warily, joined in hope, divided by fear.

The minutes stretch out and then, with a smart tap-tap, the American comes round the corner in her shiny suit, with a shiny smile on her shiny face.

'Shall we go in?'

No! Ester wants to shout, to hold onto the hope a little longer.

But Mrs Jefferson is all efficiency, sounding the bell and stepping back. The door swings open and there, peering innocently out, is a girl. She must be seven, though she's not nearly as tall as Olivia, who is big for her age. She's wearing a strappy sundress in sunshine yellow and her hair is blonde and tied in two perfect plaits with pretty ribbons around the ends, blue to match her curious eyes.

'Can I help you?'

She is polite, well trained. Well cared for. Ester and Adela gape at her, neither of them able to move, but now a woman is coming pounding down the corridor, whisking the girl behind her and trying to close the door. Mrs Jefferson puts her smart-suited shoulder against the frame.

'No you don't, Frau Werner! We have reason to believe that this child is not your daughter.'

'She is!' the German woman roars. 'She's mine and I love her.'

'Mutti?' the child cries, burying herself in the German's skirts. 'Mutti, who are they?'

Filip was right, Ester thinks. The child is shocked and, not only that, she's scared.

'She's my daughter!' Frau Werner shouts. 'Mine!'

'You know that's not true,' Mrs Jefferson says crisply, and Ester wants to clap, save for the tears running down the woman's face and, worse, down the cheeks of the blonde-haired girl.

'Don't frighten her,' Filip says and Ester blesses her husband for his beautiful soul, but cannot stop herself stepping forward all the same.

'We just want to look under your arm,' she says softly. 'To see your special mark.' The girl pushes her arms tight to her side. 'I made it, you know. I put it there with my needle.'

She gawps at her.

'Why?'

'So that your mother could find you again one day. Today.'

'Mutti?'

The girl looks up at Frau Werner, digs deeper into her

skirts. Ester feels guilt prickle her skin and then anger that, even now, on the brink of finding her child, she is being robbed of her.

'You said it was routine,' the woman shouts. 'You said it was just for social security. You lied!'

'And you stole,' Mrs Jefferson snaps. 'Frau Pasternak, if you please.'

She takes the girl with that surprising strength of hers, and prises her bare arms up to reveal the black number. Ester bends, looks at the soft dimple of flesh, reads the dark numbers. Instantly, she is back in Block 24, carving them into a tiny armpit. 4. 1. 4. 0...

6.

It is a 6.

For a moment Ester thinks about lying, about claiming this beautiful child as Pippa, but she is not Pippa and denying the tail of a numeral will not make her so.

Six steps away – six tiny, huge steps.

'She's yours,' she says to Adela.

Then she watches, frozen, as joy floods visibly through her rival before Adela leaps forward. The girl is crying, the German woman shrieking.

'She's hers,' the American echoes Ester, impassively, gesturing to Adela, who is desperately trying to cuddle the child who is, in turn, clutching at the woman she believes to be her mother.

'No!' Frau Werner begs, her voice cracking. 'Please. She's mine. I rescued her. Her mother was dead.'

'Well, as you can see, she is not dead. She was never dead, just imprisoned by the Nazi regime that you clearly supported.'

'No, I... I didn't. That is, I don't. I'm no Nazi. I'm just a mother with her daughter.'

Mrs Jefferson steps up to her, beckoning Adela.

'Show her your arm.'

Adela rolls up her sleeve to reveal the ugly number etched into her thin arm: 41406.

'You see,' Mrs Jefferson says. 'It couldn't be clearer. The numbers match. The child is this woman's, taken from her in Auschwitz-Birkenau.'

'Auschwitz?' Frau Werner gasps and in her shock she lets go of the girl. Adela instantly pulls her into her arms.

'I've found you, Katya. God be praised, I've found you.'

'I'm not Katya,' the girl cries. 'Who's Katya? I'm Heidi. Tell her, Mutti. Tell her I'm Heidi.' She squirms, desperately trying to escape Adela's fond clutches, her blue eyes swimming with fear. 'Mutti!' she cries. 'Mutti!'

She reaches out her hands, not to the mother who bore her but to the one who has brought her up for the last seven years. It is a long time. It has felt a long time to Ester, but it is this girl's whole life. It would be Pippa's whole life.

'I'm taking you home,' Adela tells her.

'I am home.' The girl stamps her foot, yanks away from Adela and runs back into Frau Werner's arms, clambering up her like a child half her age, flinging her arms around her neck and burying her pretty blonde plaits into her neck. 'I am home, Mutti, aren't I? I am Heidi and I am home. Tell them, Mutti. Don't let them take me.'

But it is hopeless. The wheels of bureaucracy have been turned, the number Ester etched into this child's armpit in the filth and despair of Auschwitz bringing the robbed mother back to her child.

And taking the child away from her mother.

Ester falls to her knees on the pavement, burying her head in her hands as the battle for Heidi/Katya rages on the well-kept doorstep. All she can hear is the child's cries – 'Mutti, Mutti, Mutti!' Imagine, if someone took Olivia from them; the pain would be unimaginable.

'Enough,' she says quietly. She looks up at Filip, crouched at her side. 'We have to stop. It's wrong to rip babies from their mother's arms. It was wrong then – terribly, terribly wrong – but it is still wrong now. We have to stop looking, Filip. For Pippa's sake, we have to stop.'

Filip wraps his arms around her and she feels his tears hot on the top of her head and grasps at him. It hurts so much. She feels as if, five years after escaping a death camp, the Nazis' poison gas is finally filling her lungs. She can barely breathe for sorrow, but this is a chamber of her choice and she can bear it. She *will* bear it.

'Maybe we can look again when she's an adult,' Filip suggests, 'when she's eighteen. Maybe then it will be different?'

'Maybe,' Ester agrees because she has to. She has lived on hope for too long to do without it altogether.

She looks at her dear husband as, behind them, Adela wrenches the child away from the weeping woman on the doorstep. Who, truly, is the mother here? Who does the daughter truly belong to?

'Let's go to Stalinstadt,' she says, standing up, stepping away. 'Let's take Olivia and Mordy and this little one inside me and go to Stalinstadt. We have more than most, Filip. We have enough.'

It is not true, they both know that, but as Heidi/Katya's wails fill their ears, they also know it is a lie they have to embrace if they are to live at peace with themselves and, more importantly, if Pippa is to be spared the same pain.

'Mutti!' the child screams. 'Please, Mutti!'

They link hands and, hearts breaking, move away from the red door and the blue-ribboned plaits and the endless pain-filled hope of Berlin.

# TWENTY-THREE

## SATURDAY, 29 JULY 1961

*OLIVIA*

Olivia stared at her mother for a long time.

'That's so sad, Mutti. Why did you have to give up your happiness?'

Ester gave an easy shrug.

'For hers. As I would for yours. We had *you*, Liv, we loved *you*.'

'But you could have had Pippa too.'

'Maybe, but that's not the point. The point is that we knew how much it would hurt you to be torn from us, the only family you'd ever known, and that's how we knew it would hurt Pippa.'

Filip leaned in.

'For us, Livvie, you pair were two sides of a coin. We decided we had to wait and we've stuck to that. But now...'

'Now you don't have to wait any longer.' His eyes were full of wonder and Olivia took his hands. 'She likes sewing, Vati. She was wearing a dress she made herself and it was lovely. She must get it from you.'

'From me?'

Tears filled his eyes.

'From you,' Olivia confirmed. 'She's your daughter too.'

'She's my daughter too,' he echoed wonderingly.

Olivia's heart contracted.

'There's no doubting it's her,' she told her parents. 'She's bright and pretty and small – petite, I mean, just like all of you. Truly, as I said, she looked just like all of you.'

'As do you, Olivia,' Ester assured her.

'Hardly. Look at me.'

She indicated her big body, made even stronger by Dynamo's vitamins and training plans. She felt so solid and imposing between her slender parents. Ester, however, shook her head.

'Those are mere bones. In your soul, Olivia, in your beautiful, kind soul, you are just like us and that, my sweet, is what counts.' She kissed her tenderly, her calm, composed self once more. 'That day, on that doorstep, with that child's cries echoing in my ears, I gave up looking for my daughter. It was the hardest thing I ever did – including surviving *that place* – but it was right. We both knew it was right and, at last, God has truly rewarded our patience – through you.' She kissed her tenderly. 'Thank you, Olivia. Thank you so, so much. *You*, my child, are the angel, the miracle, and you were under our noses all along.'

Olivia felt herself choke up and had to wipe hastily at a tear of her own. Ester laughed.

'Look at us all – this isn't a time for tears but for joy. So, let's get up, wipe our faces and make a plan. We have to go back to Berlin – but this time with both our lovely daughters together.'

PART TWO

# TWENTY-FOUR

## FRIDAY, 11 AUGUST

*KIRSTEN*

Kirsten paced Bernauerstraβe. It was drizzling again, the clouds refusing to let go of their unseasonal hold on Berlin, and this was a pointless mission, but she was so full of nervous energy that she had no idea what else to do with herself. She reached the top and saw Café Edelweiss, bright and open, its windows steamy with the breath of customers escaping the damp. It had not mysteriously closed down since she'd checked it an hour ago and did not look likely to do so in the two days between now and Sunday when she would apparently be sitting in there having kaffee und kuchen with her biological parents, her sister and her two younger brothers.

Olivia had hand-delivered a note through her door three days ago saying that Ester and Filip could join them at 10 a.m. on Sunday, 13 August. Kirsten had told Lotti and Uli and invited them along but Lotti had suggested they leave that for 'next time'. Kirsten had hugged her hard. This couldn't be any easier for Lotti than it was for her and she prayed it went well so that there *was* a next time.

She watched two women come out of the café with a tumble of small children and forced herself to stay back. She'd already been in twice to check her table booking and they might ban her if she went again. Kirsten peered up the road towards the marketplace and, above it, her sister's training ground. She longed to go and find her there again but Olivia had said it would be best not to and looked so genuinely scared that Kirsten had hastily agreed.

The track and hostel, although only ten minutes' walk from the Meyers' apartment, were both in East Berlin. Indeed, because Bernauerstraße itself was the border between the districts of Wedding and Mitte and, therefore, between East and West, her aunt, Gretchen, was theoretically in the East but, for heaven's sake, what border was going to stop them visiting her? What did it matter if the soldiers on casual patrol nearby were Soviets or Allies? Berliners had long since learned not to let them get in the way of day-to-day life.

In these last few weeks, however, Kirsten had started to realise just how different the Soviet zone was. Over here in the West, the people in the landesarchiv had bent over backwards to help her find her family. In the East, however, they'd been keeping her details from Olivia, though it hadn't been entirely clear why. Then there'd been that strange man in the café trying to bribe her to spy on customers, and the scary woman watching over the athletes at the track. East Berlin didn't look especially different on the outside, but Kirsten was starting to see that on the inside it was a very dissimilar beast, and not one to rile.

With a final glance at Café Edelweiss, she forced herself to walk back towards home. Olivia had said her biological parents had searched and searched for her. They'd scoured orphanages and refugee camps, put out appeals through every state, church and synagogue they could, but had found no trace of her. That made sense, of course, because she'd been safely tucked up in Bernauerstraße with a new name and a new mutti and not even the tattoo Ester had so carefully inked under her arm to mark her out.

Kirsten kicked crossly at a stray stone on the side of the street. Lotti had always looked so shamefaced when Kirsten had touched her scar. She'd assumed it was because she'd felt bad about letting a toddler near a hot pan, but it had turned out to be a much deeper guilt than that. That scar had hidden Kirsten's true identity as Pippa; no wonder it had always itched so much.

'Oi!' a familiar voice called into her grump. 'What's that poor stone ever done to you?'

'Uli.' She looked up with relief as her brother came towards her. 'It was a substitute.'

'For who?'

'Jan? Lotti? The Nazis? The world? I don't know!' Uli put his arms around her and she sank gratefully into his embrace. Goodness he was getting tall! 'There seem to be so many tangles suddenly, Uli.'

'There do,' he agreed solemnly, 'but some things are still straightforward.'

'Like what?'

'Like the fact that I love you.' She looked at him in surprise and he blushed. 'I never say it, but it's true. I know we're not properly brother and sister. I know we don't even share one parent, and I know you're about to meet two other brothers who share both parents with you, but, well, I love you. I thought you should know.'

Tears pricked at Kirsten's eyes and she flung her arms around him again.

'I love you too, Uli. So much. And we *are* proper brother and sister. We've grown up together, played together, shared a bedroom. It's always been you and me against the world, right?'

'Right.'

'And it always will be. All these, you know, extras, are just that. It's strange, for sure, but, you're right – some things are exactly as they've always been and you and I, we're the best one.'

Uli grinned at her.

'What you up to this afternoon?'

She rolled her eyes.

'At the moment, pacing Bernauerstraβe until I can go to sleep and forget about all this for a bit. Why?'

'I have an idea,' he said, his eyes twinkling.

'Will it speed up time?'

'Definitely.'

'Then I'm in. What is it?'

'The zoo.'

She stared at him incredulously, but then pictured Berlin Zoo, the place they'd always loved, and felt warmth steal through her.

'The zoo!' she agreed. 'You, me and Mutti, just like old times. Fantastic idea.'

Uli beamed.

'I'll be the Eurasian eagle-owl,' he said. 'Wise!'

'And I'll be a spider monkey, bouncing around all over the place.'

'You're on, let's go.'

And so, grabbing hands, they raced down the street, calling for Lotti like the little kids they had once been.


It was a happy afternoon. Lotti's eyes shone when they put the idea to her and she went into domestic overdrive, digging out goodies for a picnic and mustering waterproofs 'just in case', although, as if picking up on their mood, the sun had crept out from behind the clouds and was steaming water off Berlin.

Gretchen said she'd come too and dug out her camera and a bottle of wine to 'celebrate'.

'Celebrate what?' Uli asked.

'Being alive,' Gretchen shot back and Kirsten felt the glorious simplicity of the sentiment settle her restless mind. There might be emotional issues to face ahead, but, for now, there was nothing but giraffes and hippos and the people who had brought her up in love and security.

The zoo was quiet, visitors put off by the earlier rain, and they strolled around its familiar paths and enclosures as if they belonged to them. First stop was the hippo house to see Knautschke, who'd been a youngster when they'd first visited and was now a giant of a bull and bellowing father to a calf which was nipping at his enormous side for attention. As they stood, noses pressed to the glass, Knautschke surfaced, snorting water from his cavernous nostrils all over them and they giggled like infants.

'He remembers us,' Uli said, delighted, as the hippo seemed to give them a huge-toothed smile before sinking slowly beneath the water. 'Come on, let's go and see the elephants.'

Siam, the bull elephant, was sunning himself in his external enclosure, lazily batting a ball around with his trunk while his harem rootled for fruit in a pile of hay nearby. Suddenly he looked over at the females, picked up his big feet and trampled across to swipe a tasty apple from right under their trunks. The nearest cow gave an indignant trumpet and Siam stalked away, tiny tail swinging.

'That's men for you,' Gretchen said, and she and Lotti roared with far more laughter than the joke merited and sat on a bench to open the wine.

'Monkey house?' Uli suggested to Kirsten and she nodded and went with him, her footsteps automatically finding the right direction.

The monkeys, bored with the low visitor count, went wild

with delight to see them and swung themselves obligingly around. One cheeky chimp came right up to the glass, following them whichever way they walked, and Kirsten lost herself in the simple joy of this game. Life had been getting horribly grown up recently and it was so good to be a kid again.

'You won't go and live with this new family will you, Kirsty?' Uli asked, as they sat on the grass later, watching two giraffes nuzzle their long necks fondly together.

'Course not!' she said. 'They live in some Stalinist new town in the DDR. Why would I want to live there?'

'Lots of people do.'

'Because they don't have much choice.'

'Right. What will you do then, when you finish school?'

She wrinkled her nose.

'No idea. Become a zookeeper?'

'Really? That would be amazing! I could come and see you every day.'

She smiled.

'Not really, Uli, you have to do all sorts of qualifications.'

'So do them.'

'It's not that simple. If I could do that, I'd go to university, but you have to be clever.'

'You're clever.'

'I am not!'

'You are. You always understand recipes, and you read stories brilliantly, and you make really cool clothes.'

She leaned over, nudging into him.

'I'm not sure that's enough for university.'

'Well, it should be,' he said firmly.

She looked at him.

'Olivia says my father – my, you know, biological father – is a tailor.'

'Really? That's cool. You can be one of those then. Only here, in Berlin.'

'Maybe. Who knows. I haven't got the space to think about it with all this other stuff.'

He nodded solemnly.

'What do you think *my* biological father did, Kirsty? Apart from raping women, of course.'

She put an arm round him.

'We don't know what it was like then. Maybe he was young. Maybe others pushed him into it.'

'Even so.'

She gave him a hug.

'Even so, it's not all he did. I reckon he was probably a chess player. That's what Russians do, isn't it? And you're good at maths, Uli, so you'd be good at it too.'

'Chess?' he considered. 'Maybe I should try it.'

'Maybe you should. Now, come on, let's find Mutti and Gretchen before they get themselves besoffen, and go see the lions.'

It turned out to be too late to curb the effect of the wine, so they all giggled their way around the last of the enclosures and then Tante Gretchen had to be dragged out of the gate before she could offer the good-looking keeper a 'little treat' to let them stay longer.

'You flittchen,' Lotti told her, but fondly.

Then the man came after them and asked Gretchen if she'd like to go out to dinner and Gretchen looked at him, stunned, and then said, 'Actually, I'd love that.' On the way home, she and Lotti linked arms and Gretchen said, 'I think it might be time to look to the future, Lott. Maybe we've been widows too long.'

'I've only been a widow seven weeks,' Lotti said darkly.

'Quatsch,' Gretchen told her. 'The war took your husband. Whatever creature briefly came back was not him. Forward, Lotti, that's the way!'

And, as Kirsten and Uli followed the two women back to

Bernauerstraße, Kirsten glanced to Café Edelweiss, closed but still very much there, and thought that, with these people at her back, she could go wherever forward took her. On Sunday, she would meet her new family, but for now her old one was wonderful and she would make the very most of them.

# TWENTY-FIVE

## SATURDAY, 12 AUGUST

*OLIVIA*

The sun rose early above Berlin, blazing out its triumph over the clouds that had dogged the city all week, and the people were quick to answer its call. East and West headed out together, stepping merrily across the roads that nominally separated them, forgetting their different leaders, their different imposed ideologies, even their different currencies in the joy of a summer day in hectic, happy Berlin.

By 9 a.m. every road out to the many suburban lakes was full of cars and buses crammed with couples, families, and gangs of friends eager to enjoy the German summer once more. Olivia, looking through the track fence, could see the vehicles passing along the road below, crammed with towels and picnic baskets, chairs, umbrellas and beach balls. Children and dogs leaned out of windows to suck in the air and it made her smile, remembering many such trips with her family to the Wirchensee or Schervenzsee, singing happy songs on the way and sleeping in cosy huddles on the return. It seemed idyllic now.

*You'll see your family later*, Olivia reminded herself. They were arriving on the train at 7 p.m., once Ester's shift at the hospital had finished, and she couldn't wait. The anticipation, though, was laced with nerves and she hated that. Her family had always been her safe place, her rock, but suddenly that felt under threat in subtle, unsettling ways.

'Dummkopf,' she scolded herself and turned to run back down to the others.

Heat was shimmering across the cinder track and the whole club was training before it got too hot to bear. She made for the sprinters. Lately, Trainer Lang had asked her to do a few sessions with them to up her runway speed. Usually she was reluctant, not enjoying coming last at every burst, but today, alive with restless energy, she welcomed the chance to blast mindlessly down the track.

Franz, her fellow jav thrower, was there too and they exchanged a rueful glance as they lined up alongside the sprinters for the first of what would be ten bursts of 50 metres.

'Honestly,' Franz grumbled, 'in what competition do we ever have to run more than 15 metres?!'

'Explosive speed,' Olivia muttered – Lang's obsession – and, gritting her teeth, she waited for the coach's clap to send her out of the blocks.

She was last, as usual, but not by much.

'Good work, Liv,' Frieda said, patting her on the back. 'You're getting faster.'

'I'm useless compared to you lot.'

Frieda laughed.

'You should see me throw a jav. You'd wet yourself laughing.'

'You're on!'

They all loped slowly back to the start, getting their breath back before the next burst.

'Final comp next weekend,' one of the lads said, 'and then home for a break.'

That made Olivia smile. Tomorrow's meeting with Kirsten might be emotional, but she'd soon be back in Stalinstadt for a whole month of blissful relaxation.

'It's been a good season, right?' Frieda was saying to the lad.

'Great. I think we've stamped Dynamo on the map!'

'Shame we lost a few.'

They all instinctively looked around, but they were the only ones on this part of the track.

'More fool them,' Olivia said. 'They'll only get weaker in the West.'

Frieda frowned.

'I thought that too, but at the last comp, the girl in the next lane told me that she'd been beaten by Lisel the week before – and then she went on to win! If Lisel could beat her, she can't have got *that* weak.'

'She will,' Franz said, but with little certainty.

Again they all looked around.

'Where is Lisel now?' someone else asked.

'Hanover.'

'They've got a good club. Won a few medals at the Youth Games.'

'Not as many as Dynamo.'

'No.'

They all shifted on the hot track. Olivia's mind battered against the inside of her skull. Was this subversion or just curiosity? Did they amount to the same thing? Surely not? It was a troubling thought and for once she was glad when coach called them to the line. She wasn't, it seemed, the only one, and they were all swiftly in place and pounding up the track once more, questions forgotten in the easy burn of muscle and heave of breath. Olivia felt her lungs threaten to explode but welcomed it. It was going to be a long day's wait and she might as well spend it pushing her body to the max.

'This way, Mutti, Vati.' Olivia ushered her family proudly into her Berlin home. 'Round here, boys. That's the track.'

'Oooh, big, isn't it?'

'I suppose so. This is our hostel, though only until they complete the new one up in Dynamo proper. We can go there later and—'

'Welcome, welcome.'

Cut off in her introductions, Olivia stared in horror at the man who'd come out of the hostel, arms spread in apparent welcome.

'Klaus?' she stuttered.

He didn't even look at her.

'Olivia is an important member of our growing Dynamo team, so it's wonderful to meet her family. I hope you'll forgive the basic nature of your rooms, but we've not completed the new hostel, so cannot yet offer you the luxury you deserve.'

'Oh, we don't need luxury,' Ester said. 'It's very kind of you to put us up.'

'We consider our athletes part of our Dynamo family and that includes you too. Come in, come in.'

The Stasi officer ushered Ester, Filip, Mordecai and Ben inside, telling them how well Olivia was doing and how proud they must be of her. They chattered back, nodding earnestly at all Klaus said and shooting her admiring glances.

'I was a bit worried about how she'd cope in the heart of the city,' Ester confided. 'It's so busy after Stalinstadt. But she seems to be thriving.'

'Oh, she is,' Klaus agreed, arriving at the doors to the two rooms they'd been allocated. 'She's working very hard, being very helpful, aren't you, Olivia?'

He meant the opposite, she knew; he'd not been happy that she'd met Kirsten.

'You went behind my back,' he'd raged at her the day she'd returned from Stalinstadt.

'I didn't, Klaus,' she'd assured him. 'Kirsten found me. Ask Frau Scholz. She walked into the club and asked for me. She'd seen my picture in the paper.'

'How did she know who you were?' he'd demanded.

'Because the landesarchiv in West Berlin gave her all the details,' she'd shot back. It had sat between them like a grenade with a loose pin.

'Well, how wonderful,' Klaus had said eventually, every word laced with sarcasm.

'Isn't it?' Olivia had agreed sweetly.

'And now you want to arrange for your family to meet her?'

'I already have. They're coming next weekend.'

She'd instantly regretted giving him this information and now here he was, imprinting himself upon them, claiming them.

'I'm hugely grateful to you and everyone here for all you've done for me,' she said now, brazening it out.

Klaus smiled his thin smile and, thankfully, handed over the keys to the guest room and retreated.

'Basic?' Ester exclaimed, looking around the simple but bright room. 'It's lovely. Feel this mattress, Filip. And, look, we have a connecting door to the boys' room. You're through here, boys, see, with a view of the track. Isn't that amazing?'

Olivia's heart ached as she watched her mother settle them in. A soft mattress or cushion always delighted her and Olivia could only imagine the hard beds she'd once slept on. She wished she could wrap her up in the biggest, softest eiderdown for all time, but no one could have that sort of protection, especially in the DDR, and her mother, she knew, was harder than she seemed.

'Would you like to meet Hans?' she asked.

'Hans?' Ester turned from fluffing Ben's pillows, her eyes bright. 'Your young man? Oh, yes please!'

Hans, when he arrived, was nervous too, but his nerves were of the straightforward kind.

'I just want them to like me,' he'd said to Olivia as they'd lain in bed together that afternoon, naked but apart, the heat clogging the air too much for greater intimacy.

'They'll love you,' she'd promised. 'As I love you.'

'They might not think I'm good enough.'

'They're not like that,' she'd assured him but his worries had been touching and it was a joy, now, to see Ester and Filip draw him into the room, asking him about himself and his family, and to see him relax, open up. Within moments they were all laughing together over Hans' tale of his first competition when he'd tripped on his own feet and ended up throwing the discus into one of the poles supporting the safety net, sending it bouncing right back into his stomach.

'Did it hurt?' Ester asked, ever the carer.

'Not nearly as much as my pride,' Hans told her. 'I took a lot of persuading to try it again, but thank heavens I did.'

His hand went instinctively for Olivia's and she saw her parents exchange glances and knew they'd be whispering about her on their pillows tonight – and that they would be happy whispers. Sometimes, growing up, their father had told stories instead of their mother, and he'd often recounted the tale of how they'd sat on the steps of St Stanislaus' cathedral in Łódź every day for weeks, eating their lunch close to each other but barely daring to speak. It was only German planes tearing up the sky above them that had galvanised Filip into declaring his love, and they'd married barely a month later. It was, to Olivia's mind, the perfect romance – or it had been. Now she had her own and she hoped that her parents saw a little of their younger selves in her and Hans and that they liked it. She needn't have feared.

'He's lovely, Liv,' Filip said when Hans left for his own room. 'So kind and warm and funny.'

'And handsome?' she suggested.

'Of course handsome. I'd have expected nothing less for any man daring to come near my beautiful daughter.'

It wasn't even a joke and Olivia felt warmed to the core by their loving acceptance.

'You should get some sleep,' she said. 'Tomorrow is a big day.'

Ester's shoulders tightened and Filip put a steadying arm around them, dropping a kiss on his wife's head.

'A day we've waited for, for a long, long time,' he agreed, 'and that has come to us thanks to you, Olivia. We're so grateful.'

'It was easy,' she assured him, leaning in for a hug, and, as Ben and Mordy tumbled in too, she pushed aside the creeping thought of Klaus and his demands – demands she was sure were not yet over – and revelled in the gift she'd been able to offer her dear, kind parents. Tomorrow they would meet the baby they had lost nearly eighteen years ago. It would be a big day indeed.


She tried to sleep, tried really hard, but the awareness of tomorrow's meeting weighed too heavily on her mind to let it settle. Her mother seemed so small here in Dynamo, so fragile. For the first time Olivia felt that Ester might be growing old and she prayed that seeing her long-lost baby would bring some youth back to her or, at least, some peace. Surely one Auschwitz story could be granted a happy ending, and she tossed under her sheet, willing morning to come.

The city seemed restless too. It was always noisy on a Saturday night, but this was more than just partygoers tumbling out of bars, more than refugees heading west, or lovers seeking private corners. Olivia swore she could feel a rumble in the very ground and found herself wondering if it could be an earthquake, but Germany was miles from any fault lines, geological ones at least.

She put the light on to check the clock: 1 a.m. She'd been trying to sleep for two hours to no avail so, climbing out of bed, she went to the window to look across the city. Far off, she could make out the top of the Brandenburg Gate where the goddess of Victory was lit up in golden colours as she rode triumphantly across the night-time skyline in her four-horse chariot.

The sight of it was reassuring and she began to wonder if the strange rumble was all in her head, but then, as if God himself had flicked a switch, the lights on the great monument snapped off, many others in the city with them. Olivia imagined workmen scrabbling to put things right before the authorities came down on them for letting Germany's glory be extinguished and stared into the darkness, waiting for the lights to come on again. But there was nothing. And now the rumbling was getting louder.

Scared, Olivia grabbed her tracksuit, pulling it over her nightie, and rammed her feet into her trainers. No one else in the dorm seemed to have been woken by the noises and she hesitated but then heard voices on the street. Something was wrong in Berlin, she was sure of it, and there was one person she needed to see.

'Hans!'

She called his name as loudly as she dared and tapped on his door. There was no reply but it wasn't locked so she crept inside. Hans was fast asleep, moonlight shining across his handsome face, and Olivia longed to stand there and drink him in, but tonight was not the night for lovers' rites.

'Hans!'

She knelt on the bed and shook him gently. He started awake.

'Olivia! This is a nice surprise.'

'It isn't, Hans. Something's going on. Outside. There are noises and the lights have gone out.'

'What?'

He sat up, rubbing sleep from his eyes, and again Olivia yearned to crawl into his arms and forget about whatever was happening beyond their walls. But then there was a loud thud nearby and Hans was up and at the window.

'Is that soldiers?'

Olivia joined him.

'Where?'

He pointed and, squinting into the moonlight, Olivia saw at least fifty men in army fatigues fanning out across the market-place below the hostel.

'It is,' she said.

'What's going on?'

'That's what I want to know.'

Hans dressed as quickly as Olivia had done and, hand in hand, they took the back stairs to the fire escape. There was a security camera there, but hopefully nobody was watching as they slid out and wedged a sliver of wood into the bottom so they could get back inside. It was a trick usually used by athletes wanting a forbidden taste of the high life, but tonight the mood was grimmer.

They followed the fence until they came into the market-place and stood, frozen, trying to make sense of what they were seeing. A number of lorries were parked at the far end, perhaps the source of the rumble that had shaken Olivia, and men were rapidly unloading them. Some were handing out wooden posts, others rolls of barbed wire. More men with drills, spades and large lump hammers were ramming the posts into the ground at neatly spaced intervals and now they began to unroll the barbed wire, twisting it into vicious tangles with metal poles as they stretched it between the posts and nailed it into place.

'A wall,' Hans muttered. 'Oh my God, Olivia, it's a wall.'

'It's not,' she protested. 'It's not a wall. It's a, a...'

She failed to find a word because, in reality, it *was* a wall. There were no bricks, perhaps, no mortar, but it was still cutting viciously in front of them and already guards were lining up along it, guns slung across their chests and eyes nervously scanning the area as more people joined Olivia and Hans. On the other side, too, people were coming out of houses, pointing and staring.

'What the hell do you think you're doing?' someone called from an upper window, but the soldiers just went on stretching their coils of wire. There were a lot of them and they were working fast, clearly determined to finish the job before Berlin awoke. Already they'd covered much of the marketplace and were heading south, turning a sharp corner along Bernauerstraße.

Bernauerstraße!

Olivia grabbed Hans.

'What side is she on? Kirsten, my sister – what side is she on?'

His dark look gave her the answer she was dreading and, with a shiver of horror, she remembered Ulbricht standing before the whole of Germany – the whole of the world – and saying there would be no wall.

'They're splitting the city,' the man in the house opposite shouted out. 'It's on the radio. They're all along the border, cutting Berlin in half, keeping us from each other!'

Others were joining him, shouting angrily from their windows and pouring onto the street to shake their fists at the construction workers. Olivia wanted to shout too, but on their side were guards, guards with guns, and they were lifting them to their shoulders, looking wary but determined. No one in the East moved.

Olivia battled to process what she was seeing. It was a warm August night. People were sleeping off their days at the beach or dancing joyously in packed bars and these men, with their spiked coils, were creeping between them.

'About time,' someone said next to her and she looked over to see the sprints coach nodding in satisfaction. 'This will stop the verdammte Wessis coming over and taking all our stuff.'

'Too right,' his assistant agreed. 'And all our talent.'

'Spitzbart has shown his horns at last; socialism will be safe now.'

Olivia swallowed. They had a point. All year the DDR had been losing doctors and teachers, lawyers, accountants and business leaders, not to mention sport stars and actors. So many had been lured by empty Western promises of a better life and, in the end, it had come to this. What, she supposed, was Spitzbart meant to do if his people were too childish to give socialism a chance, but treat them as children and lock them in? Even so, Kirsten was on the other side.

'We have to get to her,' Olivia said to Hans. 'We have to get to Kirsten before it's too late.'

'You're right, come on.'

He took a few steps towards Bernauerstraβe but Olivia yanked him back.

'Mutti! We have to take Mutti. That's the whole point.'

'Right. Yes. Come on then. Quickly!'

They headed back into the hostel, with no need for the secret fire exit for the main doors were wide open as more people came pouring out to see what was going on. It was clear that, despite Dynamo being run by the Stasi, this overnight strike was as much of a surprise to the teachers as the students and Herr Braun was standing in the reception area, a shocked look on his face as he talked frantically into a telephone to someone who clearly had no answers.

'Is it permanent?' she heard him demand as they ran past. Then, 'You think so? I guess we'll have to see what the Allies do.'

Olivia shivered.

'Will this be war?' she asked Hans.

'God, I hope not. Khrushchev and Kennedy both have nuclear buttons to play with, so if it is, it might be a short one.'

Olivia clutched at his hand and he paused to shoot her an apologetic smile.

'I don't want to die, Hans.'

'Me neither, beautiful.' He pulled her into his arms. 'I want to win medals and represent my country. I want to retire into coaching or teaching. I want to have a family and get old and wizened and sit in a rocking chair poking a pipe at passing children.' She gave a half laugh but it cracked into a sob. 'And above all, Olivia, I want to do all that with you.'

'You do?'

'Absolutely. Scheiβe, I'd ask you to marry me except that I'm not sure we've the time for it.'

Two other athletes clattered past them.

'They're walling us in,' one cried.

'No,' the other told him, 'they're walling *them* out.'

'Does it make a difference?'

Olivia gave Hans a kiss, hard and fast. Her head was spinning but one thing was clear: 'We have to get to Mutti.'

Her parents were awake already, both neatly dressed and pacing their room.

'Liv!' Filip ran to her. 'Are you all right? What's going on?'

'They're putting up wire,' she told them. She wouldn't say wall, not until they knew more. 'We think Pippa might be on the other side. I'm so sorry, but we should go – now.'

'Wire?' Ester asked. 'Like a ghetto?'

'Not like a ghetto, liebling,' Filip assured her. 'It's the border, the line between East and West.'

'If you can't get across, it's still a ghetto,' Ester said grimly. 'Just a big one.'

'We don't know that you can't get across,' Hans said. 'We don't know anything much.'

'Just the way they like it,' Filip muttered darkly, but he moved to rouse the boys and within minutes they joined the flood of people heading onto the lorry-strewn marketplace.

The students were all waking each other and Olivia caught a glimpse of the Scholzes running frantically around. She looked nervously for Klaus but, thankfully, he was nowhere to be seen.

'This way,' Hans said, ushering them towards the corner of Bernauerstraβe.

They tried to turn into the street but the wire was running across the top, severing it in two. Olivia battled to see over, but the guards were thickly packed at the junction and it was impossible.

'Here.'

Hans waved Olivia to climb onto his shoulders and, with a steadying hand on a nearby lamp-post, hoisted her upwards. She stared.

The street itself was untouched and a few confused-looking Wessis were walking up it to see the wire at the end. Inside the apartments running along the Eastern side, however, she could hear shouting. Someone flung open a door and ran out.

'No doors allowed!' a harsh voice shouted after them. 'This is the border. All exits must be locked. Now.'

'A wall,' Olivia gasped. 'They're turning the actual apartments into a wall.' She scrambled down. 'This way.'

Glancing back to check everyone was following, she led them away from the wire and along Schwedterstraβe, turning right and then right again to come to the apartments from the rear. Here, all was activity. More wire stretched across the end of the side street, preventing them from getting to Bernauer-straβe and guards were patrolling the apartments, shouting at everyone within to, 'shore up your doors against the West.'

'We can't get over,' Olivia said.

They headed on down but every single street leading to Bernauerstraβe was shut off and eventually, on Ackerstraβe, Olivia stopped, feeling her insides tearing as if the barbed wire had been wound around them as well.

'That's her apartment,' she told Ester, pointing over the wire to the simple block to which she had delivered her excited note about the meeting tomorrow, the meeting that would surely not, now, be possible.

She strained to see if Kirsten was up, but the soldiers had been swift and quiet here and few people were awake. Her sister would not know until the sun crept up tomorrow that she'd been kept from her mother, again, by the desire of those in charge to control the liberties of their people.

'It's not right,' she muttered, then louder, 'it's not right!'

A guard lifted his gun and Hans yanked her back.

'Don't, Liv.'

She looked up at him.

'She's just there – ten paces away.'

'And in another whole country.'

Olivia couldn't believe it. A glint of moonlight caught in the barbs of the wire, as if they were winking cruelly, and rage filled her. She wanted socialism to succeed as much as anybody, but it didn't need this. Surely it didn't need this? She stared at the jagged wire, trying to take it in, but then a sound from behind – a raw, naked sob – caught at her more than any barbs or soldier's gun and she turned to see Ester running up to the wire, shaking her fist and screaming one word: 'Auschwitz!'

'No, Mutti!' She ran to her. 'It's not that, truly. It's a border, not a KZ. It's for our own safety.'

Ester just looked at her, eyes as dark as a hell only she, amongst them, had known.

'That's what they said last time.'

Olivia stumbled back at the raw pain in Ester's voice. What had she done? She'd thought finding Pippa would make her mother happy, but now she was trapped behind a wire fence with her baby forcibly kept from her once more.

Nothing was right about this, nothing at all.

# TWENTY-SIX

## SUNDAY, 13 AUGUST

*KIRSTEN*

'Kirsten?' Uli's voice drifted into her sleep. 'Kirsten, something strange is going on.'

'Strange?' Kirsten reluctantly prised open her eyes. The light looked low and she groaned. 'What time is it, Uli?'

'Six.'

'Six?! What on earth are you doing, waking me up at six?'

'I told you – something strange is going on. Come and see.'

She nearly told him to get lost but he sounded genuinely worried so, with another groan, she hefted herself from her nest and went with him to the window. The sun was up but still low so that it slanted into Bernauerstraβe along the side streets, casting strange, tangled shadows onto the tarmac. Kirsten squinted, trying to see what was trapping the light, but couldn't quite believe her eyes.

'Is that... wire?'

'I think so,' Uli said. 'And there are soldiers, with guns. They're on the other side but, still... I think we're trapped, Kirsty.'

'We can't be,' she snapped but, as she cast her eyes up the street, she thought she could see wire at the far end too. She had to be asleep still; this had to be some strange nightmare. 'Who'd fence off Bernauerstraβe? What have we done?'

Uli coughed.

'I don't think it's only us, Kirsty. The radio says it's all over Berlin. The DDR have closed their border.'

She stared at him.

'Can they do that?'

'No one seems to be stopping them.'

'Yet.' Kirsten threw open the window to lean out. Morning sun kissed her face, incongruously warm. 'Wait until the Americans hear about this. They won't allow it. Will they?'

'I don't see them rushing to the scene.'

She stared up and down Bernauerstraβe but he was right, damn him – the only soldiers here were the Soviet ones beyond their shiny new wire.

'Bastards!' Uli spat, Kirsten wasn't sure who at and didn't want to ask.

And now a new realisation washed over her.

'Olivia!' She grabbed at Uli. 'I'm meant to be meeting Olivia and my parents. Oh God, Uli, what if the café is on the other side?'

She ran out of her room in her light pyjamas and made for the door. Fumbling with the lock, she headed outside and up the street. She'd thought herself an idiot checking if Café Edelweiss was still there but, all along, the issue had not been if it would be there but if they could get to it.

The proprietor already had doors open and her coffee machine working hard as people spilled onto the street to see the overnight barricades. Several were standing in groups, cups in hand as they perused the ugly wire a few doors up from the café. Others were taking a less passive stance, shouting at the guards, whose backs were resolutely turned.

'KZ bastards!' someone shouted and Kirsten's breath caught.

Her mother was out there, the mother who had birthed her in a KZ and not seen her since. She ran up to the wire.

'Excuse me,' she said to the guard on the other side. He didn't turn round. 'I said, excuse me!' Still nothing. 'Oi, you!'

He glanced back. He was young, perhaps only Kirsten's age, and looked very tense.

'What?' he snapped.

'My mother is over there. I'm meant to be meeting her today. Can I get through, please?'

'Can you get through?!' He turned round, staring at her incredulously, then waved his hand along the tangles of wire. 'How do you think you're going to do that?'

Kirsten frowned.

'I don't know, but there must be a way. Isn't there?'

'Not that I know of.'

'No way through? At all?'

'No.' His voice was taut and his fingers flexed on his gun. 'Look, I don't know much more than you. I was shipped in from Dresden yesterday and told to stop people getting near the fence, so please – don't get near the fence.'

'You can't ask that,' a man said, stepping up next to Kirsten. 'Not of us. This is the West. We can do as we please.'

He shrugged.

'If you say so, sir, but you see that line?' He indicated a rough chalk mark on the ground. 'If you touch that, you're in the East and then... well, then I can't answer for what might happen.'

'You'd shoot me?' the man demanded. The soldier looked unhappy. 'You don't know, do you? You don't know what to do.'

'I know you're to stay away from that line, sir.'

The man put out a big, booted foot and scuffed at the chalk.

'What line?'

'Please, sir, don't.'

The soldier looked desperate and the man turned away with a tut.

'Christ, you're just a kid.' He turned to the gathering crowd. 'They're all just kids. Are we going to stand for this? Are we going to let them wall us into our own damned street while we stand around drinking coffee?'

Other guards were looking round now, hitching their guns nervously to their shoulders. Kirsten felt Uli tug on her pyjama top and let him pull her back a few steps. She strained to see over the wire, but it was two levels high. Oh, she could cry in frustration.

'Olivia!' she shouted. 'Olivia, are you there?' But her lone voice was lost in the growing crowd.

No one dared charge the wire, so they poured their anger into their voices instead and, at the racket, every door was opening down the street. Well, every door on their side. Kirsten looked curiously to Tante Gretchen's building across the way. There were faces watching, plenty of them, but no one was coming out.

'What's up with them?' she asked Uli, pointing to the nearest window, behind which a man was wrestling with someone preventing him opening it.

'They're in the East, poor stümper,' a woman told her.

'They can't be. I mean, their doors aren't, right?'

'Their door*steps* aren't, perhaps, but their *doors* are – the border runs literally along the line of their bricks. My Maria lives there and I've been talking to her out her window when she can escape the guards. She says they're in all the corridors, demanding entrance and taking keys away. She's got a spare hidden down her knickers, she says. She's waiting until they're distracted and then she's coming out with the kiddies. I'm waiting here to help.'

'They have to leave their home?'

'Or get stuck in the DDR. Would you want that?'

She nodded darkly to the gun-wielding guards and Kirsten shook her head.

'My aunt lives up there.'

She pointed along to Gretchen's grand apartment.

'Then tell her to get out while she still can.'

Kirsten stared at the woman, trying to take in what she was saying. This was Bernauerstraβe. Half the people living here had family on the other side; you couldn't take away their keys and fence them off. Could you?

'Kirsty! Uli! Are you all right?'

Lotti came rushing up, running her hands over them, as if feeling for injuries, and Kirsten shrugged her off.

'We're fine, Mutti, for now.'

'Which is more than I can say for your Tante Gretchen. They're holding her prisoner, actual prisoner.'

She dragged them down the road to Gretchen's apartment. Looking up, Kirsten saw her aunt's window broken in a jagged star and Gretchen waving cheerfully out of it.

'You have to leave, Gretchen!' Kirsten called up.

'I can't, schnuki. This ridiculous young man isn't letting me.'

She indicated behind her and a soldier looked sheepishly out.

'Orders, ma'am,' he said. 'It's for your own good.'

'You see. He wouldn't even let me open the window. I had to smash it with Mark's lovely old paperweight. It's made quite a dint in the brass but they can't make me close it now.'

'We can board it up,' the soldier said tightly. 'Your house represents the border of the DDR, ma'am, and that border is now closed.'

'You see,' Gretchen called. 'Tiresome, isn't it?'

Lotti clicked her teeth in frustration.

'It's more than tiresome, Gretchen. It's dangerous. You have to get out.'

'She does not,' the soldier barked. 'Republikflucht is a crime.'

'And yet once she's fled, there's not much you can do, right?'

'DDR citizens still fall under our jurisdiction even when they're on foreign territory.'

'Foreign!' Lotti shrieked. 'This isn't foreign. It's our street, our shared street.'

'Not any more,' he snapped, then grabbed Gretchen's arm. 'Come away from the window, ma'am. It's best if you don't let these Wessis try and seduce you.'

'I wish!' Gretchen told him robustly. 'They're my family and they've been through enough without your petty politics stopping me talking to them. Now, get out of my apartment!'

There was an ominous scuffle. Lotti clutched at Kirsten and Uli, but a couple of minutes later Gretchen returned to the broken window with a smile.

'He's gone.'

'So come out, Gretchen.'

'Out the window? Heavens no, someone might see my underthings.'

'Gretchen! This is no time for jokes.'

Up the street, a door flung open and a young woman came running out, two small children in her arms. The woman who'd spoken to Kirsten rushed forward, gathering them into her like a mother hen, and Kirsten assumed this was Maria, key safely retrieved and her escape made. She had a single bag on her back, all she'd been able to carry from what had, until the early hours of this morning, been a normal life, and Kirsten watched, stunned, as her mother hustled them to her side of the street.

'Get out!' Maria called back to the building in general. 'Do you want to stay at the mercy of these KZ guards? Get out, now!'

Kirsten shivered.

'Did you hear her, Tante?'

'Don't call me Tante.'

'Gretchen! This is no time to be pig-headed. You have to leave,' Kirsten shouted.

'And let them crash their boots all over my beautiful apartment? No thank you. Please don't get hysterical, Kirsten, it doesn't suit you. It'll blow over, I promise. This happened in the '48 blockade, but it didn't last. Hold tight, that's all we need to do. Hold tight and wait for the Allies, then we can be together again. Cheers!'

She raised a brandy glass to them and then she was gone and there was nothing more to say.

'Blöde kuh,' Lotti muttered.

'Do you think she's right?' Kirsten asked her. 'Do you think it'll come down again once the Allies get here?'

'What Allies?' Lotti asked darkly.

Kirsten looked around. Although the sun was climbing above the buildings and glaring down on the beleaguered street, no soldiers had arrived. For the last fifteen years Berliners had been living under the thumb of the Allies, but when they finally needed them, they were nowhere to be seen.

Furious, she marched back up towards Café Edelweiss. It was doing a roaring trade but her precious kaffee und kuchen booking would go unused. Her biological parents were the other side of the stupid wire wall ahead of her, and she glared at it. It was so flimsy, so thin. Surely they couldn't let it stand in their way?

'We have to protest,' she cried. 'We have to stand up and let them know we're not going to allow this!'

It sounded simple but, looking at the guns pointed threateningly in the direction of all their homes, she had a horrible feeling it wasn't going to be. Overnight, Berlin had been severed in two, with Kirsten's family on the other side of the dangerous divide. She and her birth mother were, it seemed, as apart as they had ever been, cruelly destined never to meet.

# TWENTY-SEVEN

## MONDAY, 14 AUGUST

*OLIVIA*

'Nice haircut, Frieda,' Julia called. 'Very modish!'

Olivia looked up to see Frieda patting self-consciously at her new, short cut.

'I thought I'd go for it now that the Wessis have to pay their own prices in their own hairdressers and we can finally have a turn over here.'

Everyone around the lunch table nodded and Olivia picked at her sauerkraut and tried to take an interest, but it was hard. Frieda's hair looked great, but haircuts didn't seem important with her mother in distress. Yesterday had been so awful. The boys had been bewildered, scared by the guns and even more so by the shouting Wessis on the other side. Filip had tried to be reassuring but it had been obvious that he was shaken too.

Was it worse, Olivia wondered bitterly, to have never seen your baby at all, or to have had four beautiful days that gave you a taste of what you would miss? Ester often smiled about the fathers who paced outside birthing rooms, nerves jangling. She told tales of men fainting when they first saw their child, or leaping for joy, or weeping. Frequently weeping.

'They're not as tough as you think,' she often told Olivia. 'That's why it's good in the DDR that things are equal – not just for us, but for men too.'

Olivia had always believed her mother because Ester was the toughest person she knew, but not yesterday. Ester told her 'stories' to cope with what she'd been through without it flooding her, but yesterday it had done exactly that. In her mind, she'd been in that horrific place again, and Olivia had seen the deep, piercing pain reflected in her eyes, and hated it.

'It's not your fault,' both her parents had kept saying to her but she'd known that wasn't true.

'I got your hopes up.'

'They've always been up,' Filip had said stoutly. 'You just gave them a chance of fulfilment when you found Pippa. You spoke to her, Liv. You hugged her. We know that she's alive and thriving and that's almost as good as meeting her ourselves.'

Almost.

That had been her father's word, chosen with care so as not to hurt her. The truth was that it was nowhere near as good.

'I have to write to her,' Ester had said as the time of their train out of Berlin had approached with no way of getting to Pippa. 'I have to explain.'

'She'll understand, Mutti.'

'Understand, maybe, but that's different from *feeling*. Letters bring hope, they keep people going.'

She'd looked lovingly at Filip, and Olivia had remembered her story about a brave woman called Mala smuggling one of his letters into her barracks in Auschwitz and protested no more. Her mother had sat down there and then at her own desk and now Olivia had a closely written, tightly folded sheet of paper burning a hole in her pocket, and no idea how she'd deliver it. Even the post was watched and one simple message of love could be enough to bring the grey vans calling.

Leaping up, she went to the window, laying her head on the warm glass to look out at the jagged tear severing Berlin, and instantly Hans was at her side, his arms around her shoulders. He'd been very attentive since her parents had been forced to take the train back to Stalinstadt yesterday without the promised meeting with their daughter. He'd even snuck into her room after lights-out to hold her while she cried herself to sleep, and hovered over her at this morning's training session, trying to stop her lifting the heaviest weights in case she dropped them on herself. It had been both touching and irritating but, then, everything was irritating now. Though not, it seemed, for her fellow students.

'I reckon the shops are already fuller,' Franz was saying. 'I was chatting to the newsagent and he says the suppliers have been offering him deals. They're not meant to do it, of course, with prices set, but for now it seems to be allowed. He had biscuits and apples and rows of Cola.'

'Vita Cola, though,' Julia said. 'No more Coca-Cola for us.'

'We couldn't afford it anyway,' Franz said, 'and Vita's OK. Besides, in a month or two, we'll have forgotten what the American stuff tastes like, so it won't matter.'

'Is that right though?' Hans sat forward. 'Is that the answer – to forget what the best stuff tastes like and be satisfied with something worse?'

'If it means everyone can have it, then yes, I think it probably is.'

Hans nodded thoughtfully.

'Sort of like everyone at a comp getting bronze.'

The athletes around the table shifted.

'No gold?' Julia said. 'I don't like that idea.'

'Me either,' Franz agreed. 'But it's not the same with sport – the whole point is to win.'

'Isn't the whole point of eating to find the best tastes?'

Franz scratched his head, then hit the table triumphantly.

'No! The whole point of eating is to be nourished, to give your body what it needs. Taste is a bonus. With sport, exercise is what the body needs to stay healthy and we, elite performers, are a bonus.'

He smiled round triumphantly.

'But we still don't get Coca-Cola,' Hans said.

'Well, no, but we have restaurants, we have good food. Coca-Cola is an empty concept, designed to divide people rather than unite them. It pretends it's there to give everyone a good time but only half the population can afford it and, for that to happen, the other half has to starve. No one starves because we're throwing the javelin a long way, right, Olivia? Olivia?!'

She blinked.

'Sorry, I wasn't really concentrating. All this is very distracting.'

She waved to the window and the empty marketplace beyond, where soldiers patrolled in front of the dark line of wire. The sun was still shining blithely but no one was heading to the beach today. In the East, everyone was at work, or huddling into their homes trying to figure out what this meant; and in the West they were out protesting.

'Why are the Wessis shouting and not us?' Olivia pondered, returning to her seat.

'Because the wire goes all the way around West Berlin,' Franz said. 'They're the ones who are trapped – a fascist island in the middle of the DDR.'

'So why are the guns pointing our way?'

No one had an answer for that and they turned back to their food in awkward silence. Olivia gave up on hers and pushed the plate away. Hans squeezed her knee.

'Maybe if the DDR keeps West Berlin fenced in, the Allies will get fed up and hand it over?'

'Is that the plan?'

'Who knows, but it could be. It's not right having a sliver of the West in the middle of East Germany. We're not at war with them and we're not preparing for war, so why can't we have our capital city back?'

'And then we could open it up again?'

'Of course.'

'And I could see Kirsten?'

'I assume so. But look, Liv, I don't know anything, so don't...'

'Get my hopes up? Oh, don't worry, Hans, I've learned that lesson. My hopes are as wired in as the rest of me now.'

Hans leaned over and gave her a slow, tender kiss.

'I'm so sorry, Liv, but, listen, I hear people at the Humboldt University can get letters through.'

'You do? Where did you—'

He kissed her quiet.

'Doesn't matter. It's worth a try, right?'

'Right,' she agreed, pulling the tiny square out of her pocket and handing it to him. 'Thank you, Hans.'

'Anything for you, gorgeous.'

She smiled sadly at him, then heard her name being called across the dining room and pulled away to see Frau Scholz waving imperiously at her. Her heart skittered.

'What does she want?'

'You better go and see.'

With a sigh, Olivia hefted herself out of her chair and threaded her way between the tables to Frau Scholz.

'Visitor for you, Olivia.'

For a glorious, happy moment, she thought it might be Kirsten and wished she'd kept the letter, but as she stepped into reception with the hausmeisterin and saw Klaus standing there, she cursed herself as a fool. Not all her hope was wired in yet, then, and it was going to hurt every time.

'Good afternoon, Olivia.'

He was smiling; it was creepy.

'Good afternoon,' she returned reluctantly.

'I thought we could have a little chat.'

'Oh, good.'

He ushered her into the usual side room and, to her surprise, she smelled coffee.

'Will you join me in a cup?' She looked at him suspiciously. Was he softening her up before he shouted at her? 'Please, be my guest. Yesterday must have been hard for you. Here.'

He slid a small pack of chocolate across the table and she stared at it.

'For me?'

'I thought you might need the consolation. Not that it makes up for, well, for what happened – or rather, didn't happen – but it should taste nice.'

The words reminded her of the students' conversation at lunch.

'Is that allowed now?'

He cocked his head curiously.

'Allowed?'

'This is Western chocolate. Is it allowed?'

'No point in it going to waste. That would be against all the principles of socialism.'

He leaned over and unwrapped it, then placed a steaming mug of coffee at its side. The mingled aromas were heavenly and, despite herself, Olivia reached out for both. Klaus smiled.

'And when this runs out,' Olivia said, 'we will eat DDR chocolate?'

'Correct.'

'Which is worse?'

He sucked in a breath. She knew she was playing with fire but was finding it hard to care.

'It is worse at the moment,' Klaus said carefully, 'because our scientists have not yet had time to develop it fully. But they will. They are the best in the world. They can make vitamins that help you to train to superb new levels, so they can most certainly make tasty chocolate.'

'Then why don't they?'

He gave a thin laugh.

'Priorities, Olivia. That is the whole point of socialism – you get society to a point where everyone is warm, safe and healthy. You make sure they have access to a good education, a decent home and proper health care. Then, and only then, do you work on luxuries.'

Olivia took another square of the chocolate, letting it melt onto her tongue and feeling the delicious sweetness run into her. That made sense.

'Can we improve Vita Cola too?'

'Of course we can. It's hardly rocket science – and we can do rocket science!'

He gave a peculiarly hearty laugh at his own joke. Olivia wanted to point out that it was the Russians who could do rocket science, but sensed that she had gone far enough and, anyway, the Russians were their friends and would help them, especially now they'd sealed off the West.

'I see that,' she said slowly, chasing the chocolate down with a gulp of coffee. It was rich and fragrant and she felt herself relax a little. She'd been too caught up in her personal issues, too obsessed with her mother's lost baby to understand what was best for the state. 'I see that,' she repeated. 'It's just hard.'

He reached out and patted her hand. She forced herself not to flinch.

'It *is* hard, Olivia. The DDR is still young. We are like you with your javelin, having to learn and make sacrifices but, in the end, it will be worth it. It will be gold.'

'Or bronze.'

'Sorry?'

She shook herself.

'Just something one of the students said at lunch – that it was better for us all to be bronze, than for a few people to be gold.'

'Which student?'

His voice had sharpened and she jumped.

'I, I can't remember. I was eating, so I wasn't paying much attention. Sorry.'

'No matter. You are upset, it's understandable.' She glanced at him, amazed by this response, and he smiled. 'We at the Ministry are not inhuman, Olivia. We just have a very hard job, though the wall will hopefully make it easier.'

'Wall?'

'It will be a wall.'

'The Allies won't stop you?'

'*Us*, Olivia. And, no, it suits them too. They get their pride at not letting go of Berlin and we get our security at containing their decadent corruption.'

'Right. Yes. It's just...'

'Your sister is on the other side?'

She nodded miserably.

'Don't worry about that. Once it settles, there will be passes.'

Her head shot up.

'Passes?'

'To visit.'

'I'll be able to visit Kirsten?'

'Maybe. More likely, she will be able to visit you. With a pass. Once things have settled and the DDR is safe.'

'Will that take long?'

'Oh no.' He waved an airy hand. 'A few weeks maybe. It's already improving.'

'I know,' she agreed. 'Frieda got her hair cut today.' He looked confused. 'Because there are no Wessis taking up all the appointments.'

'Ah! Yes. You see...' He patted self-consciously at his closely shaved head. 'A hairdresser is not something I have much need of.' It was a joke, an actual joke, and Olivia felt herself smile. He leaned across the table. 'It will work, Olivia. The wall will work. We will be safe to govern ourselves in the best way, with pure socialism, and we will thrive. It's not about everyone having a bronze medal, Olivia. Your friend has misunderstood. It is about everyone having a *gold*.'

She nodded and reluctantly drank the last mouthful of her coffee. Klaus was on his feet immediately, filling it from the jug. He really was in a remarkably good mood. She supposed she might be, too, if it wasn't for Kirsten. She glanced out the window. This room, like the dining hall, looked down onto the marketplace and she saw a family pitching a tent on their side of the wire. Klaus followed her gaze and tutted.

'Refugees. They will have to go home, back to their decent socialist towns to live decent socialist lives. And in a few weeks, you mark my words, they'll be glad they have.'

'They won't be punished?'

'No! We don't punish the innocent, Olivia.'

A picture came to her, unbidden, of the girl, Claudia, who had been imprisoned for dyeing her hair green. She could see her now, weeping on the floor as a Stasi officer, much like Klaus, tapped away down the dingy corridor with her newborn son in his arms. And she could see, too, her own mother weeping in an anguish that had torn through her yesterday.

'What's troubling you, Olivia?'

Klaus really was being very kind today; it was most disconcerting.

'I saw a woman back in Stalinstadt. She was in prison for, for dyeing her hair green.' She looked up at him. 'That seems innocent to me.'

He shook his head pityingly.

'It would, and if that was all she'd done wrong, you'd be

right, but it won't have been. The hair will have been the tip of an iceberg of subterfuge and subversion.'

'She seemed so certain.'

'She would do. You don't become a subversive without being a fantastic actor.'

Olivia supposed that was true, but even so...

'They took her baby away.'

'Ah. That would be hard. But should the baby be punished too?'

'The baby *was* punished. It lost its mother.'

'And gained a better one, a proper socialist one.'

Olivia shook her head. It felt fugged again, confused.

'That's what the Nazis said to my mother when they took her baby.'

Klaus' hand banged down onto the table, so hard and so sudden that she jumped and caught her elbow on the chair.

'We are not Nazis!'

'No, I... Sorry. I know that. I just meant...'

'What? What did you mean, Olivia? Have you been listening? This is hard. What we are doing is revolutionary. When we prove that it works, the rest of the world will have to embrace socialism and will become a better place. That doesn't come without a price.'

'No, Klaus. I see—'

'The state is more important than the individual, Olivia. You do understand?'

'Yes, yes, I—'

'We cannot pander to one person's petty, selfish needs at the expense of everyone else's greater good, can we?'

'No.'

'No. I'm sorry I made you jump, but this is vital, Olivia. We must all pull together to make it work.'

'Yes, Klaus.'

She rubbed at her sore elbow.

'So,' he went on, his voice soft again now. 'You will explain to your fellow students what I've told you?' She looked at him uncertainly. 'You know, about everyone aiming for gold.'

'Ah. Yes. I will.'

'Good girl. And you will make sure everyone understands? That no one is trying to corrupt their fellows?'

She nodded dully. This sounded familiar.

'*Is* anyone, Olivia? Is anyone trying to corrupt others?'

'No.'

'You're sure? No one is speaking against the regime, saying all that about Vita Cola not tasting good, about bronze being enough?'

She felt a tiny trickle of dread run down her spine. If she thought back carefully, it was clear that one person had been posing those questions, one person very, very dear to her.

'No! It wasn't like that. It was simply people chatting, asking questions. It's been a very confusing twenty-four hours.'

'It may have seemed like that, my dear, but you will soon find that, on the contrary, these are the twenty-four hours that have brought clarity to the DDR. It will settle.'

'And then there will be passes?'

'Then there will be passes and your sister will be one of the first to get one. I will see to it personally. As your friend.'

He smiled again and she tried to smile back, but Klaus was not her friend and, although he was right about making socialism work, she had to admit that her 'petty, selfish needs' felt important too. It was, therefore, with a heavy heart that she headed back to class to stare out the window at the guards patrolling what felt, right now, very like a giant konzentrationslager.

# TWENTY-EIGHT

## TUESDAY, 15 AUGUST

*KIRSTEN*

Kirsten filled her lungs – no mean feat in the crush of people – and sang 'Deutschland über alles' with the rest, throwing the words at the Brandenburg Gate. For two centuries that great monument had stood at the top of Unter den Linden, shouting out Germany's glory to the world; now it was strung around with wire, like a prisoner of war. The majestic view up the great avenue was severed cruelly in two and TV stations all over the world were broadcasting pictures of what the once-mighty Germans had done to their own capital. It was shameful.

Pulling her foot out from under someone else's, Kirsten waved a fist in the air and felt history shake around her. Thank God she'd come. Dieter had stormed into Café Adler around midday, raging against Spitzbart and the Ossi authorities, saying no one should be taking kaffee und kuchen while their city was torn in half. People had picked shamefacedly at their torte crumbs and Kirsten had thought he looked magnificent.

'There's to be a strike,' he'd announced, waving a copy of Bild-Zeitung. 'A general strike, at 2.15 p.m. Everyone is going to down tools for fifteen minutes in solidarity with our fellow Berliners trapped in the East, and to urge the Allies to act. What's the point of having soldiers in the city if they don't defend our basic civil liberties? Put down your coffee cups, people, and march!'

It had been most impressive. Frau Munster had clapped him on the back and said Café Adler was closing and everyone should head to the Brandenburg Gate, so here they were. Astrid and his student friends had been waiting outside with neat German flags painted on their faces and placards in their hands and Kirsten had gladly joined them in their march.

They'd stomped along the line of the overnight wire to Potsdamer Platz and into the Tiergarten on their side of the Brandenburg Gate. With most of West Berlin having done the same, there were at least twenty thousand people shouting for justice. Thanks to Dieter's energy, his group had arrived early and were near the front. Already they'd been sprayed three times with the water cannons arcing viciously over the wire from the East to try to silence them. They hurt if they caught you directly, but it was a hot day so their cooling blast was not unwelcome and everyone out of their immediate path danced in the spray, enraging the Ossis further.

Dieter had handed her a placard and she lifted it up with pride. *Es gibt nur ein Deutschland*: There is only one Germany. Others said the same, or similar, defying the men who were severing the city's roads, railways and even telephone lines. The Iron Curtain had cut off everything with its sudden fall and the only question was which Germany was more trapped. Ossis could travel freely across Eastern Europe, whereas Wessis were stuck in an island in the middle of the DDR. However, road, rail and sky offered Wessis a route to wherever else they wished to go and, much more importantly, they were free in their own homes. Kirsten knew which she'd choose but her heart still ached for her biological mother, once more at the mercy of an ideology that believed it knew better than its people.

As the clocks in the city ticked around to 2.15 p.m., a strange silence fell. Shops closed their doors, factories stopped their machines, and people poured onto the streets to stand in vigil over the horror being perpetrated on them. Kirsten felt her throat swell with emotion and snuck her hand into Dieter's. He clasped it tight.

'They have to listen, Kirsty. Look at all these people – surely the Allies have to listen?'

'Why don't we do it ourselves?' she suggested. 'There are thousands of us. What could they do if we rushed the wire?'

They knew the answer to that, though. Yesterday evening forty people on the Bethaniendamm had stormed into the Soviet sector, but they'd been driven back with truncheons and tear gas, and a number had been hurt in the crush. Even worse, when a similar group had tried it in Kreuzberg, rushing right past Café Adler, the guards had opened fire. Five Ossis had escaped but a sixth had been shot dead.

Kirsten hadn't been on shift but Sasha had told her about it this morning. She'd rushed after the group, keen to see what would happen, and had stood there with the rest, thrown into stunned silence, as a vopo had carried the dead body back into the depths of East Berlin. It had been the first casualty of the barrier, but no one thought it would be the last and if they stormed the Brandenburg Gate, where forces were strongest, many would die.

'Protest is the best way,' Astrid said. 'Mass protest. We need to let the world know how we feel.'

'Exactly,' Dieter agreed. 'The Allies brought the wretched Russians to Germany, so they have to help us deal with them and not hide away bleating about their damned Cold War from miles behind its front line. Where are the Americans?'

That was the cry on everyone's lips. A handful of US

soldiers had turned up outside Café Adler this morning with a little white hut, like an old man's garden shed, which they'd set in the middle of Friedrichstraβe.

'What's that for?' Kirsten had asked as she'd walked past it on the way to work.

'It's a checkpoint,' one of them had told her with a grimace. 'This is one of the thirteen roads still going through to the East.'

'Thirteen?'

'Yeah,' he'd confirmed gloomily. 'There used to be nearly a hundred.'

Kirsten had supposed that was a bit drastic but all she'd been able to think was that there were still thirteen routes through. Surely she could walk down one to visit her family? Where was the harm in that?

'Do they have to let us through?' she'd asked the Americans, peering up the road at the mass of border guards on the Eastern side.

'In theory, ma'am, yes. They can dictate to their own citizens, but not anyone else's, so they ought to allow Westerners in, but they're stopping everyone and if they have "just suspicions of illegal activity" they can refuse entry. Almost everyone, as far as we've seen, is suspected of that, so I'd say getting through will be difficult.'

She'd almost gone for it. She'd almost marched up the street (a street that, until yesterday, had been her normal, dull route back to the U-Bahn) and asked the DDR guards if she could go through. She should have done, but they'd had guns and dogs and dark frowns across their lean faces and she'd lost her nerve. No wonder no one in the East was coming anywhere near; these people were ruthless.

The clock ticked round to 2.30 p.m. and, with a sort of collective sigh, many of the crowd turned to make their way back to their workplaces. Life had to go on. There were wages to earn, bosses to please, families to feed.

'This is pointless, Dieter,' Kirsten said as the crowd rapidly thinned out. 'They don't care. Look at them – they're laughing at us.' She pointed to a group of vopos, standing on the top of a Soviet tank and blasting the water cannon over the fence as if they were pissing on them. 'They know we're impotent.'

Dieter ran a weary hand over his face.

'Where are the Americans?' he wailed, but the Americans were conspicuous only by their absence.

Kennedy, it would appear, did not care about Berlin and now word shot around the remaining protestors that lorries had been seen bringing concrete blocks into the city. The East had been testing the Allies, seeing what they could get away with, and the answer seemed to be whatever they wished.

'This is bad, Dieter,' Kirsten said. 'It's not going to come down.'

'You don't know that. We have to keep protesting.'

'We have to make our voice heard,' Astrid agreed, an annoying echo.

Kirsten shook her head at them.

'They're not listening. No one is listening. They're going to build a verdammte wall.'

She thought of her own street. It already looked darker with wire at every intersection, but if that turned into concrete it would be like a prison yard. And as for the apartments opposite, physically turned into a barrier...

'Tante Gretchen!' she cried. If this morning had made one thing clear, it was that this barrier wasn't going to come down; it was only going to get higher. 'I have to go, Dieter. I have to get her out.'

He looked disappointed.

'But the protest, Kirsty!'

'You've got that in hand. I'll be back once my aunt's safe.'

'It might be too late then.'

It was too late already, of that Kirsten was sure, but there was no time for arguments. She pushed her placard into Dieter's spare hand and kissed his cheek.

'I'll see you soon, yeah?'

'Maybe,' he grunted.

He didn't understand. It was all right for him, with the protection of an Austrian passport, but her aunt had only her foolhardy bravery and it was rapidly becoming apparent that wouldn't get her very far. Kirsten's heart stung as he turned back to his friends, pointedly handing the placard to Astrid with her perfect flags on her pretty face and her tuneful voice singing the anthem. Well, fine. Let them protest; Kirsten had more urgent things to do.

Bernauerstraβe was almost as busy as the Tiergarten. Wiring off the Brandenburg Gate was an outrage to the German nation, but wiring off the backstreets was a direct offence to the neighbours living either side and they were not taking it quietly.

'Kirsten, thank God!' Lotti said, when Kirsten let herself into the apartment. 'I've been so worried. There've been protestors trying to ram the wire all morning and the Russians have brought more soldiers in, tanks too.'

She dragged Kirsten to the window and pointed up the street to the mass of khaki beyond the wire at the top.

'Those aren't tanks, Mutti,' she said. 'They're armoured vehicles.'

'They're horrid, whatever they are,' Lotti shot back. 'You're to stay away, do you hear, no stupid heroics. A group of lads tried to drive a bulldozer into that end and they shot at them.'

'I don't think they had live ammo,' Uli said, coming to join them. 'There was a lot of noise, but no one seemed to go down. The DDR know there'll be trouble if they kill Wessis.'

'Ossis, however...'

He pulled a face.

'They don't seem to matter.'

Kirsten grabbed Lotti's arm.

'We have to get Gretchen out, Mutti. Don't you have a spare key for the door?'

Lotti stared at her.

'Of course I do but, what – we simply walk over there and open it up?'

'I don't see why not. The street is in the West so they can't hurt us.'

'But they could hurt Gretchen?'

'We just have to time it well.'

'Kirsten's right,' Uli agreed. 'I saw a guard jump the fence earlier – an actual DDR guard. He flung his rifle down and hurdled the wire. The photographers went mad.'

'I bet they did,' Kirsten said. 'It'll be all over the papers tomorrow.'

'And still the Allies won't do anything. People are frantic. They're jumping out of windows – look.' He pointed the other way down the street. About ten uniformed firemen were hovering beneath an apartment block with a huge, circular tarpaulin of the sort they usually used to get scared kids or stupid cats down from trees. Up on the second floor, a young couple were throwing tightly wrapped bundles into it and Kirsten watched with horror as they then edged themselves onto their windowsill.

'Are they going to jump?' she asked.

They were. The man kissed his wife and pushed himself off. He seemed to hover in the air, his legs kicking like Charlie Chaplin, but the firemen shouted instructions and, at the last minute, he pulled his legs into his chest and landed in the tarpaulin. It sagged but held and bounced him back up to a huge cheer from the crowd. All eyes then turned upwards again as the man scrambled off the tarpaulin and called to his wife.

'Jump, Elsie. Jump, meine liebling.'

Elsie shifted forward but seemed unable to take the final leap and the crowd gasped as a shadow appeared in the room behind her.

'Jump!' everyone shrieked.

She glanced behind and, as the soldier reached out, closed her eyes and launched herself. The movement was so vigorous that she leaped further than expected and the firemen had to scramble back, but their judgement was good and Elsie landed on the tarpaulin. Up above, the soldier leaned out of the window and shook his fist at the cheering Wessis below.

'People are that desperate?' Lotti asked.

'The *situation* is that desperate,' Kirsten said. 'We have to get Gretchen out. Come on!'

They stood beneath Gretchen's window for some time before the guards were sufficiently far away for her to lean out and speak. Kirsten braced herself for her aunt's defiance, but she sounded unusually cowed.

'It's horrible here,' she called as quietly as she could. 'There are soldiers in the corridors all the time and they keep banging on the door and coming in to "check". It was fun teasing them at first, but now I'm... bored.'

She'd stopped herself saying 'scared', and they all knew it.

'You have to get out, Tante,' Kirsten told her and it was a measure of her aunt's concern that she didn't pick her up on the hated title.

'How, Kirsty? I'm not jumping out of this damn window. Did you see that poor woman just now? So undignified!'

A smile tugged at Kirsten's lips. Gretchen hadn't lost all her fire then. That was good.

'Mutti has a key,' she hissed. 'It's simple. We wait until dark, then stroll across, unlock it and out you come.'

'Out I come?'

'Yes.'

'Never to go back?'

'Maybe. Maybe not.'

'You think they'll take their verdammte wall down now it's up? They're bringing in bricks, Kirsty. They're blocking up windows. It's getting dark in here – dark in every way.'

'Tonight then.'

'What about my stuff?'

'I don't know, Gretchen, I—'

'Throw it out,' Uli said. 'Say you're gifting it to Kirsten and me to create more wealth parity. That's very socialist, right?'

'Dead right, Uli,' Gretchen agreed. 'Let's give it a go.'

It was a curious afternoon, standing in the street while Gretchen threw rugs, paintings and eiderdowns out of the window. A soldier soon appeared, but Gretchen explained loudly that she was embracing socialism and no longer had any need for the 'trappings of capitalist bourgeoisie' and there was little he could say to that. After a while, drawing quite a crowd, Gretchen began throwing her wedding china to anyone prepared to catch the Dresden cups and plates. A number missed their mark and smashed onto the road and kids began running excitedly around picking up the larger bits and smashing them in turn.

'I think that might be enough now, Tante,' Uli called up. 'You still need to have something to eat off, after all.'

Gretchen offered him a big wink – Kirsten suspected she'd been finishing her brandy supplies – and agreed loudly that she did. At last, with the sun going down, she retreated inside and people meandered back to their homes, chatting and sharing the goodies they'd caught. Kirsten saw someone collect a drying towel off the wire adjoining their entrance and shivered. Already Bernauerstraße was treating the hideous barrier as if it were a normal part of life. Perhaps people were *too* resilient? Perhaps that's what the East had banked on?

They hovered in the apartment, trying to eat supper. Gretchen had said she'd light a candle in her window when the coast was clear and they sat, staring at the blank space, willing the flame to appear.

'What's she doing?' Lotti muttered.

'Stuffing jewels into her knickers?' Uli suggested, trying to keep the mood light. It didn't work.

At last, across the road, a tiny light flared. They stared at its simple brightness, then raced for the door.

'Don't forget the key,' Kirsten called to Lotti.

'In my hand!'

They tumbled outside, then forced themselves to stop and saunter, as if merely exercising a non-existent dog. Slipping into the shadows by Gretchen's door, Lotti slotted the key into the lock, but her hand was shaking and she struggled to turn it.

'Let me.'

Uli turned the key with a small rasp and they opened the door to find Gretchen standing there, wearing half her wardrobe and with a suitcase in each hand.

'Shall we?' she said calmly and then stepped out and, with total grace, sauntered across Bernauerstraβe and into their own foyer.

They scuttled after her and stood there, looking at each other.

'Was that it?' Uli asked.

'Seems so,' Gretchen agreed. 'I'm glad you left the door open. I dropped a few hints to the neighbours.'

Sure enough, when they peeked again, they saw several others creeping out, before an enraged shout split the air and a soldier came running. He stood, framed in Gretchen's doorway, staring furiously into the night. Someone shouted a joyous obscenity in his direction and he stamped his foot, slammed the door shut and, presumably, secured it again.

'You made it!'

Kirsten hugged her aunt.

'Of course I did,' Gretchen said with an airy wave, but then her voice cracked and she crumpled against her. 'I made it. I made it out.'

Kirsten stroked her back, told her she was safe now, and wished it could be that easy for everyone else. The last doors out of the East were slamming shut and the future for those in the wrong half of Berlin looked bleak. The DDR authorities were imprisoning their people in the name of socialism and she prayed that Olivia saw through it and got out while she still had the chance.

# TWENTY-NINE

## SATURDAY, 19 AUGUST

*OLIVIA*

'You were amazing.'

'No, you were amazing!'

Olivia smiled as Hans picked her up and spun her round. Today had been the last competition of the season and they'd both won their events. Olivia had been very pleased with her performance and had to pinch herself to remember that only three months ago she'd been at school in suburban Stalinstadt, captaining a provincial tennis team. Now she was competing at the highest youth level as a javelin thrower, with Trainer Lang already talking about senior selection next year if she kept up her progress. It was enough to cheer her up after the horrors of the last week and, even better, tomorrow she was heading home to her family for a month.

First though, there was the club dinner. With the wall up, the DDR's leaders were ebullient, and they had invited the athletes to their compound in Wandlitz, a suburb of East Berlin, to mark the end of Dynamo's first full season.

'I need to get changed, Hans,' Olivia mock-scolded as he tried to manoeuvre her behind the equipment shed.

His eyes lit up.

'Excellent. I'll help you. You'll probably need a shower too?'

She gave in, pulling him against her for a delicious, long kiss.

'You soap my back if I soap yours?'

'You're on!'

They snuck into the girls' bathroom together. The javelin had been the last event of the comp and most of the other athletes were long since washed and in the dorm, doing each other's make-up. They'd been issued clothing stamps for new outfits and had had a grand shopping expedition to Konsum – the state-approved store – yesterday. Not that there was much choice in party frocks in the DDR, especially for a tall and increasingly broad-shouldered javelin thrower. Olivia had bemoaned not having her father to work his magic on the few dull offerings she'd fitted into and had eventually settled for a black gown that was plain but elegant. Perhaps over the holidays Filip would add some trim or embroidery to make it prettier for next time.

As she let Hans strip her out of her competition kit, she thought of Kirsten, her lost-again sister, who'd confided shyly that she liked to sew. It was ironic – Olivia had been worrying that Ester's 'real' daughter would follow her into midwifery, when it was actually Filip's trade that had drawn her. How, she wondered – as she did at least fifty times a day – could she possibly meet her again?

'Hello there? Are you receiving me?'

She blinked back into the present to see Hans, now as deliciously naked as herself, gesturing to the steaming shower.

'Sorry, Hans. I was thinking about Kirsten.'

'Romantic!'

She grimaced.

'It's just that this time last week...'

'I know!' He groaned and banged at the tiles. 'How can it have gone up so fast? There are actual bricks all over the place already.'

'The Allies simply gave in. Did nothing.'

He nodded.

'You know the American vice-president has been in West Berlin today?'

'I know. The coaches were crowing about it. "America has come to Berlin and all they've done is take a peek at the wall from a fancy limo." They reckon it means that we're safe and socialism is protected.'

'Hmmm.'

'Hans?' He tried to kiss her but she pulled away. 'What does "hmmm" mean?'

'Nothing. Doesn't matter, honestly. I got your mother's letter to the university, by the way.'

'Really? Oh Hans, thank you!'

'Let's just hope it reaches Kirsten.'

Olivia pictured the tiny scrap of a missive and sighed bitterly. 'For all the good it can do.'

'It doesn't hurt anyone to be told they're loved, liebling.'

'True.' Olivia smiled gratefully at him and he pulled her close but then leaned back, confused.

'What's this?'

He tweaked at a hair below her left nipple and she squirmed away, embarrassed. She must have missed it with the tweezers that morning.

'It's a hair. So what?'

'So nothing,' he said hastily, pulling her into the shower but then, through its rush, asked, 'Is it the vitamins, Liv?'

Olivia jumped.

'What do you mean?'

'Oh, I don't know. Have you experienced anything else odd?'

Olivia bit her lip.

'Nothing much. I don't have periods, as you know, but everyone says that's perfectly normal.' She'd never thought she'd miss the pain and mess of her monthlies, but she had to admit their absence bothered her sometimes. 'Why?' she pushed. 'Don't you think it is, Hans?'

'I just wonder if the vitamins might be mixed with something more... comprehensive, if part of shutting off the city is being able to do things that might not be... strictly legal?'

Olivia gaped at him.

'Are you saying that the DDR is corrupt?

'Not corrupt, just... unorthodox. Oh, I don't know, Liv. I can't help wondering at a regime that can only thrive if its people aren't allowed to leave.'

Olivia turned up the water.

'Don't say things like that out loud, Hans. You never know who's listening.'

'Which is exactly the problem!'

Olivia's heart scudded. Their shower was getting less romantic by the minute. She yearned to kiss him quiet, but this was important.

'Hans, are you talking like this to other people? Other athletes?'

'No! What do you mean?'

He glared at her and her heart quailed but she had to know.

'Klaus thinks someone is encouraging people to leave Dynamo.'

His lip curled.

'Klaus, your little Stasi friend?'

Olivia flinched.

'He's not my friend.'

'He brings you chocolate. And coffee.'

'He's not my friend, Hans.'

'No, you're right – he's your spymaster.'

Olivia put her hands on her hips.

'Now you're being ridiculous.'

Hans, however, stepped out of the shower.

'Am I? Why are you asking this, Liv? Are you only here to find out more about me? Or to use me to pass your secret post, maybe? Does this relationship not mean anything to you at all?'

'No! Hans, please.' She followed him, tugging on his arm. 'You mean everything to me. I love you.' He hesitated and she pulled him down so her lips were close to his ear. 'You're right that Klaus is putting me under pressure to find who's telling athletes to leave but, even if it was you, I wouldn't tell him.'

He sighed and pressed his face against hers.

'What is this country coming to, Liv? I'm not telling anyone to leave, I promise you, but that doesn't mean I haven't thought about it.'

'Hans!' She pulled him back under the water, where their words could be washed away in its noisy stream. He looked distressed and she hated to see it. 'It *will* work, you'll see. A wall is drastic, I know, and I hate what it's done to my family just when... Well, I hate it. But it's only while socialism gets a chance to take off properly. Then, we'll be able to open again and show everyone how great it is.'

He stroked her wet hair back from her face and dropped a tender kiss onto her nose.

'I hope you're right, Liv.'

'I am! Socialism is the only decent, honest way to live. I bet you, when we come back after a month at home, that East Berlin will be a different place – a fairer place.'

'A month,' Hans groaned. 'A whole month without you. How will I cope?'

She kissed him.

'It's going to be hard. How about we make the most of each other while we're here...?'

He smiled and drew her close and, for a while at least, all was forgotten bar the rush of water and the pound of their hearts. But when they finally turned off the shower and crept out, they found Frau Scholz standing, arms crossed, by the basins.

'Boys aren't allowed in this bathroom, Olivia.'

Olivia flushed.

'No, Frau Scholz. Sorry, Frau Scholz.'

How long had the damned woman been standing there? It was embarrassing if she'd heard them having sex, but truly dreadful if she'd heard them talking.

Hans stepped forward. 'We'd run out of hot water in our bathroom, Ma, and I didn't want to go to Herr Ulbricht's dinner smelly.'

He gave her his most winning smile but for once she didn't succumb to his charm.

'Take care, the pair of you,' she snapped. 'You're being watched.' Then, with a final glare, she spun on her heels and was gone. Olivia looked nervously to Hans. 'And don't be late,' the hausmeisterin's voice drifted back. 'The bus leaves in half an hour.'

There was nothing to do but scramble for their respective rooms, but as Olivia pulled on her black dress and battled to make up her hot face, she couldn't help wishing the bus was going straight to Stalinstadt and home.

*This dinner is an honour*, she reminded herself, swirling her still damp hair into a loose bun. *A chance to meet our leaders.*

Four months ago, she would have been desperate for that; tonight she was simply scared.

.  .  .

The bus pulled to a stop outside giant gates and, as the driver spoke to two bulky guards in grey uniforms, Olivia looked out the window at the massive wall surrounding the leader's complex. Lush rhododendron bushes grew above the top but did little to soften its austere appearance. Was that, she wondered, what the wall across the city would look like by the time they got back in September? Was Hans right to question a regime that had to shut everyone in to function?

She reminded herself what Klaus had said to her the day after Stacheldrahtsonntag – Barbed Wire Sunday – as people were now calling it: 'The DDR is still young. We are like you with your javelin, having to learn and make sacrifices but, in the end, it will be worth it. It will be gold.' He was right, she was sure, and she was honoured to be a part of that process.

She pressed her face to the glass as the gates cranked open and the bus drove inside. This, then, was the leaders' complex, the perfect model town, better even than Stalinstadt. All the top people and their families lived in here in a microcosm of the state, with shops and a school, cultural and sporting facilities. This was how the children of socialism would be able to live once they settled behind the Iron Curtain.

She glanced to Hans, looking distractingly handsome in his evening suit, and hoped tonight would show him how a truly equal society could operate given the space to work as it should. She took his arm as the bus pulled up in a central parking area and they stepped out into the Wandlitz compound. It was enormous. The walls stretched into the distance on all sides, and she caught sight of guards patrolling the edges with dogs straining on leads.

Three-storey houses, in a uniform beige stucco, stood in rigid parallel rows, separated by well-tended but unshowy lawns and shrubberies – dull, but peaceful and organised, as it should be. The houses were bigger than Olivia had been expecting but she supposed their leaders had large families. To one side she spotted a run of shops, not dissimilar to those on every block back home in Stalinstadt – a laundry, a grocery store, a vet. That was a surprise as pets weren't encouraged in the DDR, but she supposed there must be guard dogs and maybe farm animals if they were growing their own food.

'This way, ladies and gentlemen, this way.' A small man in an elaborate uniform that looked like something out of the Prussian wars waved his hands towards the nearest house. 'Cocktails will be served by Herr Grotewohl.'

The students looked at each other, impressed. Otto Grotewohl was Ulbricht's co-chairman and an important man.

'VIP treatment,' Magda said gaily to Olivia as they were ushered through the door. 'Make the most of it!'

Olivia smiled, trying not to notice that Magda's shoulders, in her spaghetti-strapped evening dress, bulged with muscle. That was fine, wasn't it? She was an athlete, not a fashion model. Even so, she glanced self-consciously at the elegant and ridiculously thin lady in a stunningly elaborate dress standing inside the door to greet them.

'Private tailor?' Frieda whispered in her ear.

Olivia glanced back.

'They're not allowed.'

She knew that for sure because her father had to do all his 'alterations' very carefully so as not to fall foul of the rigid rules on equality in dress.

'Not for us, perhaps, but Frau Grotewohl's dress didn't come from Konsum. And neither did this furniture.'

Frieda gestured into the living area and Olivia looked with astonishment at the swirling carpets, old paintings and elaborate oak furniture. Not for the Grotewohls the functional tables and chairs recommended by the DDR for socialist living, but stunning pieces redolent of a more decadent age. To the right, an alcove led through to a library, panelled in highly polished wood, and to the left was a cinema-room with a huge scarlet curtain that appeared to have hundreds of sparkling discs sewn onto it.

'Are those...?'

'Coins, my dear,' Herr Grotewohl said, coming up at her side. 'Coins, ancient and modern. Do you like them?'

'Are coins not representative of capitalist decadence?' she asked.

His face darkened and, as Frieda slipped hastily away, she cursed herself. That's what they'd always been taught and it had just slipped out.

'They are,' he agreed heartily. 'Which is why I like to keep them as a reminder of what we are fighting against.'

'I see. Yes, very clever.'

'You should get a drink,' he said tightly and ushered her towards the bar.

It was an elaborate corner area, kitted out with beautiful glasses and myriad bottles of colourful spirits from all around the world. Olivia stared at it, drinking in the Italian limoncello, Caribbean rum and French cognac.

'A martini, ma'am?' one of waistcoated servers offered and she nodded dumbly and accepted the exotic cocktail, feeling dazed.

'If this is where socialism is going to get to behind a wall, I can't wait,' a voice said in her ear.

'Hans, hush!'

'Otto is very old-fashioned,' she heard a woman saying to a few of the other students. 'Such Prussian quatsch. I prefer cleaner lines in my home. My bathroom is all ebony, you know – beautifully pure.'

'Is that Red Hilde?' Magda asked, joining them.

'Who?'

'Red Hilde, Minister of Justice. Very militant.'

'And likes pure ebony.'

The three of them looked uncertainly at each other but now

President Ulbricht was arriving to a flurry of excitement and Olivia watched as he did the rounds, making sure to shake every hand and speak a word to every athlete. He was a small man, in a reassuringly dour suit, but he radiated energy.

'And what do you do?' he asked Olivia when it was their turn.

'I throw the javelin, sir.'

'Walter, please. We're all equals here. The javelin? That must be very exciting. Very powerful.'

She blinked.

'It does feel it sometimes, sir, er, Walter – when it's going well at least.'

'Like socialism.' He laughed heartily at his own wit and Olivia, Hans and Magda joined in hastily. 'We are on a great road,' he told them, raising his voice naturally for all to hear. 'Now we've cut off the decadent fascists, we can do something truly special. When you stand on the podium for the DDR, it will be for a country in which you can truly be proud. Now, shall we go and eat?'

He waved them out of Grotewohl's house and they all trooped across the compound to a huge building radiating light in the dusk.

'This is our House of Culture,' Ulbricht announced from the front of their procession. 'We have a gym, a library, a kinder-garten, and a medical clinic.' He swept them inside, waving around the shining building. 'We have a cinema, a restaurant, several hairdressers and a massage parlour. All the essentials of life.' He took them over to a big window. 'And out there, see, a swimming pool, tennis courts, a rifle range. All we need to keep us active.'

The courts were brightly lit and Olivia watched a group of four playing an enthusiastic doubles match and felt as if she were looking into her past life. Then she noticed the expensive surface, the elegant landscaping, and the sweep of the partially covered pool beyond and blinked back into the present.

'It's very smart,' Franz was saying. 'And this is what all towns will have?'

'Of course, of course, once socialism is working properly.'

'It looks good, right?' Olivia said to Hans.

'Very good. Worth a little deprivation for now, I guess.'

Olivia thought of Kirsten, trapped on the other side of the wall, but she couldn't let personal considerations intrude. If prosperity for all was on offer, it had to be worth it and she went into the opulent banqueting hall feeling a contentment that the delicious food and rich French wines only enhanced. By the end of the meal her head was swimming and she leaned over the table to Hans.

'I think I need some fresh air.'

'Do you indeed?'

His eyes sparkled and she rolled her own.

'I truly do.'

'Then allow me, my lady.'

They stepped out into the night together. The swimming pool was lit up a tropical blue, and a couple were swimming in it, a bottle of champagne cooling in a crystal container on a table nearby.

'Should we be drinking French wine?' Olivia asked.

'All German wines come from the West.'

'So it's better to buy from the French?'

'I guess so.'

'Or drink beer?'

'That's what my parents always said but, hey, Spitzbart knows best, surely?' He took a handkerchief out of his pocket and wiped his brow. 'You were right – it's nice to be outside.'

She took his hand and together they wandered down the path around the House of Culture. Olivia paused to look into a hairdressing salon, kitted out with all the latest gear, and wondered if she should cut her hair like Frieda.

'Hey, look at this,' Hans said.

He'd wandered further along and was pointing into the next window. Olivia went to join him and they stood together, staring into a veritable Aladdin's cave. It was a grocery store, but not like any other in the DDR. Coca-Cola jostled for space with Dr Pepper. Succulent burgers sat alongside breaded chicken and in the middle was a display of fresh fruit higher than Olivia had ever seen. You were lucky if you got hold of one apple in Stalinstadt, and here was an orchard-full, not to mention oranges, bananas and even something that looked like it might be a peach, not that Olivia had ever held one herself.

'Is this what we'll all have once socialism works?' she asked Hans uncertainly.

'Maybe.'

Olivia turned and looked around the compound. The concrete wall was lit up now and several guards were looking suspiciously over at them. Just beyond, she could see the plain apartment blocks of the ordinary residents of outer Berlin, their view into this compound as carefully blocked by the bushes as their access to the House of Culture was by the vast gates.

'Or maybe this is only for the top brass?'

Olivia felt a heavy sadness fall across her broad shoulders. She looked back into the window of the shop, raking her eyes over the mass of forbidden Western luxuries. Here, at the very heart of the DDR, the men who had walled the rest of the country off from the 'corrupt and decadent' West, were helping themselves to the goods they were denying everyone else.

'The other day, Hans, you said that human beings weren't capable of being fair. I thought you were being cynical. I even thought you were being subversive, but you were just being honest.'

'Not necessarily.' He gripped her hands. 'Don't give up on it, Olivia. You believe in socialism, I know you do.'

'I did,' she said wearily. 'I thought it was worth suffering in the present for a better future, but our leaders aren't suffering, are they? They aren't buying their clothes in Konsum. They aren't sitting at state-approved tables, eating state-approved food so that everyone can live in safety, warmth and good health. They're just happily taking all the wealth for themselves – like the worst of capitalists.'

'Olivia, hush.' Hans shook her. 'You're attracting attention.'

Two guards were coming over, radios in hand, and now more came running out of the House of Culture. Olivia looked around in alarm.

'You two! Halt right there. What do you think you're doing?'

'Spies!' someone else called and Olivia looked around in a panic and saw faces pressed against the banqueting hall window, among them Spitzbart himself.

'What do we do?' she gasped.

'Trust me,' Hans whispered and then he dropped to one knee before her.

'Hans?'

'Olivia Pasternak,' he said loudly. 'You are the most amazing woman I have ever met. You are strong and decent and beautiful. I cannot bear the thought of the next month without you, let alone the rest of my life, and so I ask you, humbly, will you be my wife?'

The guards froze, pulling their dogs back and gaping foolishly.

Olivia heard several people in the hall let out an excited cheer and looked down at Hans.

'You mean it?'

'I truly do.' His eyes were warm and bright as they looked

up into hers. 'Again, not quite as I intended to do it, but I truly mean it. I truly want you as my wife, forever.'

'Then, yes. Yes, please!'

Hans leaped up, grabbing her in his arms and spinning her round and suddenly everyone was rushing outside, clapping and cheering, and the guards melted back against the wall as Ulbricht himself came striding towards them.

'It seems congratulations are in order.'

Herr Braun was hot on his tail.

'Olivia, Hans – how exciting! These are our golden couple, Walter, both very talented athletes and flag-bearers for our DDR youth.'

'Wunderbar!' Spitzbart pumped Hans' hand and gave Olivia a peck on both cheeks. 'We must tell the world this glorious news. I don't allow cameras into Wandlitz – security, you know, I am quite the wanted man.' He gave a high-pitched laugh. 'But we must arrange a press conference. Good athletes, you say?'

'Both gold medallists,' Herr Braun confirmed.

'Wunderbar, wunderbar. You are exactly the sort of people we need to promote the wonders of socialism. Come and sit with me and tell me all about your lovely romance. Where's your ring?'

'I didn't bring one, Walter,' Hans said hastily. 'I've been wanting to propose for some time and was overcome by the occasion. I saw this glorious model of socialist living and I suddenly thought how much I'd like Olivia and I to move together into somewhere like this and it, it overcame me.'

Spitzbart clapped delightedly.

'How perfect. Don't worry. I will get you a ring.'

'No, no, I—'

'I will get you a ring.' He snapped his fingers and a minion darted forward. By the time Spitzbart had drawn Olivia and

Hans to the top table, the servant was back with a box full of jewelled rings. 'Pick one.'

'I couldn't,' Olivia said, 'really, I—'

'Pick one!'

And so, with the president of the DDR watching her like a hawk, Olivia selected the smallest, least conspicuous of the jewels. Even so, as Hans was encouraged to take to one knee again to place it on her javelin-calloused finger, it felt sharp and heavy to the touch and she couldn't wait to escape. Tonight, the scales of socialism had fallen from her eyes and yet she was, it seemed, more tightly drawn into its coils than ever.

'The golden couple,' Spitzbart announced.

The other students, full of French wine and rich food, cheered merrily. Olivia tried to smile, but she saw Frau Scholz looking narrowly at them and shivered inside. Staying golden was, she was now certain, their only chance of survival behind the tall, dark, deceitful Berlin wall.

PART THREE

# THIRTY

*KIRSTEN*

Kirsten looked resolutely at her book as the U-Bahn rattled through Schwartzkopffstraβe, the first of the 'ghost-stations' that now haunted Line C. She tried to concentrate on *Faust* but even Goethe's legendary scriptwriting was failing to distract from the drama around her. It was crazy. Her previous closest station had been cut off by the wall so these days she had to go two blocks north to get onto the train at Reinickendorfer-straβe and then sit, trapped with her fellow passengers, while it passed through seven closed stations until they were in the West again at Kochstraβe and the doors were unlocked. There was some-thing unnerving about the deserted platforms and *Faust* had not, on reflection, been the best choice to bring, but she had to get it read before next week for school.

The train pushed on, shooting through Oranienburger Tor and Friedrichstraβe, once lively stations in the Mitte district and now so empty it left you wondering if the city was similarly dead above them. Seeing the communists sweep in on Berlin had made Kirsten realise, in stark black and white, how sordid and corrupt their regime truly was. She couldn't believe her new family were stuck behind the Iron Curtain.

A poor young man called Günter Litfin had been shot dead trying to swim the canal the other day and on their own Bernauerstraße, 77-year-old Frieda Shulze, who'd lived above Gretchen, had narrowly survived an obscene tug-of-war between guards in her home and students scaling the building to help her jump out. Western cameras had filmed the entire episode and played it over and over on their TV stations, as well as on the giant screen the American news channels had erected near the Brandenburg Gate, set high to show over the wall in an attempt to inform the Ossis of the horrors being perpetrated on them in the name of 'eternal peace'.

It was hard to tell if it was being understood and, anyway, the poor Ossis could do little about it. Apparently, gangs roamed the streets making sure everyone 'agreed' with Spitzbart, and the Stasi were upping their vigilance. You'd have thought, with the West sealed off, they'd be able to relax, but it seemed their paranoia had only grown. Kirsten prayed Olivia was safe, her unknown parents and brothers too, but what could she really do about it?

The train passed through Stadtmitte, the last of the ghost-stations, and a sigh ran down the train as if the passengers were letting out a mutually held breath. The wall was going up fast around the city and in some places the buildings behind it were being pulled down to create an open space to deter would-be-escapees. Everyone in Gretchen's block had been given an eviction notice and soldiers were bricking up each of the one thousand windows, turning what had once been homely openings into a harsh, blank wall.

'Thank God you got me out,' Tante Gretchen said to them all at least once a day.

It was cramped in the apartment now, especially for Kirsten who had to share her room with her aunt. Gretchen's rescued clothes crowded Kirsten's few home-made items out of the wardrobe, and her make-up and lotions clattered around on Kirsten's desk.

'You don't like schoolwork anyway,' she'd said blithely when Kirsten had objected. That was true, but in this, her final year, she was trying her best to overcome her distaste. She kept the university prospectus Dieter had brought her under her mattress and was working hard to see if, by any chance, she had what it took to get the grades needed. Living with Gretchen didn't help, but it was better than watching her aunt be bricked into East Berlin so she tried to make the best of it.

At Kochstraße, Kirsten gratefully shoved *Faust* into her bag and headed out into the end of a fine September day. The sun was setting earlier now autumn was creeping up on Berlin but it was still warm on her face and she looked gladly upwards, avoiding the view of the wall being constructed on the far side of Zimmerstraße. There was, however, no avoiding the white hut right outside the café. It was rapidly becoming known as Checkpoint Charlie as it was the third US checkpoint into the DDR – Alpha being on the Inner German Border at Marienborn, and Bravo on the way into West Berlin at Drewitz. It was small and rough, but the Americans had announced it would stay that way to emphasise its 'impermanence', though there was nothing impermanent about the big buildings going up on the eastern side.

'Evening, ma'am,' the guard said in his jaunty accent, tipping his hat at her with a white-toothed smile.

'Evening,' she replied tightly.

The individual soldiers were always very charming, but she couldn't forgive the Allies for not opposing the damned wall. Every morning she thought about how close she'd come to meeting her biological mother and wanted to scream in frustration at the pointless, vicious nastiness of it all. With a sigh, she pushed open the door on a heaving Café Adler. Their position right alongside Checkpoint Charlie drew an endless stream of customers eager to enjoy kaffee und kuchen with a view into the mysterious East, and Frau Munster was overjoyed with this month's profits. Someone, at least, was benefitting from the wall.

'Evening, Kirsty,' Sasha called through the steam of the coffee machine. 'Look sharp, I'm run off my feet.'

'Coming!'

Kirsten plunged into the fray, casting a hopeful eye around for Dieter. She'd seen him a few times since she'd left him at the Brandenburg Gate, but he'd been distant and distracted. He'd given up protesting after the American vice-president had come to visit Berlin, assuring everyone of his support, but doing nothing to demonstrate it bar handing out plastic pens. He'd also stopped working at the refugee centre as the barrier had halted the flood of Ossis to a mere trickle of brave fools and, with university not yet started, she had no idea what he was doing with his time. Not spending it with her, that was for sure, and she was trying to accept the fact that he'd moved on.

She noticed a couple of his friends holed up in a corner but he wasn't with them, and neither was Astrid. Supposing she should be grateful for small mercies, Kirsten turned on her best smile and went to serve the endless stream of customers. The Ossis just up Friedrichstraβe were installing concrete blocks at intervals along either side of the road to force vehicles to zigzag slowly through the checkpoint and everyone was keen to watch. Several people had rammed their vehicles past in the first few days but these giant obstacles would make that impossible and the café was alive with discussion of how far the paranoid idiots would go.

'I've heard they're planning a death strip,' someone announced. 'A whole open area with booby-traps and watchtowers.'

'Not watchtowers,' someone else shouted him down. 'This isn't a KZ.'

'Are you sure? They shot someone else the other day – a seventeen-year-old kid who pressed his girlfriend up against the wire in a schmusen and cut it behind her back. They both got through, bless them, but the poor lad took so many bullets in his legs that they reckon he'll be on crutches for the rest of his life. What a terrible price that is for simply wanting to live where and how you choose. Bastards!'

'Bastards!' others chorused obligingly and the man ordered 'schnapps all round' to celebrate being on the free side of the barrier from hell.

Kirsten's fears for Olivia and her unknown family grew and when the crowd drank themselves noisily out into the night, she retreated to the kitchen for a breather. She was filling a glass from the tap when she heard a sound at the back and, turning, gasped to see Astrid standing in the shadow of the industrial refrigerator.

'How on earth did you get in here?' she demanded.

'I was, er, going to the toilet.'

'Behind the fridge?'

'No! But I, er, thought I heard something.'

'In the kitchen?'

'Yes.'

'You thought you heard something in the kitchen of a busy café, Astrid?'

'Yes. Something odd.'

'*You're* something odd,' Kirsten shot at her.

It wasn't her most sophisticated insult but it felt good all the same, or it did until someone else stepped through the door from the yard to join Astrid and the air was sucked from Kirsten's lungs.

'Dieter?'

'Kirsten! What are you doing here?'

'I work here! A better question is what are *you* doing here? Both of you?' They looked guiltily at each other and it was enough. Kirsten set down her water glass – resisting the urge to throw its contents onto the wretched pair – and put her hands on her hips. 'Out of here, now, before I tell Frau Munster you're lurking in her kitchen.'

'We're not lurking, Kirsty,' Dieter said. 'We're—'

'I know what you're doing, thank you. Now – out!'

'Kirsty, please, let me explain. It's the wall, you see. It made me feel so impotent and so—'

'Dieter,' Astrid snapped. 'Hush.'

Kirsten clutched at the cooker rail as she remembered Dieter's ardent hands the first night they'd been together and his apologies when Astrid had told him she was still at school. Clearly Astrid was not as innocent as her. Well, fine, see if she cared.

'I'm delighted Astrid has been able to help you with your "impotence", Dieter,' she said icily, 'but I'd rather, in future, she did it somewhere more... hygienic. Good night.'

'Kirsten...'

'Good night, Dieter. Good night, Astrid.'

'Good night,' Astrid said, grabbing Dieter's hand to pull him out of the kitchen. 'Oh, and this is for you.'

She pressed a tiny square of paper into Kirsten's hand and Kirsten blinked at it, confused. It was folded several times and crunched up to look like litter, but there, in the middle in neat little letters was one word: 'Pippa'. Kirsten gasped and then, fighting tears, sank against the wall, picked up the paper and opened it. There wasn't room for many words but she scoured the few she had been granted all the same.

*My dearest Pippa,*

*I pray that this reaches you and that you are prepared to read the words of a mother who never stopped missing you, never stopped loving you and never truly stopped looking for you, at least in my heart. I was counting the days until your eighteenth birthday to try, again, to find you, and then you, my Pippa, my daughter, my precious heart – found us. It must truly be God's will but God seems as powerless in Berlin in these fearful times as he was in the KZs.*

*I am shut in again, Pippa, and the only thing propping me up is the knowledge that you are alive and well, all but a woman yourself. When I was your age, I was cast into a ghetto, then a death camp. I did not think I would survive. I did not think you would survive. But here we both are and I wish only to let you know that, though I failed as your mother in the most basic job of keeping you safe at my side, you have always been tight in my heart.*

*I curse those who are keeping us apart, but bless the woman who has brought you up with the care that I wish I could have lavished upon you myself. I have lived too much of my life in hope but here I am again – hoping that these walls of hate come down, and that I may, finally, hold you in my arms once more. Until that day, this must suffice as a paltry but heartfelt way of expressing my care.*

*With all love and blessings,*

*Your mutti*

Kirsten held the letter to her cheek, as if she might physically feel the love passing into her. A tear formed in her eye but she wiped it fiercely away. Wall or no wall, she could not let this brave woman lose her again. Forget Dieter and forget university too. From now on, she'd focus on what was important – getting to her biological mother. As soon as she could, she was queueing for a pass. No more gliding beneath the East like a ghost; it was time to face it head-on.

Her resolve carried her all the way to the pass office – a makeshift shed near Friedrichstraβe – after school the next day, and three hours down the queue. Out of sheer boredom, she fished the battered *Faust* out of her bag and finished it. She even enjoyed it, especially once she started picturing Mephistopheles with the goatee-face of Walter Ulbricht. Finally, she reached the front and showed her ID card at the hatch.

'Reason for visit?' the clerk asked.

'To see my family.'

'Name?'

'Kirsten Meyer.'

'*Their* name, fräulein.'

'Oh. Pasternak. My sister is Olivia Pasternak and she's at the Dynamo sports school. It's only up the road from my apartment and—'

The clerk put up a bored hand to silence her. She flicked through a giant file, then paused.

'Wait here please.'

She waved Kirsten to the side.

'Here?'

'Please.'

Kirsten had seen no one ahead of her instructed to wait and looked around puzzled.

'Why?'

'You can go if you'd rather.'

'No, I—'

'So, wait. Please.'

'Fine.'

Reluctantly Kirsten stepped aside and the clerk began serving the next person. And the next. And the next. Kirsten's stomach grumbled and she shuffled her feet, very aware of the curious glances being sent her way, until at last someone tapped her on the shoulder.

'If you'd like to come inside, fräulein.'

The officer indicated a door at the back of the hut. Kirsten thought, on balance, she would *not* like to come inside.

'Why?'

'I would just like to ask you a few questions. You are quite safe, I assure you. I will leave the door open if you wish.'

'What questions?'

'Inside, fräulein, please.' Nervously, Kirsten allowed herself to be ushered into the hut, shuffling her chair as close to the open door as possible. 'You say your sister is Olivia Pasternak?'

'That's right.'

'You do not have the same name?'

'No. I was adopted. So was she, actually.'

'By Ester and Filip Pasternak?'

'Er, yes. They're my parents, my biological parents. I only found that out recently and I was due to meet them when the wall went up.'

'I see.'

'And I would like to. Meet them, that is. So, I'd like a pass please.'

He gave his head a sad little shake.

'That won't be possible.'

'Why?'

'Olivia Pasternak is on my list.'

'Your list?'

'My list of possible subversives.'

'Olivia? Impossible! She's a proper Ossi.' The officer raised a thin eyebrow and Kirsten coughed. 'That is, a proper socialist.'

'I hope you are right. Time will tell. We have an eye on her.'

'An eye on her? What does that mean?'

The soldier looked at her impassively. Kirsten thought of the Stasi man who'd tried to bribe her, first with denims and then information about her mother. He'd claimed he could help her find Ester but now his comrades were doing everything they could to stop it.

'What about my mother? Ester? Is she on your list?'

'Not yet.'

'So let—'

'But if Westerners keep trying to get in touch with her, maybe we will have to consider it.'

Kirsten gasped.

'I'm not a random Westerner; I'm her daughter. I was snatched out of her arms in Auschwitz. Has she not suffered enough?'

For a brief second the man looked discomforted but then he hardened.

'She has, which is why she must be allowed to live a safe and decent life in the DDR without being pestered by Western-ers' petty personal concerns.'

'But—'

'Pass denied. Do not try again or it may mean trouble for your supposed family. Do you understand?'

Kirsten stood up and pushed her shoulders back.

'I hear what you're telling me, sir, but I do not – and will never – understand. Good day.'

She stumbled out and past the fascinated people waiting for the pass she'd just been denied. If she'd been scared of the East before, she was even more scared now, especially for her family. But then she felt for the precious letter in her bag and set her jaw. Ester and Filip had given up so much for her; now it was her turn to work for them. Olivia must be back in Berlin for the new school year and Kirsten was more determined than ever to find a way through to her.

# THIRTY-ONE

## WEDNESDAY, 20 SEPTEMBER

*OLIVIA*

Olivia looked out of the window of her new room, straining to see the Brandenburg Gate, several miles off in the distance. She wrapped her arms around herself, suddenly cold, and longed for Hans to arrive and hold her safe in this strange new world. She'd returned to Berlin, looking forward to their cosy athletes-only set-up at the city track, and instead found herself here, in Dynamo proper. The builders must have been driven very hard to complete the new asphalt track and the athletes' hostel in time, and all just to get the students away from the dark line of the wall and the temptations of the West. It made her sad.

Arriving in the Ostbahnhof in central Berlin yesterday, she'd stepped out into a city cut in jagged half. Everywhere, the barbed wire was being replaced with concrete blocks and already, it seemed, people had got used to it. Plenty of those chatting in the shops and bars had sounded happy to be living without arrogant Wessis intruding and Olivia understood that. But it didn't mean she liked it.

If it hadn't been for that damned wall, she'd still be in a

hostel around the corner from her newly found sister. They'd have been able to meet up for coffee. She could perhaps have eaten at Lotti's apartment, Kirsten might have come to watch her compete, or they could simply have sat in the marketplace filling each other in on their lives. Instead, they might as well have been in America and Russia, so divided was life on the fraught frontier of the big powers' Cold War.

Then there was her mother.

'It's not your fault,' Ester had said to her, time and again in her month at home, but her smiles had been fiercely forced and there had been no bedtime stories. Her time in *that place* had clearly become too raw once more to even parcel out in tiny segments, and Olivia had hated to see it.

Her parents had roused themselves to celebrate her eighteenth birthday with a lovely meal and the most beautiful, blue cashmere sweater that must have taken all their clothing allowances to buy. Olivia had been very touched, but the celebrations had been shadowed by the nagging thought that her eighteenth birthday was the day on which her mother had intended to tell her about Pippa. Today they would have been at the start of the hunt and, with the border finally closed, it would have been unlikely to get anywhere. That might have been for the best.

Olivia groaned and threw herself onto her bed to stretch out her muscles, aching pleasantly from that morning's training session. She'd found herself itching for exercise at home and, wonderful as it had been to be with her dear family, she'd had to force herself to sit still and play Meccano with her brothers or chat around the table. It was good to be back, even though she knew she'd be aching tomorrow.

'Knock, knock – is there a fiancée in there?'

She leaped up, all pain forgotten.

'Hans!' Throwing open the door, she fell into his already open arms. 'I'm so glad you're here.'

'The train was held up for ages in Wittenburg. It was so frustrating.' He took her face in both hands and kissed her tenderly. 'It's been a long month without you, beautiful.' To her embarrassment, Olivia found tears welling up in her eyes and tried to bury herself in his chest to hide them but he simply kissed them away. 'Are you all right?'

'Just happy to see you.'

'And I you.'

Hans pushed her gently back into her room and kissed her again, longer and harder. Olivia let her body curve into his, loving the feel of him. Now she felt safe. Now she felt warm and loved and sure of her place in even upside-down Berlin.

'I've got something for you, Liv,' Hans said when they finally pulled apart. She raised a cheeky eyebrow and he laughed. 'Not that! Well, yes, that, but first...' He drew a small box out of his pocket. 'Last time I asked you to marry me it was... fraught. May I?'

He reached out to ease Ulbricht's ring off her finger and she nodded gladly. She'd been wearing it out of love for Hans and pride in her engagement, but it reminded her every day of that dark night in Wandlitz when she'd seen their leaders' hypocrisy laid bare before her and she was glad to remove it.

'Good,' Hans said. 'I warn you, this one won't be as expensive, but it will be... honest.' She nodded him on, tears threatening again. 'So, Olivia, I want you to marry me, not because the state threatens us – though, Lord knows, I want to do everything in my power to protect you – but because I think you are the most wonderful girl I've ever met, because you've made my life feel complete, and because I want us to be together for always.'

He opened the lid and she saw a beautifully simple gold band, studded with small aquamarines.

'Oh Hans, it's beautiful.'

'It reminds me of your lovely, sparkly eyes.'

Blushing, she held out her finger and he slid the ring carefully on then moved to kiss her. She stopped him.

'You should know that I want to marry you too, Hans, so much. You're strong, you're brave, you're fun. You dare to ask questions and you dare to push for all that is good and true and I cannot think of a better man to spend the rest of my life with.'

She turned to her bedside drawer and drew out a small box of her own. Many men had started wearing rings in the war, symbols of their loved ones to cling to on faraway battlefields, and it was a tradition being encouraged in the DDR. Not everyone was keen, though, and she prayed Hans liked it. His eyes widened and, heart thudding, she opened the box to reveal a simple band, carved with foliage.

'They're oak leaves,' she said. 'Strong and vibrant – just like you.'

He stared down at it and she thought perhaps she'd misjudged him and felt slightly sick but then he looked up, eyes shining.

'I love it. I never thought... Isn't it amazing, that I get to wear a symbol of your love too?'

He did like it!

'Not everything in the DDR is corrupt and equality seems a good ideal to me. May I...?'

She slid it on and kissed him and then he was pulling her to him, clasping at her as if his hands wanted to touch every last bit, and she drew him down onto the bed and lost herself in him – her friend, her love, her soon-to-be husband.

'When shall we marry?' she asked him afterwards.

'Tomorrow?'

'Hans!'

'I would if I could.'

'Me too, but I think our parents might have something to say about that, don't you?'

He smiled ruefully.

'My mother would kill me! I can't wait for them to meet you, Liv. They're coming to the inaugural competition. Are yours?'

'I hope so. I've written to tell them about it and I'm sure they'll come if they can.'

'Perhaps we can all have dinner? Make plans. Do you think we could marry at Christmas?'

'Definitely,' Olivia agreed, warmth stealing through her again. 'Then I'll be Olivia Keller.'

It was a strange thought. She would have a new name, a new family. Bonds didn't, after all, need to be carved out of blood and there could, surely, be no such thing as too many people to love?

'Do you think we'll be allowed a shared room once we're married?' Hans asked.

'I sincerely hope so. I want to sleep in your arms every single night for the rest of my life.' He kissed her and stroked his fingers down her spine, but then paused, his hand halfway down. 'Is something wrong?' she asked.

'No,' he said, but too hastily.

Olivia sat up. 'There is. What's wrong?'

'Nothing's wrong, Liv. It's just... Well, you have hair on your back.'

'What?'

She twisted, trying to see, but of course it was impossible. She'd spent ages this morning with the tweezers being sure that nothing marred her chest before she saw Hans again but now this. She pulled the sheet up, ashamed, but Hans eased it gently away again.

'It's only a little. And it's very soft.'

'That's not the point,' she said, tears stinging.

'Then what is? Talk to me, Liv, this is important.'

She didn't want to but this was Hans – he knew every bit of her and loved her all the same.

'It's not just the hair. It's the missing periods. It feels wrong, somehow, as if my eggs are being, I don't know... stifled. I think you might be right about the vitamins, Hans.' She took a deep breath and spoke her worst fear to him on a whisper. 'What if they stop me having babies?'

He drew in a shocked breath.

'That would be bad. That's to say, I'd cope if we couldn't, I'd still want to be with you, always, but, well, children would be nice, right?'

'Right,' Olivia agreed. 'I want to have babies with you, Hans. Not yet, definitely, but one day. I want us to be a family.'

He kissed her.

'Me too. Do you think, perhaps, you should stop taking the vitamins, just for a bit, just to see?'

She bit her lip.

'What if I can't throw?'

He thought about it.

'You could throw before you took them.'

'Not as far.'

'That might be technique. How do we know? It's worth a try, isn't it, just to see? You can always start them again. Tell you what, I'll stop too.'

She gave a small smile.

'You don't have periods, Hans.'

He nudged at her.

'True. But, even so, I think they make me aggressive and I don't like it. How about a pact, Liv – we both stop taking them for the next two weeks and see what happens?'

Olivia swallowed. If the club found out, they'd be furious. It was probably subversive and they were under enough suspicion already. On the other hand, if those tiny blue pills were damaging her womb, she wanted nothing to do with them. A javelin was just a javelin; it was her life with Hans that truly mattered.

'Yes,' she said.

Already she felt lighter, but then a bang at the door made her jump out of her skin.

'Olivia?!'

Olivia looked to Hans in horror. Frau Scholz had, sadly, made the transition to the new hostel and was proving as intrusive as ever.

'Yes, Frau Scholz?' she called sweetly.

'There's a journalist here to see you.'

'A journalist?'

'She's been sent by Herr Ulbricht, so I suggest you don't keep her waiting.'

'Er no, of course not. I'll be right there.'

'Excellent. They want Hans too. Any idea where he is?'

Olivia looked at Hans, naked next to her, and suppressed a giggle.

'I'm sure I can track him down.'

'Good. In the conference room in ten minutes please.'

Then she was gone, tapping off down the corridor leaving them laughing together, though not for long.

'Why does a journalist want us?'

'Only one way to find out. Oh, and Liv.' Hans touched a finger to her ring. 'Dearly as I love seeing you wearing this, I think you'd better swap it back. If Spitzbart has sent this journo, it might be politic to wear his ring, not mine.'

Olivia's heart ached at the thought but Hans was right and sadly she pulled her beautiful new engagement ring off her finger and slid Ulbricht's back on. It was a nice ring, she reminded herself, and it had been kind of the president to give them it, but she couldn't help wondering where all the jewels in that box had come from and what sort of socialist thought it right to keep them.

Jumping in the shower to cleanse off the effects of her varied exercise, she pulled on her Dynamo tracksuit and together Olivia and Hans headed to the conference room. Both the Scholzes and Herr Braun were hovering around a middle-aged woman in a smart suit. With her was a cameraman who, to Olivia's horror, was setting up an elaborate screen and set of lights. She touched a hand self-consciously to her damp hair, pulled back into a stern ponytail. What on earth was going on?

'Ah, Olivia! Hans! The golden couple! Come in, come in.' The woman ushered them obsequiously into chairs. 'I'm here to interview you for *Neues Deutschland*. We're doing a feature on the new track and the upcoming competition and we'd love to include something about your engagement. You *are* engaged?'

'We are,' Hans agreed. 'And our love is sealed with a ring provided, so very kindly, by Herr Ulbricht himself.'

He put an arm around Olivia, who dutifully held out the finger that, only moments ago, had borne her true engagement ring. Life in the glare of the DDR, she was learning, was a web of lies and you had to make sure that yours were the strongest to survive. She glanced nervously to Frau Scholz, wondering how long she'd been outside her door, but the hausmeisterin looked blandly back and the interview began.

They were asked all sorts of questions about how they'd got into athletics and their aspirations for the future and they both spouted all the right things about wanting to bring honour to the DDR. Herr Braun and Herr Scholz soon slid away and Frau Scholz took a seat in the corner and, to Olivia's surprise, pulled some wool out of her pocket and began crocheting. The sweet domestic activity was so at odds with her stern hausmeisterin that she almost laughed, but then the door opened and Klaus came in, killing any amusement dead.

The questions were over and it was time to have their photo taken.

'Can I not put on some make-up?' Olivia asked.

'You do look pale,' the cameraman agreed, but the journalist waved this away.

'You're perfect as you are, fresh and clean-living.'

'Not as clean as all that,' Hans whispered in her ear, bringing a welcome blush to her cheeks. Still, though, it was hard to avoid Klaus leaning against the wall, arms folded and dark eyes following her every move, and she had to be urged, several times, to smile.

'Look like you're in love!' the cameraman ordered and Hans chuckled and tickled her, making her fold helplessly against him as the camera clicked away. 'Marvellous,' the journalist finally concluded. 'You're free to go, thank you.'

Olivia made gratefully for the door but Klaus stepped in front of her.

'Not yet, you're not. This way, Olivia.'

He ushered her outside. Hans tried to follow but Klaus put up a hand with a stern, 'not you', and he was forced to stop at the door, watching nervously as the Stasi man guided Olivia onto the open space of the Dynamo car park.

'It will be a touching article, I'm sure,' he said. 'You make a lovely couple – a golden couple.'

'Thank you,' she said stiffly.

He leaned in.

'It's very clever, Olivia, but it won't work. Gold soon scratches off in the DDR.'

She sighed. Would this man never go away?

'I'm not here to make trouble, Klaus. I'm here to train and to compete. That's all.'

'I'm not so sure. Your sister, Kirsten...'

'What about her?'

'She's been trying to get a pass into the East.'

'She has?'

Olivia's heart pounded; this was wonderful news.

'It was refused, of course.'

'Why?' she wailed. 'Why would you stop her?'

'I told you – gold soon scratches off. We want you to prove

your loyalty to the DDR, Olivia, and meeting up with Westerners is hardly the best way to do that, is it?'

Olivia stamped at the ground, furious now.

'I *am* loyal, Klaus. I just want to see my sister. And I want my mother to see her. Is that so hard to understand?'

Klaus frowned.

'You're over-emotional, Olivia. That won't do. Come, your mother has done without this girl for nearly eighteen years, so what's a few months more?'

'What's a...?' Olivia shook her head. 'You really don't get it, do you, Klaus? The bond between mother and child cannot simply be severed with a few blocks of concrete.'

Klaus' eyes narrowed.

'You are protesting against the wall?'

His voice rasped like a file across a knife and Olivia glanced to Hans, hovering nearby, and forced herself to stay calm. She lifted her hand, flashing Ulbricht's ring.

'I'm *not* protesting against the wall. I'm *not* protesting against anything in the country I love and am working hard to be allowed to represent.'

Klaus gave a grudging nod.

'I'm glad to hear it. Keep up the good work, Olivia, but remember, I'm watching you.'

He spun on his shiny heel and strode off across the car park. Olivia watched him go, thinking of that other Stasi officer taking away Claudia's baby, of her mother's baby, stuck behind a wall, and of the babies she might herself one day have and the world she wanted them to grow up in. It did not, she was sure, look like this one and she turned wearily back into Dynamo.

Spitzbart's tame journalist came past, waving a cheery goodbye, and Olivia clutched at Hans' hand. They were the 'golden couple' and they had to stay that way, not for pride, honour or triumph, but for their own most basic safety.

# THIRTY-TWO

## FRIDAY, 29 SEPTEMBER

*KIRSTEN*

Kirsten mopped the floor behind the bar with studied concentration, using every fierce sweep to try to think up a way into the East. It was doing the tiles the world of good, but not getting her very far. She couldn't get in to see her family without a pass and she couldn't get a pass because of her family; it was an endlessly frustrating loop. She shouldn't even be here. She had no lessons on Fridays this year and had been planning to catch up on homework, but Frau Munster had begged her to cover for a poorly Sasha and, seeing as it was impossible to concentrate on Faust's metaphysical quest, she'd agreed. What did the works of a dead playwright matter when there was urgent live drama here in Berlin?

She paused, looking out the window to the new viewing platform on Zimmerstraße. The curious could climb up the small structure made of scaffolding poles and wooden planks, and look down into the East. At first it had been West Berliners, but recently tourists had started arriving from all over Europe and even America, keen to see the wall and even keener to look into the mysterious land behind it. They'd be disappointed. The ground on the far side was a rubble-field and, although you could look at the growing DDR border controls, the officials were shielded with fences and all you'd see were a few shadows. Perhaps it was more exciting that way.

Kirsten watched the tourists pointing and snapping pictures of the crazy wall and felt bitter. They could pack up their suitcases and go home to tell everyone about the curious island city behind the Iron Curtain; for West Berliners, this was life.

It was still better than being in the East though.

'Another coffee please, Kirsten.'

Kirsten put her mop aside and rushed to serve the glossy girl in the window seat. Dieter had come into the café the day after she'd caught him in the kitchen, but she'd refused to speak to him and eventually he'd left. He hadn't been back, but Astrid seemed quite happy to still order her black coffees from Kirsten and, although she couldn't quite bring herself to say thank you for delivering her mother's letter, she was grudgingly offering her best service instead.

Coffee delivered with a forced smile, Kirsten set to tidying the counter, tutting at the crumpled newspapers all over it. Trying to untangle several pages of *Neues Deutschland*, she laughed at a picture of Spitzbart spouting quatsch from some podium and looking exactly like her imagined picture of Mephistopheles. It was actually quite a good play, *Faust*, when you got into it and her thoughts were turning to her essay when she picked up the next page and stopped dead.

Olivia!

Her sister was in the paper again, looking rather austere in a stark ponytail, but laughing up at Hans in an open way that left no doubt about how happy they were together.

'GOLDEN COUPLE!' the headline shouted. All *Neues Deutschland* headlines shouted, but this was different from the usual political crap. This was a feature on Olivia and Hans and how they'd got into athletics. Kirsten read it, fascinated. She'd only had about an hour with her newly discovered sister and they'd been so busy talking about Ester, Filip and the boys that she'd had little chance to quiz her about her own life. It seemed she'd only taken up the javelin five months ago and was already the best junior in East Germany. Much was made of her strength and the quality of her training at Dynamo and she was touted as a medal chance at the Tokyo Olympics in three years' time.

Kirsten felt a surge of pride, followed by a rush of shame. Olivia was working towards the Olympics and what was she doing? Putting off writing an essay on Goethe that might, or more likely might not, get her enough marks to apply to university to sew pretty dresses. Perhaps it was better if her biological parents didn't meet their Pippa; she'd only be a disappointment.

'Oh, get over yourself, Kirsty,' she scolded under her breath. 'Self-pity is very unattractive.'

It was something she'd heard Gretchen say a few times recently, mainly to herself as she edged around their cramped apartment trying to pretend she wasn't pining for her old, luxurious space. She had, at least, been on her date with the zookeeper and had come back pink and amusingly giggly, which Kirsten and Lotti had taken as a good sign. Life went on and Kirsten had to put her head down and work and hope her future became clear in time.

She read more of the article and got to the astonishing fact that Olivia was engaged. God, there was no stopping the girl. She'd bagged that handsome Hans, while Kirsten had caught Dieter getting it on with someone else. She needed a bit of what the paper called Olivia's 'fire and dynamism'. Maybe she should get herself a spear and see if that helped!

*You can see Olivia and Hans in action at the brand-new Dynamo athletics track in Hohenschönhausen on Wednesday, 4 October*, the article announced. Kirsten's heart stopped. Could she? Of course not. The wretched Stasi were blocking her pass. Maybe she should have helped the fox-man after all. She read the final lines: *Their parents will be proudly watching on as this golden couple show us what the DDR has to look forward to. Tickets just two Ostmarks on the door. All welcome.*

'Ha!' Kirsten spat and flung the paper down in disgust.

Her sister was going to be throwing the javelin nearby and her parents were going to be right there and there was no way she could get to them.

'Something wrong?'

Kirsten looked up to see Astrid standing at the counter looking curiously at her.

'Yes,' she spat. 'My family are all going to be at this athletics event next weekend but it's the other side of the verdammte wall so I can't get there.'

'Get a pass. I know it's a long queue but if it matters that much to—'

'I can't!' Kirsten snapped. 'I've stood in their dummkopf queue but they won't let me. They don't like me trying to connect with my family – think I'll corrupt them with my decadent Western ways or some such crap.' She grabbed at Astrid's arm, furious now. 'I was born in Auschwitz, Astrid. I was snatched away from my mother after four days. Four days! Have we not been through enough? Is it not fair to want to see each other?' Astrid gave a little cough and Kirsten shook herself and let go of her arm. 'Sorry.'

'Don't be.'

'Sorry?'

'Don't be sorry.' Astrid smiled; it was most disconcerting. 'It must be horrible for you.'

Why was she being so nice? Was she feeling guilty about Dieter? Well, good.

'It is,' Kirsten agreed. 'It's horrible and frustrating and so damned stupid!'

'I agree.'

'You do?'

'Of course. All reasonable people would. This wall is an abomination. Our lives are being ruled by corrupt communists on one side and lazy-arsed Allies on the other.'

Kirsten blinked. A tiny, childish part of her thought, *Astrid said arse!* But she told it to shut up.

'That letter you brought – er, thanks by the way – was from my mother saying how dearly she would like to see me, and this weekend she's going to be less than an hour's walk away but I can't get to her. If only there was a way to get a pass.'

Astrid leaned in.

'There might be. That's to say, there *is*.'

Kirsten stared at her, confused. 'My name's on a list, Astrid.'

'Yes, but mine isn't. And I have a permanent pass because I'm doing a research project with a group at Humboldt University in the East. I got your letter from them, by the way, they're doing a good run in secret post across the border.'

Kirsten was still confused.

'Why would you want to go to the competition, Astrid? Do you like athletics?'

Astrid laughed, a merry tinkle, as pretty as every other thing about her.

'No, silly! You can take my pass.'

Kirsten gaped.

'I can?'

'I'd say so. The photo is tiny and we look fairly alike.'

This was blowing Kirsten's mind. She looked nothing like glossy Astrid and, besides...

'Why?' she asked. 'I mean, why would you do that?'

Astrid gave her a sad smile.

'Because you're suffering a huge injustice. Because I hate what's being done to this city. Because I can't bear the thought of your poor mother being deprived of meeting her baby after losing her in such terrible circumstances. I'm not as nasty as you think, Kirsten.'

'No. I...' Kirsten fought to process this. 'Are you sure?' was all she could manage.

Astrid nodded.

'I'm sure. Next Saturday, yes?' Kirsten nodded. 'Then I'd better teach you a few basics of physics so you can dazzle them into silence if they ask awkward questions at the border.' She looked around. 'It's pretty quiet, so how about now?'

'Physics? Now? Why not!'

Kirsten accepted the piece of paper that Astrid tore from her notebook and picked up a pen. She'd been jealous of this young woman for so long and now she was going to *be* her, to walk into the East as her. She swallowed the lump of fear rising in her throat and fought to concentrate as Astrid started feeding her soundbites about Newton's law of motion. She might not have fire and dynamism like Olivia, but she could rustle up spark and determination. Her mother and father were going to be at Dynamo next weekend and, God help her, so was Kirsten.

# THIRTY-THREE

## WEDNESDAY, 4 OCTOBER

*OLIVIA*

Olivia paced the bottom of the runway, her javelin over her shoulders as she tried to stretch the myriad nervous knots out of them. Glancing across to the fence, she saw her parents leaning on it, watching her intently. There was a fancy stand along the 100 metre straight, but the best place to watch the javelin was immediately behind the runway and they'd found that instinctively, keen to be close to her. They smiled and waved and she felt their love seep into her aching muscles and reminded herself that this was only sport, the same as all the tennis matches they'd come to watch her play over the years.

Only it wasn't the same.

The stakes were so much higher under the spotlight of a regime that was prepared to wall in its citizens with no warning. She'd stuck to her plan of flushing her vitamins down the toilet every morning and could swear the hairs had already stopped growing but there was no doubt she was feeling weaker. She was having to push herself extra hard so that Trainer Lang didn't notice and was so tired every night that she'd taken to going to bed not long after dinner.

Hans often went with her and the others assumed they were having wild sex, but he was tired too and they usually just lay in each other's arms making plans for their future until they fell asleep. Frau Scholz invariably checked on her at lights-out and turfed Hans back into his room but often even that didn't rouse her enough to offer him more than a brief peck goodnight before she was asleep again. What would this mean in terms of the distance she could throw today?

She was called up for her first attempt and battled to block out everything but the runway, the javelin, and the blue skies into which she would launch it. She glanced to her parents again, just in time to see someone step up at their side. Klaus was all obsequiousness and her parents shook his hand with innocent enthusiasm.

'Fräulein Pasternak, you must take your turn,' the official nagged.

Olivia shook herself and turned back, but she was flustered and messed up her crossovers so that she hit the white line too soon and had to chop her run-up. The javelin came out of her hand sideways and wobbled its way pathetically to around the 30 metre mark. Olivia kicked at the fancy asphalt in annoyance. All the strength in the world wouldn't help if she didn't get her run-up right.

'Well done!' Ester called and Olivia's heart ached for her mother's simple pleasure in her.

She jogged over.

'That was rubbish, Mutti. I messed up my steps.'

'It looked good to me,' Ester said stoutly. 'Went miles up in the air.'

'Thank you, but it wasn't good enough.'

Filip patted her arm.

'I'm sure you'll get it right next time,' he said calmly.

Olivia nodded.

'I will, Vati.' She glanced sideways at Klaus. 'I definitely will.'

By the end of the first round, Olivia was in third place. Good but hardly golden. Trainer Lang was shouting instructions at her and she was very glad when Hans came jogging over. His discus wasn't until the next day but Herr Braun had roped him into helping with registrations.

'Sorry,' he panted. 'Only just got free. How's it going?'

'Badly.'

She glanced to Klaus and Hans understood immediately.

'You need to block out everything else, gorgeous. It's just you and the jav, yes?'

Olivia nodded. She strode over, took her javelin out of the holder and did a few practice thrusts. Her muscles protested and she had a sudden picture of fourteen blue pills in the bottom of a toilet. The girl before her launched her javelin and it went flying out to 40 metres. The crowd around the fence clapped and Olivia felt her heart thudding hard against her Dynamo vest. She heard the official call her name and the stadium announcer tell everyone to watch as the golden girl was about to throw. Her vision blurred and she stepped up to the runway in a daze.

'It's all for the state,' she heard Klaus say in his thin voice to her parents. 'We ask them to do it all for the state.'

That had been true when she'd first arrived, but in the last few months the state's demands had become tangled too tightly with her own.

'Just you and the jav,' she told herself sternly and, throwing herself into her run-up, thrust the spear into the air with all her might.

The gasp of the crowd told her it was a good throw and she opened her eyes to see it sailing well past the 40 metre mark – and landing just outside the sector. The official put up a red flag and his colleague yanked the javelin out of the ground unmeasured.

'What's going on?' Ester asked. 'Why aren't they telling us how far it is?'

'It was a foul, Mutti,' Olivia said heavily.

'Olivia!' Trainer Lang was steaming. 'What was that? You flung it like a cavewoman. Where's your finesse?'

Olivia hung her head.

'I was trying too hard, Trainer.'

'Or not trying enough. This is a three-throw comp, girl. You've only got one more to get it right.'

'I know!'

Olivia felt tears itching at the back of her eyes and retreated to the other competitors.

'That was amazing,' the girl in the lead said to her.

'It was out,' Olivia said dully.

'Well, yeah, but it went miles. You'll nail it next time.'

Olivia smiled at her.

'You're very kind.'

The girl spread her hands.

'It's tough this stuff, right? We make it look easy to that lot but we know the truth. I'm Suzanne Bauer, from Hanover.'

She stuck out a hand and Olivia shook it.

'Olivia Pasternak. Dynamo.'

'Home crowd then – that can be tough too.'

Olivia glanced to her parents, Klaus still ominously along-side them.

'It feels it today,' she admitted. 'Hanover's in the West, right?'

'That's right. Long trip here but Dynamo paid our expenses so, why not?!'

'I think one of our sprinters joined you in the summer – Lisel?'

Suzanne nodded.

'I know her. She's good. She couldn't come today though – for obvious reasons.'

Olivia nodded, scuffed at a stray lump in the new asphalt.

'Do you like it at Hanover?'

'It's great,' Suzanne said instantly. 'My coach is Almut Brömmel. She went to the Olympics last year. Threw over 55 metres. She's dead strict but lovely.'

Olivia looked at Trainer Lang, brooding as he waited for her to take her final turn. Suzanne got up to throw and Olivia wished her luck, then watched as she improved her distance out to 42 metres. She could beat that, if she got it right, but her heart was thudding, her vision was fuzzy around the edges, and all she wanted to do was run out of there and beg Ester and Filip to take her back to the safety of Stalinstadt where the needs of the state did not press on her too-broad shoulders all the time.

'Olivia Pasternak,' the official called.

Ester blew her a kiss and Olivia tried to smile. Her parents were here to watch. That, surely, was the most important thing about today. Not being a 'golden girl', not filling articles for Spitzbart and his Wandlitz cronies, not even doing it for Dynamo. The irony, though, was that her parents wouldn't care whether she won or not, only if she was happy doing it. And right now, she wasn't.

Taking her javelin from the holder, she walked to her marker on the runway, feeling dread clutching at her heart. One more throw. She saw Klaus lick his lips and it was hard not to feel like prey beneath his claws.

'You can do it, Liv,' Hans called.

She looked at him, drinking in his care, his belief. And then someone stepped up at his side. Olivia stared.

Kirsten.

She'd only met her sister once, but she'd recognise her anywhere and, seeing her near her mother, it was clear that this was the girl who'd been snatched from Ester as a newborn. They had the same slight wave in their straw-blonde hair, the same slim nose, even the same way of leaning on the fence.

'Go, Olivia!' Kirsten shouted.

Olivia saw Ester turn and smile at the girl standing in the shadow of Hans' big body. She didn't know who she was, but she would. As soon as Olivia got out of here, she could introduce them. They could meet. Her heart soared. Kirsten had got here. Somehow, she'd fought her way past Klaus and his blockades and got to her side. If she could be brave, Olivia could too.

'Let's go,' she said to her javelin, lifting it high.

She looked down the runway, seeing not Dynamo's fancy scarlet asphalt but the scruffy school sports field where Eric Ahrendt had first put a javelin into her hand and she'd felt its magical power.

'Throw it through the point, Olivia,' he'd told her.

It wasn't about power, not really. It wasn't about extra muscle, or bigger lungs, but about technique. She stared at the silver tip glinting in the autumn sun, flexed her arm in readiness, and ran. She knew as soon as the javelin left her hand that it was sweet. She heard Lang bark, 'yes', heard the crowd roar and Hans shout out in joy, and she stood there watching the javelin soar way past the 40 metre mark and land, point first, into the middle of the 50 metre one. She gasped.

'It's a whopper of a throw from Dynamo's golden girl,' the announcer cried. 'Surely no one can beat that!'

'No one can,' Suzanne Bauer said, coming over to shake her hand. 'Nice throw, Olivia. Told you you'd nail it.' Olivia gave her a hug and Suzanne held her tight. 'If you ever decide you want to, you know, change club, we'd love to have you at Hanover,' she whispered. 'I could do with a training partner who's not a sweaty boy.' Olivia stared at her. 'Think about it,' Suzanne said and then she was pulling her off the runway to let the last couple of girls have their throws, a mere formality as it was already clear that Olivia had won.

'That was wonderful, kindchen!' Ester said when Olivia jogged over to them.

'Wonderful,' Filip agreed. 'You looked like an Amazon throwing that spear.'

'Thank you, Vati,' Olivia said, kissing his cheek as Klaus, robbed of his prey, stormed off.

Right now, though, she didn't care about javelins, or medals; right now there was something far, far more important to focus on. Jumping lightly over the fence, she reached for Ester's hands.

'Mutti. There's someone here I really think you should meet.'

# THIRTY-FOUR

*KIRSTEN*

'In here. It's a bit small but it's private.'

Kirsten followed Olivia, Ester and Filip into a neat cubicle of a bedroom and they stood there, staring at each other like creatures in Berlin Zoo.

'Pippa?' Ester put out shaking hands. 'Pippa, is it really you?' She touched a fingertip gently to Kirsten's cheek, her eyes shining. 'You're a miracle.'

Kirsten smiled.

'Not really. I'm just me. That is...'

She wasn't entirely sure who 'me' was any more, but she drew the photo of her tattoo from her bag and held it out to Ester. Her birth mother peered at it, then quietly pulled up her sleeve to reveal, etched roughly into her arm, the same number: 41400.

'It *is* you. Oh, my dear, my child – we searched for you for so long. We didn't give up, I promise, not until we thought it would be kinder to do so. We hated that decision every day, truly we did, but now, here you are. Here you *are!*' She moved to hug Kirsten and then held herself back. 'I'm sorry. This must be very strange for you. You've got your own life, your own identity. I can't rush in and, and...'

Kirsten's heart swelled. Ester, her mother, was so slight and sweet, and her eyes were shining with such joy. She couldn't quite believe she was truly the cause of it, but there was no doubting the number that matched her own and emotion bubbled within her. There was guilt, yes, for Lotti who had brought her up with such love, but also a fizzing joy at finding this missing part of her life story. She had grown inside this woman, been brought into the world by the efforts of her Nazi-tortured body, then been torn from her by indescribable cruelty. Yet, here they were, defying all the horror at last. Stepping shyly forward, she held out her arms and Ester fell into them.

'Oh my girl, my child.' She pulled back and looked her up and down. 'You're so beautiful.'

'Hardly,' Kirsten protested but Ester was turning to her husband.

'Isn't she beautiful, Filip?'

'Beautiful,' he agreed, stepping forward. 'I've never met you before, for which I apologise.'

'It's hardly your fault,' Kirsten assured him.

'Perhaps not, but fathers are meant to protect their daughters, fight for them.'

Kirsten patted his arm awkwardly.

'Some things are too big to fight. And it doesn't matter – we're here now.'

He smiled, his slim face lighting up.

'We *are* here now. And you *are* wonderful.'

Kirsten thought she might cry.

'I'm really not,' she said. 'I'm just, you know, ordinary.'

Filip spread out his hands.

'As are we – wonderfully ordinary. Well, perhaps not Olivia; she's golden.'

'Don't,' Olivia snapped, making them all jump. 'I'm sorry. I... I don't like all that, the press and everything. I might want to win gold medals but I don't want to be "golden".'

Ester looked at her in concern.

'Are you all right, kindchen?'

'Fine,' Olivia said quickly – too quickly, Kirsten thought. 'I'm very happy. I have Hans and, as you saw, the throwing is going well.'

'You seemed tense,' Filip said.

Olivia gave a shallow laugh.

'It was a competition, Vati – they're tense things.'

'You were never tense playing tennis.'

'Yes, well, it's, you know, a bigger deal here. Dynamo take it all very seriously. They're putting a lot of money into us.'

'That doesn't mean they own you.'

Kirsten thought Olivia was going to cry, but then she gathered herself.

'I know that, Vati, but thank you. It'll be fine, really. It's just been an emotional day. Please – we're not here for me now.'

'We're *always* here for you,' Ester told her firmly. 'But you're right, today we need to find out more about Pippa. That is, about...' She stumbled, then recovered herself. 'You're Kirsten now, is that right? It's a nice name.'

Kirsten heard the strain in Ester's voice and thought how hard this must be for her. Unbidden, a memory of Jan came into her head, pressing her face against the white wall and telling her he was expected to believe it was black now. His issue had been with Nazi ideology, which was hardly the same as this poor woman trying to accept that her daughter had a whole identity without her, but there was a parallel. Life was not as it should have been.

'I can be Pippa too,' she offered.

Filip leaned in.

'A name is just a name. What counts is that you're alive.

Alive and well.' He shook his head. 'You look so like your mother.'

Kirsten looked to the wall where a small, square mirror reflected her and Ester. It was true. Meeting this woman was like looking at a picture of herself some years down the line and she felt some of the pieces of her life, so scattered recently, settling into their new places.

'Tell us about yourself,' Ester urged. 'What do you do with your time? What do you enjoy? What makes you smile?'

Kirsten sat awkwardly on the bed, one new-found parent on either side while Olivia sat on her desk-chair opposite. She looked around them all, overwhelmed with the impossible task of filling in nearly eighteen missing years for these kind, generous people.

'I, er, I live in Berlin with Lotti, my mother. That is, my, er, adopted mother, and Uli my brother. Or, rather, the boy I thought was my brother...'

She ran out of words. This was impossible. But then Filip took her hand.

'Olivia says you like to sew, Kirsten.'

'I do,' she agreed, snatching gratefully at the subject.

'Did you make that?'

He indicated the dark green dress she'd taken so long choosing this morning, keen not to stand out at the border but to look good for her parents, especially for her tailor father. Now, looking down at its simple lines and hand stitching it felt meagre.

'I did. It's not very good, I know, but—'

'Stop right there.' She stopped, surprised by the force in Filip's voice. He reached out to the hem and turned it back, examining it carefully. 'This is excellent,' he said. 'Really, Kirsten, the quality of this stitching is very fine – so neat and regular. And I love the way you've put in the darts. You've given just enough tuck to accentuate the shape without clinging. Subtle but womanly.'

He caught himself and Kirsten wasn't sure which of them was blushing more.

'You really think so?'

'I know so. I'm speaking not as your father...' another blush, 'but as one professional to another. You have talent. What are your plans?'

Kirsten ran her hand self-consciously down her dress and looked around the three people listening intently to her.

'There's a course in design at the Technical University in Berlin,' she admitted. 'It looks amazing, but I don't think I'd be good enough.'

'You are!' Filip seemed to startle himself with his own vehemence. 'Sorry,' he said more softly, 'but you really are. Put together a portfolio and apply. They'll be delighted to take you, I'm sure of it.'

'A portfolio?'

'Photographs of your work. Can you do that? It's expensive, I realise, unless you know anyone with a camera?'

'My aunt has one. She brought it with her when she fled her apartment.'

'She did what?' Ester gasped.

Kirsten sighed.

'She was on the wrong side of the wall. That is,' she corrected hastily, 'not our side.'

'The *wrong* side,' Olivia said darkly. Everyone looked at her. 'If she wasn't with you, I mean. Family are important, right?'

Kirsten reached out a hand to her newly discovered sister.

'Right.'

Olivia held her hand so tightly she thought the blood might drain from her fingers and she looked at her in concern, but Filip was still talking and Olivia let go again.

'If your aunt has a camera that's excellent. Take photos – of you in your work, of it laid flat, of any patterns you might have created. If you can add in small swatches with samples of your stitching that would be good. Anything to show off what you can do.'

'You really think I could?'

'I do.'

'And that I should? I sometimes wonder if sewing is, you know, important enough. Oh God, sorry, I'm not saying what you do isn't important. It's just the people I know seem to study chemistry and physics and grand things like that.'

'Scientists are amazing,' Filip agreed, 'but they still need clothes.'

He winked at her and she smiled gratefully.

'And, besides,' Ester put in, 'sewing *is* important. It saved Filip's life.'

Kirsten looked from one to the other, battling to take all this in.

'How?'

Filip looked self-conscious and Olivia leaned forward. 'Vati was in Chelmno, towards the end of the war, part of a gang having to shovel ashes out of the incinerators.'

'Ashes?'

'Of corpses,' Olivia told her. 'Awful.'

Kirsten stared at Filip, her mind spinning at the thought of this kind, gentle man having to sort through the clothing of his dead compatriots.

'But then they found out I could sew,' Filip said hastily, 'and I was moved to the tent where they were sorting through people's belongings. The officers' wives liked to come down and rifle through for anything they fancied. They despised Jews, of course, but were happy enough to take their goods.' Filip's voice soured but he pulled himself together. 'Anyway, they found out I could do alterations – needless to say, they were fleshier than the poor people coming in from the ghettos – and that's what kept me alive. So, you see, tailoring is vital.'

He gave a wry smile and Kirsten returned it.

'Your skill made you useful, even to your enemies.'

'Exactly. And it was only my skill because I'd followed my passion. If I tried to throw a javelin like our amazing daughter here, I'd be last every time. You have to do what you're best at, and what you're best at is usually what you love.'

'Wow.' Kirsten put out a hand to touch his knee. 'Paternal wisdom.'

Filip laughed.

'I don't know about that but life-learning perhaps. And excitement at seeing you, my daughter, as such a consummate needlewoman.'

He was blushing again, saying 'daughter' tentatively, as if he wasn't sure he had the right, and it warmed Kirsten's heart. Jumping up, she threw her arms around him in a hug, which was instantly returned. A picture of Jan, spitting bile and fury, flashed across her mind and she held gratefully onto the man who was her true father, then looked awkwardly over to Ester.

'Can you tell me about my birth?' she asked her. 'Can you tell me about Auschwitz?'

Ester winced but nodded.

'I can tell you, Pippa – Kirsten – but it's not pretty. I had to deliver you into hell, I'm afraid. Do you know, when Ana and I first arrived, they were drowning babies in a bucket, plucking them from between their mother's legs and holding them under with meaty hands until they wriggled no more.'

Kirsten felt bile rise in her throat.

'Ester, gently,' Filip warned.

She clapped a hand over her mouth.

'I'm so sorry. We're not here to rake over the past, but to celebrate the present. We got out. You, me, Olivia, we all got out of *that place*, and I should not dwell on it.'

'Nobody drowned me in a bucket,' Kirsten said. 'That must have been because of you, right? You must have kept me safe?'

Ester shook her head.

'Not me. That was Ana, the midwife. God bless her, she was amazing – stood up to them all and told them our job was to bring life into the world, not to snuff it out. After that, the babies weren't drowned and they started taking some of them away. Like you.'

'Yes. Why?'

In reply, Ester reached out and twirled a strand of her hair.

'You got lucky and inherited my blonde hair. My sister has it too. It's more common amongst Jews than you'd think, but the Nazis convinced themselves that any child with this most Aryan of traits couldn't possibly be Jewish. They needed babies, you see. By winter '43 the Reich was losing thousands of men a day on the Russian front and they wanted fresh meat to restock the Aryan larders.'

Kirsten winced and, again, Filip leaned in.

'My wife can be a little... blunt.'

Ester grimaced.

'I'm so sorry. Ana and I promised ourselves when we got out of *that place* that we would tell the world how it was, that we wouldn't let the Nazis hide their shame behind fences any longer. I've stuck to that – ask my children.' She gestured to Olivia who gave a nod. 'But if it's new to you, I must seem very crass.'

'Not crass,' Kirsten said hurriedly. 'Just honest.'

'They took you away from me,' Ester said, her blue eyes burning. 'You were four days old and they snatched you away and carried you out into the snow. That's the last time I saw my precious Pippa – until today.'

Kirsten smiled awkwardly.

'You know that my father – well, not my father, but the man I knew as that – was the one who—'

'Hauptsturmführer Meyer,' Ester spat. 'I know he took you and gave you to his wife. His fancy Nazi blood couldn't breed, so he took a Jewish cuckoo. It's almost funny, when you think about it.'

It was clear no one found it funny. Kirsten dug her hands into Olivia's bedspread and wondered how to go on, but then Ester took her fingers in hers, soothing them with the gentlest of touches.

'I'm sorry. This isn't your fault, dear girl. None of this is your fault.'

'He's dead now,' she offered. 'He shot himself.'

Ester nodded.

'I'd like to say I'm sorry, but I'm not.'

Kirsten grimaced.

'I don't blame you. He was a schwein.'

'But Lotti – your mother – she was good to you?'

'*You're* my mother,' Kirsten said awkwardly but Ester waved this away.

'I gave birth to you; she raised you. It was the same with my dear Olivia.' She reached out, pulling Olivia closer. 'She had a mother, Zofia, who gave birth to her, and myself who raised her. Both are valid. I realised that the day I watched Number 41406 be torn from the only mother she'd ever known.'

'That's when you gave up looking for me?'

'Paused,' Filip said gently.

'Paused,' Ester agreed. 'It was impossible to stop but we just had to trust that God was keeping you safe with someone kind.'

'He was,' Kirsten agreed awkwardly. 'Mutti is very kind.'

'I'm so glad.' Ester smiled. 'I felt sure no one could love you as I had – as I *did* – but that day I decided I was wrong. After all, I could not love Olivia more.'

'It was a terrible sacrifice.'

'Not as terrible as losing you to a bucket of water.'

'Ester!' Filip warned but she shrugged.

'It's true. So many people lost their entire family in the KZs and look at us here, together. Who spent more time with whom is the least of our concerns. There are worse things than having two mothers, and far more ties than mere blood. I only survived *that place* because of the love of Ana and our friend Naomi. They stood as my family when I was torn from my own, and kept me strong enough to keep going. That and my love for your father.' She moved to Filip, who curled an arm around her waist and Ester sank onto his lap, looking for a moment like the girl she must have been when they met. 'Ask Olivia how I always end my nasty little stories,' she said to Kirsten.

Kirsten looked to her sister.

'Love won,' Olivia said simply. 'That's how they always finish – "and in the end, love won".'

'And it did. Here we are. Here *you* are, my Pippa, my miracle,' said Ester.

They all looked at each other, huddled together in a cubicle of a bedroom in East Berlin and laughed, all the tension and awkwardness falling away with the sheer joy of the moment, but then there was a noise in the corridor and Olivia leaped up, on instant alert.

'How did you get here today, Kirsten?' she asked.

'Astrid,' Kirsten told her.

'Sorry?'

Kirsten fished Astrid's pass from her pocket and showed it to them.

'Isn't that dangerous?' Ester gasped.

'A bit, but I so wanted to see you. And I'm so glad I have.'

'Me too.' Ester hugged her again. 'I can't believe you two girls found each other. It goes to show that it will take more than a wall to separate people who love each other.'

'Absolutely,' Kirsten agreed.

Olivia just looked at her feet and that was when a knock shook the door.

# THIRTY-FIVE

*OLIVIA*

'Open up, Olivia, now! We believe you have unauthorised guests in there.'

Olivia leaped up and reached for the door. It was Frau Scholz's voice but she had no doubt who would be standing at the hausmeisterin's shoulder. She was afraid, yes, but more than that, she was angry. She'd invited her parents to see her sparkling life at Dynamo and instead they were going to be subjected to suspicion and hostility. She yanked the door open.

'I'm with my family, my invited family.'

Klaus stepped forward and waved a slip of paper.

'Your invitees are Ester and Filip Pasternak.'

'We were told to invite family. These are my family.'

'That girl,' Klaus pointed a sharp finger at Kirsten, 'is not your family.'

'She's my sister.'

'Not according to DDR records.'

Olivia turned, ashamed, and saw Ester and Filip closing

protectively around Kirsten. It warmed her heart but made her feel horribly alone. She was the only one who knew what was going on. Worse, she was the one who'd brought it all upon them by associating with Klaus.

*Only because you asked after Auschwitz records,* she reminded herself. That wasn't a crime. It was just that these people were experts at making you feel you'd done something wrong.

'Mutti,' she said, keeping her voice as calm as possible. 'Could you show our visitors the number on your arm?' Ester stepped next to her, rolling up her sleeve to reveal the ugly black numbers. 'And, Kirsten, could you show them the number in your baby photograph?'

Kirsten presented the picture. Frau Scholz leaned over to look but Klaus pushed her behind him.

'Your story is very tragic, Frau Pasternak,' he said to Ester. 'And we in the DDR would like to do our best to help, but these young people have gone against the state for their own needs.'

Olivia tensed but then she felt her mother's hand slide into hers and saw Ester straighten her slender back in a tell-tale way.

'These young people, sir, have been bold and brave and good. They have worked together, despite obstacles put in place by people with an agenda wider than their own, to reunite me, a grieving mother, with the baby stolen by the Nazi oppressors. In what way is that wrong?'

Klaus squirmed. Olivia would have smiled to see it save that every ounce of his humiliation was likely to be paid back on her in double measure.

'Your daughter. This one.' He waved at Olivia. 'Asked for my help to find her sister and then went rushing ahead herself.'

'Thus saving you a job. You're an important man, I'm certain, and don't need to be wasting your time on our tiny family tragedy.'

'It's kind of you to say so,' Klaus said, through gritted teeth, 'but I'm afraid your other daughter, Kirsten Meyer, is a cause of concern to us. Fräulein Meyer, can I see your pass?'

Olivia looked anxiously at Kirsten as she stepped forward, but her sister, despite her slight stature, clearly had something of her birth mother's steel in her spine for she stood as unwaveringly before Klaus as Ester had.

'You may see it, but it is not, as you already know, in my name. I stole it.'

'Stole it?'

'From Astrid, a customer in the café in which I work. I stole it from her purse. I knew Olivia was competing and I knew my parents were coming to watch and I wanted to see them, so I stole it. That's it. There's no mystery, no conspiracy – just a child looking for her parents.'

She spread her hands wide and Klaus tutted.

'Stealing an identity is a criminal offence.'

'And one committed in West Berlin, so to be judged there.'

'Where you are going right now,' Klaus shot back. 'And if you cross through again, it will be prison – *our* prison. As for you,' he snapped at Olivia, 'you are aiding and abetting a criminal.'

'She didn't know,' Kirsten said.

'So you say. Shall we see how that stands up under Stasi interrogation?'

The whole room went silent. Olivia felt her guts slither inside her at the memory of a windowless grey van and a corridor full of metal doors. How had it got to this? All she wanted to do was train, be with Hans and see her family.

'I've done nothing wrong,' she protested.

'So you say,' Klaus said again, his voice icy.

She could see she'd really offended him this time. Klaus had thought her naive and biddable, and she had been, but things had changed and she didn't want to be his stooge any longer. She looked desperately to her mother, who smiled softly and stepped up to Klaus.

'I thought socialism was going to take us forward into a better future,' she said, deceptively lightly, 'but the way you tell it, it seems to be sucking us into the past. And the past, for Germany, is not a good place to go, believe me. I was there, sir. I was in Auschwitz at the end, huddling in a dark, bare barrack around a pot of soup made from rotting turnips. I was there dragging corpses outside so they didn't infect those of us clinging on to life. And I was there when, at last, Russian soldiers broke through the gates and freed us. Freed us, sir. That's what they said. A "liberation force", it was called, a "salvation". And it was – or at least, it felt like it. And yet here I am, sixteen years later, behind barbed wire, watched over by gun-toting guards and being made to live my life to a roll-call of fear. Is *that* liberation, sir? Is *that* salvation?'

Klaus shrank back in the face of Ester's passion.

'It will be,' he stuttered. 'When socialism has a chance to thrive.'

Ester looked at him sadly.

'And how will it do that when men like you are drowning it in a bucketful of distrust at birth?'

'Ester, enough.' Filip stepped protectively in front of her. 'My wife is emotional, sir,' he said to Klaus. 'She has met her daughter for the first time in nearly eighteen years. It is a beautiful story, is it not? *Neues Deutschland* would love it, I'm sure.'

'*Neues Deutschland* has done enough harm already,' Klaus growled, refusing to be mollified. 'Frau Pasternak, I am sorry for your distress, but suggest you return to your home to recover and… regain perspective.'

'It is not my perspective that—'

'Thank you,' Filip said firmly. 'I'll see that she does.'

'As for you, Fräulein Meyer, I will be personally escorting you to the border.'

'No!' Ester clutched at him. 'Please, don't take Pippa away. Please don't take her away again.'

Klaus shifted uncomfortably. A crowd was gathering in the corridor, despite Frau Scholz's attempts to hold them back, and he did not like it.

'I am merely obeying orders. You can, of course, if you wish, come to see her off.'

Ester didn't hesitate.

'We wish,' she said. 'All of us.'


They went in Klaus' car, a smart Trabant similar to the one in which Herr Braun had driven Olivia down these same roads into Berlin back in May. Life had seemed so straightforward then, she thought. She'd been happy, believing in the utopia that both school and the FDJ presented, because why wouldn't she? It had made sense. Even now, socialism made sense. It wasn't fair for some people to have excess when others had nothing at all, but it seemed that in the DDR, as in Russia, socialism was just a way of making sure different people had the excess. And they still had no actual intention of sharing anything – not food, not comfort and certainly not power.

'We're here.'

Klaus stopped outside Friedrichstraβe station, once the hub of all travel in Berlin and now the clearest symbol of its division. Its U-Bahn was a ghost-station through which Westerners could only pass in a locked-box of a train, and its S-Bahn was split by a vast glass screen running through what had once been a bustling concourse. In the centre was a narrow gate manned by two clerks and watched over by a guard with a slavering Alsatian.

'This way,' Klaus said, taking Kirsten's elbow.

'Are we not allowed to say goodbye?' Ester demanded loudly.

Again, Olivia was astounded by her mother's audacity. Had she learned this in *that place*, or had it been there already, an iron core that had enabled her to survive in the jaws of hell? Klaus hesitated.

'Five minutes,' he conceded. 'I am right here. And so, are they.'

He clicked his fingers at the guards, who snapped to attention. Everyone in the queue waiting to return to the West eyed their group suspiciously, but Ester simply took Kirsten and Olivia's arms and drew them a few paces away, with Filip in tow.

'In *that place*,' she told them quietly, 'I learned to build a synagogue in my heart. In this place, it seems, I must build a home there too.'

'What do you mean, Mutti?' Olivia asked.

Ester reached up to peck her on the cheek.

'You are in danger, my sweet one,' she whispered. 'I can see it. Through no fault of your own, you have offended that weasel of a man and he will make a bad enemy. The gates are closing on you, Liv, and you must get out before they do so.'

'Get out?'

'Sssh, kindchen. I've seen this before and it's the only way. Once they have you on their list, you are doomed, however unjust it may be.'

'But you...'

'Will still be here when this madness ends.' Ester kissed Olivia again and turned to Kirsten. 'It has been such a joy to meet you, Pippa. Kirsten. It matters little what you are called and everything who you are. For so long I've had this well of love dammed up inside me and to see you today, to have such a beautiful young woman to pour it into at last, has brought me peace.'

Kirsten wiped tears from her eyes.

'It's been a joy for me to meet you too, both of you.' She looked from Ester to Filip. 'I didn't even know you existed until a few months ago and I'm sorry for that. I would have looked sooner if I'd known.'

'Sssh, kindchen,' Ester said again. 'You've been very brave. Finding me has put you in danger, Olivia too, but you will be safe together.'

'Together?' Olivia asked. 'What do you mean, Mutti. What—?'

Ester reached up and held her shoulders, her midwife's fingers lean but strong.

'You have to leave, Liv,' she whispered. 'You have to get away.'

'No!'

'Just for now, while this man is hunting you, because once people like him have you in their sights, they do not stop until you are dead.'

'Mutti, don't!'

'It sounds harsh but it's true, believe me. Kirsten – you were amazing to get to us today; now can you help us get Olivia out?'

Kirsten stepped up.

'I can help. I can find a way to keep her safe.'

'Thank you.' Ester kissed her. 'Thank you so much.'

Olivia grabbed at her arm. 'Mutti, please, no.'

She couldn't bear this. She had found Pippa for her mother and now, because of it, her mother was having to give her up too.

'Fret not, Liv,' Ester said softly. 'Of course I would rather have you both together with me. Of course I would like a hundred sunny days ahead to chat, to laugh, to tell stories, and to hug, especially to hug.' She threw her tiny arms around them as if they were as wide as the branches of an oak, and Filip drew in on the other side, completing the circle. Olivia sensed Klaus twitch but he did not break through. 'But, above all, I want you to be safe,' Ester went on, her voice low, 'and to think of you two together, protected and happy, will keep my mother's heart whole until those days come.'

'Mutti,' Olivia protested, her heart cracking. 'I don't want to leave you.'

'You couldn't leave me if you tried, for we have a home in our hearts, remember? Now come,' she raised her voice, 'enough tears. We have been granted today and I am most grateful. To see my lovely daughters together has been a blessing and one that I hope – once the state is assured of our loyalty – to repeat.'

Klaus bustled forward.

'I hope so too, Frau Pasternak. Now, Fräulein Meyer, if you please...'

He indicated the gate but Kirsten clung to her newly discovered parents and, in the end, Filip detached her from Ester and, offering his arm, escorted her to the gate. The dog snapped at his legs but he ignored it, calmly kissing Kirsten on each cheek and bowing her through. She hesitated on the borderline but, as the guards lifted their guns, she gave them a hasty wave and was gone.

Before Olivia knew it, Klaus was ushering them back to the exit, back to the East. She clutched at Ester.

'I can't let them force me away,' she hissed.

'No,' Ester agreed, kissing her, 'which is why you are going to go before they do so.'

'I can't leave you, Mutti.'

'It won't be forever. Just until the world sees sense and the wall comes down. It will, you know. It will fall just as Auschwitz fell. Evil cannot endure, not while good people resist it.'

Olivia prayed that she was right, but, looking at Klaus glowering beside his car, she knew for certain that she was not safe here, in the land of the grey vans. Even so, she couldn't believe she had to choose to go away, choose to leave all she loved in pursuit of a life that would, surely, never be complete. She'd found the missing piece of Ester's family but, in return, would have to go missing herself. It was a hard, cruel reward for them all.

# THIRTY-SIX

## SATURDAY, 7 OCTOBER

*KIRSTEN*

'And then what happened?' Uli asked.

Kirsten groaned.

'I've told you,' she said for the umpteenth time. 'They put us all in a car, drove us to Friedrichstraβe station and posted me through the gate with the guards brandishing their guns and a great big Alsatian looking at me like it wanted me for dinner. The moment I was through I ran, but I needn't have worried. It was the same station, Uli, the same damn concourse, but on our side of the glass, I was safe. How can that be?'

'It's mad,' Lotti agreed, 'but you are not to do it again. Promise me, Kirsty – promise me you won't do it again.'

'I'm not sure I can,' Kirsten said, leaning over the table to take her hand.

They were in Café Adler but, for once, on the customer's side of the counter. Kirsten was due on shift in half an hour but Uli had needed new school shoes so he and Lotti had come into the centre with her and, being a boy, he'd picked his shoes in about three minutes, then demanded cake. It was nice to sit with them, but Kirsten had no time for happy chatting today.

'It's not safe for Olivia in the East,' she told Lotti. 'There's a Stasi man who doesn't like her.'

Lotti sucked in her breath.

'That's not good. Frau Epstein's son got on the wrong side of the Stasi last year and one night he disappeared. He came back three months later but hasn't been the same since. Sleeps with the light on and had to give up his job as an accountant and become a janitor. Panic attacks.'

Kirsten stared at her.

'That's not helping, Mutti.'

'No. No, I see that. Sorry. You were talking about Olivia?'

'Olivia, yes. And Ester. Do you know why she stopped looking for me, Mutti? Because she watched another girl taken from the mother she'd grown up with, to be with her birth one, and saw how much it hurt the child. She didn't want that for me. She didn't want me taken from *you*.'

Lotti bit her lip.

'I think perhaps your birth mother is a better person than me, Kirsten. I stole you from her. Not directly perhaps, not knowingly, but by turning a blind eye. I feel bad for that, schnuki. I hope that I'd have had the good grace not to do it if I'd known, but I can't be sure because, oh, I'd have hated missing out on you, my sweet girl.'

Kirsten felt tears sting her own eyes.

'It's complicated, Mutti.'

'It is but I'd like a chance to make it up to her, somehow.' She tutted at herself. 'Stupid thing to say, sorry. How could I ever make up for taking her child?'

'Well...' Kirsten said. 'Now you mention it, there is something you could do.'

'There is? Name it.'

Kirsten squeezed her hand.

'Like I said, Olivia isn't safe in the East any more. I want to get her out.'

'Goodness, and you want me to, what, dig a tunnel? Hide in the boot of a car? I'm not very good at that, Kirsten, though I could, perhaps, flirt with a guard?'

Kirsten shook her head incredulously.

'You'd do that?'

'If it helped you out.'

'No flirting needed, thank you. And no digging either.'

'Phew. It's terrible for your nails, you know.'

'I'm sure.' Kirsten squeezed her hand again. 'All I need from you, Mutti, if Olivia makes it, is somewhere for her to stay.'

'The apartment?'

'Yes. Just for a bit. Oh, and maybe Hans too.'

'Hans?'

'Her fiancé.'

'She's engaged? Goodness! I've heard they go for it young in the East, but eighteen?!' She considered. 'Actually, I was eighteen when I married your... when I married Jan. Not that that's exactly a good advertisement for marriage.'

Kirsten hid her impatience. She hadn't realised before quite how hard it was to pin down her mother.

'So can she – they – stay in the apartment?'

'It's cramped already, schnuki, with your aunt spreading herself around the place.'

'Mutti...'

She put a hand up.

'But of course she can stay. We'll manage somehow. Honestly, every time I look out the window and see those poor people being bricked in on the other side, my heart aches for them. I'd have them all to stay if it helped and most certainly this Ester, your... your mother.'

Kirsten looked fondly at Lotti and thought that might be true. She was easily distracted, yes, but her heart was huge. She flung her arms around her in a full hug and although Lotti batted her off, fretting about getting strudel on her best jacket, she was clearly pleased all the same.

'Honestly,' she said, 'those so-called socialists bang on about community and shared responsibility but then they turf people out of their homes without a by-your-leave. Where's the shared responsibility in that?'

'Where indeed, Mutti,' Kirsten agreed. 'More cake?'

Uli's eyes lit up but Lotti shook her head.

'I've got to stay trim. Tante Gretchen says her zookeeper has a friend and we're going out for cocktails next week. Cocktails, me! What'll I wear?'

Kirsten smiled.

'Leave that to me, Mutti. I'll soon run you up something nice.'

Lotti patted her hand.

'You're a good girl, Kirsten.' She picked at her apfelstrudel. 'Is she, Ester, your, you know, other mother, very clever?'

'What?'

'Because you're clever. You don't think so, but you are, and I'm not. I'm a dummkopf. So, I wondered if she was, you know, clever.'

Kirsten's heart went out to her mother. Ester had certainly seemed more composed and perhaps more academic than scatty Lotti, but it had taken a lot of nous to bring up two children alone in post-war Germany and she hated to see her underestimating herself.

'You're cleverer than you think, Mutti,' she assured her. 'And, besides, I barely got to talk to Ester before that man came knocking. My father though, Filip, I talked to him about sewing. He thinks I'm good. Well, he said "excellent" but he was just being kind. He says I should get a portfolio together.'

'A port-what?'

'A collection of photos of things I've made. I've asked Tante

Gretchen to help me and then... then I can apply to the university.'

'Wonderful idea!'

Lotti's easy acceptance made Kirsten love her even more. She slid around the table to hug her.

'You know Ester will never replace you, Mutti. I feel sad for her and I like her. If I could, I'd probably want to see her more but, well, I can't. Even if I could, though, she'd never replace you.'

Lotti's eyes shone.

'We're a funny lot, us three, aren't we? I'm not proud of how I got either of you, but I've done my best by you, right?'

'Right,' Uli and Kirsten agreed.

'And, you mean the world to me, both of you.' She dabbed at her pretty blue eyes with a handkerchief and then looked up with new resolve. 'You've coped with all of this so well, you know, Kirsty. You just give me the nod when your, er, sister, is on her way and we'll get them sorted. Frau Epstein has camp beds, and your aunt has enough bedding to sleep a harem, so it'll be good for it to get some use.'

She kissed Kirsten's cheek then stood up, brushing her immaculate self down.

'Come on, Uli, while we're in town, let's look for some new underpants. Yours are getting quite ragged. Heaven only knows what you do to them.'

'Mutti!' Uli wailed, mortified.

Kirsten laughed and waved them out, then, gathering up their crockery, ducked under the counter and made for the kitchen. It had been good to spend time with Mutti and Uli and at least Olivia now had somewhere to stay if Kirsten could get her over the border. The question was, how was she ever going to do that?

It was getting busy in the café and a queue was forming at the counter.

'I'll dump these plates and be right with you, Sash,' she called, squeezing past.

'Lifesaver,' Sasha said, juggling coffee cups. 'I keep telling Frau Munster we need more staff now we're spy-central, ideally all young and male.'

Kirsten laughed, though she couldn't stop her mind going to Dieter so, for a moment, when she walked into the kitchen, she thought she'd actually dreamed him up. When he stepped forward, however, she came to her senses and had to hurriedly put the crockery down before she dropped it.

'What are you doing in here, Dieter? Again!'

'Kirsty, please, let me explain.'

'Please do.'

She folded her arms, waiting, but then someone else came out of the pantry – a young woman with her hair in two long plaits and a very schick beret.

'Oh!' she gasped. 'You're rampant, Dieter Wohlfahrt. Does Astrid know about this?'

She felt a wicked shiver of pleasure that Astrid was being cheated on too but then a second girl stepped out.

'What the...?'

Dieter leaped forward, clamping a hand over her mouth. She struggled but he was strong and she felt her heart thud with fear.

'Sssh, Kirsty. Please.'

'Why?' Kirsten tried to say but his fingers were tight over her lips so it came out as a mumble and now a third figure was emerging, a young man this time. What on earth was going on? Was Frau Munster running some sort of bordello out the back?

'It's not what you think,' Dieter assured her.

'How do you know what I think?' Kirsten tried to say, to no avail.

'I'll explain,' he said. 'In fact, even better, I'll show you. Only please don't make a noise until you understand.' Kirsten turned her eyes to the full café, only steps away, and nodded. Dieter cautiously removed his hand. 'Good. Thank you. Now, this is Elke.' The girl with the beret smiled. 'And these two are Karen and her boyfriend, Emil. We went to school in the East together a few years ago.'

'Right.'

'We'd better go,' Elke said. 'Thank you so much, Dieter.'

Kirsten watched as the three of them squeezed past, shaking Dieter's hand with tears in their eyes. Stranger and stranger.

'Nice beret,' she said to Elke.

'Thanks!'

Then they were gone and Dieter took her hand and led her to the back of the kitchen.

'Dieter, whatever you're doing in there, I don't—'

'Sssh!'

He pulled her through the back door and into the little yard beyond and there, between the bins and the gas bottles, was her answer.

'A trapdoor?'

'It leads to the sewers, Kirsten.'

'Right. And the sewers lead...?'

'To the East.'

She stared at him, working it all out – him and Astrid, the letter from her mother, his recent distance; it all made sense now.

'So when you said you felt impotent you meant, erm, politically?'

'I did. You were right, Kirsty, protesting wasn't enough; I had to do more.'

'You're not getting with girls back here then?'

'No!'

'Not even Astrid?'

'Definitely not Astrid, she's far too scary.'

'She is,' Kirsten agreed, 'but very pretty.'

'Not as pretty as you.'

Kirsten filed that one to consider later, when she had more time to focus. For now, there was the trapdoor. She peered down into the inky depths before Dieter shut it and shuffled a barrel across the top.

'We've been smuggling people out of the East for a couple of weeks,' he whispered. 'There's a trapdoor in the back of a cabaret theatre on Friedrichstraße that leads into this same pipe and the owner turns a blind eye to those who, let's say, don't come out the same way they went in. Frau Munster has been amazing and we've got nearly twenty people out so far. I can get into the East on my Austrian passport and Astrid with her Humboldt pass—'

'About that,' Kirsten said awkwardly.

Dieter waved her quiet.

'They've given it back, warned her to be more careful where she leaves her purse.'

'Thank God.'

'I expect someone pulled some strings. She's very highly regarded at the Humboldt.'

'Of course she is.'

'Her father's the dean.'

Kirsten laughed out loud. She looked around the little yard and thought of Astrid with her ridiculous advantages in life, and of Olivia in danger, and of Dieter buzzing around Berlin rescuing people. This trapdoor wasn't just the answer to why Dieter had been so distant, but to something far, far more important. She grabbed at his jumper.

'Dieter, I need your help.'

'With what?'

'My sister. She's stuck in the East and she's in danger. The Stasi are threatening her and all just because she was looking for me. I have to get her out.'

Dieter smiled.

'Then you've come to the right place.' He pulled a small notepad from his pocket. 'Shall we make a plan?'

'Yes!' Kirsten said. 'Yes please!'

Ester would have said that God had delivered Dieter to them. Kirsten wasn't so sure she believed in a god of any sort, but she believed in Dieter, and she believed in the justice of their cause, and she prayed to all that was good and fair, that they would succeed.

# THIRTY-SEVEN
## THURSDAY, 12 OCTOBER

*OLIVIA*

Olivia wiped sweat from her brow and focused on the dumb-bell. She could do this, she *had* to do this. Everyone else had gone up a weight and she was barely holding onto this one. She felt tired and faint but she couldn't fail. Already Trainer Lang had been asking questions and she'd only got away with it because of some raucous teasing about her sex life.

'The first day I was here the nurse told me sex was good for the circulation,' she'd said, figuring joining in was her best cover.

'She didn't mean five times a day though, Liv,' Franz had teased.

'I wish *I* could do it five times a day,' Frieda had moaned.

'I'm right here for you, sweetheart!'

It had all been laughed off and Olivia had survived another day, but it was tense. On the other hand, she had no more weird hairs on her body, she'd had a hint of a returning period, and she felt less charged. No less scared though.

Straining, she grabbed the bar, and jerked it clean into the air, forcing every sinew in her body to keep it high.

'Not bad, Olivia.'

She dropped it with a sigh of relief and went for her water bottle, hoping it would magically douse the fire in her poor arms.

'Five minutes and then, Olivia and Franz, you're off for sprinting. The rest of you, circuit training.'

Olivia groaned and nodded gratefully as Hans gestured to the doors that led outside. Following him, she leaned on the top of the low fence, sipping her water and drawing the fresh air into her lungs. The sprinters were gathering on the far side and she was in no hurry to join them.

'Hey there!'

They both looked up as a young man came jogging towards them on the outside of the fence. He was dark-haired and lean, but had a most peculiar running style and was panting as if it wasn't something he was used to.

'Are you all right?' Liv asked him as he came to a halt next to them and put his hands on his knees, trying to catch his breath.

'I will be in a minute.' He looked up. 'Tell me, is there a toilet around here anywhere?'

Olivia thought.

'There are plenty here but I'm not sure non-members are allowed in.'

'Typical!' He looked at her more closely and added, 'Are you Olivia Pasternak?'

She jumped.

'I am, yes.'

'Thought so. I saw you in the paper.'

'You're famous, Liv,' Hans grinned.

'As are you. Hans Keller, right?'

'That's me. D'you want our autograph or something?'

'Great idea!'

The man produced a piece of paper from a pouch strapped

around his waist and dug in it for a pen. Olivia looked at Hans. Was this for real?

'I'm Dieter,' he said. 'Big fan. Wish I could throw like you two. Just here please.' He passed the paper and pen over the fence. 'Reckon these'll be worth a fortune when you win the Olympics!'

'You're too kind.' Olivia laughed and bent to write her name. As she did so, the runner leaned in and, in a low voice, said, 'I'm here from Kirsten. If you want to escape, be at the Cabaret Die Distel on Friedrichstraβe at 10 p.m. tonight.' She froze. 'Keep writing.'

Hand shaking, Olivia wrote, *Best wishes*, signed her name with a flourish and handed the pen back.

'You too,' Dieter said to Hans.

'Me too?'

He nodded urgently.

'Die Distel, 10 p.m.' He lifted the paper, looking ostentatiously at it before reaching over to shake both their hands. 'So cool to meet you,' he said loudly. 'I better go and find that toilet now!'

Then he headed off with his peculiar, loping style as Trainer Lang came out to join them.

'Who was that?' he demanded, eyeing him suspiciously.

Olivia forced herself to laugh.

'Some runner who recognised us from the paper. He wanted our autographs, can you imagine?'

'Get used to it,' was all Lang said. 'You're going to be superstars. Or, at least, you are if you get your arses back to training!'

'Yes, sir!'

They snapped to it, Hans heading inside for circuits and Olivia jogging off to join the sprinters, her head spinning and her legs bursting with renewed energy. 'I'm here from Kirsten,' the man had said. 'If you want to escape...' Did she? She looked around the track. She loved training, loved throwing the javelin, loved her fellow athletes. She even liked Trainer Lang, plus, of course, her parents and brothers were here in the East. If she left tonight there would be no going back, no seeing them for maybe years, until the wretched wall came down. Could she bear that?

Olivia glanced up to the clubhouse and saw Frau Scholz standing there like a carrion crow, her dark eyes following her, and knew she had no choice. She didn't want to escape, but she *needed* to. When the time came, she was not giving birth to Hans' baby chained to a pipe in a Stasi basement, and she was not having it taken away from her, as Pippa had been taken from Ester. History could not be allowed to repeat itself, however hard the authorities seemed to be trying.

'Cabaret Die Distel,' she muttered under her breath as she lined up with the sprinters. '10 p.m.' Then the coach clapped, and she was off.

The only way to get to the theatre unnoticed, they decided after agonised whispering in the shower, was to go as a group. That had its own risks, but they were unlikely to be allowed a pass into Berlin alone, especially with Klaus stalking the school. So that afternoon when they were all lounging in the athletes' common room, Hans produced the culture section of *Neues Deutschland* and said, 'Anyone fancy a bit of comedy tonight?'

People looked up keenly and Hans showed them the advert for Cabaret Die Distel, a well-known theatre in East Berlin, famous for its irreverent comedy skits.

'Great idea,' Franz said. 'I laughed so hard when I was there before, I nearly wet myself.'

'What an advert!' Magda said. 'I'm in.'

'Me too,' Frieda agreed and several others nodded.

'We'll have to ask the Scholzes,' Franz pointed out.

'It'll be fine if Hans does it,' Magda laughed. 'Ma Scholz loves him.'

'Loves who?'

They all jumped as the hausmeisterin herself slid, uncannily, into the common room.

'President Ulbricht, of course,' Magda said smoothly. 'As do we all.'

Frau Scholz looked suspiciously around but they all smiled sweetly back.

'Are you lot after something?' she demanded.

'We are, Ma,' Hans agreed. 'Could we possibly go to Die Distel tonight? We're two weeks into winter training and we're all knackered. Some comedy might be the perfect thing to pep us up.'

She peered at the advert in the paper.

'I've heard bad things about that place. They can be very rude about the DDR.'

'But fondly.'

Olivia watched Hans turning his charm on Frau Scholz and crossed her fingers behind her back, willing him on.

'I'm not sure it's a good idea. It sounds a bit subversive.'

A bead of sweat formed on Hans' temple. 'Tell you what, Ma,' he suggested. 'Why don't you come too, then you'll know what it's like.'

She tipped her head on one side, considering.

'Oh, very well then. But if it's too rude, we're leaving. Deal?'

'Deal,' Hans agreed, beaming at her before turning to send a grimace Olivia's way.

Having Frau Scholz with them was not going to make this easy and they had to pray the comedy was good enough to keep her there until 10 p.m. and prevent her noticing two of their party slipping away to... To where? Olivia had no idea how Dieter was going to get them out and already she felt ten times more nervous than she had at even the Youth Games. There was a lot more at stake here than medals and Olivia could only pray that Dieter was who he said he was and that he was up to the escape he'd promised.

Because if they were caught, Klaus would have them both in prison immediately. And once in a Stasi prison, there was no coming out.

It was a huge effort for Olivia and Hans to laugh and chat with the other athletes as they arrived at Cabaret Die Distel at 8 p.m. that evening. Luckily, everyone else was enjoying the rare treat of being out, so they could let them carry the mood. Both the Scholzes had come and were nearly as giddy as the students, even buying everyone a drink at the bar as they waited for the show to start.

'We have the best theatre here in the East, don't we?' Hans said to Frau Scholz, gulping at his beer as they made for their seats.

'Slower, Hans. You'll give yourself hiccups. And yes, we do. The state believes in enriching our lives with the arts and it's very good for us sporting types to participate sometimes.'

'Enlarge our souls as well as our muscles.'

'Exactly, Hans, very good.'

She beamed at him, and Olivia, worried they'd get stuck next to her in the theatre, held him back to let a useful surge of others separate them.

'Have you seen Dieter?' he whispered.

'Not yet.'

Her nerves were jangling and she barely heard the actors. Everyone else rolled with laughter at the show but she had to force her chuckles and try not to look too often at her watch. Thankfully they'd been allowed to wear their own clothes and she was in the soft blue jumper that Mutti and Vati had given her for her eighteenth and that felt, just a tiny bit, like their arms around her. She was wearing trainers, in case she had to run, and had the photo of her family tucked into the inside of a coat it was really too warm to wear.

It was a risk, bringing the photo with her, but one she was prepared to take. Her DDR-donated ring was on her finger and the one from Hans on a chain around her neck. Hopefully she could sell the Spitzbart one to buy a few things, but for the rest they would be relying on charity. Kirsten hadn't hesitated in telling Ester that she would have them to stay, but what then...?

Clapping burst into Olivia's tortured thoughts, signalling the interval, and they all trooped out to the bar, chattering about their favourite jokes. She looked frantically around for Dieter but could see no sign of him.

'All well, Olivia?' Frau Scholz asked.

She pushed herself to smile.

'Do you know where the loos are? I'm desperate!'

'Right there.'

She indicated the clearly apparent doors and Olivia grimaced.

'Oh yes! Won't be a minute.'

There was, of course, a queue for the ladies but Olivia was glad of it. Frieda and Magda joined her but luckily it seemed that Frau Scholz's bladder was as iron as the rest of her and she stayed away. Olivia scanned the crowd. Nothing. It was 9.30 p.m., half an hour until Dieter's stated time, but the theatre was big and they still had no idea where they were meant to be.

'What do we do, Hans?' she asked unhappily as they retook their seats for the second half, but he placed a hand over hers to silence her and, when the show started up again, leaned in to whisper in her ear.

'I met Dieter in the men's loos. I know where to go.'

Olivia's heart calmed and then raced all over again. It was going to happen. If all went well, in half an hour she would be heading for the West. It was only 100 metres down Friedrich-straβe and yet it might as well be the moon.

'Do you know how?' she whispered back.

His answer was one word: 'Sewers.'

Olivia looked to the red and gold ceiling of the theatre and wondered what on earth her life had come to. The actors came back on stage but all Olivia could see was Ester – Ester hugging her and teasing her, cooking for her and talking to her from the end of her bed. Ester coming to her tennis matches – her biggest supporter, her loudest cheerleader. Could she do this? Could she leave her behind?

'The wall will fall,' Ester had told her, 'just as Auschwitz fell. Evil cannot endure, not while good people resist it.'

She was right, she had to be, but in the meantime why was it also the good people who suffered?

Hans' fingers squeezed hers.

'Now,' he said and, before she could think about it, he was leading her up and out of their seats.

Frau Scholz leaned forward immediately, glaring down the line at them. Olivia mimed needing a wee and the haus-meisterin tutted but turned back to the actors, who were thankfully in the middle of a very funny skit about rabbits' sex urges, leaving Olivia to stumble blindly out into the auditorium.

'Hans, are we sure...?'

'We're sure,' he said and led her on, around the bar and into the back corner where Dieter was waiting.

'This way.'

He led them through a side door and down dimly lit stone steps into the cellar. They traced their way between barrels of beer until Dieter rolled one aside and there, before them, was a metal hatch.

'Down there?' Olivia asked.

'Yes. It's going to be tight for you broad-shouldered pair, but you'll make it. I'll go first with the torch and you stay right behind. Hans, can you pull the trap shut?'

'Of course.'

Hans did not, Olivia knew, like this any more than she did, but his chin was stuck up high and he was refusing to look back. She'd met his parents on the second day of the inaugural competition and they'd been lovely people, his father a bear of a man from whom Hans clearly got his physique, and his mother a tiny, smiley woman who had fussed around Olivia telling her how delighted she was to be acquiring another daughter. More bonds, Olivia had thought, but for now they were bonds that would have to survive across a barrier – a barrier under which they were about to pass.

They slid into the tunnel. It was dark but Olivia was grateful as she didn't want to see whatever was squishing into her trainers as she reached the bottom of the iron ladder.

'Stay to the side,' Dieter cautioned, turning on his torch. The thin beam lit up a pipe wide enough to travel down with your back bent over. 'It's not far. Come on.'

They set out, Olivia's heart beating so hard that she could hear it echoing against the concrete tube that was their unglamorous route out. She didn't care. At the other end of this pipe was freedom.

'Nearly there,' Dieter said. 'Just round this...' He turned at a crossroads where their pipe joined another and stopped dead. 'No!' he gasped.

Olivia came up behind him and saw, lit up in the beam of his torch, a shiny metal grid.

'Is that meant to be there?'

Dieter shook his head.

'Bastards!' He rattled at the grid but it was fixed into place with huge bolts and it was clear there would be no getting through. 'They must have found out we've been using this route.'

He looked around, his eyes pale with terror, and Olivia felt her heart quail.

'What do we do now?'

Dieter shook his head.

'I don't know. That is, I do know. We have to go back.'

'Back?'

'There's no choice. And we need to be quick in case they're patrolling. I'm sorry. I'm so, so sorry.'

Olivia looked to Hans. This was a disaster.

'If we're quick,' he said, 'they might not even realise we've been gone.'

Olivia thought about it. She felt as if they'd been out of the theatre forever but it had probably only been five minutes. And, besides, what choice did they have?

'Our wet feet!'

'We'll think of something.'

He was trying to protect her but she could see her own panic mirrored in his eyes and, as they climbed the ladder back upwards and pushed open the trapdoor, she fully expected to see Frau Scholz standing there, awaiting her prey.

There was nothing. They scrambled out and into the bar. Muted laughter was still coming from the auditorium but even as they stood there, the door opened and Herr Scholz stepped out.

'Here!'

Hans yanked Olivia into the men's toilets and pushed her into a cubicle, pulling up her top and tugging at her trousers.

'Hans!'

'It's our only excuse, Liv.'

He was right and, every nerve screaming, she forced herself to let out a loud moan. The door flew open and Herr Scholz stormed in.

'What the hell do you think you're doing?'

He raked his eyes over them and Olivia pushed Hans away,

scrabbling at her clothing and, conveniently, catching her soggy trainers in the toilet bowl.

'Sorry, sir,' Hans said, making a show of buttoning up his trousers. 'We got, er, carried away.'

'So I see. I thought you wanted to come and see a show?'

'Sorry, sir,' Hans said again. 'We just got carried away.'

Olivia looked around, wishing the ground would open up and swallow her, but now the door opened again and Frau Scholz joined her husband.

'They're here,' he said. 'Apparently having sex.'

Frau Scholz looked at Hans and then Olivia. She put her hands on her hips and Olivia closed her eyes and waited for her to say Klaus would have to be called.

'Was this you, Olivia?' she demanded. 'Asking for sex?'

Olivia forced her eyes open.

'Erm...' she stuttered. What was going on here? Was Frau Scholz jealous or something? 'It was,' she tried. 'That joke about the rabbits had me gasping.'

It felt such a ridiculous thing to say but Frau Scholz nodded earnestly.

'I'm getting this a lot,' she told her husband. 'These athletes have a ridiculous sex drive, especially the girls. It's all the train-ing, it does things to them.'

Olivia did her best to look like a rampant sex goddess, but it was hard with sewage on her trainers and fear coursing through her veins.

'It's true,' Hans said. 'She wears me out, sir. Not that I'm complaining of course.'

Herr Scholz looked at them a moment more, then laughed.

'What's the world coming to, hey? In our day we had to get married, right, Leonie?'

Leonie! A tiny part of Olivia's tortured mind registered the surprisingly feminine name.

'I suppose you pair are engaged,' Leonie Scholz said, 'but

it's still no excuse for this sort of behaviour. Imagine if a member of the public had come in and caught you? It would bring Dynamo into ill-repute.'

'Yes, Frau Scholz,' they said. 'Sorry, Frau Scholz.'

'Don't do it again. Now come on, back into the theatre before we miss the end.'

She shepherded them ahead of her into the auditorium and, out of the corner of her eye, Olivia saw Dieter slinking off down the stairs and felt as if all her hopes had gone with him. The rest of the audience were laughing uproariously, but this was no joke for Olivia. They weren't in prison, but they weren't out either and, with Dieter's escape route sealed off, it was hard to see how they would ever be. She was trapped, trapped in the East and trapped in the sights of the Stasi; they might as well have a gun pointed straight at her.

# THIRTY-EIGHT

## SUNDAY, 22 OCTOBER

*KIRSTEN*

Kirsten peered out of the window at Checkpoint Charlie, watching a white VW Beetle pull up and the driver pause to chat to the guards. That would be Allan Lightner, the American Chief of the State Department Mission, and his wife Dorothy. They were always heading into the East, using their military immunity to go to the theatre and ballet. Sometimes they stopped in Café Adler for a schnapps before they went through and they were lovely people, but Kirsten couldn't help being jealous of them.

She considered asking them if they'd put her sister in their boot and bring her across. How hard would it be? The vopos on the border weren't allowed to stop them in a US car so there was almost no risk. A nice trip to *Swan Lake* for them and freedom for Olivia – easy. Dorothy was a feisty old lady, and Kirsten was pretty sure she'd be up for it; she just had to find the right time to ask.

She served two men mint tea and butterkuchen, then looked out again. The Lightners were zigzagging their jaunty little car through the concrete blocks towards the Eastern checkpoint, fifty metres up Friedrichstraße. It wasn't fair. They weren't even Berliners and they could ride around as they wished, while she was stuck here and Olivia was stuck over there.

Kirsten had waited ages in the backyard of the café the night they'd been meant to escape, peering at the trapdoor and willing her sister and Hans to come popping up out of it. But it had never moved. In the end, Dieter had arrived at the café with the terrible news of the grid.

'What about Olivia?' Kirsten had wept. 'What will happen to her now?'

Dieter had assured her that he'd seen them emerge from the toilets with their teachers and go back into the theatre. It had all seemed all right, he'd assured her, but Kirsten wasn't convinced. She'd met that Klaus man and hated the thought of him preying on her sister. They had to get her out but with the escape routes tightening all the time, it was hard to see how.

'I'm working on it,' Dieter told her every day, but every day more wall went up and more guards arrived.

The apartments on the other side of Bernauerstraße were all empty now and word was they were going to pull them down for a death strip.

'What a waste!' Gretchen had raged when she'd heard. 'What a stupid, senseless waste. Have they seen my wallpapers? They were from the KaDeWe!'

Kirsten wasn't sure the lost wallpaper was the main problem, even if they had come from Berlin's most prestigious store, but she saw Gretchen's point.

'Fräulein?'

'Sorry.'

Kirsten tore herself away from her tortured thoughts and took the customer's order. When he'd gone to join friends in one of the window seats, she forced herself to return to the form she'd tucked beneath the counter and scanned it for at least the fiftieth time. She'd checked and re-checked her application but was still nervous she'd got something wrong. The university would never let her in if she made a mistake on the damned form, would they? She'd be straight on the scrapheap before she'd even had a chance to show them the portfolio she and Gretchen had spent ages putting together.

She rubbed her eyes and looked to the clock. It was Sunday evening and the café was quiet. She'd love to shut up shop and go home to bed but there was an hour before closing time and Frau Munster would not be impressed.

'What's going on out there?' one of the men at the window said.

'Lightner's arguing with the guards,' another supplied. 'Looks like they're stopping him from going through.'

'He won't be happy if he's late for his ballet,' someone else said and they all laughed, but nervously.

A staff car screeched up to Checkpoint Charlie and the Adler customers pressed to the windows to see the US provost marshal get out, lit up by the East's paranoid searchlights. There was more arguing and much frantic radioing by the sentries in the white hut, then two armoured vehicles drew up. Eight GIs jumped out, guns slung over their shoulders, and marched off to join the Lightners' white Beetle and the provost marshal's car.

'Is this war?' one girl asked.

Kirsten waited for someone to tell her not to be silly, but no one did because now, pulling up behind Checkpoint Charlie, were four US tanks with huge guns pointing up Friedrichstraβe right alongside the café's windows. Kirsten swallowed back fear. She'd been worrying for Olivia and suddenly she found herself at the centre of a stand-off. The Lightners were still arguing fiercely with the Ossi guards in the centre of the road and now a bristling Dorothy stepped out of the car and two of the GIs escorted her back towards the hut. She thanked them and then, to everyone's delight, came into the café. A space was instantly cleared in the centre and Kirsten hurried out to welcome her.

'Can I fetch you a drink?' she asked.

She had to admit that, scary as those massive tanks were, this was rather exciting.

'Schnapps, please, dear,' Dorothy said. 'A double. Those ridiculous Ossis are refusing to let us go to the ballet!'

'Can they do that?'

'They cannot,' she said robustly. 'Under the terms of the treaty, only a Soviet officer has the right to ask for our papers. The cocky vopos are getting above themselves and it has to stop!'

Kirsten felt a thrill. Was this it? Was this the day that the Allies finally put their foot down and challenged the wall? Ester had said it would fall and maybe it would be sooner rather than later – though if the tanks were going to start firing, she'd really rather be further back.

Outside, the GIs were marching out to take up an armed guard on either side of the Beetle and the vopos were, it seemed, relenting. Lightner drove through their barriers and disappeared slowly up Friedrichstraβe, still escorted by the soldiers.

'He better not go to *Giselle* without me,' Dorothy said indignantly, but ten minutes later her husband was back.

It was rammed in the café now and out on the street a crowd had gathered. There were press jostling for position on the viewing platform and leaning out of the windows of the Press Association building opposite, eager for photos of armed soldiers penetrating the East. This was a big thing. It could even be a declaration of war if the Ossis chose to take it as such, and now Allan Lightner was turning his Beetle around in the delighted crowd and heading over once more.

'Stubborn mule,' Dorothy muttered proudly. 'More schnapps please!'

Kirsten hurried to serve her and was very grateful to see Frau Munster coming down from her flat to join the excitement. Sasha would be gutted she'd missed this – though, that said, it didn't look as if it was going to be resolved any time soon.

Sure enough, trouble rumbled around the border all week, with military personnel coming and going in an ever-escalating stand-off. Café Adler was packed and Kirsten had to work every evening so was there when, on Thursday, General Clay – the magnificently bullish special envoy for President Kennedy – drove ten shiny M48 tanks up to Checkpoint Charlie to ensure his military vehicles could get through unchecked by the East German guards. After much rushing around, a Russian officer arrived and reluctantly lifted the barriers. Round One, it was felt, to the Americans.

The Ossis then responded by rigging up floodlights, and pointing them direct into the West to make it hard to see what was going on behind them. General Clay, making his stand from the tiny hut outside the café, responded by summoning an American truck with a floodlight so bright that the vopos staggered back, crying in physical pain as they shielded their eyes. It used so much power it drained the grid and every light down Friedrichstraβe turned off. Kirsten and Sasha had to rush around Café Adler lighting candles, but shortly afterwards the Ossis turned off their light and Clay sent the US one back. Round Two also to the Americans. The whole of Berlin was on tenterhooks, convinced that, at last, the matter of the hideous wall was coming to a proper head.

On Friday, her home-study day, Kirsten got up early to try to tackle the schoolwork she'd neglected in the week but Frau Munster sent a message saying that now the Ossis had tanks too and it was going to be a crazy day. Was there any chance Kirsten could make it in?

'Try stopping me,' Kirsten said.

'Me too,' Uli agreed. 'Need an extra hand?'

'Why not?'

'What if it's dangerous?' Lotti wailed. 'What if someone shoots at you? I couldn't bear to lose you.'

'Who'd shoot at a waitress?' Gretchen scoffed. 'Come on, let's all go. It'll be fun.'

It wasn't fun.

By the time they arrived, the guards on the East side had cleared the concrete zigzags and five unmarked tanks were lined up in their place, pointing menacingly at Checkpoint Charlie and, indeed, at Café Adler to its side.

'I didn't know the Ossis had tanks,' Lotti said.

'They don't,' Uli told her. 'But the Russians do.'

'Russians?' Lotti went pale.

Uli nodded.

'They said in school yesterday that thirty-three T-54 tanks had been seen down Unter den Linden. Some American linguist went to talk to them. He got no answer in German, but an instant response when he spoke Russian. They're right behind this, no doubt about it.'

Lotti sank back against the wall of Café Adler.

'Not the Russians.'

'It's all right, Mutti,' Kirsten said, taking her arm and pointing to General Clay standing, legs akimbo with five of his own tanks ranged behind him. 'The Americans are here.'

'What about that makes it all right?'

'The Ruskies won't dare shoot at America.'

'Are you sure?'

Even as she spoke, they heard a loud rumble and turned to see more tanks lining up on the Eastern side. General Clay barked instant orders to the two guards in the hut who got straight on to a radio.

'Oh, my goodness,' Lotti said, flapping at her face, 'we are literally on the frontline of the Cold War.'

'Best then, Mutti, that we get inside.'

Kirsten shepherded them into Café Adler and fought her way to the counter where Frau Munster was serving at speed.

'Kirsten, thank heavens! I need three erdbeerrolle cutting up, the coffee machine emptying and those American cookies arranging on a plate. Horrible things, but this lot seem to like them.'

'The world is about to end and she's worrying about cookies!' Lotti cried.

'Mutti, hush!'

'What if they drop a nuke?'

'Then we've all had it and you might as well go out eating cake,' Gretchen said. 'Come on, sis, sit down and let these people get on with their jobs.'

Kirsten gratefully left her aunt tending her mother and ran to help Frau Munster. She was happy to take on Uli and sent him out to collect and wash plates and cups. More tanks arrived until both sides had twenty lined up, barrels pointing straight at each other.

'Twenty is all the tanks the Allies have in Berlin,' Uli said when they grabbed a ten-minute break.

'They can bring in more.'

'Only if they can get them into the DDR through the Alpha and Bravo checkpoints. The Ossis could hold them there for days if they want to.'

'Whereas the Russians...'

'Can roll straight in from the East.'

Lotti grabbed Kirsten's hand.

'You know, don't you, that the most likely endpoint of this kaffee und kuchen stand-off is that the Russians will win. The Russians will win and they will trample into West Berlin and they will, will...'

She broke down in tears and Kirsten felt awful for dragging her poor mother into this. She'd forgotten, in the drama, what had happened to Lotti the last time the

Russians had taken Berlin and she threw her arms around her.

'It won't be like that, Mutti. Even if they did take West Berlin, it wouldn't be like that.'

'How do you know, Kirsten? You weren't there. You haven't seen what it can be like. Do you want your virginity taken by ten Russian soldiers in a row?'

Kirsten shivered.

'How do you know she's a virgin?' Gretchen asked.

'Not helping, Gretchen,' Lotti growled.

It was Uli who calmed things.

'This is not 1945, Mutti. Berlin is not stranded and alone. The world is watching us now. They're not, perhaps, doing as much as they should to help but they're watching and that is a protection too.'

Lotti looked up at him, then reached out and pulled him down to kiss his cheek.

'When did you get so wise, son?'

'I only know what you've taught me, Mutti. Don't fret, I'll protect you. The son who was forced on you, will not let anyone do it ever again.'

They all stared at him, then Lotti wept once more, but this time through smiles. Kirsten thought that, with this poetic pride, it was the most Russian she had ever heard her brother sound, but there was no way she was speaking that out loud. Instead, she finished her sandwich and went back to work. If the world was ending, it was making people very hungry and there was little time to rest.

Uli escorted Gretchen and Lotti home, and Kirsten served on. Customers blurred into one as she worked the coffee machine into the ground until one voice pierced the fug.

'Any doughnuts for a poor student?'

'Dieter!'

She looked up, delighted, and he leaned over and tucked a strand of loose hair behind her ear.

'You're run off your feet, you poor thing. Do you need a hand?'

'Do I ever!' She lifted the counter and he slipped underneath. A thrill ran through her as his hand brushed against hers, but this was no time for romantic nonsense. It was just five months ago that she'd first flirted with Dieter over doughnuts, of all things, but she felt five *years* older. 'What's going on out there?'

'Not much. A lot of posturing and gun-waving but no one looks inclined to actually advance. I heard one of the journos say that Washington is on the line to Moscow, so pray those talks go well.'

Kirsten ground her teeth.

'It's insane. Two power-hungry men are playing silly games with each other from thousands of miles either side of us and *we're* the ones with the tanks in our backyard.'

'Put like that, it does sound a bit insane.'

'Do you think the Allies will give up West Berlin, Dieter? It would be easier for them, right?'

'Right,' he agreed reluctantly.

'And if they do, we'll be Ossis just like that? The wall will come down, but we'll be on the wrong side of the Inner German Border?'

'I guess so.'

'And there'll be nothing we can do about it?'

'Nothing that doesn't involve getting shot, no.'

Kirsten grimaced and he put his arms around her, holding her close.

'I don't think that will happen, Kirsty. It would have been easy for the Allies to give up Berlin when Stalin blockaded it in 1948 but they didn't. They flew supplies in every day for eight months to keep it in the West, and they've kept troops here protecting our rights. Why, after all that effort, would they give up on us now?'

Kirsten looked up at him. His eyes were so brown, his chest so strong and his lips so close to hers.

'You really think so?'

'I do.'

'I hope you're right but, just in case you're not, Dieter, and they press the big red button and blast the whole of Berlin into non-existence...'

'Yes?'

'May I kiss you?'

He smiled.

'I thought you'd never ask.'

The kiss was bliss for three horribly short seconds before it was cut off by Frau Munster bustling in, concerned for her profit margins.

'Enough of that, thank you very much. If that boy is back here, he can make himself useful cutting cakes.'

She nudged them determinedly apart.

'You're such a romantic,' Dieter told her, but picked up a knife all the same. 'Later,' he mouthed to Kirsten and the thought of it kept her going through two more gruelling hours of serving.

Finally, cakes gone, coffee machine groaning and all the schnapps drained, even Frau Munster had to call it a day.

'Can I walk you home?' Dieter asked Kirsten.

'I'd like that.'

They came out onto Friedrichstraße and walked towards the U-Bahn, threading their way past the tanks lined up between the shops and bars of central Berlin.

'Have you heard?' one journalist said to his cameraman as they passed. 'Kennedy and Khrushchev are going to call it off. It's simply a matter of when.'

Dieter and Kirsten stopped.

'The Russians won't swarm West Berlin?' Kirsten asked them.

'Doesn't look like it,' the journalist said. 'But, then again, the Allies won't swarm East Berlin either. This will be it. If this comes to nothing, Berlin is in stasis, divided forever.'

'Not forever,' Kirsten protested.

'Until the Cold War ends, which might amount to the same thing.'

Kirsten looked at him unhappily and Dieter pulled her away and on past the back tank. A group of soldiers were playing cards on its bonnet, bottles of beer resting against the barrel of the giant gun, and, seeing them, Kirsten knew the journalist was right. This was a mere show of power by both sides before they backed off to their respective corners on either side of the globe and left Berlin stuck unhappily in the middle.

Khrushchev wasn't torn from his family, or stopped from seeing his friends. Kennedy wasn't barred from half his city, refused entry on the say-so of officials wielding their petty power with glee. No, that was the Berliners, and even having Dieter's hand in hers couldn't cheer Kirsten up as she made for the severed street she called home.

'I'm worried, Dieter,' she said. 'After all this posturing, the Ossis are surely going to shore up the border even further?'

'That's true. I was talking to my friend Elke about just that earlier today.'

'The one in the kitchen with the cool beret?'

He squinted at her.

'Erm, yes, I suppose so. Anyway, she said exactly the same as you and she's keen to get her mother out before it's too late. She used to live in the suburbs at Staaken and she reckons there's a weak spot there – a country road with only wire fences and not much in the way of lighting.'

'You think you can get her out there?'

'Maybe. I'm going to look tomorrow.'

'And if you think it could work, might there be room for two more people to squeeze through?'

'There might be, if they were quick and strong and brave.'

'Oh, they're all that.'

'Your sister and her fiancé?'

Kirsten clutched his hand tighter.

'I have to do something, Dieter. I have to get them out before the Stasi...'

She shuddered and he bent and kissed her softly.

'Then let's try. I owe you, Kirsty, for not trusting you with the escape plans. If I can get your sister out this time, will you forgive me?'

She brushed her finger across his lips to silence him.

'I forgive you anyway. You were doing what you thought best.'

This time the kiss was longer, deeper.

'Let's give it a go,' Dieter whispered when they finally parted. 'If it makes you happy, it will make me happy.'

Kirsten swallowed, nervous again. She was scared for Olivia, stuck at the mercy of the DDR, and even more scared about what would happen if she was caught trying to escape. But what choice did they have?

'You'd just cut the wires and run across?' she asked.

He nodded.

'Mad?'

'Maybe.' She looked back down the line of Friedrichstraβe, bristling with pointless military might. 'But it seems like the rest of the city is mad too, so it might be our best option.'

# THIRTY-NINE

## SATURDAY, 9 DECEMBER

*OLIVIA*

'Where does it hurt?'

Trainer Lang prodded at Olivia's shoulder.

'Ouch!' Olivia said.

'There? Odd. Are you doing all the stretches?'

'Yes, Trainer.'

'Warming up fully?'

'Always.'

'Taking your vitamins?'

'Of course.' She knew better than to hesitate for even a beat. 'Though I did have a stomach upset last week, so that might have had an effect?'

The lie was dangerous but not as dangerous as the truth. Without the vitamins she felt so much more in control of herself but there was only so long it could continue to go unnoticed and this injury might be her undoing.

'We can't have you out of action as we go into the hardest part of the winter regime,' Trainer Lang grunted. 'This is where the groundwork is done, Olivia, where your strength is built as a platform for the next season.'

'I know,' she agreed. 'I'm as unhappy about it as you are.'

That much, at least, was true, if for different reasons. She was trying desperately to keep her head down and praying that Klaus would lose interest in her. The wall was up, the Americans and Russians had done their strange tank stand-off at the intersection they were calling Checkpoint Charlie, and somehow the DDR, or so *Neues Deutschland* would have them believe, had won. The West were backing off. They were hoarding their half of Berlin for now, but they'd get bored. Capitalists always got bored.

In the meantime, more death strips were being cleared along the wall, and more people were getting caught trying to escape, and it looked as if Olivia and Hans were stuck. They'd missed their window by maybe twenty-four hours. Now, their only hope was to stay under the radar. Actually, their only hope was to stay *above* the radar – to keep performing well for Dynamo and stay as Spitzbart's golden couple – but without the vitamins that was going to be hard.

'I hear Hans Keller is injured too,' Trainer Lang said. 'Is it something you two are getting up to in your own time?'

She blushed.

'No!'

He shrugged.

'Well, if it is, stop it! For now, we'll get you to the physio and she can run some tests.'

'Tests?'

'Blood levels and all that. Maybe we need to adjust your dose. The scientists will know more than me.'

'Scientists?'

'Of course. You don't think we'd leave anything to chance, Olivia?' Was it her imagination or was he staring her down, telling her he knew what she was doing – or not doing? 'It'll all come out in the lab,' he added and now she was sure. He knew and he was giving her a choice – start taking the vitamins again, or face the music.

'It will be great to get it resolved, Trainer,' she said brightly.

'Yes, well, until we do, you're sprinting.'

'Really?' she groaned.

'Really! Off you go.'

Olivia rolled her eyes, for form's sake, but gladly made her escape to Frieda and her gang. It was cold but bright and they were on the top bend doing what looked horribly like 200 metre runs. That might not hurt her shoulder but it would be hell for her thighs and she reported reluctantly to the sprints coach.

'You can join in at the next one, Olivia.'

'How many are there still to do?'

He grinned sadistically.

'Six.'

'Fantastic!'

She watched the others finish their sprint and start a very slow jog around the rest of the track back to the start point. Herr Braun was showing around some dignitaries on the back straight and, to her horror, she saw Klaus in the group. She hadn't been summoned since the day of Kirsten's visit back in October, but she often saw him around and knew he was biding his time to pay her back for not kowtowing to his demands. Her stomach squirmed as she watched him approach and then she saw Frau Scholz heading down the main straight, carrying some papers. They looked set to converge right at the 200 metre start.

Olivia started some determined stretching and, for once, wished the sprinters would hurry up and reach her. She looked around for Hans and that's when she spotted him – not her fiancé but the gangly figure jogging awkwardly around the outside of the waist-high fence. Dieter!

Her heart pounded. Dieter stopped across from her, rubbing his leg as if easing out cramp. His gaze found hers and she knew he wanted her to go over but how could she? She threw her eyes towards the dark-suited group, hoping he'd get the message and come back later, but he looked flustered and now, to her horror, he pulled a piece of paper out of his pocket and waved it.

'Olivia?!' he called. 'Olivia Pasternak?' Everyone looked over, or so it felt to Olivia. She saw Klaus stiffen, Frau Scholz too. 'Olivia, over here!'

What could she do?

'Can I help you?' she asked awkwardly.

'I want your autograph, here, on my picture of you.'

He waved the paper again and she saw that it was a cut-out from the 'golden couple' article in *Neues Deutschland* last month. It was a good ruse, she supposed, but surely one he'd used before? It wouldn't take Klaus long to find out who he was and track down a link to Kirsten, then he'd be back at her door and she'd be straight into a Stasi basement. Her skin crawled.

'I don't think that's appropriate,' she said, turning her back on him.

Herr Braun's group were close and Klaus was detaching himself, his eyes laser-sharp, and heading for Dieter.

*Go*, she willed him but it was too late, for Frau Scholz had put on a surprising turn of speed and grabbed him by the collar of his running vest.

'Right, young man,' she said crisply. 'You're coming with me.'

Olivia felt her legs collapse from underneath her and, crumpling to the track, had to swiftly twist herself into a back-stretch to cover her fear. This was it. Frau Scholz had Dieter and she would not stop until she got the whole story out of him and then Olivia would be in the back of a grey van on the way to the darkest depths of the DDR. Hans too.

*I'm sorry, Hans*, she told him in her head. All he'd done was care for her and she'd dragged him into terrible trouble.

Dieter was struggling wildly, shouting something at Frau Scholz, and now he twisted out of her grasp and shot off. That was one mercy, she supposed, but then Frau Scholz's piercing voice rang across the track. 'Olivia, my office – now!'

This was it – the guillotine falling. Olivia forced herself up, all the sprinters staring curiously, and Klaus smirking from behind the shiny suits.

'And Hans Keller, please.'

They were doomed.

She reached Frau Scholz's office before Hans. It was a step up from the hausmeisterin's scruffy table in the old hostel but still very plain, the only decoration a DDR crest and a picture of herself and her husband shaking hands with Walter Ulbricht.

'Take a seat.'

Olivia sank into a chair, looking at the dull brown floor until Hans came in and she jumped up and ran to him.

'Hans, I love you.'

'And I you,' he said gently. 'What's wrong?'

He looked from her to Frau Scholz and she saw realisation crash across him. He went pale and she tangled her fingers in his as tightly as she possibly could, though it would never be tight enough to keep them together once Klaus got here.

'Close the door please, Hans.'

Hans did as he was asked and Fran Scholz steepled her fingers.

'That man,' she said, 'was a Westerner, an enemy of the DDR.'

'He was?' Olivia tried but Frau Scholz waved a thin hand dismissively.

'You know he was. He was trying to contact you about an escape to the West. An escape! How ungrateful are you?'

'We didn't—'

'Hush,' she snapped. 'You are instruments of the state and cannot be allowed to be corrupted in this way.'

'Frau Scholz, please, we never—'

'Silence, fool girl! I cannot have this, you hear! You will be locked up in this office until we can decide what's best. It is very disappointing, after all we have done for you.' She rose. 'Think very carefully about your defence – if you have one – for I am certain that Ulbricht himself will take an interest if his golden couple have let him down.'

'We haven't—'

'Think!' she roared. 'And repent.'

'Frau Scholz, please.'

The hausmeisterin gave her a withering stare and reached for the door handle. Olivia felt the bitter cruelty of the DDR closing in on her. Klaus would put them in his car and drive them to the Stasi prison. They'd be separated and they'd disappear. She'd never see Hans again, she'd never see her family again, she'd never run or throw or hug or laugh or kiss ever again. She would be hollowed out and made to confess to whatever they wanted and then... Then her poor, dear mother would have one daughter behind the wall and one in a grave.

'Please,' she gasped again. 'We've done nothing wrong.'

'We'll let the state decide that,' Frau Scholz sneered.

She opened the door but, at the last moment, thrust something at Olivia. The lock clicked shut behind her but neither Olivia nor Hans noticed because there, in Olivia's hand, was a small piece of paper with an address written on it in the hausmeisterin's unmistakably neat hand. And the key to the window.

'What...?'

Hans kissed Olivia quiet. His eyes were as wide as hers but, as they parted, he blew another kiss after Frau Scholz and winked at Olivia.

'What the hell have you done?' he demanded, deliberately loud.

'Nothing,' she shouted back, as they moved together to the window. 'I've done nothing. I've no idea who that man was.'

'He knew who you were all right, asked for you by name.'

'Only from the paper. He must have been some crackpot,' Olivia replied, keeping up the pretence.

Hans slotted the key into the lock, turned it.

'Crackpots don't try and get people out to the West.'

'We only have Frau Scholz's word that's what he was trying to do. I don't even want to leave the DDR.'

'*I* certainly don't. No one else can train us like Dynamo can, and now you've put that in jeopardy for me!'

Under cover of his raised voice, he pushed the window open and looked out. It opened onto the yard at the back of the hostel, a scruffy area where anything that spoiled the club's shiny image was stashed. Just below the window was a big wooden box containing spare weights.

Olivia let out an angry shout as Hans helped her onto the windowsill.

'I'm not talking to you if you're going to be like this.'

'Fine, don't.'

He joined her, lifted an eyebrow, and together they let themselves down. Once they reached the ground, Hans turned and opened up the box.

'What are you doing?' she whispered.

'We can't leave Ma Scholz to take the rap.'

Lifting out a dumb-bell and wrapping it in a dirty old towel, he smashed it into the window, sending glass tinkling to the floor. Shoving the weight and towel back, he closed and locked the broken window, then grabbed her hand.

'Now, we run.'


Olivia had no idea how they'd get to the address – the intersection of Bergstraβe and Hauptstraβe in the far-out suburb of Staaken. Her mind was too fogged with fear to think straight and she could only follow Hans as he twisted her around endless side streets and alleyways.

'It's west,' he said, 'so as long as we follow the sinking sun, we'll be getting closer.'

They stopped in someone's garden, watching intently to be sure the coast was clear before darting in and grabbing clothes off the line. Olivia got a housedress in a hideous grey check that was rather short but, thankfully, wide enough for her javelin thrower's shoulders. Hans got a grimy shirt and a pair of trousers with well-darned knees. They felt terrible for robbing from what were clearly poor people but didn't dare leave their Dynamo tracksuits in case it implicated them in some way. Instead, they carried them bundled beneath their shabby new clothes and dumped them in a public wastebin.

Night fell, bringing welcome cover, and they took to a slightly larger road, scanning the fronts of buses until, to their huge relief, they saw one with 'Staaken' on the front.

'This way.'

They linked arms, trying to blend in with commuters heading home from work while checking every street name to find one of the two marked on their precious piece of paper. At every heartbeat, Olivia expected to hear pounding footsteps and voices calling out their names, but there was nothing and eventually there it was, Hauptstraße.

'All we need to do now,' Hans said quietly, 'is follow this until we get to Bergstraße and then wait.'

Olivia nodded. The waiting would be the worst bit. No one hung around on street corners in the DDR and it would only take one nosy neighbour calling the Stasi for it all to be over.

'What will we do if he doesn't come?' she said to Hans.

'I don't know,' he said. 'But we can't go back now.'

That much was obvious. Their only choice would be to head into the countryside and try to cross somewhere along the hundred miles on the edge of East Germany, but even there they would come up against a border every bit as well-defended as the one splitting their city.

'I'm so sorry, Hans.'

'For what?'

'For dragging you into this, for putting you in danger.'

'Oh, liebling.' He stopped and kissed her, pulling her tightly against him. '*You* did not do this, *they* did. You did nothing wrong trying to see your sister. That's not a crime. It's only them who've made it seem so.'

'Even so, it's not been the perfect start to our engagement.'

He let out a choked sound, half laugh, half sob.

'You can say that again, but I'd still take it. I—'

'Hans!'

Olivia pulled him in against the hedge, heart pounding. Up ahead, in the silvery light of the moon, a slim young man was leaning on a street sign smoking a cigarette. The sign said Bergstraβe, and the man was Dieter. She looked up at Hans, hardly able to believe this might work, and he kissed her again.

'Easy does it, Liv. Easy does it.'

Arm in arm, they strolled up to Dieter who gave them a nod, studiously calm.

'Nice evening,' he said.

'Not bad for the time of year.'

'I thought I saw a badger a minute ago – just up there.'

'Up there?'

'Yup.'

'Right. Well, we're going that way, so we'll keep our eyes out.'

'You do that. Lovely creatures. Vicious of course, if need be, but beautiful. Night.'

'Night, then.'

Hans steered Olivia in the direction Dieter had indicated, moving slowly, scanning the undergrowth as if looking for nocturnal animals. There was no one about but they didn't dare speak, clinging to each other as they traced their way along. Shortly, they came to an open patch of land lined by a wire fence. On the other side was a small, cobbled road, and on the other side of that a second fence, and then...

Freedom.

They heard footsteps behind them and spun round, but it was Dieter, whistling a quiet tune.

'Glad you made it,' he whispered. 'You ready?'

'Ready.'

'My friend's mother should be here very soon. I got Elke out two months ago and I'm told she's keen to join her. I don't know what's kept her, but it doesn't matter. We can cut the fence and go and it'll be there for her when she comes.'

'How...?' Olivia started but Dieter had stopped moving.

He put a hand to the wire and she looked through it to the cobbled road. Dead opposite, behind the second fence, two people emerged from a clutch of trees. One was a girl with glossy hair, long legs in lovely denims and two pairs of wire cutters in her hands. The other was...

'Kirst—' she started, but Dieter's hand was over her mouth before she could speak her sister's full name.

'There's no time to lose. Stand back.'

They did as he bid and the other girl flung a pair of cutters with impressive accuracy over both fences. They landed at Dieter's feet and he swept them up and made for the wire on their side, snipping a line up the diamond pattern. Hans ran to help, prising the wire away to create a gap and Olivia saw that, on the other side, Kirsten and her friend were doing the same. She looked frantically around. No one.

'Two snips more,' Dieter gasped. His hand slipped and he missed the wire but quickly corrected himself. 'That's enough. Now go – go, go, go!'

Hans grabbed Olivia's hand and, ducking low, pulled her

through. A spike of wire caught on the back of her horrible housedress but she yanked hard, heard it rip, and was free again.

'Come on,' Kirsten urged in a hoarse whisper, holding out her hands.

They made it into the middle of the cobbled road. Olivia thought she heard a voice somewhere, a footstep even, but perhaps it was just in her fear-racked mind because now Hans was reaching the fence and bundling her through and she was falling into Kirsten's arms and the other girl was laughing and saying, 'Welcome to the West,' and it seemed they'd done it, they'd made it.

And then the shot rang out.

# FORTY

*KIRSTEN*

Hans fell to the ground at Kirsten's feet.

'Hans, no!' Olivia screamed, letting go of Kirsten and dropping to her knees at his side.

'I'm all right,' he said, stumbling up. 'I'm all right.'

'You're not shot?'

'No.'

'Then...?' Kirsten scrambled past them, staring through the fence. A searchlight slammed on, illuminating Dieter, crumpled against the cobbles of the dark little road on the outer edges of Berlin.

'Dieter!' Kirsten sprang forward, but Astrid grabbed her and pulled her back into the shade of the trees. 'We can't leave him,' she protested, struggling.

'We can't go to him, Kirsten. Look!'

It was hard to see much with the searchlight in their faces but Kirsten could make out several pairs of jackbooted feet beneath the giant torch and now another gunshot rang out.

'Traitors!' someone called. 'We know what you're doing. A

good comrade informed on you, stealing her child away to the West!'

'Elke's mother!' Astrid gasped. 'How could she?' She clasped at the tree they were cowering behind, then shook herself and turned to Kirsten. 'We shouldn't be here.'

'We can't leave him!'

Kirsten was fixed on Dieter. He wasn't moving, and blood was running from a hole in his chest, forming a pool beside him. His eyes stared at them, milky pale, as he held up a hand, scarlet with his own draining life.

'Stay back,' he gasped. 'Go!'

'No.'

Kirsten longed to run to him and hold him in her arms. He was dying, that much was clear, but she didn't want him to do it alone on a cold street in the glare of a vicious spotlight.

'We must be able to do something,' she begged the others.

Olivia was weeping and Hans looked distraught. Only Astrid had recovered herself.

'Dieter and I talked about this when we decided to help people escape. We made a pact that if one of us was hit, the other had to leave. No point losing more than we have to. Does it help Dieter if he dies in your arms?'

'Yes!' Kirsten wailed.

'Not if you're dead too.'

It was a stark, merciless fact. Kirsten turned her eyes back to Dieter, willing him to find the strength to crawl to them, but knowing that if he moved a muscle, the bastard guards would shoot him again. They were only leaving him there now to try and lure them, his friends, onto Eastern ground where they could shoot them too. She wouldn't give them that satisfaction, but if they could rob Dieter of the comfort of her arms, they couldn't take away her words.

'You're a good man, Dieter Wohlfahrt,' she called from behind the tree. 'A good, noble, kind man. You will die a hero and we will honour you. We will put up a cross right here, and we will come and we will celebrate you. They will not win while people like you are here to fight against them.' Was it her imagination or did she see a glimmer of a smile on Dieter's pale face? 'I never had a chance to love you, Dieter,' she called, 'but I would have, of that I'm sure. And others love you – Astrid, your friends, your family. I'll tell them, Dieter, that you died bravely and boldly. We will remember you.'

Dieter twitched and she leaned forward as far as she dared. Another shot rang out, ricocheting off the cobbles.

'Go!' he urged again, then he closed his eyes, his blood-red hands relaxed into the cobbles, and he was gone.

'Bastards,' Kirsten flung across the wire to the handful of guards. 'What does it matter to you what side we live on? What use to you is the death of a fine young man? I'll get a gun and I'll hunt you down for what you've done.'

'Kirsten, hush.' Olivia pulled her into her arms. 'Hush now. He's gone. He's at peace.'

'No thanks to them. Bastards!'

She took a step forward but another shot rang out.

'Stay back,' a guard growled.

'I want my friend's body to bury,' she shouted. 'He's not yours. He's on neutral ground.'

'He *is* ours. Your fence is the border. Ours is added security.'

A young guard was pushed through the hole in the wire. He was pale and uncertain in the glare of the Ossi light and Kirsten held out a hand to him. He looked at it with something like longing, but they both knew that if he tried to step forward, he would be dead. Instead, he bent and hefted Dieter's slender body into his arms, cradling it awkwardly.

'He will be buried,' he said gruffly.

Then he turned and walked back to his bosses. Two more guards ran out with metal clips, pulling the holes in the fences shut as if they had never been, then the light snapped off and Dieter was gone, into the darkness of the East.

'No!'

Kirsten's anger drained from her, leaving only sadness, and she fell to the floor. Dieter was dead. All he'd wanted was to help people and he was dead. Olivia crouched at her side, cradling her.

'I'm so sorry, Kirsten. This is all my fault.'

'No,' Astrid said. 'That's not true. If Dieter hadn't been helping you, he'd have been helping someone else. Now you must honour him by living the freedom he won for you.'

She offered a hand to Kirsten, who clasped it and let herself be led away, Olivia and Hans following behind. They had done it, they had got Olivia out, but the price had been high indeed and it was with a heavy heart that she made for home.

'Kirsty, oh Kirsty, I'm so glad you're back. And this must be your, er, guests. Come in, come in. We have cake, wine. Gretchen – this is Gretchen – went to the shops to have something to welcome you to—'

'Mutti,' Uli said, stepping forward and looking at Kirsten with concern. 'Ssh a minute.'

'Why? What's happened?'

'Dieter died,' Kirsten told her, the stark words stinging her tongue. 'They shot him right there in the road and they left him to die in front of us.'

'No.' Lotti's hands went to her mouth. 'Oh, my child, my poor, poor child.'

She tugged Kirsten into her arms, stroking her hair and kissing her cheeks, but Kirsten resisted. She didn't deserve this care. Dieter's mother would never hold him again and all because of her and her quest to find the mother she'd only learned about at the start of this long, hard year. But then she looked at Olivia, pressed against Hans, glancing uncertainly around the tiny apartment that would be her new home, and told herself not to be ungrateful. She was the luckiest girl alive. She had not one, but two caring mothers. She was loved and she was free to love and she had to embrace that. For Dieter.

'Mutti,' she said, pulling back from Lotti's arms once more, 'this is Olivia, my sister.'

Lotti smiled, let go of Kirsten, and went to Olivia, taking both her hands and pulling her into the warmth of her easy embrace.

'Welcome, Olivia. You must have been scared.' Olivia nodded. 'Well, there's no need to be scared now. You are with me and you are safe.' She drew Olivia onto the sofa, gesturing for Kirsten to join her. 'This year has taught me much,' she said. 'I am not a clever woman...'

'Mutti, you—'

'Hush, Kirsty, let me say this, please. I've been thinking, a lot. It is a painful business, but important.' She looked to Olivia. 'Your mother had to give up her baby. She had to give her up to me and I'm sorry for that. If I'd known she was still alive I would – I hope – have returned her, though I cannot swear to that because I am a weak woman and, God help me, I love my Kirsten so much. Not that she is *my* Kirsten, not really, but I hope I have cared for her as best I can.' She shook herself. 'What is done, is done. It's how we go forward that matters. I swear I will also care for you, Olivia. It's a tiny return for your mother's suffering, but it's all I have to offer and I hope you will accept it?'

She looked shyly at Olivia.

The girl smiled.

'I will be very grateful.'

'There now!' Lotti wiped at her eyes. 'Don't be grateful, it's so wearing. Just have fun.' She looked to Hans. 'This is your fiancé, yes? Lucky you! Welcome, Hans. Come, we must celebrate. We must celebrate the life of this poor young Dieter, and we must celebrate your escape and your love and the life that lies ahead, yes?'

Olivia looked to Kirsten.

'Yes,' she agreed.

And then Uli was stepping up to pour the wine like a grown man, and Gretchen was passing streuselkuchen around, and Lotti was fussing over seating and plates and, somehow, Kirsten's new family were melding with her old one and growing into something far bigger and more magical than either had been before. They were divided still, but not in their hearts, and one day they would be together again.

# FORTY-ONE

## SATURDAY, 23 DECEMBER

*OLIVIA*

'Don't fidget, you'll get pollen on the dress!'

Olivia looked fondly at Kirsten as she fussed around in the simple porch of the registry office. She could swear her sister was more nervous than she was, even though it was her wedding day.

'Leave it, Kirsty, it's perfect.'

'Is it though? These long sleeves were very hard to get right and I'm not sure the bodice is lying flat. I think you've lost weight.'

She looked accusingly at Olivia, who laughed.

'That's usually a good thing in brides.'

'Not for their dressmakers.'

Olivia laughed again and pulled Kirsten in for a hug, ignoring her squeaks of protest.

'It's beautiful – every bit as good as my father would have made it.'

'Truly?'

'Truly. He's so proud of you for getting your place at the

university. He says that you're to work really hard and get really good and then, when the wall comes down, you can set up a business together.'

'He does? We could have our own brand. We could call it Pippa.'

They both welled up and had to hastily pull apart as mascara would be far worse for the dress than pollen! Beneath her sole, Olivia felt the brautschuh coin that Ester had managed to enclose in a precious letter sent via a chain of people (a doctor in Stalinstadt, the dean of Humboldt University, and his daughter, Astrid) to keep Olivia's family free of the 'taint' of associating with her. The thought of them suffering for her escape had tormented Olivia and it had been a huge relief to hear all was well.

'We will be so sorry to miss your wedding,' Ester had written, 'but so happy it's taking place. Your father and I have found such joy in each other over the years, and such strength. I could never have made it out of *that place* without an awareness of him on the other side and I can only thank God that you will not have to live apart from your husband.' Olivia looked through the half-open door to where Hans was fidgeting at the front and smiled, remembering the last of her mother's words: 'We will be there in your heart at the ceremony, sweet one, and we will be there on the other side.'

It wasn't the same, but their love was, surely, strong enough to cope and Olivia smiled at the feel of the coin beneath her sole. It was a traditional symbol, meant to bring prosperity to the bridal couple, and this one was an Ostmark and all the better for it. The authorities might wish to separate the people of Germany, but the people knew how to share.

'Ready?' the registrar asked and Olivia nodded and took Kirsten's arm.

Her throat constricted as she pictured Filip, and she wished her father could be here to walk her up the aisle but at least she had her sister to stand in. Uli had offered and Olivia had been touched, but choosing him would have felt treacherous to Mordecai and Ben, stuck in Stalinstadt. Besides, this was Pippa, her parents' blood child and the one who had found her, and she was happy to defy convention for this special day.

'I could do with you, Uli,' Hans had said and Uli had proudly agreed to stand as his best man.

The registrar disappeared into the main room and then the doors opened, music played, and she and Kirsten stepped out together. Well, not quite together because Olivia's stride was so much longer than her sister's, but, giggling, they sorted it out and, besides, it was only ten steps to the front of the small room so it mattered little.

'Olivia!' Hans said, stepping so eagerly forward to take her hands that the congregation chuckled. 'At last!'

'Worth the wait?'

'You're beautiful. My Christmas angel.'

Olivia smiled.

'I'm no angel.'

'Even better.'

'Hans!'

The ceremony was short, but perfect in its simplicity, the registrar asking them only if they were willing and free to marry each other. Olivia replied loudly and clearly that she was, thinking of how much they'd had to go through to be so.

The registrar spoke a few words more, invited them to sign the register and then asked them to swap rings. They had both worn their engagement rings on their left hands, leaving their right free for the golden wedding bands they'd bought with the proceeds from selling Ulbricht's dirty jewel. The registrar pronounced them married and everyone cheered. Olivia wondered, momentarily, what a synagogue wedding would have been like, but she'd long since learned from Ester to keep her synagogue in her heart and she knew God blessed them however the words were spoken. Then, to her surprise, Lotti stood up, nervously adjusting her floral dress, as she pulled a book of poetry from her pocket.

'Olivia and Hans' parents cannot, as we know, be here with them today. I, for one, am proud to stand in their place and bless this lovely young couple and I'd, er, I'd like to share a poem with you.' She gave a nervous laugh. 'It's not like me but, well, it seemed right. Anyway, this is "Morgen!", by John Henry Mackay, one of a collection of songs that Strauss gave to his wife as a wedding gift. I thought it was, er, perfect for today.'

Heart swelling, Olivia nodded her on. Lotti bit her lip, then lifted the book high and read:

> Tomorrow morning the sun will shine again
> on the path I tread through life.
> It will unite us once more
> upon this sun-blessed earth
> and to the shore, the wide, blue-waved shore,
> we will descend, quietly and slowly.
> We will look mutely into each other's eyes,
> and the silence of happiness will settle upon us.

Olivia felt her eyes fill with tears at the simple beauty of the words.

'Oh no,' Lotti said, 'did I not do right?'

Olivia leaped forward and clasped her hands.

'You did perfectly, truly.'

'Thank heavens for that!' she cried, and the congregation – a small but merry group of their new friends and adopted family – laughed fondly.

Then it was time to head outside, into the icy air of a Berlin December to where Astrid and the other students were dragging the traditional log to the front of the registry office on a metal sawhorse.

'Really?' Olivia said. 'It's freezing.'

'It's tradition,' Kirsten insisted. 'A symbol of marriage as a joined labour of love. Besides, it should be no bother for you strong pair.'

That, Olivia had to concede, though she'd never had to saw a log in a long dress before. Gamely taking one end of the two-handed saw, she stepped up to the sawhorse, Hans opposite her, and together they set to the cutting. The saw buckled.

'Come on,' Astrid called, 'put your back into it.'

They tried again, but again it buckled.

'I thought you two were top athletes?' Uli laughed.

Olivia looked at Hans, he looked back, puzzled, then grinned and reached out to feel the edge of the saw.

'Blunt as an old dog's teeth,' he said. 'Give us the proper one, you idiots!'

With more laughter, a far shinier saw was produced and this time it took only a handful of cuts to bite into the wood and not many more to saw right through it. The two halves crashed to the ground and their guests cheered.

'Still got it, hey, Liv?' Hans said, stepping through the gap to sweep her into his arms and kiss her to even greater cheers.

'Still got it,' she agreed when she came up for breath.

'And without any blue pills either?'

She shook her head, picturing Dynamo and their suspect regime and, for a moment, seeing Frau Scholz who had, all along, been watching them for their own safety and had saved them at the crucial moment. She'd seen a photo of Dynamo in the paper recently and spotted both Scholzes standing at the back, so it seemed Hans' towel trick had worked and Leonie was safe too, for now at least.

In the new year she and Hans were going to Hanover, to train with Almut Brömmel and her team. They would have to get jobs, pay their own way rather than being cosseted as they had at Dynamo, but that fazed neither of them. Suzanne Bauer had been in touch several times and had found them an apartment, which Gretchen had insisted on paying for.

'You can't do that!' Olivia had protested.

'Course I can. I got all these jewels out of the scheiße DDR and they'll be far more use getting you somewhere to live than weighing down my old fingers! Besides, I might have a new ring for that soon enough...'

She'd looked to Heinrich, her zookeeper, and he'd rolled his eyes, but happily. He was taking Uli on as an apprentice next summer and the family was, it seemed, expanding in ever wider and more enjoyable ways. Kirsten, Lotti, Uli, Gretchen and Heinrich were already planning a trip to Hanover and Olivia couldn't wait to welcome them into her very own home.

'We'll call it the liebesnest,' Suzanne had said merrily. 'I'll get a sign made.'

Olivia had laughed that off but, in truth, she hoped Suzie had done it anyway. 'Liebesnest' was a very soppy name but, hey, they were newly-weds so it was allowed.

'Time to toast the happy couple's health?' Heinrich asked.

Olivia sobered.

'Not quite yet,' she said. 'We have somewhere to go first.'


It was a bright procession behind the beautifully dressed bride and groom and everyone else on the tram north smiled and pressed their best wishes on them. It soon became apparent that many were going the same way and when Olivia, Hans and Kirsten turned the corner onto a darkly familiar patch of land, they were astonished to see a great crowd gathered. Spotting their arrival, the priest at the front waved them over and people parted gladly to let them through.

It was the shortest day of the year and the sun was already dropping between lowering clouds, casting a golden light onto the wooden cross erected as memorial to Dieter Wohlfahrt, and glinting in the brass plaque bearing his name and the date of his tragic death. It reminded Olivia of that hideous Ossi spotlight lighting up his poor, dying corpse, and she staggered, but Hans was at her side, holding her firmly, and, in turn, she wrapped her arm around Kirsten's waist and they stood together at the front as the priest stepped forward.

He spoke a welcome to the hundreds of Wessis who had gathered to honour Dieter's memory and then, with a smile, turned and faced across the wire, across the cobbles, across the great divide carving its way through Berlin, and spoke a second welcome to a similar crowd of Ossis standing bravely on the far side. He named no names – it would have been dangerous to do so – but at the front Olivia saw a weeping couple who must be Dieter's parents and there, just along from them, a second pair who brought tears to her eyes.

'Mutti,' she whispered, 'Vati.'

'We will be there,' Ester had written. 'We will be there on the other side.' And here they were. Even better, Hans' parents were standing with them, in-laws joined against the laws keeping them from their children.

Guards were patrolling and Olivia dared not cry out but, as she stepped forward with Hans and Kirsten to lay her wedding bouquet before the memorial to the brave young man who'd made today possible, she looked to Ester and Filip, saw them smile, and knew her wedding day was complete.

It was Ester, she thought, who started the singing. Ester who opened her mouth for the first line of 'Silent Night', a little strained, perhaps, a little tear-laced, but loud and clear. Instantly, the crowd took it up and voices rose either side of the wire, joined to plead for calm, for peace. Olivia thought of her mother's story of *that place*, of a Christmas gift of hate and a counter-song of love, just like now. She thought of Ester giving birth to Pippa in squalor and cruelty, and of the baby being snatched from her. In two days' time it would be Kirsten's birthday and they would have to celebrate it in the West, both of them far away from Ester and Filip, who had gone eighteen long, painful years, only to come full circle to a new KZ. This time though, surely, it was one that the world would not allow for long.

The wall had divided them but not split them apart, and it would fall. It would fall just as Auschwitz had fallen. Evil could not endure, not while good people resisted it and, as Olivia blew a secret kiss to her family across the wire, the first flakes of snow crystallised in the air and fell on East and West alike.

# EPILOGUE

## AUSCHWITZ-BIRKENAU | SPRING 1990

*ESTER*

The car pulls up as the first streaks of dawn shine incongruously rose and tangerine through the stark wires of Auschwitz-Birkenau and I stare at the long, dark shape of it ahead.

'Are you sure, Mutti?' Olivia asks, turning to me from the driver's seat.

I'm not sure at all. Fear is creeping across my skin like lice and rats and typhus fever, but this is not 1940. This is not even 1960, but 1990, and Auschwitz is nothing more than a museum now. For most people at least.

'Everyone deserves to know where they were born,' I say, 'even if it was here.'

From the back seat, Kirsten places a quiet hand on my shoulder, but it still feels hard to leave the sterilised safety of the car.

'There are no gates there now,' a young voice says quietly. 'No one can shut you in, Oma.'

I look back. Smile.

'You're right, Pippa my dear. Thank you.'

I see Kirsten pat her daughter's knee. She was delighted when, after twin boys, she gave birth to a girl. She wrote to me in glee that she had borne a Pippa and I felt the weight of the name I'd once given her and was sorry for it. Pippa was a legacy of a person Kirsten did not know how to be and this new child, born past the conflict, has been a resolution for us both.

'Come on,' Pippa says, bouncing out of the car with the insouciance of her eighteen years, 'we're here now. Let's go.'

It's simple to her. She's grown up in the cherished freedom of West Berlin, living with her parents in the Tiergarten, not far from Berlin Zoo where Onkel Uli runs the monkey houses, or where Oma Lotti and Groβetante Gretchen live with their second husbands. She is a child of David Bowie and Whitney Houston, of tie-dyed tops, ra-ra skirts and stonewashed jeans. Not for this Pippa the privations of rationing or conscription or a life behind a curtain of fear. And thank God for that.

Both my daughters have carved out good lives in the West. Olivia threw the javelin at the Tokyo Olympics, Hans competed too, and we shouted ourselves hoarse watching it on the television set they sent us. Hans went on to a wonderful coaching career and Olivia opened a sports club for the under-privileged children of Hanover and now supervises branches in cities all over Germany.

Kirsten became a designer, known across Europe for her bright children's clothes, made popular by Jorgie, the fantastic photographer she went on to marry. They send us lovely photos of all our grandchildren looking very swish and, more impor-tantly, very happy. And, of course, Filip follows every fashion show, cuts out every article on her designs, and cherishes every shirt and jacket that she sends him.

'See the stitching,' he always says, just as he did that first – and only – day we met her. Until now.

I'm sure the stitching is very fine but I always turn to the label for her logo – a small, black number, erased from Kirsten's armpit but not from her life. A mark from the place we are finally visiting.

Kirsten helps me from the car and there is no turning back now. We've been granted early access to avoid the crowds and are the only ones here as we head slowly beneath the now infamous arch. I lead the way, leaning on my stick, blaming the arthritis that plagues my seventy-year-old limbs, though in truth it is far more likely to be the memories of this dark place that will trip me up.

I know, in reality, that it is silent here at this early hour, but for me the place fills instantly with sounds. A dog snarls, a guard barks orders, a reluctant orchestra plays grotesque marching tunes as a hundred exhausted men and women limp back to the stark wooden boards they have to call beds. I smell the stink of dysentery, sweat and urine, taste rotting turnip soup and the endless rasping pain of eternal thirst and see the dark smoke of Jewish lives curl up into the sky above us.

'Oma?'

Pippa takes my arm and I lean into her, letting her youth flood through me, seeing this place through her eyes – just lines of empty wooden huts, powerless fences and the broken remains of once omnipotent crematoria.

'This way,' I say and head off, my footsteps taking me unerringly two lines left and down towards the hut I was condemned to call home for two long years. I wish Filip could be here, but the doctor told him it was too far to travel and, besides, I'm not sure I could bear the pain it would cause him. My own is almost too much already.

I glance back and see Kirsten and Olivia just behind – my daughters, mothers themselves now. They were shocked, I know, at how old Filip and I look. But we have had twenty-eight years apart and, likewise, I am horrified at them – not their appearances, for they are beautiful women, but the evidence of how much of them I have missed. There are laughter lines in the corners of both their eyes that tell me of playtimes with toddlers, trips to the park, birthday parties and school plays. They speak of the highs and lows of touchlines, of holidays, of evenings with their husbands, and of many, many meals around family tables. All forever lost to me.

If we had known, when the wall went up that dark night in August 1961, that it would have stayed in place until 1989 would we have acted differently? Could we have done? Even when travel passes were granted in the eighties, the DDR stubbornly refused such privileges to us, and we wouldn't let Kirsten or Olivia step behind the Iron Curtain. Stasi lists are written in indelible ink and we could not risk them being caught.

'This one.' I stop in front of a dilapidated shed, every fibre of me knowing it. 'This one was Block 24.'

I put a hand to the door frame and Kirsten and Olivia rush forward to support me but, curiously, I feel stronger here.

'Don't fret,' I tell them, 'the memories are sharp but as many of them will lift me up as knock me down.' I take a step inside and, although bad smells still crowd my senses, they are tempered by the sounds of love, friendship, support and even, just occasionally, laughter. I smile.

'This is where I used to sleep with Naomi and Ana,' I tell them, pointing. 'This is where I kept the one letter from Filip that got smuggled into me by Mala Zimetbaum – until they sprayed the mattress with disinfectant and it disintegrated. That was the day I realised I was pregnant with you, Pippa.'

'Me?'

Kirsten's daughter, my lovely granddaughter, looks at me, confused.

'Not you, my dear, your mother. Though the seed of you would have been already inside the baby inside me, just as the seed of the next generation is already inside you. Life, you see, is always ready and waiting to happen.' I stroke Pippa's young face. 'I was eighteen like you, my dear, when the Nazis invaded my homeland. And your aunt and mother were eighteen when the Russians, our so-called saviours, turned tyrant and walled us off from each other.'

Pippa looks alarmed.

'What's going to happen to me then, do you think?'

'If God is merciful, nothing dramatic at all.'

Pippa thinks about it.

'I was in Berlin when the wall came down last year, Oma,' she offers. 'I danced on top of it as the hammers tore it apart and the cameras broadcast Berlin's reunification to the world. Will that do?'

I put a hand on her head, caressing her soft blonde hair, so like my own white tresses once were, and cherishing the fact that, finally, I can touch my own flesh and blood.

'That will do very well, my dear. When that wall came down it wasn't just the end of a divided Berlin but the end of this – of leaders thinking they had the right to put fences around people who'd done nothing wrong at all. No one should have power of life and death over others. No one.'

They gather closer around me and I pull my gaze from the relics of my past to the people who have brought me back to face them. All are looking at me with love. 'The fences are down and we must keep them down. That will be up to your generation now, Pippa.'

'We'll do our best, Oma.'

'And we will keep reminding you why you must,' I warn her. 'It will sound like the ramblings of the old but, I hope, when you are rolling your eyes at your Opa and I droning on, you will remember this visit. Remember why it matters.'

'I will,' Pippa promises.

'You're a good girl.'

I'm blessed in all my grandchildren, especially when you

think of the thousands of grandparents, and would-have-been-grandparents, who perished in Auschwitz-Birkenau.

'I'll show you the cattle carts they shipped us here in shortly,' I tell them. 'I'll show you the remains of the gas chambers where they herded so many of us to our deaths, and the great warehouses where they clawed through our worldly goods, seizing wedding rings and lockets and even teeth, as if they mattered more than the person who'd treasured them. I'll show you the gallows where they hung the brave ones who tried to escape, and the wires where those driven mad by this hellhole frazzled themselves against the electrics. I'll show you all that.'

I am overwhelmed suddenly by everything I have to bear witness to, then I look at them and remember what truly matters. Taking Kirsten and Olivia's hands, I draw them further into the stark room.

'See this?' I pat the low concrete rectangle running the length of the long hut. 'This is the most precious place in Birkenau.'

Kirsten squints at it, confused, but Olivia runs an awed hand along the rough surface.

'I know this from your stories, Mutti. It's the stove.'

I laugh bitterly.

'They called it that, certainly, but it was rare we ever had wood to fuel it.' I point to one end where a metal log-burner is rusting. 'You were meant to light that and the heat came along the pipe beneath the concrete and warmed us all up. Ha! We were lucky if we ever got it more than lukewarm to the touch.'

'But even like that it was the most precious place?' Pippa asks.

'Oh yes,' I agree. 'Because it was on here that the babies were born, that my babies were born, both of you.' I look from Olivia to Kirsten, seeing these beautiful middle-aged women as tiny, perfectly formed newborns. 'It was on here, in the very centre of Auschwitz-Birkenau, that miracles took place – miracles of hope. For while we could bring forth life, we could hold back death.'

They sit down either side of me.

'And then we were taken away?' Olivia asks.

'By the man I thought was my father,' Kirsten adds.

I hear her guilt and pain echoing mine, but she has nothing to feel guilty for. None of us do.

'He came in a car,' I tell her, 'rapped down these wooden boards right here and snatched you as if you were no more than a ring or a necklace or a tooth – just another commodity to feed the ravenous Reich. But we'd marked you – an ugly, jagged mark on a baby's newborn skin, perhaps, but the mark of the hope you'd brought us, the hope that we'd one day meet again.'

'And we have,' Olivia says. 'The divisions were longer and darker and more tangled than they should ever have been, but they're over.' She puts an arm around me, as strong as ever, and Kirsten and Pippa crowd in too, a huddle of comfort against the bleakness of the past. 'The wall has fallen, just as the wires fell, and we can be together, free to love each other.'

'Free to love each other,' I agree. 'And that, in the end, is the greatest miracle of all.'

I look around the death camp that failed to kill me and that now stands as a powerful reminder of what can happen if we fall slave to hatred.

'You see,' I tell my girls, 'Mutti is always right.' They squint at me and I laugh, a clear, merry bell sounding out across the broken remains of a dead death-camp. 'I told you, my beautiful, wonderful girls, I told you how it would end, how it must surely always end.'

I stand and walk out of Block 24, out of the Auschwitz Museum and into the sunshine. With my family around me, the sounds, smells and tastes of the past finally fade away.

'Love wins,' I tell them with a smile. 'Our love, finally, wins.'

# A LETTER FROM ANNA

Dear reader,

I want to say a huge thank you for choosing to read *The Midwife of Berlin*. I was overwhelmed by reader response to *The Midwife of Auschwitz* last year, and it was when one reader messaged me saying they were desperate to know what happened to Pippa that the idea for this sequel was born. Many other readers have asked the same question since and, although Pippa and Ester are fictional characters, I'm delighted that their story has touched people enough for them to care about where it ends and really hope that this new story satisfies. If you want to keep up to date with all my latest releases, just sign up at the following link. Your email address will never be shared and you can unsubscribe at any time.

*www.bookouture.com/anna-stuart*

When I worked out that both Pippa and Olivia would turn eighteen in 1961, the year the Berlin Wall went up, it was too good an opportunity to miss. The Wall, and the terrible Cold War that brought it about, is a significant part of modern European history and I was especially interested in the way this darkly grand political creation impacted the lives of the individuals caught on either side of it. The chance to embody that through Pippa and Olivia, and their complex families, was tough but rewarding.

Inviting Stalin's Russia onto the Allied side in 1941 was a crucial part of defeating Nazism but it brought another terrible, oppressive regime into Europe. The fall of the Berlin Wall has been, rightly, much celebrated and written about, but I was very happy to step back and explore the terrifying events around it first going up.

I hope you enjoyed reading this novel and, if so, I would be very grateful if you could write a review. I'd love to hear what you think, and it makes such a difference helping new readers to discover one of my books for the first time. I also love hearing from my readers – you can get in touch on my Facebook page, through Twitter, Goodreads or my website.

Thanks,

Anna

www.annastuartbooks.com

facebook.com/annastuartauthor
twitter.com/annastuartbooks
instagram.com/annastuartauthor

# HISTORICAL NOTES

As with all my novels, I have done my very best to portray the settings, events and feelings of the period as accurately as possible. For this one, however, I had to enter a world of very complex political and geopolitical issues. I really hope that I made the situation in Berlin, as an occupied city, clear enough for the reader to enjoy Olivia and Kirsten's story, without boring them! For those who are interested, here are a few more historical details.

## East and West

Most of us will be aware of the definition of East and West Germany during the time that the Berlin Wall was up, but the situation in Berlin before its erection was complex and hard to convey. I was forced to put more 'fact' into the novel than I would normally like to try and make it clear, but here is a little more explanation.

When Germany signed the surrender in 1945, they lost the right to govern their own country. Germany was split, with Russia getting control of the Eastern half and the other Allies

(Britain, America and to a lesser extent France) controlling the Western half. The line ran clearly down the centre of the country but the problem was that Berlin fell well into the Eastern zone. As the capital, it was made a special case and was also divided into a Soviet and an Allied zone (originally there were four zones, one for each Allied country but Britain, America and France rapidly joined theirs into a 'trizone').

Routes into Western Berlin were kept clear by road, rail and air, although, crucially, only the air channels were written into the formal treaty meaning that when, in June 1948, Stalin tried to close off Berlin in a bid to take it all for himself, the only route in was by plane. For eight long months, in the 'Berlin Airlift', Western countries supplied the people of besieged Western Berlin with all basic supplies via hundreds of planes a week, until Stalin grasped that they weren't going to let it go and allowed the roads to open again.

Meanwhile, Stalin, who had taken full control of almost every Eastern European country, was dropping the Iron Curtain (named by Winston Churchill in a speech to Westminster College, Missouri, in March 1946, but rapidly adopted as a worldwide term) by erecting a wired, manned, fence/wall all along the borders with the West – including that of East Germany (the IGB or Inner German Border). This left West Berlin as, quite literally, a tiny Western island within the sealed-off Eastern Bloc. And because there was no hard border between Eastern and Western Berlin, it was possible for anyone in East Germany – indeed any of the Eastern Bloc countries with a little effort – to get into East Berlin and simply walk across the border into West Berlin from where they could get a train, plane or car into Western Europe and beyond.

By 1961 this was becoming a huge problem as thousands of Easterners were 'illegally' leaving Eastern Germany every day. Significantly, most of those choosing to flee were young, well-educated professionals so the East was losing all of its doctors, teachers, academics, scientists and financial experts. It was a brain drain that would make the economy hard to sustain and the government were desperate to stop it. They tried posting guards on the soft border to stop anyone with suitcases. They tried to ban people crossing to work in the West and they tried heavily taxing anyone moving between the sectors, but still they fled. The Berlin Wall – the final piece in the Eastern Bloc's existing hard border – was the solution and it had to happen in secret to prevent even more people leaving in the weeks preceding its erection.

### The Wall

The Berlin wall – or at least the barbed wire version that preceded the final structure – truly did go up overnight and was a near total surprise to almost every inhabitant of Berlin. Only a handful of the government elite knew about it before 12 August, when the first briefings were held for those who, unbeknownst to them, would be carrying out the operation. Top government officials were told around 5 p.m. that Saturday at a 'garden party' out beyond Wandlitz, with no one allowed to leave until the construction work had started. City commanders opened sealed orders at 8 p.m. and briefed battalion commanders at 9 p.m., with unit commanders not getting their orders until midnight for action stations at 1 a.m.

There had been rumours, of course, and Walter Ulbricht denying that there would be a wall in a press conference on 15 June is absolutely true. Indeed, I used his exact words (in translation), but behind the scenes all was activity. A commission to consider the option was first set up in January 1961, the idea most likely coming from the Russian leader, Nikita Khrushchev, with Ulbricht's eager agreement. The disingenuously named 'Operation Rose' was organised by Erich Honecker, Secretary for Security in the DDR politburo, and was given the rubber-stamp in Moscow at the start of August.

There were clues – for example, a reference in the East German parliament on 11 August about 'impending measures to protect the security of the DDR and to curtail the campaign of organised kopfjägerei (head hunting) and menschenhandel (human trafficking) orchestrated from West Germany and West Berlin' – but it was summer and, with elections due in September, no one truly thought anything would happen until autumn. That was part of the genius of the cruel plan.

Honecker had to coordinate many groups in order to erect the 156 kilometres of wire around the outside of West Berlin and the 43 kilometres across the centre of the city in one night. Around 32,000 men were employed from across the Nationale Volksarmee (the National People's Army), the Volkspolizei (East German police), the Grenzers (the Border force), the Betrieb-skampfgruppen (the part-time factory fighting units), and the Freie Deutsche Jugend (the DDR youth movement). They were backed by at least 8000 Soviet troops, guarding the constructors to prevent an uprising. Thousands of soldiers, like the one Kirsten talks to in the novel, were drafted into Berlin from units all over Eastern Germany without knowing what they were there to do until midnight struck and they were sent into Berlin's streets with rolls of barbed wire.

A chosen few in the transport services were in the know so they could be ready to seal off the S-bahn and U-bahn lines between East and West, leaving many partygoers stranded on the wrong side, and ultimately creating the 'ghost stations' shown in the novel. The only others aware in advance were the executive staff of *Neues Deutschland*, the DDR government's tame, communist newspaper. When the rest of the staff were dismissed at 10 p.m., this skeleton crew stayed on to produce a new edition, announcing the closing of the border. This became almost the sole information about the new rules going forward, including for the border guards expected to enforce them. It was a highly effective way of informing Berlin, fast, about its new formation and I suppose credit must be given to Honecker for the extreme efficiency of his hateful plan.

## Checkpoint Charlie

This is perhaps the most iconic symbol of the Berlin Wall and, indeed, the entire Cold War, and it is all credit to the Americans that, despite their counterparts twenty metres up the road erecting a phalanx of border buildings, they kept theirs as the small, white hut that we still see today in order to emphasise its 'impermanence' – for all twenty-eight years of its operational existence! Café Adler (now Einstein Kaffee) is also still there, its original décor largely preserved, and I would recommend a visit. However – a word of caution...

I had a wonderful trip to Berlin to research this novel, but spent far too much of it pondering Checkpoint Charlie as what I was seeing before me did not make sense with what I knew of events in the area in 1961 – and how they are told in the novel. The checkpoint was on the junction of Friedrichstrasse and Zimmerstrasse, with Zimmerstrasse in the West and where the viewing platform mentioned in the novel was built. However, the sign announcing that 'you are leaving the American zone', today stands before Zimmerstrasse. It didn't make sense.

In the end, with the help of wonderful old pictures in the Checkpoint Charlie Museum which looks directly out onto the street, I worked out the simple answer that the sign has been moved! Presumably for better photo opportunities (and, to be fair, traffic control), it is now almost next to Checkpoint Charlie, rather than across the street. So if anyone, after reading this, has the good fortune to visit this iconic area, do bear that in mind.

## Bernauerstraße

This, to me, is one of the most fascinating streets in Berlin, at least in the context of the Berlin Wall, and is also worth a visit to see the well-recorded photos and stories of its place in the rapidly unfolding drama of 13 August 1961. The street had long been the border between the districts of Wedding and Mitte, but that had never mattered a jot until Wedding was assigned to the French and Mitte to the Russians in the post-war carve-up. Even then, despite one side being nominally 'Western' and one nominally 'Eastern', life on the street went on as it always had, family and friends crossing to visit each other all the time, and many widows on the Western side visiting their loved ones' graves in the cemetery on the Eastern side daily. The nominal border had no meaning – until the DDR put barbed wire up along it overnight.

Even more ridiculously, the actual border was along the line of the houses on the Eastern side. The entire street was in the West, the doorsteps of the Eastern side were in the West, their front doors opened straight into it, but the actual apartment blocks were part of the border and, therefore, technically under the control of the DDR. Soldiers really did march in and demand doors were locked and keys surrendered. People really did jump out of windows, from higher and higher storeys as the lower ones were boarded up – including Frieda Shulze, shown in the novel. Within weeks, all apartments were commandeered, blocked off and eventually torn down to make the infamous death strips that were a hideous later development of the Berlin Wall.

When, on visiting Berlin, I discovered that the athletics stadium was – and still is – just at the top of Bernauerstraße, it seemed far too good an opportunity to miss, so I housed Kirsten on one side and her aunt on the other. When I then brought Olivia to the stadium, I hope it intensified the drama and showed how absolute the separation of the wall was, even for people living bare metres apart.

## Good things about the East

I have tried very hard in this novel not to present the East as a 'bad' place and the West as its counterpoint 'good' one. The core idea of socialism/communism is, and always will be, a strong one – everyone being paid a fair and equal wage based on how hard they work rather than the perceived value of what they do. What I believe the post-war period in Eastern Europe proved (like other attempts at communism both past and present), however, is that human beings are not capable of being inherently fair enough for it to ever work on a large scale.

With Germany's relatively developed initial economy and industrial skills, as well as the classic Teutonic organisational abilities, it was famously said that if anyone could make communism work, the East Germans could. And there was much to like about their regime, at least at first. For women, in particular, it was a truly equal society in which boys and girls were educated in the same subjects and with the same rigour, then both expected to work and both expected to contribute to home life. The state provided universal and effective childcare (albeit with a good dose of indoctrination built in) and women were encouraged to succeed.

This led to far more open sexual attitudes and I point any interested reader to Kristen Ghodsee's excellent book 'Why Women have Better Sex Under Socialism'. The core argument goes that in traditional Western relationships, sex is barter: women give it to men in return for being kept. This results in a psychological imbalance, with women giving and men receiving. If you take that away, both parties come to the bedroom as equals, leading to far more open, trusting and ultimately satisfying relations. I paraphrase, clearly, but do read the book for a more nuanced exploration of a fascinating phenomenon that I tried to portray through Olivia's relaxed attitude to sex with Hans.

Other strong elements of life in the East were that all the basics of life were taken care of by the state. Health, education and culture (the DDR was huge on art, music and literature) were provided at low cost and everyone was encouraged to partake. There was – or should have been – no elite. Doctors lived alongside factory workers and they all went to concerts together. Sadly, of course, those in charge were unable to follow their own doctrine and resist giving themselves privileges – creating a new, equally corrupt elite. I tried to show Oliva as a true, idealistic believer in all the best elements of communism, building to her sad disillusionment in Wandlitz and the resultant dangers to both her and Hans.

I have, incidentally, portrayed the Wandlitz compound exactly as described in records and accounts, down to Otto Grotewohl's Prussian taste in furniture and Red Hilde's ebony bathroom. As the post-wall era went on, the compound was kept a closely guarded secret and it is probably unlikely that the athletes would have been invited in, even this early on, despite being under the charge of the leader of the Stasi. However, it felt important that I showed the corruption of the leaders to both Olivia and the reader directly, so I hope they will forgive the poetic licence.

True social equality is an admirable aim but, unfortunately, communism does not encourage people to achieve beyond the minimum required of them and it then fosters distrust and, ultimately, surveillance. In the DDR, with the now infamous Stasi, this reached unprecedented and horrific levels and I tried to show this in the opening scene with Claudia and then the rising threat of similar imprisonment for Olivia. That does not mean that there were not many earnest, hard-working people who were devoted to the cause and wanted it to succeed. Many East

Berliners were, as shown, delighted when the wall went up and stopped greedy Westerners coming and using their cheap services and believed that it would allow communism to thrive. It is their tragedy that their leaders let them down in this and that it cost so many of them their lives.

Interestingly, there has been much debate in the press recently about a residual resentment from Ossis (the term genuinely used for Easterners in Germany), because when the Wall went down, the East was subsumed into the West, the implication being that everything about it had been bad. Many, even today, are still proudly Ossi and I think it is important to approach any consideration of life in East Germany and, indeed, the whole Eastern Bloc, with nuanced, careful thinking. I hope I have done so here.

## Dynamo

Dynamo Football Club, and its later development into athletics, swimming, gymnastics and other big sports, was indeed run by Erik Mielke, the vicious head of the Stasi, who was passionate about football in particular and success in general. The compound exists today, with the old Dynamo FC stadium still standing, as well as the original central buildings as shown in the novel, although there is also now a beautiful modern sporting facility on the large space.

Promising young sports people were taken into this facility, and several others in the DDR, and given amazing training, nutrition and medical support – and a little more besides. This novel was not the place to fully explore the corruption and exploitation of the doping regime in East Germany, which was only really starting in the 1960s. I wished, however, to include something of the 'little blue pills' that were systematically given to the athletes to stay true to their experiences and to show the pressures that both Olivia and Hans were under to succeed, initially to justify their place at Dynamo, then later for their safety and very survival.

## Stalinstadt

Stalinstadt is a real place, created as a new town to service the vast iron works on the banks of the River Oder. It was an idealistic, socialist town, crammed with services for young families and promoting genuine equality. It still exists today, under the name Eisenhüttenstadt (Iron Foundry Town) that it was given when Stalin was discredited by his successors (the name change was actually instigated in 1961 and I initially included it in the novel but it added nothing to the narrative so I chose to leave it out.)

I went to visit Eisenhüttenstadt when researching this novel and it is a truly fascinating place. Getting out of the car there felt like stepping back in time to a world of seventies buildings, shops and services. That said, the grand apartment blocks, each around their own grassy courtyard with barely a car within the residential space, felt open and friendly and I can see how it must have been a safe, exciting place for thousands of young families looking for a new start after the horrors of the war. If any reader visits Berlin and has a day to spare, it is not far to go and well worth a look. It stands, perhaps, as testimony to the optimism of true communism, a sad counterpoint to the corrupt, vicious, endlessly paranoid regime it ultimately became and that cost so many innocent Ossis their happiness and their lives.

## Dieter Wohlfahrt

Dieter is the only one of the main characters in this novel who was a real person. His testimony can be found at the Wall Memorial on Bernauerstraße and I believe a plaque, at least, still stands where the cross to his memory was erected, as shown (with poetic licence) in the novel.

Dieter was, as portrayed here, a young man with an Austrian father, studying chemistry at the Technical University in West Berlin. After the wall went up, he worked with several other students to get people out of the East, at first via the sewers and then, when they were closed up, via any method they could manage. He was shot, as shown, on 9 December 1961, and left to die (in reality for around an hour with no one daring to help) on the cobbles in the middle of a deserted street in the suburb of Staaken – one of the early deaths of what were to become far too many on the Wall. He was, it seems, betrayed by the mother of a schoolfriend he had already rescued and this tragic story seemed to fit perfectly with my own, fictious one.

I hope I have done Dieter and his compatriots honour, and would like to conclude these notes with a tribute to their bravery in the face of persecution and injustice. The Berlin Wall and all its horrors should still scream to the world about the dangers of an inhuman curbing of basic freedoms, but I fear that many cannot, or are choosing not, to hear. I hope this novel is a reminder that kindness, care and understanding should be the guiding principles of managing families, nations and the entire, divisive world. Love knows no borders.

# ACKNOWLEDGEMENTS

My first thanks for this novel must go to Detmar, Penny and Sascha Owen, who not only kindly and generously put me up for my research visit to Berlin, but also provided huge knowledge and assistance. They drove me to Eisenhüttenstadt for a wonderful day out, introduced me to their fascinating Ossi neighbour, and provided an invaluable translation service with guides, articles and information boards to greatly enrich my understanding of Berlin. This book would not be half as detailed without their kindness and wisdom, so thank you to all three Owens. Also to Brenda, my trusty and wonderfully persistent research assistant, without whom I might never have tracked down the correct positioning of the bafflingly elusive Checkpoint Charlie. Thank you, Brenda, for friendship, support and saving me from geographical madness!

Credit, as always, must go to my family and friends for always being right behind me, but in this book, I would particularly like to thank the brilliant people I work with in this crazy book industry. I'm very lucky to be surrounded by a talented, friendly and great fun team so this one is for all of you!

This novel is dedicated to my wonderful agent, Kate Shaw, of the Shaw Agency. Kate first responded to my work back in 2003, when I sent her an extremely rough first novel and she was kind enough to see promise in my writing and encourage me to develop it. Her sharp editorial suggestions were key in helping me to hone that book over the next few years and, after much toing and froing (and at least three babies between us), she took me on in 2010.

We failed to attract a publisher for that novel – a contemporary story – and Kate, bless her, didn't blink an eye when I told her I fancied writing historical fiction – medieval historical fiction! Again, she helped me to hone my novel and again we failed to sell it, but did attract some praise and invitations to submit another. This we did and finally, in 2014, we secured the long-awaited publishing contract under the pen-name Joanna Courtney. Not only that, but thanks to Kate ringing me up the day before submission and asking if I thought I could 'come up with an idea for two more books to go with it', we secured a three-book contract. Our publishing journey together had finally begun.

It has been a long and winding one, taking us from the medieval period, into Shakespeare's queens, then forward into contemporary fiction and the creation of a second writing persona, Anna Stuart, who has herself now moved back into the endlessly fascinating and fertile period of World War II. Throughout all this, Kate has been at my side, offering editorial wisdom, commercial nous and emotional support. It hasn't all been plain sailing – two 'strong women' will clash at times – but we have come out of it all even stronger and more united. Kate, I cannot thank you enough for being with me throughout everything, and I look forward to many more years working together.

Another crucial piece in this convoluted writing story is my brilliant editor, Natasha Harding, who was one of those early editors who invited us to submit again, and the one who (when working at Pan Macmillan) finally took me on as Joanna Courtney. She was also the one who persuaded me into writing about World War II and I am over the moon to be working with her again, some years down the line, at Bookouture. Her eye for a plot, her commercial genius and her all-round wonderfulness mean so much to me. Thank you, Natasha.

And so to Bookouture – what a fabulous publisher! I have never worked with a company more proactive, forward-thinking, open, fair and exciting. Everyone in the firm is bought into the success of their authors and they use hard-working, clever, commercially-engaged techniques to secure it. Plus, they all seem to genuinely love their work and are passionate about the company. This is huge credit to Jenny Geras and all who work beneath her. I thank you all and am very excited about our next ventures together.

Made in the USA
Coppell, TX
06 March 2024

29846481R00236